BURNING
NATION

BURNING NATION

TRENT REEDY

ARTHUR A. LEVINE BOOKS
AN IMPRINT OF SCHOLASTIC INC.

Library of Congress Cataloging-in-Publication Data

Reedy, Trent, author.
Burning nation / Trent Reedy. — First edition.
pages cm
Sequel to: Divided we fall.
Summary: Idaho is a war zone under Federal occupation, and Danny Wright and his friends in the Idaho Militia are determined to fight back, running guerrilla missions against the army — but what at first seemed like a straightforward battle against governmental repression quickly grows murky, and Danny finds that even winning the war does not mean an end to tyranny.
ISBN 978-0-545-54873-1 (alk. paper) — ISBN 978-0-545-54875-5 — ISBN 978-0-545-54876-2 — ISBN 978-0-545-75282-4 1. Idaho. National Guard — Juvenile fiction. 2. Government, Resistance to — Juvenile fiction. 3. Guerrillas — Juvenile fiction. 4. War stories. 5. Idaho — Juvenile fiction. [1. Idaho. National Guard — Fiction. 2. Government, Resistance to — Fiction. 3. Guerrilla warfare — Fiction. 4. War — Fiction. 5. Idaho — Fiction.] I. Title.
PZ7.R25423Bu 2015
813.6 — dc23
2014027134

Littoral combat ship image by James R. Evans via Wikimedia Commons. Public domain.

10 9 8 7 6 5 4 3 2 1   15 16 17 18 19
Printed in the U.S.A.   23
First edition, February 2015

This book is dedicated to
the memory and honor of
Staff Sergeant Joshua William Pratt
(1980–2013).

"All able-bodied male persons, residents of this state, between the ages of eighteen and forty-five years, shall be enrolled in the militia, and perform such military duty as may be required by law, but no person having conscientious scruples against bearing arms, shall be compelled to perform such duty in time of peace."

Constitution of the State of Idaho
Article XIV, Section 1

A tracer round sliced a bright red streak through the black night in front of me. I grabbed Sweeney and Cal by their coats, pulling them down behind our bunker. Machine guns and rifles opened fire from both sides of the Washington-Idaho border. Given that I had just two months of basic training, a handful of National Guard drills, and a few weeks of sentry duty, I hadn't really practiced fighting a battle to stop the US Army from invading my state.

"Aw yeah, dude!" Cal shouted near my ear. "This is the real deal!"

Sweeney hit me in the shoulder. "Danny, you're the soldier. Just tell us what to do. We'll follow your orders."

I was packing my .45. Cal had Schmidty's AR15. Sweeney still needed a weapon. "Stick with me! Stay low!" I yelled over the roar of gunfire.

The screech of a jet fighter shot past overhead. Cracks like thunder exploded close by. We pushed forward into my squad's bunker.

Inside, PFC Luchen fired his SAW, while Specialist Sparrow sent heavier rounds downrange with her .50-cal. Sergeant Kemp was helping them reload as they burned through their ammo belts. They were both holding down the trigger so long that I worried they'd melt their barrels.

Kemp spotted me. "Wright! What are you doing here!?"

"Here for the fight!" I shouted back. "Got my boys with me."

Kemp handed me and Sweeney M4s, probably Luchen and

Sparrow's regular weapons. "Come on!" He led the way to the firing window. "One shot! One kill! Pick your targets to save ammo."

"Seriously? Just like that? Just jump in?" Cal took aim.

"Yeah!" Kemp said. "But you have to aim carefully so —"

"I can shoot." Cal aimed and pulled the trigger.

At least a whole company of Federal infantry had crossed into Idaho, shooting as they moved through the valley below our firing position. They were supported by machine guns on the Washington side, which opened up to offer suppressive fire. I'd shot an Army staff sergeant back in Spokane to save my friends. Was that the right thing to do? Who knew? To win this fight now, to protect my state, I would have to do it again and shoot as many of the enemy as I could. I'd have to use my best skills to kill American soldiers.

"Let's go, Wright!" Luchen said. He held down the trigger and mowed down a whole charging fire team. "Get in the fight!"

I'd wanted in the war. I hated the damned Fed. A bunch of rounds shattered against the rocks next to me. I lined my sights up on the shadowy form of an advancing Fed and pulled the trigger. Clipped his leg. I found another target. Fired. Pegged his chest. Knocked him down. I fired again and again.

"Aw shit!" Luchen yelled, and pointed way down the hill to our company's base. "They got a mick-lick!" An MCLC was a Mine Clearing Line Charge, a little trailer with a small rocket that pulled a line of C4 charges out over a minefield or wire barrier. The rocket would explode the obstacles and clear a path for the advancing army. With the mick-lick, they could take out our wire obstacles and open the road to our bunker.

Three of our guys ran out, ready to fire an AT4 rocket launcher. One of them was hit twice and fell. A few steps later, another took a round through the throat. The last soldier aimed and fired a rocket.

The mick-lick burst into white-hot flame. The crack of the explosion slammed us a second later.

"Yeah!" Luchen shouted. He high-fived Cal. "Awesome!"

An Apache helicopter gunship swept through the sky, and another rose up from behind some trees. They dodged around firing at each other until one of them went down with its engine burning. The surviving bird dipped down and turned its thirty-millimeter chain gun and Hellfire missiles against the Fed lines. Hundreds of soldiers exploded all over the field.

"We got 'em!" Cal said. "They ain't got a chance!"

But our Apache exploded into fiery pieces seconds later, and five M4B Schwarzkopf main battle tanks pushed through the woods from Washington. The tanks fired, and our side of the border erupted. Down the hill, our TOC tent went up in flames. The farmhouse by the road collapsed as well. A second mick-lick moved into position, firing its rocket. Seconds later, its C4 rope exploded and Fed soldiers poured through the gap.

"There's more Feds than we got bullets!" I shouted.

One of the Schwarzkopfs turned its turret and raised the huge barrel of its main gun toward our bunker.

"Fall back!" Sergeant Kemp slung a full rucksack over his shoulder, an AT4 strapped to the top. "Grab your stuff! We're bugging out!"

"Bullshit! We can take 'em!" Cal fired six more rounds.

No we couldn't. I pulled Cal away from the firing post. Sparrow started to take the .50-cal off its tripod.

"Leave it!" Kemp yelled. He pushed her out of the bunker through the crevice in back. I followed Sweeney and Cal. Luchen was right behind me, carrying his SAW. Kemp covered our six. "Go, go, go!" he shouted.

Behind us, the hill where we'd built our firing position exploded and we were all thrown to the ground. The little radio clipped to Kemp's chest squawked, *"All 476 elements, all 476 elements, this is 476 actual! Fall back! I say again, fall back! Evac truck charlie mike in five. 476 actual, out."*

"That's the go code!" Kemp yelled. "The whole force is evacuating. We don't make that truck, we're screwed!"

We all bolted through the woods as fast as we could. I fell once, and my M4 hit a log, bouncing up and smacking me in the face. I scrambled to my feet in seconds and ran after my group.

We reached the road only to find our Army five-ton truck speeding away, its tarp in the back on fire. Soldiers inside used fire extinguishers, trying to put out flames that only flared up more in the wind. The truck sped off and disappeared around a bend.

"Shit! That was our last ride!" Luchen yelled. "What do we do now?"

"I parked my truck a ways back there," I said. "We can get out in that."

Kemp nodded. "Let's go."

I turned and led the way back through the woods toward the Beast. I slipped in something as I ran, and then I saw what I'd slipped in.

It wasn't snow. It was some guy's guts. Even worse, the guy was the other team leader in my squad, Sergeant Ribbon. He had a wide-eyed, openmouthed look of shock on his face. Dead.

There wasn't time to mourn him in the right way. Sparrow grabbed his rifle. I took a couple extra thirty-round magazines out of his ammo pouches. Then I closed his eyes.

"I'm sorry," I whispered. "I'll hit 'em back for you. For all of us."

"Hey, over here," said Cal. A moment later, another flash revealed PFC Nelson from my squad, soaked in blood and clutching a chest wound.

"Wright?" said Nelson. "You gotta help me."

Another low groan came up from the ground nearby.

"Wright, come on!" Luchen called from up ahead.

"Wait! We got wounded back here!" I went toward the groan and stopped when my feet hit something soft. In the darkness, I bent down. "Hey, you okay?"

"Wright? Private Wright?"

"Yeah."

"It's Danning. Been shot. Leg. Stomach." His words and breaths were tight, like someone was pressing on his chest. He held his giant prized .50-caliber rifle. "I bandaged . . . myself. I think."

"Okay. Okay," I said. What was I supposed to do? The Feds were right behind us, but I couldn't leave the guy like this. "Hey, if you're well enough to bandage yourself, you're fine. You're gonna be fine. You got a radio?"

"Naw, man. I —" Danning's voice seized up like he was in pain. "Drone hit us. Sergeant Ribbon. Nelson, Jamison . . ."

"Sergeant Donshel, where are we going?" came the gravelly old voice of First Sergeant Herbokowitz from behind a nearby stand of trees.

"I don't know, First Sergeant. Silver Mountain, maybe. We might hide there."

Donshel was my squad leader. These were my guys. "First Sergeant, this is PF —" I remembered I'd been busted in rank the last time I was with the Guard. "Private Wright," I called out.

The first sergeant came out of the tree line with Staff Sergeant Donshel. Three other guys followed them. "Private Wright, what the hell are you doing here?" He turned behind him. "Anything on the radio, Specialist?"

"Negative, First Sergeant," said Crocker. "We were getting a ton of chatter on the radio in the TOC, but since we've been on the move,

I'm hearing nothing." That was Crocker. The jackwad never had a clue what the hell he was doing.

"Come on," said Sergeant Donshel. "We got to go."

"Yeah, let's go, guys," said an unarmed man I didn't know. "They'll be here any second."

"Who are you?" I asked.

"Martin Bagley," said the man.

"Civilian Corps guy," said Luchen.

"Come on!" said Donshel.

"Danning and Nelson are wounded," I said.

"We'll have to carry them," said Sparrow.

"Okay," said First Sergeant Herbokowitz. "We'll move out and double-time in a squad wedge formation. Private Luchen, you take point. Staff Sergeant Donshel, Specialist Smith, you fan out to the left."

Specialist Smith from second squad was here? Where were the rest of his guys?

"Our evac trucks have rolled out already, but Wright's got his own ride," said Kemp.

The first sergeant continued, "Sergeant Kemp, Specialist Sparrow —"

Weapons fire opened up from the tree line my guys had just come out of. Herbokowitz screamed and fell. A parachute flare went up above us, a burning ball floating in the sky, lighting the whole field. A round sliced through Donshel's throat. I whirled with my M4 and shot back. Sparrow and Luchen fired too, Luchen unleashing quick bursts with his SAW.

Cal let it rip with Schmidty's AR15. "Come on!" Two more shots.

Sparrow had Nelson hoisted up over her shoulders in a fireman's carry. Kemp had done the same with Danning. "Donshel's dead," he shouted. "We're moving. First Sergeant?"

First Sergeant Herbokowitz stood up, his leg bleeding. "I'm fine!" He started hobbling away.

Luchen pulled the pin on a grenade. "I was first team all-conference in baseball." He smiled and whipped the grenade toward the trees. Without even waiting for the thing to explode, he grabbed another, pulled the pin, and threw it. Sparrow, Cal, me, and Sweeney kept firing for a few more seconds. At least one Fed got off another shot because Specialist Smith screamed and fell, grabbing at his groin area.

"Come on!" Sparrow ran with her weapon in tow and Nelson on her back. Cal picked up Smith and we all followed her. A few shots rang out from behind us.

"Ow! Mother-frraaah!" Luchen staggered as he took a bullet. His SAW swung from his shoulder and he clutched his ass, but he was a tough, wiry little bastard and stayed standing. Me and Sweeney turned around and shot back while Crocker ducked under Luchen's arm and half carried him away.

"Let's go," Cal said.

"Sergeant!" I called out. "My truck's up here!" I led my guys to the Beast. I hadn't had the chance to switch out the bloodstained upholstery after our border run, so a few more wounded guys wouldn't mess it up too much.

Cal laid Specialist Smith down on the cold ground next to the Beast. "Guys, he ain't breathin'." He felt around his neck. "I can't find no pulse or nothing."

Specialist Sparrow set Nelson down next to Smith and pushed Cal out of the way, crouching down to place her fingers at Smith's throat. "He's dead. Bled out."

"Shit." Cal was soaked in blood. He stared at Smith.

"Come on! Get in the damned truck!" Herbokowitz yelled.

"We can't leave Smith behind like this!" Sparrow said.

The first sergeant shoved her toward the Beast. "We just left our whole damned company behind. Move it, Specialist."

Herbokowitz and Sparrow somehow fit in the back with Luchen's SAW and Danning's .50-cal rifle. Kemp rode shotgun with his M4 out the window and his rucksack on the floor in front of him. Cal, Sweeney, Bagley, and Crocker wedged into the backseat, with Luchen lying on the floor under their feet and Danning draped across their laps. Nelson lay with his legs over the center console and his head and shoulders over Danning. My fingers were sticky on the steering wheel with someone's blood. When I brought the Beast out here, I never dreamed I'd be turning around so soon, driving back in a bloody-clown-car-from-hell type situation.

"Hold on, boys." I fired up the Beast and threw her in drive, guiding her around some trees until I reached the highway. Then I hit the gas. "The Fed'll be right behind us, and this ride could be all jacked up."

"Lucky for us, Wright's a champion bull rider," said Sweeney.

"I still say we should go back there and fight those bastards!" Cal shouted.

I felt a little weird with Cal yelling around my first sergeant and team leader. I would never dream of telling those guys what to do. Since the Battle of Boise, my military life had kept creeping into my civilian world. Now my civilian friends were mixing with my Idaho Guard circle. All the lines were blurring.

We sped down the highway, piled in my truck, people on top of gear on top of people, racing along at a hundred miles an hour. When the highway went up around Silver Mountain, it would be too curvy to go this fast.

What had I gotten us all into? What had I started? How many people were dead because I had accidentally pulled the trigger at that protest in Boise? And now — how had I been stupid enough to believe that the Idaho National Guard could possibly hold back the entire United States military?

We rode quietly for a while, the only sounds the wind and the groans from our four wounded. As we rolled along, people did their best to bandage those who were hurt, but we needed to get them to a doctor.

"Where do we go?" I asked everyone. "I mean . . . If the Fed wins this battle and takes over Idaho, we're really criminals now. Me especially, I guess."

"We can't just give up!" Cal said. "We could set up an ambush somewhere. We could —"

"We don't need tactical advice from untrained civilians," Sparrow said. Cal was about to say something back, but she didn't give him the chance. "Some of us *do* need medical attention. We should go to a hospital. Surrender there."

"I'm not —" Luchen said, but his statement ended in a gasp. "No way. I'm not surrendering. The Fed can go to hell."

"Luchen," said Sparrow. "I've got most of the bleeding stopped for now, but you need more than a bandage."

"Rather . . . die than give in to the Fed," Luchen groaned.

"Me too," said Cal.

"If we surrender, we might be treated better than if they catch us," said Sergeant Herbokowitz. "But if we're charged with treason, we could be looking at life in prison or worse."

A half-dozen well-armed guys on motorcycles roared toward us, heading to the fight. They were all wearing black bands on their upper right arms. I swerved so I wouldn't hit them. "Idiots," I mumbled. "Whoever they are." I gripped the steering wheel tightly. I didn't know what the hell I was going to do, but one thing was clear. "The Fed blockade has been starving us out for months now," I said aloud. "They cut off our food supply. Same with our gas. With everything. They came after my friends, after my girl. They killed my mother. You guys can do what you want. I'm not surrendering."

"Then we need a place to hide," said Sergeant Kemp.

I remembered the bunker under Schmidty's shop. "I got a place," I said. "It's got food, water, ammo, everything we need. They'll never find us there."

Sweeney cleared his throat. "I know I'm only a civilian, but it looks like the Idaho Guard is gone and you're all civilians now. Technically felons . . . and fugitives too. If Danny's hiding place is where I think it is, anyone who is not committed to hiding with us needs to say so now. We'll drop you off someplace on the way, but we're not going to let you know where this place is, so you can just surrender or be captured by the Fed and give up our location."

That was a good point. Smart. I had to start thinking that way if we were going to survive this.

"With you all the way, buddy," said Cal.

"I . . . I don't know," said Bagley. "Can I think about it? I mean —"

"Yeah, you can think about it until we get to Freedom Lake," Cal said. "After that, in or out."

"No choice," said Luchen. "I'm not giving up."

Kemp and Herbokowitz said they were in. "Sparrow?" Kemp asked.

She only nodded.

Eventually everyone agreed to come with us. I slowed down as the highway went into a long, rising curve. The road would snake up the mountain, go through a tunnel about halfway to the summit, and then wind back down before it straightened out and headed southeast into Freedom Lake. The Beast's tires screeched when I took a tight turn too fast.

"It's too quiet," I said finally. "I can't take this tension." I turned on the radio. A deep computerized voice was speaking.

". . . Idaho residents. All Idaho military, militia, and law enforcement personnel must surrender to federal authorities immediately. All Idaho civilians must disarm, remain in their homes, and await instructions from federal authorities. Failure to comply will be met with deadly force. Continue to monitor this frequency for further information. This message will repeat. Attention Idaho residents. All Idaho military —"

I tried to change the station, but the same message was all over the dial, the only thing on the air. "Sorry." I shut the radio off and felt around under my seat for my dad's old CD. I'd added over a thousand songs to my collection in the cloud, but with our Internet shut off, I couldn't get to any of them. "Gotta have some music." Nobody answered me, and a few seconds later the hard guitars of AC/DC's "Highway to Hell" came on, sounding a little off since one of my speakers was still busted from the last time I'd been on the run from the Fed.

"How *old* is this music?" Sweeney asked.

"Hey, this is some good stuff," said Herbokowitz.

I turned up the volume and the heat, as we were all shivering in the late November cold, rounding Silver Mountain in my truck full of holes.

"Hey, turn it down," Sparrow said about halfway through the song.

"Just let him play it," Sergeant Kemp said.

"No, listen! Out there!" Sparrow shouted.

I turned the music down a little before I heard it — the unmistakable *whump-whump-whump* of a helicopter. "Oh shit!" I hit the brakes to slow us down enough to shut off the headlights and drive by the light of the moon. "Did they spot us?"

"Apache's right on our ass, coming in fast. They know we're here," Herbokowitz called from his place in the back.

"They're gonna light us up!" Cal shouted. "We should ditch the truck. Go on foot."

"No, hang on! I got this!" I flicked the headlights back on, cranked the music, and floored it. "Come on, you Fed sons of bitches. Eyes on me. Come and get me."

"The tunnel?" Sweeney asked.

"It's all we got," I said. To Kemp, I added, "Hey, get that AT4 ready."

"Yeah . . ." Luchen groaned. "Let's waste the bastards."

"You ever fire an AT4?" Herbokowitz asked. I shook my head. "The live rocket's nothing like that little nine-mil tracer they use for training."

"If you get a clear line of fire, the bird will have guns on us too, and they have a lot better weapons," Sparrow said.

A new roar tore through the sky above us, and the road in front of us burst with sparks and chunks of pavement. I swerved into the left lane as bits of blacktop peppered the truck.

"Their weapons aren't that great," said Cal.

"They're trying to make us stop," I said. I put the pedal to the floor. The tunnel was in view.

"They're speeding up!" Herbokowitz yelled.

Seconds later, the Apache dropped down out of the sky in front of us, hovering a few feet off the ground.

"Look out!" Kemp yelled.

"Nice try," I said. The gunship hadn't turned its thirty-millimeter cannon on us yet, so I drove straight for it. My big, heavy truck with its reinforced body traveling at eighty miles an hour, up against this stationary helicopter with its thin hull? I'd knock it back to the mountain if I had to.

"Badass, dude! You're playing chicken with an attack helicopter!" Cal yelled.

The Apache swooped up into the air and we rolled under it. Moments later, we were deep into the tunnel, gunning it around the curve. Finally, I hit the brakes and brought us to a stop.

"We're trapped," Sweeney said.

"He'll fly up over the mountain and down to the other end of the tunnel," I said. "Let's take the AT4 up the back side of the mountain and blast him."

"I'll fire the rocket," said Sergeant Kemp. "I'm the only one here without a wounded leg who has actually used the thing before."

"I'll go with you." I climbed down out of the truck, leaving the keys in the ignition. "Cal, you're driving. You hear that helicopter blow, you pull forward out of the tunnel and stop to pick us up."

"Got it," Cal said.

"Right! Let's go!" I took off at a sprint back the way we'd come. Kemp ran right behind me, carrying the rocket launcher. As we approached the mouth of the tunnel, we stopped to listen for the Apache. Nothing. Only the sound of explosions, like thunder off in the distant night. Someone was still fighting back there. Me and Kemp nodded to each other and ran out of the tunnel, scrambling up the rocky bank on one side. In Idaho, just being in the woods always meant making your way up and down some serious slopes. We moved through the scrub brush up the rocks faster than I'd ever climbed before.

As we neared the crest of the ridgeline, we could hear the helicopter again. I dropped down behind a boulder and eased my way up to peek over the top. Sure enough, the Apache was hovering about thirty feet above the road and about fifty yards from the mouth of the tunnel.

"There you are, you Fed bastard," I whispered. "Can you hit him, Sergeant?"

"Doesn't look like I have much choice," Kemp said. "I'm only going to get one shot at this. If I miss . . ."

If he missed, we'd both be dead seconds later when that Apache lit up the whole mountain. Sergeant Kemp moved the covers on the side of the AT4 so the targeting sights popped up. Then he pulled out the safety pin from the back of the launcher, pushed the cocking lever forward, flipped it down, and held the forward safety. He put the weapon on his right shoulder and aimed. For a second I thought about praying that he would succeed, but was it right to pray for someone else to die?

"Back blast area clear," Kemp whispered in a tone like *here goes nothing*. A shrieking whistle ripped the air all around us.

Then fire burst out of the center of the Apache's rotors and the bird whipped into a reverse spin as it fell. When it crashed by the side of the road, it seemed to shred apart for a second before it exploded. Kemp and I ducked as pieces of the helicopter pelted the hillside.

"Got him!" I said. "Let's go!" We scrambled down the mountain, half climbing, half tumbling, our path lit by the burning wreck of the gunship. When we hit the pavement, the Beast was already there, waiting for us. Me and Kemp squeezed in.

"Go, Cal, go!" I shouted.

Wounded and exhausted, we raced on through the night toward Freedom Lake.

CHAPTER
TWO

As we rolled into Freedom Lake, I was shocked to see that the town looked like a war zone. Whatever gas was left in the pumps at the Gas & Sip was on fire, but people were still fighting each other to scramble in and out of the shop, trying to get the last of whatever supplies the Fed blockade had left us with. The grocery store was the same. Looters stepped over the unconscious bodies of the two police officers who had been assigned there to enforce rationing. Gunshots echoed from another street.

"Everyone is out of their minds," Sweeney said.

"Panicked," said Sergeant Kemp. "Like us. They're realizing we're on the losing side of . . . of whatever this is."

A cold emptiness dropped into my stomach. If people were going this crazy before the Fed had even arrived, what would happen after the US Army showed up? No place was safe. "JoBell," I said.

"Yeah, we better go get the girls," said Sweeney.

"What are you two talking about?" Sparrow asked.

"Some friends of ours," Cal said.

"Wright," said Sergeant Kemp quietly. "Maybe this isn't the time for —"

"I'm going to get them! When the Fed takes over, they'll be in trouble because of me. I can't leave them out here. I'll make sure you're all safe, and then I'm going to get JoBell and Becca."

"Me and Sweeney are coming too," Cal said.

"You guys don't have to —"

"Shut up," said Sweeney.

Cal drove the Beast to the shop, where Schmidty was waiting with the bay door open and a cigarette dangling from his lips. "Well, hurry the hell up, would you?" he said.

We pulled in and the bay door closed behind us. I hurried to the driver's seat while everyone else crawled out of the Beast. "Schmidty, we got wounded here! You have to help get them downstairs. We gotta hide."

"Don't get blood on the floor," Schmidty said. "The Feds are gonna be all over this place, and they'll ask too many questions if they see blood."

"This is your big plan!?" Sparrow yelled at me as she reached to help Luchen out of the truck. "Take us right where the Feds will be looking?"

"Calm down, Specialist," Kemp said. He and Schmidty were back at the closet with the secret hatch in the floor. "This is as good a place to hide as any."

"It's better than most," said Schmidty. "The hatch is damned near impossible to spot when it's closed. It locks. There's food and running water down there. Electric if the Feds ever turn the juice back on. A flush toilet. Even a tunnel to escape if you need to. So stop bitching. Wright, cut the engine and get down there!"

"We have to go get JoBell and Becca at Sweeney's," said Cal.

"Well, you better hurry up!" Schmidty yelled.

"Don't forget the drones." Kemp pulled a bunch of thermal cloaks from his ruck. "If you have to go on foot, wear these to hide from their infrared cams."

"You get caught out there and we're all screwed," said the first sergeant.

"Then I won't get caught," I said.

A few seconds later me and my boys were rolling out. I floored it, the Beast roared, and we headed toward the lake and Sweeney's house as fast as we could. Three times I had to swerve around people running out into the street in the dark. I suppose they might have spotted me better if I'd had the headlights on, but I thought the sound of the engine would have warned them away.

We pulled into Sweeney's driveway so fast that the tires skidded when I hit the brakes. With no electricity and the evergreen trees blocking the moonlight, Sweeney's place was entirely dark. I climbed down out of the truck with my M4 at the ready.

JoBell's voice came from the trees. "I have all three of you in my sights right now. If you're not who I'm looking for, you're dead."

"Kitten, is that any way to talk to your best friends?" Sweeney said.

I heard JoBell sigh. "Eric, you make me wish I really had a gun."

"Thank God you're all okay." Becca ran out from the trees. Sweeney and Cal caught her in a hug. She leaned close and looked at the blood on their coats. "What happened? There's blood everywhere. Are you guys okay?"

"Shh," Sweeney said. "We're cool. Some other guys got hurt. We were helping them."

Becca let out a breath of relief. "What happened with the fight?"

"We lost," Sweeney said. "Idaho is beat. The Fed will be here any minute."

A column of moonlight made my JoBell shine as she came down through the trees, wearing jeans and a Freedom Lake Minutemen sweatshirt. Her long blond hair was pulled back in a ponytail. We met on the front lawn, and she slid her hands up through my hair, kissing me hot the way she had after I had been gone for two months at basic training. When we finally separated, I noticed the others watching us. "I'm glad you're okay," she whispered.

"If the Fed is coming," Becca said, "maybe we should hide."

"I got a safe place we can go," I said. "A bunch of guys from my unit are already there."

Gunshots echoed from back toward town.

"Help me get some stuff." Becca led Sweeney and Cal into the house.

"Right!" I said. "Grab what you can. We're rolling in five minutes." I started following the others inside.

"Wait!" JoBell grabbed my arm. "Danny, hang on."

"We don't have a lot of time," I said.

"Baby, I'm not coming with you."

I froze. "What?"

"I'm not going to become some kind of rebel, Danny. I went on that blockade run to protect you and help your mother. I won't get involved in this war by hiding with you. And you shouldn't let Becca get into this either. You gotta hide. I get that. But if Idaho is beat and the Feds have won, why should Becca and I join up now?" Tears welled in her eyes. "Anyway, you have a better chance if you have fewer people to worry about, fewer people eating your food and stuff."

"But you shot at the Feds on that border run," I said. "They'll be after you."

"It's been two months since that happened. Dad said if the Feds were going to press charges about that, they'd have done it already. Plus, they'll have plenty of other people to deal with, active fighters. I'll be low on their list." She looked down. "Even if they are after me, I'm not about to add to the list of charges they might raise against me by joining some rebellion. I'm . . . I'm keeping out of this, Danny. On moral grounds."

"JoBell, this is stupid. Come on. We're staying together." I took her hand and tried to pull her along, but she threw herself at me and hugged me. We kissed, and then she kissed my cheek. She took a step back and touched the new stains all over her sweatshirt that I'd pressed on her from the blood of all our wounded.

"You really want to drag Becca and me into this?" she said. "I never wanted this war, or to be a part of it, or for you to be part of it."

"You think I wanted this?"

"No, of course I don't."

"You're all I ever wanted," I said.

"I know. I love you. And when things cool down, we can be together again."

"I can't believe —"

JoBell stepped close and whispered, "Becca won't understand. She'll want to go with you guys. Don't let her. Please, Danny. Don't drag her into this."

I wiped the tears from her cheeks. The others had come out of the house, but stopped in the doorway when they saw us. "I don't know how long it will be before I see you again," I said. "If I'll ever see you again."

"You will," she cried. "Somehow. I promise."

"What's going on?" Becca asked.

"You and JoBell are staying here," I said.

"Like hell they are," Cal said.

"We're sticking together, Danny," Becca said. "The Fed is coming. We gotta get moving."

"No." I swallowed against the tightness in my throat. "I'm not bringing you two into this."

"I'm already in it!" Becca shouted. "I'm staying with the group. My parents are trapped out of state. I have nobody. I'm not going to lose you guys. What did you tell him?" she yelled at JoBell. "I don't care what she said. I'm —"

"What the hell did we even come here for?" Cal shouted. "They have to —"

"It's my call," I said, unable to look at JoBell. I waited for Sweeney to argue, but he only nodded. "It's my shelter. You two are going to stay, in society or whatever you call it. Try to live normal lives. Whatever that means anymore."

Becca grabbed my hands, crying. "Danny, don't do this. Come on. We're coming with you."

I hugged her. "I'm sorry, Becca. This is the way it's gotta be. We came out here to say goodbye."

JoBell put her arms around Becca and pulled her away from me. "Come on, Becca. It will be okay."

"We should go, then," said Sweeney. "We're kind of in a hurry." He hugged both girls together, picked up the box he'd carried from the house, and ran to the Beast.

Cal stood still, looking pissed off with his fists tight at his side. Finally he snapped out of it. "Bye, girls. Be careful." He hugged them and joined Sweeney.

I was the last to say goodbye, and again Becca tried to hold on to me. "Please, Danny. Don't go."

"Goodbye," I said to them both. Then I pulled JoBell to me for one more kiss. "I love you," I whispered. The horn honked. "Take care of yourselves."

I climbed up into the driver's seat and sat there for a moment with my fingers on the keys in the ignition. JoBell stopped on Sweeney's doorstep and looked back at me.

"Dude?" Sweeney asked from the seat next to me.

"I'm just worried that I'll never see her again."

"The girls should be coming with us," Cal said from the back.

Sweeney shook his head. "JoBell's made up her mind. You know her. Let's go, Wright. We gotta hurry."

I started the truck and peeled out in reverse, backing onto the highway. Then I clenched my fingers around the steering wheel and hit the gas to head back toward town.

The road from Sweeney's wound along through the woods above the shore of the lake. I drove as fast as the Beast would go, right down the middle of the road. We rolled along for several minutes like that, and I was glad things were calmer out here than they were in town.

Then bright white floodlights lit up the whole road. *"UN-AUTHORIZED VEHICLE! THIS IS A WELL-ARMED AND ARMORED CONVOY OF THE UNITED STATES ARMY! STOP YOUR VEHICLE IMMEDIATELY OR WE WILL FIRE! THERE WILL BE NO FURTHER WARNINGS!"*

"What is it?" Sweeney asked.

I couldn't see anything ahead. The light was blinding. I flipped on my brights and sped up, swerving in what I hoped was a surprise move onto the right shoulder. A machine gun opened up. I could hear the bullets rip through the air to our left. A bunch of what must have been rifles started shooting too. A few bullets pinged the car.

"Oh shit!" Cal shouted.

I swerved back to the left as the machine gun fired again, but only veered for a second before cutting back to the shoulder. I had to keep them guessing. If that machine gun hit us, it was over. We'd almost reached the floodlights. I dodged hard to the right, another quick left, a fake to the right, and then an intense move to the left to get us around the vehicle.

"It's a damned Stryker," I said when I could see the armored eight-wheeled monster without its lights blinding me. A dull clunk and scream told me I'd just hit someone, a soldier probably.

"Go, Danny, go!" Cal yelled. "They're spinning the gun turret."

"Shit, is that a fifty-cal?" Sweeney asked.

"Strap yourselves in. Now, now, now!" I ignored the stop sign at the highway crossing and hit the gas again, whipping the fastest, tightest turn I'd ever tried. The Beast's thirty-six-inch super swamper tires squealed until we'd made the corner.

Sweeney checked the mirrors. "They're going to follow us."

"It'll take that big thing forever to turn around," said Cal.

"There must be hundreds of other Fed vehicles out here," Sweeney said.

He had a good point. I hit the brakes and slowed down just a little. "Hold on to your shit. Time to lose them by off-roading it."

"But we can't outrun radio," said Sweeney. "They've called us in already. Other units and drones will be on their way."

The Beast's engine revved higher as I jumped her off the side of the road into an open field. "I'm doing the best I can!"

"I don't think it's going to be enough," Sweeney said.

"You saying we should just give up?" Cal asked.

"I think we're going to have to do something you're not going to want to do, Danny," Sweeney said. "The Beast's engine is going to show up on every drone's infrared scanner. Let's head for the old Bethelman rock quarry. We can ditch the truck there and then go on foot. The cloaks will keep us hidden."

"What?" I gripped the steering wheel hard as the Beast rocked over a big bump. "Just leave my truck at the quarry for the Fed?"

"We can't let them find it. They'll know we were out here. They'll know you survived the attack."

"Then what —"

"He means we gotta sink it in the pit," said Cal.

"Sorry, dude, but there's no other way," Sweeney said.

"I can't . . ." I started, even as I turned toward the quarry. The Bethelman quarry, or "the pit" as most of us called it, was an abandoned rock quarry, basically a huge, deep pond ringed with basalt.

The perimeter of the land was marked by about a billion NO TRESPASSING signs, but that had never stopped us from sneaking in there in the summer for swimming, cliff jumping, and even skinny dipping. "This truck is my baby. I restored her from practically a wreck. Right there in the backseat, me and JoBell first —"

"You gotta turn up here," Sweeney said.

The access road was blocked by a rusty, swinging bar gate that was chained and padlocked to a pole. I gunned the engine and smashed right through it, sending the bar whipping back to the side. "Get all the shit we're gonna need out of the back." I stopped the truck. "I'll take it up to the jumping cliff and get rid of it."

Cal opened the door and climbed out. "How are you going to —"

"Just hurry up!"

When the guys had unloaded the truck, I hit the gas and sped away toward the jumping cliff. It was a solid twenty-foot drop from the cliff to the waters in the deepest part of the pond. But driving fast up the rough hill with no headlights, it was really tough to tell how close I was to the cliff. If I was still in the Beast when it went over the edge, I'd have to stay in the vehicle until it broke through the ice. Then I'd have to escape the sinking wreck as the freezing waters poured in around me. In other words, I'd be dead.

The Beast bumped along, hitting rocks and crashing through low shrubbery the whole way. I kept my hand on the door handle and gave her gas. Any second now.

I felt the slope level out a bit and knew I couldn't wait anymore. "Goodbye, baby. I'm sorry." I threw the door open and shoved myself to the side. But I was stuck. "Shit!" Seat belt. I fumbled for the release. Found it. Tossed the belt aside and jumped.

Rocks and gravel hit my knees, my back, my legs, and my face as I skidded along the ground. The Beast's engine whined as she fell out of sight. A huge crack and splash below. Then my legs were out in the open and dropping. The edge! I swept my hands along the ground, reaching for something. Anything. Finally I caught hold of a rock, clinging for life. My legs still dangled in the air over the cliff. I let out a breath and pressed my cheek to the cold stone.

I crawled to my feet and looked down at my awesome truck's watery grave. "You were the best, girl," I whispered. "Thanks for everything."

I limped my way back to the guys.

"Damn, Wright, I thought we lost you!" Cal handed me a thermal cloak and I put it on.

"Yeah. I mistimed it a little."

Sweeney had been scanning the area. He turned back to me. "You look like shit, dude. You're bleeding everywhere." He paused. "Sorry about the Beast."

"No time to worry about that now." I took my M4 back from him.

We headed out, wearing the bulky thermal cloaks, carrying our weapons and what food and supplies we could manage. While the cloaks would hide our heat signature, we would still be visible in the bright moonlight, so I led the way from tree cover to tree cover, moving quickly and quietly the short distance into Freedom Lake.

We paused to catch our breath at the Huffs' house, crouching down between two cords of wood at the back. The ground shook and I peeked around the woodpile to see an infantry squad — nine well-armed soldiers — marching beside an M4B Schwarzkopf. I'd read up on those tanks before I shipped to basic training last summer. They had a 120-millimeter cannon, a .50-cal, and a couple M240 machine guns. The tank had enough firepower to level Freedom Lake by itself.

"Shit, we messed around too long back at the quarry," Sweeney whispered. "They're already here."

Cal said, "How are we going to get all the way across town to the shop?"

"Attention!" A loudspeaker on the tank called out into the dark. *"All Idaho military, militia, and law enforcement personnel must surrender to federal authorities immediately. All Idaho civilians must disarm, remain in their homes, and await instructions from federal authorities. Failure to comply will be met with deadly force."*

"We'll wait until they pass," said Sweeney. "Then cross the street and cut between the Blake and Reese houses. There's a fence, but when Mary Beth invited me over, all I had to do was reach over the gate and pop a latch."

"No way," said Cal. "I was hanging out with Tucker Blake once, and he had a big thing for Mary Beth. Must have been after the two of you broke up."

Sweeney shrugged. "Eh, we were never really going out."

"Yeah, well, me and Tucker were going to see Mary Beth one night, and when we cut through the yard, the motion sensor light turned on. If that happens with those soldiers around, we'll —"

"Cal," I said. "The power's out. The only lights will be on the Fed tanks."

"Oh yeah," Cal said.

The tank was out of sight by now and moving farther off. A few gunshots went off down the street. Seconds later, a bunch of rifles and machine guns cut loose. Then it was quiet. Whoever had taken a shot at that squad had paid for it the hard way.

"Okay," I whispered with a shaky breath. "Weapons ready. Do not shoot unless they do. We don't want to give away our position."

"And we really don't have a chance fighting these guys," Sweeney said.

"That too," I said. "Ready?" My friends nodded and picked up our stuff.

I came out from between the two cords and crouched-ran through the Huffs' yard. The street looked clear, but in basic training we'd learned about crossing linear danger areas, long straight pathways or streets that made handy places for the enemy to set up a machine gun. Anyone who tried to cross one could get mowed down.

I ducked down beside the Huffs' front porch and motioned for the others to do the same. Cal crouched right beside me, so I whispered to him, "I'm going to run across the street first. If I make it, I'll set up on the other side to cover you crossing. We go one at a time, so we're not all clustered together in one target." Cal nodded and I sprinted across the street, looking both ways, but mostly keeping an eye out for that tank and squad. When I dove under the bushes in front of Mary Beth's house, I aimed my M4 down the street and motioned for Cal to follow. In that way, one at a time, we crossed the street. Then we rushed around the house, popped the latch on the gate, and ran through the Reese family's backyard.

That's how it went all across town. We spotted two more patrols, each with two armored gun Hummers and a dismounted squad. They'd sent at least one platoon, maybe two, to conquer Freedom Lake.

We paused again in Mr. Shiratori's backyard. His daughter had a little playhouse there, and the three of us managed to creep inside to catch our breath.

"You guys okay?" someone whispered from the playhouse door. We all freaked and aimed our weapons. "Take it easy. It's Coach Shiratori."

"Geez, Coach!" Cal pointed his rifle downward. "You about got yourself killed."

"What are you doing out here?" Sweeney asked.

Mr. Shiratori frowned. "I should ask you the same question. The Army is everywhere."

"We're in trouble," I said. "We're going someplace to hide."

He crawled the rest of the way into the cramped playhouse. Everybody shuffled to give him room. "Where?"

Me and my friends looked at each other for a second. "We can't tell you," said Sweeney. "We have to keep it a secret."

"Makes sense," Coach said.

"But listen, Coach," Sweeney went on. "Can you do us a favor?"

I frowned. What was he talking about?

"I need you to talk to Travis Jones. Tell him to tell Dave Schmidt that I said he's a guy Schmidty can trust."

"What?" I shifted where I sat. "Come on. We don't need to get TJ wrapped up in this."

"I know you two have had your problems," Sweeney said to me. "Everybody else knows it too. That's why nobody will suspect him. And we're going to need someone to be our eyes and ears outside. Unless you want to risk the girls' lives?"

I couldn't think of a good comeback.

Sweeney said to Coach Shiratori, "So when it seems safe, talk to TJ about Dave Schmidt."

"I think 'safe' is going to be a relative term for quite some time," said Shiratori. "But I'll pass along the message."

Cal picked up his AR15. "I'd say we've rested enough. Unless we're staying in this playhouse forever, we'd better move."

"Yeah, it'll be light soon," I said. "From here on out, it'll be pretty much a fast sprint to the safe house."

"I'm faster than you," said Sweeney. "I can handle it."

I started moving toward the door. "Then let's go. If anyone asks, Coach, you didn't see us. You've been inside all night." Shiratori nodded. "And one more thing. JoBell. Will you please look out for her? Help her if you can?"

"I'll do my best. You boys be careful."

We grabbed our gear and left the playhouse. When we were all ready, we took off, our thermal cloaks flying out behind us like capes as we ran. It was only a couple blocks, but it felt like the longest run of our lives. When we finally reached the shop, I checked the street to make sure nobody was watching. Luckily, the shop was kind of at the edge of town, across the street from some giant steel grain bins. There were no houses around. Nobody to spot us.

I could hardly see in the darkened shop, but I knew the place so well that it didn't matter. I opened the back closet door and knocked on the floor hatch.

It lifted a crack. "Wright?" Sergeant Kemp asked.

"Yeah, we're back," said Cal. "Barely. Let us in."

Cal went below, but Sweeney stopped at the hatch. "You coming?" he said to me.

"I'll be right there." I stood in the empty shop where I used to park the Beast and looked out through the little round window in the garage door. The sun was just coming up, and in the distance I heard the rumble of a tank. A Chinook helicopter descended somewhere over near the high school, probably coming in for a landing on the football field, possibly carrying another whole infantry platoon. Freedom Lake, my hometown, was now under federal military occupation.

Sweeney put his hand on my shoulder. "Come on," he said. "It's over, for now."

I sighed and went with my best friend into the basement, wondering when I'd next see the sun.

THREE

The bunker was lit by the dim light from a battery-operated survival lamp. I surveyed the room. Luchen lay on his stomach on a cot in a corner across from the stairs. His pants were down and a T-shirt bandaged his ass. Danning, Herbokowitz, and Nelson occupied cots in a row near the stairs, with Specialist Sparrow sitting on Nelson's cot next to his feet, her head in her hands. That Bagley guy sat with his back against the wall near the entrance to the escape tunnel, his arms around his drawn-up legs.

The rest of the guys sat on folding chairs next to the cook stove and microwave in what I guessed was going to be our kitchen area. Crocker was fiddling with the hand-crank emergency radio Schmidty had put down here. Everybody was quiet, kind of in shock, so I guessed it was up to me to take charge.

"What else do we need to do for the wounded?" I asked. "We can't just sit around if —"

"Hey, Wright," Cal said quietly. "Your friend is dead."

"What? Who?" Then I focused on PFC Nelson, his still chest, his calm face no longer twisted up in pain. "Why? What happened?"

"Where? When?" Sparrow shouted. "What the hell do you think happened to him, moron? Massive chest wound. He lost too much blood. There was damage to his insides. How the hell should I know? I spent three weekends at a combat lifesaver course that taught me to stop bleeding, treat for shock, and run IVs. I'm not a damned doctor!"

"Whoa." Sergeant Kemp went to Sparrow and put his hand on her shoulder. She shrugged him off, but he stayed by her side. "Easy, Specialist. Nobody's blaming you. You did all you could."

"Which was precisely dick!" Sparrow said. "The only real bandages we have left are trying to stop the bleeding in Danning's gut and leg. Everybody else is patched with T-shirts or scarves or whatever. We need to get these people real medical treatment or they're gonna —"

"Hey, Wright. Where's your girlfriend?" Herbokowitz asked me.

"She's at Sweeney's for now, I guess until the Fed lets people outside. Then she'll go home to her dad."

"I thought you were bringing her here," said the first sergeant.

I hesitated before replying. "She wouldn't come."

"Damn it, Wright," said Herbokowitz.

"What?"

"Now we're really screwed," said Sparrow.

"What's the problem?" said Cal. "We said goodbye to the girls and came right back. Nobody saw us."

"You tell them where we are?" Herbokowitz asked. "Do they know about this place?"

"I don't . . ." My cheeks felt hot. "I didn't tell them we were here. I don't think I did."

"Oh, great," said Sparrow. "He doesn't *think* he did."

"I didn't tell them where we were going!" I said. I looked at Cal and Sweeney.

"I didn't," said Sweeney.

"Me neither," said Cal.

"But they've been to this shop before. They might know about this place," said Sergeant Kemp.

Did they? I racked my brains, trying to remember whether I ever told JoBell or Becca about Schmidty's hideout. Had I just condemned us all?

"Well, it ain't like the girls are going to run to the Fed and tell them where we are, even if they do think we're here," said Cal.

"The Fed might not give them a choice," said Herbokowitz, "not if they want information bad enough. And it doesn't seem like they're really concerned about people's rights as long as they stop us rebels."

"I'll go get them," I said. "Bring them here. It'll be fine." I headed for the stairs, but Sparrow and Kemp jumped in front of me. I shoved Kemp aside, but then Sweeney joined Sparrow.

"Dude, no way," said Sweeney. "We barely made it back here. You'll never get all the way to my house on foot without being caught. And even if you did, you'll only get yourself and the girls killed trying to come back."

"Plus, you ain't never gonna convince JoBell to go with you," said Cal.

"Wright," said Herbokowitz. "No more cowboy shit. We have to work as a team if we're gonna make it through this." He sighed. "Nothing left to do but wait."

Sweeney held out a beer to Sparrow. "While we wait, want a cold one? We don't have any fridge. Might as well enjoy these now. Might help, you know, to take the edge off."

Sparrow snatched the brown bottle from his hand and chugged half of it right away.

"Where did you get that?" I asked.

"Brought it from my place." Sweeney grinned.

"On the run for our lives, and you still can't do without beer?"

"I *could* do without it," said Sweeney. "But why would I want to?"

Herbokowitz bit his lip in pain as he sat up on his cot, leaning against the cement block wall. The scarf around his injured leg was solid red. "I could use a beer right about now."

"You probably don't want alcohol after you've lost that much blood, First Sergeant," said Sparrow.

"Thank you for your expert medical opinion, *Specialist*." Herbokowitz accepted a beer from Sweeney and closed his eyes as he took a drink. He held it up and looked at the bottle with raised eyebrows. "It's got a bite."

"I brew it pretty strong." Sweeney smiled. "Why mess around?"

Sweeney passed beers to everyone who wanted one. I'm not gonna lie. Mine tasted good and helped me calm down after all the insanity with the Fed.

"Hey, everybody," Specialist Crocker said. "Um, I think maybe we should listen to this. Something different is coming on the radio."

"More stupid Fed shit?" Cal said.

"Who cares? Turn it up," Kemp said.

Crocker looked to the first sergeant, who didn't seem interested but didn't object, and turned up the radio.

> ". . . listening to the official broadcast of the Federal Idaho
> Reconstruction Authority . . ."

"The federal what?" Cal yelled.

"Shut up!" Kemp and Sparrow said together.

> ". . . on multiple radio frequencies across the AM and FM
> dial and streaming to screens and COMMPADS to ensure a
> peaceful transition toward a stable and unified United States.
> All Idaho residents are advised to continue to monitor this
> broadcast in order to remain in compliance with federal
> regulations and instructions from the Reconstruction Authority.
>   "Residents of Idaho, please stand by for a message from
> the President of the United States, Laura Griffith."
>   "My fellow Americans. Throughout the long and
> illustrious history of the United States, many American

presidents have begun to address the people with those three words. 'My fellow Americans.' This morning, those words hold an even greater significance than they might have in the course of normal events, for these are not normal times. Last night, after lengthy deliberations with my cabinet, congressional leaders, and senior military advisors, I brought about an end to the standoff in Idaho by ordering a precise and overpowering military strike against rebel forces in that state.

"The idea of ordering military action against Americans is contrary to every instinct in my being, but after months of negotiations and peaceful pressure applied by my predecessor, it was clear that the rebel leadership in Idaho had no intention of complying with constitutional mandates. To allow this insurrection to continue would only worsen the situation in Idaho, and offer a dangerously destabilizing precedent for the future.

"Now, although there have been regrettable losses of life both in federal forces and in the Idaho State Militia, I'm pleased to report that with careful surgical action designed to keep military and civilian casualties to a minimum, the United States has prevailed. Former Governor James Montaine's attempt to defy the rest of the country has collapsed, and the state of Idaho will soon be safely in compliance with federal law.

"Early this morning, I summoned lawmakers to an emergency joint session of Congress, where the House of Representatives and the Senate passed a series of measures to broaden and enhance the Unity Act. Under the provisions of the Unity Act, I have, as president, wide discretionary powers for the purpose of bringing the existing insurrection *to an end and preventing future rebellion in the United States. Peace, order, freedom, and unity are being restored.*

"To that end, as commander in chief of the United States military, I have ordered the creation of the Federal Idaho Reconstruction Authority. Soldiers from the US armed forces are in Idaho communities to guide residents through this transition period. Reconstruction Authority soldiers will also seek out any and all rebels to bring them to justice.

"To the residents of Idaho, I say this. The ill-advised, illegal, and dangerous resistance to federal authority is at an end. You loyal American citizens have nothing to fear. The presence of the United States military in Idaho brings an end to the blockade, and food and supplies will be provided to all residents who accept the federal identification card and comply with efforts to locate and apprehend rebels. Federal Idaho Reconstruction Authority soldiers in your community will provide you with more information about the card and the food program, and they are ready and willing to answer questions and assist you in this difficult time.

"My fellow Americans, as President Gerald Ford once said, 'Our long national nightmare is over.' America is united once more. And though we still collectively face many challenges, I do see the dawn at the end of our long night. I ask you to join me in welcoming the new day. May God continue to bless the United States of America."

Crocker switched the radio off. We sat in silence for a moment.

"That's it, then," I said quietly, to myself as much as to the others. "It's over. We lost."

After all that work, dodging the president's attempts to arrest me or the governor, building up our defenses on the state line and then freezing on border guard duty. After Mom was killed trying to come home. After so many Guardsmen had died fighting to defend our home. For what? It was all for nothing?

What would happen to us now? I looked around at the people trapped with me in this dim dungeon, at our wounded. The soldiers in the room had chosen to fight on this side, but would they have had to make that choice at all if I hadn't accidentally fired that night in Boise? And my friends — what were they now? Rebels? Criminals? Fugitives, at least. All because of me.

And I'd left JoBell and Becca out there. What would happen to them? Would the Fed take them in? Interrogate them? Torture them?

I took a swig of the beer, but it tasted flat and was already getting warm. It sat wrong in my stomach and threatened to come back up. I leaned over and put my hands on my knees.

"The Fed's coming after rebels. We're in deep trouble," said Kemp. "They mean to punish us."

"But what's that mean? Who's a rebel?" Sweeney asked. "It's not like we signed up for a rebellion. Our names aren't on a list somewhere."

"Ours are," said Sparrow. "All of us in the Guard were supposed to report to the US Army for federal active duty. They've got our names, especially Wright's."

"And this Unity Act," Kemp said. "Sounds a lot like the Patriot Act back after 9/11. Something with a great-sounding name. Who doesn't want to be a patriot?"

"I don't!" Cal said.

Kemp nodded. "But who would oppose patriotism? Nobody. Then we found out it was a set of laws that allowed the government to spy on our phones and computers and comms." He coughed. "The president said this Unity Act gives her broad powers. To do what? Shut off our electricity? Decide for herself who is a rebel? Send soldiers to shoot us in the street without probable cause? Ignore our rights as much as she needs to in order to apprehend or kill us 'rebels'?"

Nobody said anything for a while. Danning was already asleep, or passed out maybe. I held my hand close to his face. He was breathing, at least.

"What are we going to do?" Luchen asked.

Sergeant Kemp stood up and surveyed the contents of the two rows of metal shelves off to one side of the room. "Well, it looks like we're pretty well supplied for rations. And we have running water. Bottled water if that fails."

"No," Luchen said. "I mean, how will we tell our families that we're safe? How long will we be trapped down here?"

Nobody answered. Nobody knew how long the Fed occupation would last. Even if the US Army left town, we'd still be considered wanted criminals under Fed law.

Sergeant Kemp returned to the table and sat down. "Maybe we should take it all one step at a time. We're safe for now. Let's take care of our wounded and get some sleep. Then we'll figure out what to do next."

A Fed fighter grabbed my shoulder, ready to plunge the knife into my back. I clutched my .45 and sat up to shoot. Then someone held my wrist and a bright light shined in my face.

"Wright!" someone whispered. "Wright, it's me, Eric. Relax. You're okay."

I lowered my weapon. "Get that damned light out of my face, Sweeney. The hell you doing?" It took a moment for me to realize I wasn't fighting Feds in the woods. I was racked out on a cot between the two sets of steel shelves.

"Shh." Sweeney held a finger to his lips. My eyes had adjusted to the dim light cast by his flashlight, and I could see him crouched next to me, holding his M4. From upstairs I heard a muffled shout. "Someone's up there," he hissed.

I rolled to my feet, still holding my .45. It would be a better weapon if we had to fight in close quarters. I motioned for Sweeney to follow me, and we quickly but quietly went up the stairs to the hatch. It was made of thick steel, but hopefully we'd be able to hear something through it.

"Go ahead and search everywhere," Schmidty said above us, his voice sounding muffled. "I got nothing to hide. I'm no rebel. I got an American flag flying outside the shop, and soon's I get a chance, I'm going to get my federal ID card."

"The Feds are here," I whispered to Sweeney. "Go wake up the others."

"But we have wounded. Even if we can all get out through the tunnel, how will we get away?"

"Just do it!" I hissed. There was a rumbling sound above me, like someone moving stuff around on top of the hatch. I'd told Sweeney to wake the others mostly to give him something to do. If we were caught, I didn't want my best friend right here in the line of fire. This would be the end. We'd never get away on foot. Holding the .45 up with both hands folded over the pistol grip, I rested my forehead against the cool metal of the barrel. *Oh, God, please don't let them find us. Please keep us safe. Please protect JoBell and Becca.*

Kemp joined me, holding his M4. He didn't say anything, but the look on his face said it all. He knew we had no chance if the Fed found us down here.

We waited.

And waited.

Finally my head dipped, and I jerked awake. Kemp elbowed me. "They must have left," he whispered. "It's been three hours, and the shop isn't that big. They'd have found us by now. Most everybody else has gone back to sleep. We should post a guard here under the hatch, just in case. I'll take first shift. You go rack out."

My hand ached as I finally released my grip on my gun. They'd searched the shop but hadn't found us. They didn't know we were here, which meant they probably hadn't gotten any information from Becca and JoBell. At least, not yet. The not knowing was killing me.

The next time I woke up, Sweeney was poking me with an aluminum pole from the end of one of the cots. "Thought this would be safer than shaking you awake," he said. He handed over my .45. "Just to be safe, I took your gun first. Maybe you shouldn't sleep with a weapon."

"Can't sleep without one," I said. The lamp was on and everyone was awake. "What's going on?"

"Hey, Wright."

I turned and saw TJ sitting on the stairs. He wasn't exactly the guy I wanted to see when I first woke up. "What are you doing here?" I said. "Were you followed?"

"Relax, Wright," said Cal. "I took over guard duty from Kemp. Schmidty knocked on the hatch, said the Fed were gone, told me to open up. The lock was a bitch, but when I opened the door, Schmidty and TJ were there."

"Coach Shiratori said I was supposed to tell Dave Schmidt that I'm a guy Sweeney can trust," TJ said with pride. It was the same tone he would use to brag about making a good play in football.

I shook my head. "Have you talked to JoBell? Becca? Are they okay?"

"The Fed allows you to go outside?" Sergeant Kemp asked TJ.

TJ looked around and frowned. "You have wounded down here?"

"And some dead," said Sparrow.

I took a few big steps closer to TJ. "The girls. Do you know what's happened to them? They were out at Sweeney's. Are they okay?"

"The Fed arrested them," TJ said. "Hauled them into the cop shop at the end of Main Street." Panic started to surge through every one of my muscles, but he went on, "They're cool. They're fine. Relax."

"Relax? They've been arrested!" I yelled.

"They're going to talk to the Fed eventually," Sparrow said.

"The Fed let them go!" TJ shouted quickly before everybody started up. "They were detained for about six hours. Then they were released and allowed to walk home. I haven't had a chance to talk to them yet —"

"That's the very next thing you're going to do," I said.

"Just let me explain." TJ sounded like a whiny little kid. "I couldn't talk to them because Coach got me that message about Schmidty as soon as we were allowed out of our houses. By that time, the Fed had the girls. They released them, but they're still watching them. There's a black car parked on the street, just a couple houses down from JoBell's. I'm guessing the same is true out at Becca's farm."

"Is that where Becca is now?" Sweeney asked.

TJ sat back down on the stairs. "Yeah. At least, she started walking out of town in that direction."

"Damn," said Cal. "That's like four miles."

TJ shrugged. "Nobody's allowed to drive."

"Becca shouldn't be alone out there," said Sweeney. "In the dark with no power."

"I think I have some nasty old carrots. I could take them out there for her horse as an excuse to go see her. If the Feds stop me, I can say Becca's my girlfriend and I'm going to make sure she's okay."

I spun one of the metal folding chairs around backward and sat down, my chin on my folded arms on the backrest. Just when I thought the whole situation couldn't get any worse, Travis Jones had become my only link to the outside world.

"Whatever you do, you have to be careful," said Kemp. "Does the Fed know you're here now?"

TJ brushed a strand of his long hair out of his eyes. "When I got Sweeney's message, I took the spare tire off my dad's truck, let the air out of it, and carried it down here to the shop so that if anyone stopped me on the way, I could explain that I was getting it fixed. It had to look legit. There's a Fed gun Hummer parked just down the street from the shop, I guess waiting for you guys to show up."

"Why did the Fed let the girls go?" Sparrow asked. "Wright's been all over the news. They know he and JoBell are hot for each other. They have to know both girls were on that stupid border run you guys did." I rubbed my aching hand and wrist, struggling to focus on the present. Sparrow continued, "Maybe the girls cut a deal."

"With the Fed?" Luchen asked.

"No, a record deal." She rolled her eyes. "*Yes*, with the Fed."

"Hey, you better watch it with that shit." Cal stood up. "Those girls are like my sisters. No way they'd sell us out."

If Sparrow noticed Cal's tough-guy act, she didn't show it. "Then why did the Fed let them go?"

"I don't know, but not 'cause they ratted us out!" Cal yelled.

I hated that the girls had been put in this position. Worse, Sparrow was kind of making sense. Why *had* the Fed let JoBell and Becca go?

I shook my head. No way was I even going to start thinking that way.

Kemp stood up. "Whoa. Calm down, everybody. TJ, how long ago were the girls released?"

"Like last night."

"That would have to be *after* the Fed searched the shop," Sweeney said. "So the girls didn't tell them about this basement or they would have found us. They were searching the shop just because it's Wright's shop."

"Wait, what day is it?" Luchen asked.

"Monday," TJ said.

I was glad Luchen had asked. It was hard to keep track of that kind of thing down here.

"So that's it?" Sparrow said. "The Fed let those girls go instead of sending them to prison, and they just gave up asking them any questions after a few hours? You believe that?"

The back of the chair was pressing into my arms, cutting off my circulation. My hands and wrists ached and my fingers were going numb. But I pushed down harder and took in the pain. "Bait," I said. "The Fed let JoBell and Becca go because they're going to wait until one of us . . . until *I* make contact with them."

Nobody said anything for a moment, and I pressed on the back of the seat even harder. "So I can't make contact with them," I finished. The Fed had ruined my whole life, and now they'd even taken my girlfriend away. I could feel everyone else watching me, and I hated it. They could shove their pity. "You got anything else?" I finally asked TJ.

He pulled out his comm.

"Is the Internet back up?" Sweeney asked.

TJ showed us the screen. "Only for reconstruction information. Here are the new rules. Nobody is allowed outside their house from eight p.m. until six a.m. Except for hospitals, nursing homes, schools, and places like that, no outside-the-house gatherings of more than four people are allowed."

"What about the First Amendment?" Crocker said. "The right to peaceful assembly?"

"They'll just say everyone in Idaho is a rebel, and so any gathering is *not* peaceful," said Kemp.

TJ shrugged. "And I don't think this Unity Act is too concerned with the Constitution. Anyway, the Fed is shipping in and basically giving away food. Unless people have canned stuff or can butcher their own livestock, they'll have to take the Fed handout if they want to eat. But to get the food, they have to sign up for the federal ID card, and they have to allow their home to be searched for" — he made air quotes with his fingers — " 'evidence of association with rebels or rebel groups.' What else?" He swiped his finger to scroll down. "Nobody is allowed to drive without a federal ID and a special driving permit, and without filing a driving plan. Even then the vehicle has to have a special marker on the outside and must have a location tracker on board."

"What!?" Cal said. "That's bullshit! They can't do that!"

TJ read on. "And everyone ages five through twenty-one who does not have a high school diploma is required to register with and attend a public school full-time. This includes dropouts and home-schooled students. This rule goes into effect tomorrow, and I think they have enough soldiers out there to enforce it."

"The easiest way to control teenagers who might start to cause trouble when forced to live in a police state," said Kemp. "Keep them all in one location. Teach them Fed propaganda."

" 'All firearms except for nonfunctioning collectible antiques must be turned in to federal authorities,' " TJ read.

Cal held up his AR15. "Come try to get this one, assholes."

"Did they say when they're going to turn the rest of the Internet back on?" Sweeney asked. "At least so we can make comm calls? Right now, we can't even let our parents know we're okay."

"You couldn't even if the comms worked," said Herbokowitz. "The Fed will be recording everything. You hook your comm to the network, they'll find your location in seconds."

"TJ, can you at least go to my house, tell my dad I'm okay?" Cal asked.

"But don't tell him where he is," I said. "Nobody can know where we are."

TJ nodded. "No problem."

"You have to be careful," Kemp said. "You shouldn't come here that often. Maybe only if you really have to, like if we absolutely must know something."

"You need to get us medical supplies," said Sparrow. "Or maybe just take these wounded guys to the hospital. All of them need medical attention, but Danning's in real bad shape."

Luchen craned his neck to look at Sparrow. "Kiss my wounded ass! I'm not going to the hospital. The Fed will arrest me in ten seconds."

"It's not that I'd mind getting arrested," Danning said quietly. "But I know that . . . they'd try to make me tell them where you are. We can't . . . risk it." He pushed out each word with an exhausted breath. "Fed questions would be such . . . a pain." Danning coughed. "Get it? A pain?"

Cal laughed. Luchen gave a thumbs-up. "I hear ya, buddy."

"Then get medical supplies," Sparrow said to TJ.

He looked helpless. "From where? There's a first-aid kit in the science room at school. I could check —"

"Does it look like these people need basic first aid?" Sparrow asked.

"Well, I don't know. What do you want me to do, walk damned near thirty miles to rob the hospital in Coeur d'Alene?"

"They seem mostly stable for now," Sweeney said.

"Danning's abdominal wound is seriously bad," Sparrow said. "If we're going to be stupid enough to not get him to a hospital, then we might have to figure out how to get the bullet out of him and close him up ourselves. Everybody else needs stitches and clean bandages at the very least. If we don't do something, we're going to have some serious problems with infection."

I looked at the bloodstains on the cot where Nelson used to be. Kemp and Cal had hauled his body out in the dark sometime after the Fed left the shop. They couldn't risk being caught, so instead of taking the time to bury him, they put him inside the shell of a junked Chevy van sitting behind the shop near the creek.

"Can you just do your best?" I said to TJ. "Even some clean white sheets for bandages would be an improvement over what we got."

"Yeah, and maybe like some real hard-core alcohol to clean wounds? I saw that on a movie once," TJ said. "But I better go, in case the Feds outside start wondering why this simple tire job is taking so long."

Cal held out his fist to bump TJ's. "Thanks for helping us, man. Keep it cool out there. You get caught or in trouble, we're all screwed."

"Oh, and TJ," Sweeney said as TJ started up the stairs. "Can you see if you can find us some old board games or paper books or something? All we have is an old issue of *Turbo Truck* magazine and this book called *Surviving the Final War*. It sounds like we're going to be stuck down here for a while. It could get pretty boring."

"Okay, hold him down," Sparrow said. I helped Cal pin Danning's shoulders to the cot. Kemp and Sweeney held his arms. Crocker and Bagley grabbed his legs.

"Hey, Sparrow," Danning said. "I don't . . . Maybe . . . You know, I think this could just heal on its own. Like we could just leave the bullet in there." Sweat slicked his whole body.

Sparrow held her bayonet and a pair of basic, drugstore-issue tweezers. A set of regular kitchen tongs had been sterilized and set on a clean cloth on a folding chair.

We'd been in the dungeon for a week. Schmidty had taken the federal ID card so he wouldn't seem suspicious and so the Fed would allow his power to be turned back on. Once we could see a little better with the fluorescent lights on the ceiling, we'd noticed Danning was in trouble. His wound had dark streaks running out from it, and the skin around it was dry and dead. Worse, he was turning kind of yellow, like maybe jaundice, all over his body.

"We got to get the bullet out," Sparrow said. "We don't know what it messed up in there. We might have to sew up some internal organs."

I hoped to God she didn't have to go that far. She and I had taken turns using an Army sewing kit that Schmidty had down here to close up wounds, but neither one of us had had to touch an organ so far. From up in the shop came the shriek from the steel grinder. Schmidty had agreed to make enough noise to cover Danning's screams.

Herbokowitz sat in a chair next to Sparrow, shining a flashlight on Danning's quarter-inch-diameter wound. I looked down at Danning from where I stood by his shoulder. "Ready, Will? We got to do this now." His eyes were wide, tearing up. He nodded, his breathing heavy. "Cal?"

Cal held a thick stick to Danning's mouth. "Bite down on this."

Danning clamped down on the stick with a moan. Sparrow checked the picture in Schmidty's old survival manual one more time before she looked at the rest of us. "Everybody knows their job? You get sick, turn away, but don't stop doing whatever you're doing. Here we go." Sparrow moved her bayonet toward the bullet hole. "Got to open it up a little."

The next five minutes were awful, for Danning and for us. I kept my eyes focused on his face as he bucked and screamed. His face went about as red as his blood when Sparrow extracted the bullet. We sterilized the wound with the last of Herbokowitz's eighteen-year Macallan single-malt Scotch from his flask. The pain made Danning finally pass out, and Sparrow sewed him up.

"Okay, that's it," she said at last. "We'll let him sleep."

Cal pulled the stick out of Danning's mouth, holding it up to show the deep bite marks.

"I'll go tell Schmidty he can stop it with whatever metal he's grinding up there," I said. I looked around at the group, everybody filthy and sweaty and totally fried. I only hoped Danning would survive.

↜• *From the worldwide coverage of ABC News."*

"Good evening. I'm Dale Acosta, and this . . . is Night Time. *Welcome to our first show after a fifteen-hour total broadcast lock-out imposed by the federal government. Open military conflict in Idaho. No word yet on the number of casualties. The president insists this is a police action and not a civil war.*

"And the Unity Act. For residents of Idaho, it means, among other things, that this and all our other programs will not be seen. But what does it mean for the rest of America? We'll tell you about some of its restrictions on the way we bring you the news. Reporting and thoughtful analysis on all that, ahead on the program for Monday, November 22. •↜

Nick Tilly ★ ★ ★ ☆ ☆

Okay, I just posted to complain about "the law that shall not be named" and it was deleted like a minute or two later. Sorry if I believe in the First Amendment. I'm not a f@cking rebel! And look at my star rating, cause a lot of people agree with me. You'd think the government would have better things to do than police the whole Internet.

★ ★ ★ ★ ★ This Post's Star Average 4.95   [Star Rate][Comment]   17 minutes ago

---

Gabby Stillhorn ★ ★ ★ ★ ☆

What do you expect the President to do? She has to pull back on our freedoms a little to keep the country in one piece. Lincoln did this during the Civil War and FDR did it during World War II. If we can't save the country, then there won't be any Constitution to guarantee our freedom anyway. I just hope this will all be over soon so we can get back to normal.

★ ★ ☆ ☆ ☆ This Comment's Star Average 2.25   [Star Rate]   3 minutes ago

*┤—• Breaker one nine. Nobody truckin' with the Fed drive ban.
Anyone know how to deal with these drones? They took out a whole
Brotherhood squad. Come back now, hear? •—├*

┤—• Welcome back to the Sam Harrison Show *on the* Fox News
Channel, *government censorship edition. You know, from time to
time, I feel like I need to remind people that I am a conservative first
and a Republican second. That is, I stand in support of certain
ideals like freedom and limited government. While most of the time
these ideals are supported by the Republican party, I feel that I
have a duty to my viewers and the listeners of my radio program to
point out when the Republican leadership has strayed far from the
ideals upon which they were elected. Right now, our* Sam Harrison
Show *lawyers and legal analysts are busy poring over the so-
called Unity Act that our Republican lawmakers helped to radically
expand — at least, those parts of the law that aren't classified. And
I never thought I'd have to say something like this in America, but
I'm afraid. I'm afraid of saying something that our government
doesn't like and then being punished for it.*

*For the record, I believe Idaho's bid for independence is crazy.
It is wrong. This entire situation should have been negotiated
and resolved peacefully months ago. Now Americans are killing
Americans in Idaho, and the rest of the nation faces unprecedented*

restrictions on its citizens' rights, or should I say former rights, to free speech and assembly.

The Unity Act is something that I would expect from liberals and Democrats who believe that the solution to every problem is more government, more control from Washington, DC. Tonight I am deeply ashamed of Vice President Jim Barnes and the rest of the Republican leadership who signed this secret bill at the last second and without any time for public debate.

I am horrified and saddened to have to warn my audience not to publicly object to the Unity Act, because I honestly fear what our government will do to dissenters. We can only pray that this law will be struck down by the Supreme Court. But as we've learned in the past, holding out for help from the Supreme Court is often futile. •—⌁

⌁—• Tom, I'm on Interstate 84, northwest of Ontario, Oregon. My video crew and I have been trying to cross the border into Idaho, but we are still being stopped by a military blockade. Media personnel aren't even allowed to enter Ontario, and everyone is being kept well away from the Idaho border. We're being told this is for our own safety, and that while Idaho is under federal control, rogue insurgents still pose a threat. At least one news agency attempted to send a small cam drone toward Idaho, but it was quickly shot down. We'll continue doing our best to try to get you the story, but at present that's proving to be a real challenge. •—⌁

⌁—• Here on Comedy Central's Top News, we take a fair and balanced approach . . . to laughing at Republicans. And at Fox News. It's usually too easy. But tonight, perhaps for the first time, I, Jerry Simpson, must confess . . . I can hardly do it . . . I must confess that the time has finally come when I agree . . . with Sam Harrison.

At least on one issue. Um, sort of. And it is hard to joke about, because I worry that maybe jokes that are critical of the government might be one of those things forbidden by one of the classified sections of . . .

THE UNITY ACT.

You like that? That big echo effect? We have to try to make jokes somewhere. Sam Harrison says he is ashamed· of the Republican leadership for passing the Unity Act. Yes! I agree! I'm also ashamed of the Republican leadership.

But . . . the joke stops there. Because in fact, I'm ashamed of every member of Congress and of President Griffith for passing such a law. And if you want to take me off the air for saying so, that's fine by me. I don't know what disgusts me more, this law, or the fact that I'm forced into a position where I am in agreement with someone like Sam Harrison. •⌁

⌁• I'm going to turn it over to questions now. Um, there in the front."

"Bibi Sahar, New York Times. Vice President Barnes, I think it's fair to say that many people were surprised when President Griffith nominated you for the vice presidency. The two of you had been fierce political opponents. Now you seem in lockstep with the president on her policies. Can you explain this sudden reversal in your position?"

"Great question, Bibi. The answer is that this isn't a reversal at all. Look, the president and I disagree on several issues. Abortion. Gun rights. But one thing we both feel very strongly about is staying the course. While a peaceful solution is possible, I always advocate for peace. But President Griffith and I both believe that was no longer an option in Idaho. And I admire the president's leadership in quickly working to end this rebellion. Did I help convince my Republican allies to vote for the expansion of the Unity Act? Absolutely. Because we need this law at this time, and when something is the right thing to do, I try to convince everyone to support it. Next?"

"Molly Williams, National Public Radio. Mr. Vice President, what about the reports from a number of sources that say southern Idaho is not actually under federal control?"

"Molly, at times like these, there are going to be more rumors than bottles of maple syrup in Vermont and New Hampshire combined. Next question."

"Tyler Glover, ABC News. Mr. Vice President, part of the Unity Act places total restrictions on firearms in Idaho, with provisions in the law that would make such restrictions easy to expand to other states. In the past, you've strongly opposed gun control. Can you explain this reversal?"

"You see, this is the kind of thing that we, as Americans, need to look past right now, these petty issues that divide us. I have held an A rating from the National Rifle Association throughout my entire political career. I firmly believe in the right of the law-abiding individual to keep and bear arms as guaranteed by the Second Amendment. What I do not support are rebellions against this country. We have a dangerous situation in Idaho, and I know that many or most of the people living in that state love America and support the Constitution. For our troops' safety as they go into that dangerous place to try to restore order, to try to bring food and freedom to the people of Idaho, I support the provision to outlaw firearms only . . . only in those states deemed to be in a condition of rebellion.

"That's about all I'm at liberty to discuss at this time, but I want to remind all Americans everywhere of the importance of unity and cooperation. Together, we will get through all of this, and I truly believe America will be a stronger nation as a result. Thank you. •⟶⥿

⌁• Reaching a decision quickly, a five-to-four majority in the US Supreme Court upheld the Unity Act today. The majority opinion said that restrictions on certain rights have always been permissible in the presence of a clear, present, or imminent danger. The court did caution, however, that great care must be taken to ensure that the Unity Act is applied equally and not used to target any Americans based on race, gender, nationality, political affiliation, sexual orientation, or religion. The minority opinion argued that the rights guaranteed by the Constitution are absolute and cannot be restricted without due process, especially in times of great nationwide fear or uncertainty. Analysis on this landmark decision when NPR's Everything That Matters continues."

"Support for NPR comes from •⌁

CHAPTER FOUR

"First Sergeant, haven't you finished that magazine yet?" Crocker asked from over near the gun safe, fiddling with his radios as usual.

"I've read the survival book and this whole magazine twice already. Nothing else to read," Herbokowitz said.

"Aimee Hartling," Sweeney said to me. Him and me were laying on our backs on cots by the kitchen wall, staring up at the swirls in the concrete ceiling above us. Sometimes I could kind of see pictures. "Wright."

"What?" I tried to focus on what he'd been saying. I could hear the sounds of Sparrow taking a dump on the toilet under the stairs. More than anything, I wished we had more than a thin sheet to wall off that little space. That and an exhaust fan.

"Aimee," Sweeney said.

"What about her?" I asked.

He hit me in the arm. "I think maybe she was the one, man."

Bagley and Cal sat at the table playing cards. Kemp usually joined them, but he was on guard duty. The guy took extra shifts a lot of the time. Maybe he liked to be alone. It was as close to privacy as we got in the dungeon.

"Luchen, when you gonna join in the game?" Bagley asked.

"Soon as my ass is good enough so I can sit in a chair, and soon as you play a real game."

"Bagley, would you go already?" Cal said. "And this *is* a real game, Luchen."

"Fine." Bagley looked over his hand. "You got any threes?"

"Go fish yourself," Cal said.

"You dated Aimee Hartling?" I asked Sweeney.

"Oh yeah," Sweeney said. "Around Christmas last year, remember?"

I scratched an itch on my head, and my fingers came away greasy from my filthy hair. "I thought you were going out with Caitlyn Ericson then. Didn't you get her a scarf or something?"

Crocker poked his head out from around the end of the shelves. "He does so have a three. Three of hearts, has that frayed corner and crease near the bottom from when him and Sweeney got in that argument last week."

Cal slapped his hand down on the table and flicked the card at Bagley. "Man, Crocker, what the hell!? Go back to your corner, you little troll."

"And maybe I'll play when y'all stop cheating!" Luchen said.

The stench of blood, sweat, death, and shit hung over the whole basement. It stuck to our clothes, soaked into our hair, ruined our food, and even sneaked into our sleep, stinking up our nightmares.

I propped myself up on one elbow to check on Danning. He was asleep, but his color had improved a lot since the surgery. And when he was awake, he had a lot more energy. I was glad he was feeling better, but if I had to listen to him explain one more time how him and his dad once saw Seattle beat Denver in the Super Bowl, I would go upstairs to the shop and crush my head in a vise.

The toilet flushed, and a few seconds later, Sparrow crossed the room to join Luchen in the corner, where the two of them had side-by-side cots.

"You just want to mess around back there with your girlfriend," Cal said to Luchen.

"Riccon," said Sparrow, "you may be strong, but I've been trained in hand-to-hand combat, and if you give me and Luchen any more shit, I'll rip off your arms and shove them up your ass."

Cal shook his head. "Never thought I'd say this," he said, "but I miss my job. Spending all summer on the dock. All the girls coming to rent kayaks and paddleboats, checking out my muscles. Taking rides in my boss's seaplane. He even let me take the yoke a couple times and fly it a bit. That was so much better than this stinky-ass dungeon."

"Shit. Yeah. Caitlyn loved that scarf," said Sweeney. "Silk. Cost a fortune. Maybe Caitlyn Ericson was the one."

I rolled onto my side, facing away from Sweeney. This was how every day had dragged on down here for nearly four weeks. Waiting. For nothing. And I guess I was glad that I at least had two of my best friends with me, but I'm not gonna lie. I would have given anything to just lock myself away from everyone to be alone. If this continued much longer, the Fed wouldn't have to kill us. We'd die of boredom.

It happened again. Some dirty Fed's hand brushed my shoulder, reaching for my neck in the dark. I sat up with my knife and sprang to my feet as I slashed at him. Sweat stuck my filthy clothes to my armpits, crotch, and back as I looked around for the danger.

"Whoa, take it easy!" a whiny, nasally voice said in the dark.

"Crocker," I said, taking deep breaths to try to calm my pounding heart. "I told you to poke me with the cot pole to wake me up. You're going to get yourself killed trying to grab me while I'm sleeping." It was rare enough that I slept at all. The hard Army cots and the cement floor down in the freezing cold dungeon were as uncomfortable as it got, even though we had sleeping bags and blankets.

When I did sleep, the nightmares came. They were distorted images of the protest in Boise that had gone wrong, where I'd accidentally fired the shot that had led to the war. Or I'd dream of that horrible day I'd first had to kill a man so I could bring my mother home to Idaho. Then my sleeping brain made me relive the moment the Fed shot her. In my dreams I could still hear her screaming, still see the blood.

Crocker picked up his flashlight from the floor. "You awake? Sorry to scare you. It's zero five. You're on guard duty."

I took the flashlight. "Yeah, have a good sleep."

The flashlight cut through the darkness as I found my way to the stairs and our guard position. Everyone had a thermal cloak, but the stupid things rustled so much that we just kept one hanging there by the stairs to cut down on noise during the shift change. Like all our clothes, it needed a wash and stank pretty bad. I slipped it on anyway. Nobody went on guard duty without a therm. It was mandatory. No exceptions.

I climbed up the stairs and turned the handle to unlock the trapdoor above me. It only moved about half of the quarter turn needed to make it unlock. The metal in the latching mechanism must have warped or something. I pushed the handle harder. No good. "Damn thing," I whispered. I braced my back against the wall and pushed with all my strength. Finally, the lever moved and the hatch unlocked.

My job for the next hour, until someone turned on the lights at six a.m., was to sit here and listen in case Feds came into the shop. I wasn't sure it would matter much if I heard something. If the Fed knew we were here and sent soldiers to take us down, we wouldn't be able to mount a real defense anyway. I sat there for a long time, wrapped in that stinking therm, letting the hour crawl by.

A tap on my foot made me jump. I ducked down the hatch to see Sweeney.

"Merry Christmas," he whispered.

"Already?" When nothing we did had any meaning, it was easy to lose track of the days.

He came up and joined me, half sitting in the closet under the thermal cloak. "Christmas Eve."

"I'm sorry I got you into this, man. I ruined your life."

He turned to look at me. "The hell you talking about?"

"I started this whole war, standoff, occupation, or whatever. I dragged you into it with me."

"You might have been a spark, but the fuel for this fire has been building for a long time. If not you, then someone else would have taken the first shot. The end result would be the same. And nobody drags Eric Sweeney into anything." He shrugged. "Except for a beautiful woman dragging me to bed."

"Yeah, and I've even made that impossible. Sparrow doesn't seem interested."

"The feeling's mutual. Besides, she seems pretty hung up on Luchen and his wounded ass." We laughed quietly. "And you've kept me alive, making it possible for me to find my one true love someday."

I grinned. "Your twelve true loves, maybe."

Sweeney chuckled. "Maybe in the past, but this war's got me thinking maybe it's time to find that one special girl, you know? You have JoBell, missing you through this, and where are all my old girlfriends? Do they even remember me? Do they even care if I'm alive or dead?"

It was quiet for a long time, and I thought about JoBell, as I often did. I hadn't seen her or heard from her in weeks. Was she okay? Did she miss me? When would I see her again?

"Listen, man," said Sweeney. "I think we need to do an op."

"A what?"

"An op. I saw it on TV one time. It means operation. We should do an attack or something. You know, like an ambush against the Fed. Schmidty said their headquarters is in the cop shop at the end of Main Street while they build a permanent base. Kemp's got a backpack with thirty pounds of C4. We could blast those bastards."

Had Cal and Sweeney somehow switched brains during the night? "That's insane," I said. "It won't work."

"You don't know that. We haven't looked into it enough. Anyway, we can't stay down here forever."

"We won't," I said. "We can go somewhere else when the Fed occupation is over."

"But what if they stay for a year? For ten years? We're not going to make it down here. You know that. Besides, don't you want to put the hit on these guys?"

My left hand had pretty much healed from the wound I'd gotten the day the Feds killed my mom, but it ached now. "Nobody hates the Feds more than me. Nobody. I'd kill every one of those bastards if I could."

Sergeant Kemp's watch alarm went off. A few seconds later, the lights went on below. I pulled the thermal cloak tighter around us. "But we'll never pull it off," I whispered. "Fed drones are all over. We'd be spotted and shot before we even got started. Anyway, what would be the point? The war's over, Sweeney. We lost."

"Come on, man," Sweeney said. "You can't just give up."

Kemp joined us by the stairs. "Hey, guys." His voice sounded wilted. He fell to take a seat near our feet without even looking up at us. "Will Danning is dead."

"I told you that we should have taken him to the hospital!" Sparrow shouted a little later, after everyone was awake. Her eyes threatened to spill tears. "I told you! Now he's dead."

"I don't get it," said Cal. "I thought he was getting better."

"Infection, you moron!" Sparrow yelled. "He's had shit medical attention."

"But you cleaned your —"

"I dipped kitchen tongs in hot water!" Sparrow said. "This whole room is filthy. We should never have tried to get the bullet out by ourselves. I basically killed him."

"The Fed killed him!" Cal said.

"Enough!" shouted First Sergeant Herbokowitz. "None of this will bring Danning back!"

Bagley picked up his sleeping bag, crumpling it into a wad instead of rolling it up. "That's it. I've had it. I gotta get out of here."

Cal yawned. "We've been over this, Bagley."

"No, I'm serious. I can't stand it one more day, lying around doing nothing. I'm not gonna die down here like him!" He unlatched and started to swing up the steel plate that closed off the two-foot-by-two-foot escape tunnel.

I crossed the room to slam the tunnel lid back down with my foot. "You're not leaving!"

"You can't keep me here! You got no right to keep me here! I ain't your prisoner! Let me out!" Bagley tried to move me aside, but he was a skinny guy. I pushed him back so hard he fell on his ass.

"Dude, I'm sorry, but we can't let you leave," I said. "If you get caught by the Fed, you could tell them where we are."

"I won't!" Tears streamed down his face. "I promise I won't." He was quieter now. "I promise. I won't tell. You gotta let me go." His voice, his whole body, had fallen into a shuddering whimper there on the floor, and he pulled his sleeping bag up over his head to hide himself.

"We'll have to get Danning out of here," said Herbokowitz.

"Danning was a good guy," said Kemp. "He deserved better than this."

Sparrow wiped her eyes. "We won't even be able to give him a decent funeral."

"We should do something, though," said Luchen. "We shouldn't just dump him like we're tossing out the trash."

"Why don't you say a few words before you take him out?" Herbokowitz asked me. "It's your place and all."

Me? I was no preacher. What could I say that would possibly do justice to this loyal Idaho soldier who had held on for so long? Still, everyone was looking at me, waiting.

"Specialist Danning, um . . . Will Danning was a great guy. He took a stand and fought for his home." I was ruining this, just like I'd ruined everything else. "Um, I remember he used to tell a lot of funny jokes. Biggest Seattle Seahawks fan in the world." Some people chuckled. "He was a great soldier. A hero. He was our friend."

The only sounds in the dungeon were Bagley's sniffles and the hollow hum of the fluorescent lights.

I folded my hands in front of me and bowed my head. "Let us pray." Everyone but Sparrow joined me. "Lord, please look after Danning for us. Please don't let him hurt anymore. God? . . . Please help us. Amen."

Moments later, we pulled Danning's dog tags and zipped him into his bloodstained sleeping bag. Then I holstered my .45, me and Kemp put on therms, and we dragged Danning out through the escape tunnel that led to the vacant lot next door to the shop.

I'm not gonna lie. Mixed in with the sadness over losing Danning and the misery of dungeon life, I felt a sliver of excitement at the chance to see the sun again. Of course, it was still mostly dark by the time we came out of the tunnel by the slag heap. A faint glow had begun to brighten the eastern sky, and the snow surprised me. There were at least six inches covering the ground and more coming down pretty fast. So, no sun, but at least our trail would be covered.

We carried Danning back to the junked cars near the creek ravine, where we had the cover of trees. It would take all day to hack a grave in the frozen ground, so the best we could do was put his corpse in the old van with Nelson. The cold would preserve the bodies and keep the smell down. Come spring, we'd have to dig them graves. If we were still alive.

"It's getting pretty bright out," Kemp whispered after we'd made sure the guys were covered in car seats, old mufflers, a spare car door, and other junk. "We should get back."

I closed the door to the van and pressed my hand against the cold metal. "I'm so sorry. Goodbye, Will."

We'd only taken a few steps down the little creek ravine, retracing our footprints, when we heard a branch break. Someone said, "Shh."

I drew my .45 and froze, completely still except for the pounding of my heart. We should have been safely out of sight down by the creek, but who knew? Maybe a drone had spotted us and given away our position. Maybe this was a random Fed patrol. Out of the corner of my eye, I saw someone step up to the edge of the ravine, and I aimed at his heart.

The intruder stopped and put his hands up. I sighed and lowered my gun. TJ.

He slid down the snowy slope with a big dumb grin. "Merry Christmas, Wright." What was so merry about it? "Got a present for you."

I noticed the backpack-shaped bulge under his therm. Since we weren't using all our cloaks, we'd agreed TJ should take a bunch of them to help with his runs or in case the girls got in trouble and needed them. I hoped he brought us some real food.

"Well, let's get inside," I said.

"Hang on," said TJ. "Just don't shoot."

I was about to ask him what he meant when I saw the cloaked figure of my JoBell step over the ridge.

I wanted to drop to my knees right there. JoBell smiled. I reached out to her, and she slid down the slope right into my arms. Nothing in my whole life had ever felt so good as holding her right then.

"I missed you so much," I whispered. She wrapped her cloak around us, and in that small space we kissed. Who cared if Kemp and TJ were right there watching? They could deal with the show. JoBell's kiss was warm, and wet, and hungry. For a moment, I thought about taking her upstairs to the front office of the shop so we could be alone, but that room was almost all windows, and we couldn't risk the Fed finding us.

That reminded me that we needed to get moving. I smiled again when I saw Becca carefully working her way down into the ravine. We hugged, and I was surprised a little at how tightly she squeezed me. "It's so good to see you again, Danny," she said.

"This is touching," Kemp said, "but we have to hide."

We all crawled through the tunnel, and soon Becca, JoBell, and TJ were happily greeting Cal and Sweeney down in the dungeon. I was jazzed, but I checked my smile when I saw Crocker and Bagley looking miserable. How could I be happy to see my girlfriend and one of my best friends when they hadn't seen their loved ones for weeks? When we'd never see Danning alive again? How could I feel like celebrating on the day of our fellow soldier's funeral?

"Are you insane?" Sparrow came out of the corner she shared with Luchen. "What the hell are they doing here?"

"It's okay," TJ said.

"Bullshit it's okay," said Sparrow. "They're going to bring the Fed down on us."

"TJ made it here fine before," said JoBell.

Sparrow folded her arms. "Yeah, princess, but he wasn't watched twenty-four hours a day. He didn't cut some shady deal to get out of a Fed prison cell."

"Hey!" Cal said. "Take it easy."

"We didn't cut any deals!" Becca said. "They screamed at us for hours, asking where Danny was, but we didn't say anything! We said we hadn't seen him since he went off to the fight!"

"Maybe that's what *you* told them," said Sparrow. "But I'm not so sure about her." She jerked her head at JoBell.

"Come on, Sparrow," I said. "Lighten up a little."

Sparrow rolled her eyes. "I heard you whining to Luchen back when we were on border duty about how your girlfriend was so against the Idaho Guard, how mad she was. Then you go get her to bring her here, and she doesn't want to come. Then the Fed arrest her and just let her go?"

JoBell threw her thermal cloak off, and for a moment I thought she was ready to fight. Sparrow thought so too, because she widened her stance into a combat position. When JoBell spoke, her words were tight, calm, and controlled. Her eyes locked onto Sparrow's. "I didn't tell the Fed where you were because I did not know. As for today, maybe it's because of Christmas, maybe something else, but the Fed car usually watching my house is gone. We were very careful coming here, and we took a very indirect and slow route until we were sure we weren't being followed."

It was a little weird that the Fed would just give up watching the girls, but Sparrow was full of shit thinking JoBell had sold us out. I could tell when my own girlfriend was lying or telling the truth. Then the idea hit me. "Sparrow, if JoBell wanted to turn us in, she could have done it a long time ago."

"Are you really that stupid?" Sparrow asked. "If she didn't know where we were, she would have to wait until TJ brought her here."

"Specialist Sparrow, that's enough. They're here now. This isn't getting us anywhere," said Herbokowitz from where he lay on his cot.

"Oh, yes, First Sergeant." Sparrow saluted. "Since we're not in the Army anymore, I will of course do whatever you say."

"Actually, before anyone says anything they might really regret, I have something to show you. Something important," said TJ. "This is seriously great. Like Christmas-miracle great." He held both hands up. "So a few days ago, I was walking to JoBell's house to join her on the walk to school." I tensed up, but JoBell squeezed me. TJ went on, "This guy comes up to me, checks to see if anyone else is around, and then holds his left hand up the way Wright did that day." He put his own hand up in a clenched fist, the way I'd held it in that video that had gone all over the Internet. "Anyway, the guy says, 'Travis Jones, you're friends with Daniel Wright.' Like that. He wasn't asking a question. It was like he knew."

"What did you say?" Herbokowitz sounded worried.

"What do you think I said? I figured he was a federal agent. I said I had known Wright in school, but I hadn't seen him in months and heard he was dead. The guy was real quiet when he spoke again. He handed over this old-as-hell iPod nano and said there was a message for Daniel Wright on it." TJ pulled the red iPod out of his pocket.

"You brought that thing here!?" Kemp said.

"You idiot!" Sweeney jumped to his feet. "That guy could have been CIA. The iPod probably has a tracking device on it. It's a good bet the Fed knows where we are."

"Whoa, guys. Calm down," said JoBell. "It's not tracking us. Hear him out."

"Of course, *she* tells us not to worry about the Fed finding us," said Sparrow.

Herbokowitz reached for the iPod. "How do you know if —"

TJ pulled it away from him. He plugged a little speaker into the device and tapped play.

We all gathered around as a tiny video of Governor Montaine came onto the screen.

"Is this current?" Kemp asked. "Is the governor alive?"

"Quiet," Herbokowitz said with some of his old authority. "We need to hear this."

Montaine nodded into the camera. He pointed out the date on an actual paper copy of a newspaper, the *Idaho Statesman*.

> Today is December fifteenth. This message is for Private
> Daniel Wright of the Idaho Army National Guard.

I grinned at hearing my name and rank again. After a few weeks in the dungeon, we had all mostly dropped the rank and protocol thing. The governor put the newspaper down.

> Private Wright, if my operative has succeeded and you are
> now watching this video, then let me say, I'm glad you're
> still alive and free. Be assured that the same is true for me,
> General McNabb, and the majority of the Idaho National
> Guard and the Idaho State Militia. The federal government
> thinks it can keep us helpless, uninformed, and out of touch
> because it's shut down Idaho's Internet and electricity. But
> the Fed is wrong, as I hope to prove by sending you this
> message. I'm working with a resistance group called the
> Brotherhood to distribute similar devices throughout
> occupied northern Idaho to patriots just like you, who are
> hiding in the dark and looking for hope.

"What's the Brotherhood?" Luchen asked.

"Probably just some code name. Now shut up! We need to hear this," said Herbokowitz.

> Take heart. You are not alone, and help is on the way. Private
> Wright, I wanted to send you this personal message, because
> from the very beginning, for better or worse, you've been at
> the center of this struggle. Time and time again, you've
> proved your loyalty to Idaho, and many have come to see you
> as an example of the strength and resilience of our people.
> That's why I'm asking you to listen to a very important radio
> announcement that I'll be making soon. I know this situation
> is tough, but hang in there. Idaho isn't beaten, and we
> need you.

He smiled and the video froze.

"That's it?" said Crocker. "How are we supposed to listen to his radio message if he didn't give us the frequency?"

"His operative did," said TJ. "I guess they didn't want to leave the frequency in the message in case the Fed captured the iPod. Maybe if the Fed knew about the broadcast in advance, they could jam it? I don't know. But the man told me to listen to AM 1040 at noon on Christmas Eve."

"You're sure?" I said.

"Yeah, I'm sure! He made me repeat it three times."

Herbokowitz stretched his injured leg, then stood up straight. "Specialist Crocker, get on the radio and make sure we can pick up that station. It might not come in so good down here, and you might have to rig some kind of field-expedient antenna." That old grouchy first sergeant sound was back in his voice.

"Yes, First Sergeant," Crocker said.

Herbokowitz put his hands on his hips. "Private Luchen, how's your ass?"

"It's pretty sexy, First Sergeant!"

The old man held back his smile. "No, dammit. I mean can you move if you have to?"

Luchen stood up with Sparrow's help. "Let me stretch out a little, First Sergeant. Then I think I'm ready to go."

"Great. Get yourself stretched out and dressed. Then assist Crocker if he needs help with the radio. After that, let's make sure our weapons are cleaned and ready to go. We're still in the Army, people! We want to be prepared for whatever the governor asks of us."

"Yes, First Sergeant!" I shouted with the others, happy to be back in action.

CHAPTER FIVE

"Wait a minute!" Becca said. "Before you all go into battle, it's Christmas Eve, and we didn't just bring news from the governor."

"We brought some supplies," TJ said.

"You bet we did." Becca pulled a small white box from her backpack. "Cal's dad smuggled us some amazing treats. Check out this smoked salmon. And I even brought a twelve-pack of beer."

They unpacked some basic survival food for us, canned vegetables and a couple MREs. But there was also a jar of real pickles, a can of cashews, a little box of chocolates, and five whole potatoes. Along with the canned ham we'd been saving from Schmidty, it was shaping up to be an even bigger Christmas feast than we could've hoped for.

While we cleaned our weapons, TJ, JoBell, and Becca shared news from the outside, though most of it was really just rumor passed along by Fed soldiers on the street, or by smugglers or the handful of people whom the Fed allowed to drive. The latest rumor was that the federal government was debating dissolving Idaho as a state. Under this proposal, northern Idaho would become part of the state of Washington, while the rest would go to Oregon. There were huge arguments about whether or not that was constitutional and how eliminating the state would help or hurt the Republicans and Democrats.

"How are the other states reacting to all this?" Kemp asked.

"Well, we don't really know," TJ said. "Like JoBell said, news is in short supply."

JoBell pouted. "I miss Digi-Eleanor."

The Feds were now using the high school gym for a CRC, or Civilian Relations Center. They'd shipped in food and other stuff that had been in short supply since the blockade, but for people to get any of it, they had to register with the federal government, accept the stupid identification card, and volunteer to have their homes searched for weapons, contraband, and evidence of cooperation with rebels.

Hearing about the searches and the way the Fed were trying to starve out anyone who didn't totally obey them made me want to run out of this dungeon, guns blazing, and shoot down as many Feds as I could. If they'd stop holding us all at gunpoint, we could feed ourselves.

Becca, JoBell, and TJ organized our food for a Christmas Eve dinner while the rest of us cleaned the dungeon. We even did the best we could to clean ourselves. I was grateful for the work, not only because it finally gave us something positive to do, but also because it helped kill time until the radio announcement.

Finally, we all gathered around the table in the kitchen area. After we had gotten the damned sticky hatch open, Specialist Crocker had risked a trip up into the shop, where he had found enough copper wire to run a big loop antenna all the way up the stairs to the top of the closet. Now he stood by the old boom-box-style radio, smiling.

"I don't get it," Luchen said to him. "What are you so happy about? I don't hear nothing."

"Exactly!" said Crocker. "You don't hear any static. It's completely quiet. Someone's broadcasting on this frequency, but they're broadcasting dead air."

At 12:02 p.m., I started to doubt if the governor was going to pull this off. Finally, there was a crackle of static and a popping sound.

People of Idaho, stand by for an important announcement
from your capitol in Boise. Ladies and gentlemen, here's Miss
Kayla Foster.

"Who?" Becca said.

"Shh," said JoBell.

Some somber piano notes played and then a sweet voice began to sing.

Idaho, Idaho
Land where freedom lovers go
From fertile plains to mountains tall
Brothers, sisters one and all

Idaho, Idaho
Light of hope in darkness glow
We will defend our liberty
Idaho, our lives for thee

The music ended and a little shiver ran through me, the kind I used to get when the national anthem played before our football games or a rodeo.

"That's not the old Idaho state song," Becca said. "I learned it for a 4-H project once. This is completely new."

The governor's voice came over the radio.

People of Idaho, I am James P. Montaine. I bring you
greetings this Christmas season, a time traditionally
dedicated to peace and hope. While the government of the
United States will not, at present, allow Idaho any peace, at
this time I offer you all a message of hope. Despite the United

States federal government's best efforts, southern Idaho remains free of the US military. Northern Idaho faces a harsh occupation, but even now, the resistance is building, and the time will come when the military forces of the United States are sent back where they came from.

My people, Idaho survives. Freedom survives!

Months ago, suspecting that the federal government of the United States was preparing to invade Idaho, I worked in cooperation with the military leadership of the Idaho National Guard to prepare a plan to seize control of Mountain Home Air Force Base and its military assets. Thanks to the excellent preparation and professionalism of Idaho Guard forces, and to carefully placed allies inside the base, Mountain Home was taken with minimal loss of life the moment the United States military invaded Idaho. In addition to the Idaho National Guard's A-10 ground attack airplanes and its advanced Apache attack helicopters, our skies are now protected by three squadrons of F/A-35 jets, nearly one hundred of the world's most advanced fighters.

On the ground, southern Idaho is protected by Idaho Guard and Militia forces. Infantry soldiers and combat engineers are working with artillery and armored units. Idaho has the advantage of fighting to defend our home on rugged terrain that is familiar to us, but a difficult challenge for a large portion of the federal military. In the dangerous chaos following the federal attack, Idaho forces rallied at the Battle of White Bird. In and around that tiny mountain valley town, we made our stand and held our ground, stopping the federal advance and securing our freedom.

Since some of Idaho's electricity is produced out of state, President Griffith was able to order a significant blackout across much of Idaho. However, emergency electrical generators were employed to maintain power to military outposts, hospitals, and other critical installations. Idaho's electrical grid is being rerouted and restored, and in the future we will rely more on our natural gas resources as well as on solar power. In time, we will even establish our own computer network so that Internet feeds to our COMMPADS and screens can be restored. Despite President Griffith's and the federal government's best efforts, we will have the freedom to communicate and once again live our lives as we wish.

Protecting our freedom has been our only goal since this crisis began. We would not accept the unconstitutional invasion of our privacy when the federal government tried to force us all to use their trackable federal identification cards. We would not allow the federal government to arrest Idaho Army National Guard soldiers who had committed no crime. To stop this government overreach, to stop these violations of our rights, we joined together to use the minimal force required to enforce Idaho's Constitution, preventing all armed federal agents and military personnel from entering the state. We then worked in good faith with the federal government, doing all we could to seek a peaceful resolution to our disagreements.

President Laura Griffith's brutal attack on Idaho has not been without cost. Our infrastructure has been damaged. Many of our soldiers have been killed. Many of our civilians are dead. Many survivors, already endangered by the harsh federal blockade of food and other supplies, are now forced to live with no electricity or information from the outside *world, save for false propaganda from the Griffith administration.*

In all of my years of public life, I have always done what I thought was best for the state of Idaho. I loved the United States of America as well. But now, President Laura Griffith has designated Idaho a rebel state. This has given the Idaho state legislature and myself no choice but to declare our home to be the fully independent Republic of Idaho. We hereby dissolve all formal ties with the United States of America and establish our own representative democracy, maintaining the borders and all forty-four counties that our state held before the United States invaded.

Yesterday, solid majorities from our thirty-five counties that are fully or partially free of United States occupying forces voted to elect me interim president of the Republic of Idaho. We look forward to the day when all of Idaho is free to hold another election for our first president to serve under the terms of our new constitution. To that end, we will, for the time being, continue to abide by the Idaho state constitution with only a few emergency amendments. The people from our thirty-five free counties have voted to allow their representatives in the state legislature to begin drafting a new constitution, subject to ratification by all our counties. This constitution will ensure our freedom and way of life for generations to come.

And now, I want to speak directly to those of you huddled in the dark, suffering under the tyranny of the so-called United States Federal Idaho Reconstruction Authority. My message to you is this. Hold on. Stay the course. You are not alone, and you are most certainly not forgotten. Help is on the way. And I have a Christmas present for you. Because the scientists and engineers at Idaho Electronics helped develop many of the control and communications systems for military-grade drone aircraft, they were able to devise a number of countermeasures against the federal drones. The Republic of Idaho has already seized control of many of these drones, forcing them to crash, landing them safely in Idaho, or, in some cases, even using them against the US military. With this technological threat neutralized, it is the hope of all the citizens of Idaho that you will have more freedom of movement. It is our hope that you will double your efforts to fight back.

That is my message to all of my fellow citizens of the Republic of Idaho. Fight back! Fight back against a military intent on destroying you. Fight back against the United States' intent to enslave you.

The struggle ahead will be difficult. Freedom is neither painlessly won nor easily maintained. That is why I am currently invoking Article Fourteen, Section One, of the current Idaho State Constitution, in which the original authors of that document wrote, 'All able-bodied male persons, residents of this state, between the ages of eighteen and forty-five years, shall be enrolled in the militia, and perform such military duty as may be required by law.' The clause continues, 'But no person having conscientious scruples against bearing arms, shall be compelled to perform such duty in time of peace.' We unfortunately are not in a time of peace, but in a time of dire war, and so all able-bodied Idaho men will be required to serve the Idaho military in some capacity. Conscientious objectors have the option to serve in noncombat roles. Additionally, though I will follow the law as

it was written, I would ask able-bodied women to volunteer
to join our forces as well. We need you. We need all patriotic
Idahoans in the coming fight.

This Christmas, we celebrate the birth of our Savior, and
we also celebrate the birth of our new nation, asking for God's
help in our struggle to be free. May God bless all of you and
the Republic of Idaho.

The previous announcer's voice came on again.

We will continue to broadcast news and information about
Idaho and the United States on this frequency. If the United
States succeeds in blocking the broadcast, please monitor
other frequencies, as those Idaho patriots working with our
network of stationary and mobile broadcast equipment will
never relent in their efforts to keep you and all Idahoans
connected. The news is next, but first, another rendition of
our new Idaho national anthem.

The same girl's beautiful singing voice came back on.

Idaho, Idaho
Land where freedom lovers go . . .

Sweeney reached over and slowly turned down the volume on the
radio.

"So, Governor Montaine really did it," JoBell said. "Declared
independence. All-out civil war."

"*President* Montaine," said Cal. "And it ain't a civil war. It's . . .
What do they call it?"

"A resolution!" said Luchen.

"Revolution," said Sergeant Kemp.

"Only if it succeeds," said Sparrow.

Herbokowitz coughed. "It will succeed. It's our job to make sure that it does."

I stood up. "First Sergeant Herbokowitz is right," I said. "This revolution *will* succeed. It's time to fight back. We'll have our Christmas celebration, and then we'll start making plans."

SIX

There was a moment of silence, then everyone started talking at once.

"Yes! About time we started fighting back!" "What will we hit first?" "We have a fifty-cal rifle. Let's do some sniper attacks." "We have explosives, right?" "Sniper attacks will only take out one soldier at a time." "We could blow up their HQ on Main Street." "It's hard enough to rig explosives when you have time and there's no danger." "What about the people this will hurt?" "Who cares? They're Feds. They deserve it." "I think we're missing the point." "Maybe we can contact the gov — er — the president to see what we should hit." "What if there's some nineteen-year-old file clerk working the office? Does she deserve to die too?"

"This is a military operation!" Sparrow shouted.

"Yeah!" Luchen cut in. "You civilians let us handle this."

"Atten-TION!" First Sergeant Herbokowitz boomed. All of us soldiers and even Bagley sprang up straight with our fists at our sides. "All right, lock that 'soldier versus civilian' shit up right now!" He pointed "blade hand" at Sparrow, with his thumb and fingers in a tight vertical line. "Do you want to die, Specialist Sparrow?"

"First Sergeant?" she said.

"Do you want to die!?" Deep red splotches flared in his neck and face. He snapped a fast movement so his face was inches from Luchen's. "How about you? You want to die, Private Luchen? Want to spend the rest of your life in a federal prison? A permanent cell in Guantanamo Bay with your nuts wired to a car battery?" He moved to the middle of the room, rubbing his bad thigh for only a moment. "We can rot in this basement, we can rot in a federal prison, or we can fight back. To fight back, we will have to attack United States soldiers. We'll have to kill them. We can't fight them head-on, so what does that leave us? IEDs, sniper attacks, sabotage, and hit-and-run stuff. Those are our options, and we'll have to make the best use of them we can." The first sergeant came to the position of attention. "Now, on the command of 'fall out,' fall out and engage in a reasonable discussion. Fall out!"

We all laughed and relaxed our postures.

"First Sergeant, what you describe sounds like terrorist tactics," JoBell said.

Herbokowitz frowned. "Terrorists. Insurgents. Whatever you want to call them. Their methods are effective, the only tactically sound option when facing a vastly superior force. Trust me, I know. My company lost a lot of good guys to IEDs and snipers and shit during our year in Kandahar Province."

"So you're okay with becoming one of them?" JoBell asked.

I closed my eyes and shook my head. That wasn't going to go over well.

Herbokowitz stiffened. "You better watch —"

"What?" JoBell said. "You gonna hit me because I disagree with you?" She turned to face the rest of us. "Listen, this announcement from the governor —"

"President," Luchen said.

"From Montaine," she said. "Maybe it's good news. Maybe it just means that a long bloody war will drag on for a lot longer. But it doesn't have to change anything for us. We don't *have* to start fighting. Violence isn't the answer."

Luchen and Sparrow looked at each other and rolled their eyes. "Of course you'd take the side of the Fed," Sparrow said.

I spun to face her. "Would you stop accusing my girlfriend of shit?" This was getting out of hand.

Herbokowitz grunted. "Listen." He seemed to have calmed down. "I wish that was true, that fighting didn't have to be the answer. I pray all the time that that could be the way things are. But I've been on two combat tours, one in Afghanistan, the other in Pakistan. In Pakistan, we were all fired up about helping the poor people in these villages, about building them schools and getting education for the kids. We lost two soldiers setting up one of those schools, but we got it done. We even put up big cement walls around the place for the students' safety and privacy. The colonel patted us all on the back, saying 'mission accomplished' and all that.

"And two weeks later, the damned Taliban crashed a truck full of explosives through the wall. Then they stormed the school and raped and burned every girl in there who had dared to try to learn to read." His face was flaming red and his eyes were watery. "Those little girls *trusted* us! It was our mission to help make their lives better, and they got a fate worse than death! And now, I gotta stand here and listen to you tell me violence isn't the answer!? You better wake up, sweetheart. This whole world is controlled by physical force. Whoever is toughest makes the rules. Whoever wins the fight, or wears his enemy down until the enemy is tired of fighting, decides how things are."

"George Washington and all of the Founding Fathers might have been called terrorists if the word had been around back then." Specialist Crocker shrugged. "But they won the war and started a country, and so our history books call them patriots or revolutionaries."

"Unless Idaho wins, we spend the rest of our lives like this. Always on the run. Never able to go home and live freely," Sparrow said.

"That's why we have to fight the Fed," Cal said.

"Exactly. See, now it's like we're those good people in that village in Pakistan," said Herbokowitz. "We gotta protect ourselves. The world is ruled by the power of the gun."

"I'm so sorry for those kids, those girls in Pakistan, and for the soldiers you lost," JoBell said to him. "But it doesn't have to be this way. The gun is not the only truth, or the only option. Or at least, it doesn't have to be that way for us. We could stay out of the war."

"You want us to stay down here for decades?" Bagley asked with panic in his voice.

"No," said JoBell. "But we don't have to fight. Now that we have more freedom of movement, we could go somewhere safe where it's easier to live."

"My parents have a cabin about an hour's drive north. We could go there," TJ said. "If we could drive."

"That's a long walk in winter," Luchen said.

JoBell continued, "I'm just saying that war doesn't *have* to be the inevitable nightmare. We can choose peace. For ourselves, anyway."

I watched JoBell saying all this, impressed, as I always was, by her passion and by how well she made her case. But I couldn't understand how, after all we'd been through, after all the Fed had taken from us and what they'd *tried* to take from us, she could still think this could go down without a fight. Maybe that was the point of being a soldier. We were the ones to go out and fight the war so that people back home could live in peace, with the freedom to think like JoBell.

"I get what you're saying, Jo," Sweeney said. "But I think we're past the point of peace now. Even if we could find a better place to hide, the Fed would find us eventually. Violence is the only way we're going to get them to leave us alone."

"So said every terrorist in modern history," said JoBell.

Luchen slowly lowered himself onto a folding chair, sitting on his butt for the first time since he'd been shot. "We're nothing like terrorists."

"That's not how the president will see it," said Becca. "The president of the United States, I mean."

"The difference between terrorists and soldiers are the targets they choose," said Sergeant Kemp.

Herbokowitz smiled at the sergeant. "Exactly! Terrorists deliberately target civilians. Shopping malls. City buses. Skyscrapers. We'll be engaging military targets only."

"America always says that," JoBell said. "In every foreign war, we use smart bombs or guided missiles or drones to go after the bad guys, but over and over again we hit the wrong house and accidentally kill families. Children. We call it 'collateral damage,' but that really means 'innocent people that we've murdered.'"

"We'll be careful," said the first sergeant. "If there are too many civvies in the area, we'll go for a different target. But to win this war, to stay alive, we're going to need to throw out the old rule book. That's what the Fed will be using, and we'll have to use that against them. We're going to rely on civilians, not target them. We'll be liberating them from Fed control." He pointed at JoBell. "You said yourself that the Fed was violating the Constitution to enforce this occupation."

JoBell folded her arms. "Danny, you've been quiet. What do you think?"

I was thinking I wished she wouldn't have asked me that. I was thinking how much better life would be if we were back to arguing about whether to listen to Hank McGrew or the news on the radio, or if we couldn't decide which movie to watch on our comms. I looked at JoBell, hoping she'd understand. "I'm sorry. I wish it was possible to get out of this without a fight. I wish this had never happened or that it could be over. But the Fed has proven that they're not interested in peace. Who knows if we could find another safe place to hide? What does 'safe' even mean during an occupation? They'll kill whoever they have to kill to force us to obey them. They killed my mother. They've killed most of our unit." I shook my head. "We don't have a choice. Now that I know I still have a country to fight for, I'm going to make those Fed sons of bitches pay."

JoBell shook her head and walked down the narrow aisle between the supply shelves. I started to follow her, but Becca caught my wrist and shook her head. "Just let her be," she whispered. "Give her a chance to adjust to all this."

Cal actually raised his hand. Sergeant Kemp and First Sergeant Herbokowitz laughed. "This isn't a class, son," said Herbokowitz.

"Well, sir, you were talking about soldiers and civilians, and I was thinking about what Govern — about what *President* Montaine said. About all men older than eighteen having to enlist. I'm eighteen. I want to enlist."

"Me too!" TJ said. "I want in."

"This is bullshit!" said Sweeney. "My birthday's in April. You're telling me I have to wait four months? Wright's only seventeen and he's enlisted."

JoBell came right back out from behind the shelves. "Do you think it's a good idea to actually be signing up?" she said.

"Jo," said Sweeney. "We've been over this. We're joining the Militia, the Guard, the Idaho Army. Whatever it's called."

JoBell shook her head. "I get that I can't stop you from doing this stupid thing. But what I meant is that we shouldn't be writing a whole bunch of contracts with our names on them, saying we're joining what President Griffith calls a rebel army."

"What's she going to do about it?" Cal asked.

"No, she's right," said Sparrow. I had to smile. Finally, she and JoBell had agreed on something. "If the papers fall into Fed hands, you guys are all guilty."

"Never mind that — we don't have enough paper to write contracts. We'll just swear you in," said Herbokowitz. "Here, someone give me the truck magazine and that pencil that was floating around. I need to try to remember what's in the oath. I've sworn in enough soldiers to figure it out, but we'll have to make some changes, and I want to do this right."

The first sergeant and Sergeant Kemp worked together on the oath. I reached out to take JoBell's hand, but she pulled away and went back behind the shelves again. Crocker kept monitoring the radio. Cal, Luchen, Sparrow, Sweeney, and TJ gathered around the table to talk about possible op plans. Bagley went on guard duty. Becca seemed to have assigned herself the cook's job, and I joined her at the corner stove to help prepare Christmas Eve dinner.

I couldn't find the key thing that was supposed to open the canned ham, and using the damned can opener turned out to be impossible. Becca laughed when it slipped off the can for the fifth time. "How's that working?" She sliced the potatoes into a pan for frying.

I got the thing back on the lip of the can and cranked it. "I think winning the war will be easier than getting this . . ." It slipped again. "Damn it . . . this meat product out of this stupid can."

She laughed again and touched my elbow. "You want me to help?"

"No, I got this," I said.

She moved a step closer to me. "Listen," she said quietly. "I didn't want to bring this up in front of the others, because emotions are already running pretty high. . . ."

I smiled. Maybe peace was impossible between the Republic of

Idaho and the United States, but Becca would never stop working to cool off fights between her friends.

She pushed the potato slices around in the frying pan. "I'll go along with whatever you all decide. I mean, whatever you, JoBell, Cal, TJ, and Eric decide." She started working her magic with seasonings. "But what if JoBell is right, Danny? I'm worried about you. About all of us, if we get back into the fight. Maybe we can all go find a better place to hide. Or if we can move around more freely now, why not take off by ourselves? Your soldier friends could go south maybe, link up with the Idaho Army down there. But we could just stop fighting."

"I swore an oath," I whispered. "I'm a soldier. It's my duty to protect my home."

She touched the purple butterfly hair clip that she always wore. "You sure that's what this is about? Duty and not revenge for your mom?"

I looked into Becca's eyes. Sometimes it was like the girl could see my thoughts, and I wasn't sure how I felt about that. "This time duty and revenge work out to pretty much the same thing."

She was quiet for a moment. "Well, if that's the way it's got to be, then for what it's worth, I got your back."

We didn't say anything else for a long time, and I finally got the ham out of the can. I showed it to Becca, but she only smiled sadly. "What's wrong?" I kind of laughed at my own question. "I mean, what's bugging you more than everything else that's been going on?"

"Christmas," she said. "And I have no idea where my parents are. No way to contact them to tell them I'm okay, and they still can't come home." She leaned a little closer to me and whispered, "I mean, I'm sorry. I know my folks are still alive, and what I'm going through is nothing like what you've had to deal with, but still, it's —"

"Hey," I said quietly, patting her arm. "Don't apologize. I know it's hard."

She looked up at me. Becca was really pretty great, the best female friend in the world. I noticed the subtle shading on her cheeks and around her eyes. "Are you wearing makeup?" I asked her.

Her cheeks flushed redder than any powder or whatever. "Is it dumb? I don't know. I found this old stuff from a long time ago kind of wedged in at the bottom of my bag. I'd forgotten it was even in there. I thought I'd try it for once. You know, it's Christmas and everything. I should wash it off, I guess. I've never been good at all that girly stuff."

"Whoa. No, it's cool. You look good." I shrugged. "I mean, makeup, no makeup. It's all good." I looked around to make sure nobody was listening. "Maybe I could set you up with Crocker or Bagley over there."

She laughed. "Yuck."

"Okay, I think I've got it," said the first sergeant behind us. "Everybody who was already in the Idaho National Guard or the Idaho State Militia is still a member of the new Idaho Army." He pointed to the floor a few feet in front of him. "Anyone else who is interested in joining, please form a line here shoulder to shoulder."

Sweeney, TJ, and Cal rushed to the line. Becca rubbed my back real quick, smiled, and joined them. They waited on JoBell, who stood by herself off to the side.

"Jo?" Becca asked after a moment.

"I'm sorry," JoBell said. "I can't be a part of this. I'm not a soldier."

"Why am I not surprised?" Sparrow said quietly.

"Easy, Specialist. It's everyone's free choice," First Sergeant Herbokowitz said. "Sergeant Kemp, you'll be platoon sergeant here.

Let's get a formation." He looked around the basement. "I wish we had an Idaho flag somewhere." When Sergeant Kemp had all of us Guardsmen plus Bagley standing shoulder to shoulder at a right angle to the line of four who were about to swear in, Herbokowitz called out, "Fall in!" We snapped to attention. My friends and TJ did their best to imitate us, even if Cal couldn't wipe the dumb smile off his face. "Attention to orders," Herbokowitz continued. "We are about to issue the oath of enlistment. New enlistees will raise their right hands and repeat after me. I, state your name . . ."

"I, state . . . er, Calvin Riccon," Cal repeated. The rest got it right.

The first sergeant fought to hold back a grin. "Do solemnly swear . . . that I will support and defend the Constitution of the Republic of Idaho . . . against all enemies foreign and domestic . . . that I will bear true faith and allegiance to the same . . . and that I will obey the orders of the president of the Republic of Idaho . . . and the orders of the officers appointed over me . . . according to Idaho law."

They all repeated his words, line by line.

"So help me God," said the first sergeant.

"So help me God," said the others.

"Welcome to the Idaho Army. Let's give them a round of applause."

Even though we weren't supposed to do anything like this at the position of attention, we all clapped and cheered. "First sergeant, do they get a sign-on bonus?" Luchen asked.

Herbokowitz laughed and returned to the position of attention himself. "On the command of 'fall out,' fall out for a Christmas celebration, and let's resume planning to kick a little Fed ass. Fall out!"

We all broke formation, laughed, high-fived, and shook hands with the new soldiers. TJ stepped up in front of me.

"Congratulations . . . Private," I said. He reached out his hand and I shook it. I'm not gonna lie. I felt weird shaking hands with TJ and congratulating him. I was so used to hating him that it bothered me a little that he was a soldier like me. Yeah, he hadn't been through basic training, but with everything that was going on, all that training crap just seemed kind of babyish. TJ had been putting his life on the line a lot since the Fed invasion. Every time he sneaked us news or supplies, he risked being arrested or worse. "Thanks for all your help," I said.

He shrugged. "No problem."

I laughed. "Bullshit, no problem."

A little bit later, we all sat down to an almost old-fashioned-family-type Christmas dinner. The mood in the dungeon was better than it had ever been. I was on a cot with my JoBell on my lap, Becca on my left, and Sweeney on my right. Cal and TJ took up the cot across from us. The remaining members of my Guard unit sat on chairs and cots around the table. The dinner was small — the ham and potatoes with smoked salmon and pickles on the side, some canned pears, and the almonds and chocolates for dessert. But while we never ate our fill anymore, nobody complained today.

When we were all finished, we sat around enjoying our beers. It was just cheap PBR, but better than nothing. Cal leaned back in his chair with his feet up on the table. "I remember one Christmas when Dad was on the road, my brother told me Dad hit Santa's sleigh with his semi. He said Santa and all the reindeer except for Rudolph had been killed, and Rudolph was hurt so bad that his glowing nose was all that still worked on him, so Dad had to shoot him in the head. I cried and cried. Always a bunch of fun, my brother."

"I was thinking about proposing to my girlfriend this Christmas," said Kemp.

"Really? Tom, that's great. How long have you two been together?" JoBell asked.

Kemp slumped in his chair. "No, see, she broke up with me when I was on duty guarding the border."

"What? I'm so sorry." JoBell rubbed my back as she spoke. "That must be tough."

He shrugged. "It's for the best. I want her to be happy, you know. I'm not going to be able to be with her anytime soon. It's probably best she thinks I'm dead and moves on."

"Hey, man," Sweeney said. "When this is all over and we get out of here, I'll find you dozens of girls. Trust me."

Kemp didn't seem encouraged.

"Well, as you all know . . ." Herbokowitz took a drink of his PBR. "Being at war, you miss out on a lot of life. My oldest daughter was three years old the Christmas I was in Pakistan. I promised her the best present ever the next Christmas when I was home." He sat up in his seat. "I had a bunch of deployment money saved up, so I bought her this toy horse. It was covered in fur, about this big" — he held his hands about four feet apart, then he drew an imaginary horizontal line about five feet above the floor — "with a big brown mane. When she petted the horse, it made these whinny and snort sounds. It would stretch out its neck and nuzzle her with its nose. Its eyes blinked. I mean, this thing did everything except piss and shit." We all laughed.

"The Real Rider horse!" Becca said with a huge smile. "I grew up with horses on the farm, but I still wanted the Real Rider! You got that for her?"

Herbokowitz sat back in his chair, took another drink, and stared up at the ceiling. "She woke up first on Christmas morning, of course. I flew out of bed after the loudest, most eardrum-splitting scream I'd ever heard. I got . . . got downstairs, and she was jumping around in her pajamas like a little frog. 'Daddy, Daddy, look! Look! A horsey!'

she yelled over and over. I could hardly get her calmed down enough to even get on that horse. Once I did, she stayed in the saddle all day until she finally fell asleep." Herbokowitz wiped his eyes. "She's twelve now. I hope she's okay."

We went on like that, talking about our great memories of Christmases past, until we all sank into silence, weighed down by the thought of all we'd lost.

Finally, Herbokowitz clapped his hands. "Right! Now then, I know we all want to launch an attack against the Fed, but before we run out there, I think we ought to have a plan."

"What gun will I get?" TJ asked.

"None," I said.

"What?" TJ said. "I just swore in. I should —"

Sweeney closed his eyes and pinched the bridge of his nose. "Danny, I know you two haven't always been the best of friends, but —"

"It ain't about that," I said. "The Fed aren't looking for you, TJ. You can go wherever you want around town without drawing suspicion. You can get into the school to see what they're doing there. You risked a lot bringing these supplies here, and none of us could have pulled that off."

"You're our spy." Sparrow nodded.

"Hey," he said. "Maybe I haven't been through training, but I'm not afraid to fight."

"Then you're a dumbass, just like I always knew you were," I said. " 'Cause fighting the Fed is scary as hell."

"Travis, is it?" Kemp asked.

He nodded. "You can call me TJ."

"Right. TJ, Wright's plan makes a lot of sense. And it's not about courage. In a lot of ways your job will be the most dangerous of all. The risk of getting caught will be a lot greater for you. You could really help —"

"Okay, okay! Enough! I'll do it," TJ said.

"And no doing stupid shit!" Cal said. "Any of us. It's like all those old zombie movies and TV shows." I exchanged a look with Sweeney, and we both laughed. "I'm serious," said Cal. "People trying to survive a zombie apocalypse are always doing *stupid* shit! The humans have their camp set up, then one guy goes off by himself into the dark woods to investigate a weird noise or take a leak. What happens? Oh, surprise, you dumb son of a bitch, a zombie bit your dick off! Now that guy is going to scream and draw a bunch more zombies, or he's going to crawl back to camp, bleeding out on the way so that he turns into a zombie and starts killing people. I mean why can't —"

"Right!" JoBell said, trying to hold back her laughter. "Rule number one. Nobody goes alone."

"Except me," TJ said grimly.

"Yeah, but that's different," said Kemp. "You'll be mixing with civilians, and you'll be just fine."

"This isn't some dumb horror movie," Sparrow said.

"No," I said. "But the idea is the same. If one of us goes off by himself, he has no one to look out for him or help him if he's in trouble."

"Okay," said Sergeant Kemp. "We're agreed on rule number one."

"The other thing the idiots in those movies do is go around without guns," said Sweeney. "They might be somewhere they think is safe, but the zombies have sneaked in somehow, and then they're in all kinds of trouble that they could easily have solved" — he made like he was shooting a finger gun — "if they'd only remembered their weapon."

" 'If they only had a gun,' " Cal sang to the tune of "If I Only Had a Brain."

"That's a pretty standard Army rule," said Herbokowitz. "Rule number two. Never go unarmed. Anything else?"

"Always post a guard," I said. "In the human camps Cal's talking about, lots of times everybody goes to sleep, or they're all eating dinner or something, and nobody is keeping a lookout for trouble."

"Right!" said Luchen. "Then suddenly the zombies are all up in their shit, sneaking into their tent or camper or whatever, eating one guy at a time, and the group never figures it out until like half of them are dead." Cal grinned and slapped Luchen on the shoulder.

"Okay, rule number three," said Kemp. "Always post a guard. Solid. Those are good ideas that will help us avoid most problems. I guess now it comes down to choosing targets for an op. What we'll do first is recon. We go out in small groups and gather as much information about the Fed as we can. Watch for their routines. Do they ever leave their vehicles unguarded? Do they drive the same routes a lot? If so, we could bomb their vehicles or set up IEDs."

"We should also monitor the radio, both Fed and Idaho signals, to get as much information as we can," I said. "I think there's another old radio upstairs in the front office. I could bring that down so we could listen to both stations all the time."

"Right," said Herbokowitz. "Crocker. Bagley. Monitoring the radio is your job."

"Yes, First Sergeant," said Crocker. Bagley only studied his shoes.

"Don't worry, Bagley," said Herbokowitz. "We'll make sure you get some time out there. If we're going to start going topside, then all of us should get a chance to get some fresh air. But we gotta remember situational awareness at all times. Feds are everywhere."

"Yeah," I said. "We'll be careful. But let's find a bunch of targets. Hopefully stuff we can hit all at once. That way, the Fed won't have time to go on high alert."

"Cal, we should talk to your dad," TJ said. "You all are going to need more supplies, and he has a bunch of stuff that" — he made air quotes — "'fell off the truck' when he was making smuggling runs for the Idaho Civilian Corps."

It bothered me a little that Cal's dad had been stealing on ICC business, but if what he took helped keep my people alive, I guess I could live with it.

Christmas Eve had begun as one of the worst days of my life. It was the first Christmas without Mom, we were trapped in the dungeon, we'd lost Danning, and we thought we'd lost the war before we'd even had a chance to fight. But starting Christmas morning, things were going to change. The Fed better look out. I was coming for them.

⌇—• *In the aftermath of self-proclaimed 'President' Montaine declaring Idaho an independent country, the White House has been under extreme pressure to explain its apparently false assertions that the Idaho rebels had been subdued. Joining us in the studio is NBC's Idaho Crisis correspondent Rebecca Cho. Rebecca, the president is expected to address the nation in just a few minutes. What do you think we'll hear from President Griffith tonight, and what response can we expect from the Republicans?"*

"Thanks, Byron. Quite simply, the president needs to explain why she has misled the American people. It's very difficult to gauge the public mind-set on this issue since so much of our media is subject to censorship under the Unity Act. There have been reports that comments on FriendStar and Shout Out about the Idaho Crisis are often deleted, possibly by the federal government, and the increase in these reports might indicate a surge of public unrest in the wake of the revelation that Idaho has not been subdued. As to the Republican response, I think we can paradoxically expect more agreement with the president now that Jim Barnes has been confirmed as vice president. Perhaps that was the president's intention with that surprise nomination. But it is worth pointing out that the last time America had a president and vice president from different political parties was with Republican president Abraham Lincoln and Democratic vice president Andrew Johnson during our first Civil War. When Andrew Johnson became president, he —"

"Going to have to stop you there, Rebecca. Thank you. Going now to the White House for President Griffith's address, live from the Oval Office."

"Good evening. My fellow Americans, I bring you greetings. Soldiers, airmen, sailors, and marines, wherever you may be serving tonight, I salute you and your families. As you face these

difficult times, I ask you to remember that you carry with you the hope of a grateful nation.

"I speak to all Americans on this night when Christmas is celebrated by many across our country. It is for the sake of the preservation of our great country that I recently made the decision to engage in a tactical deception, declaring the Idaho rebellion to be at an end. I made this decision in order to demoralize Idaho insurgents and discourage insurrection in other parts of our country. I executed this tactical deception in an effort to save the lives of Americans on both sides of this great divide, to more quickly bring an end to this destructive conflict.

"To that end, I once again applaud the United States Supreme Court for upholding the Unity Act, without which I would not have the legal means to disrupt the communications of terrorist insurgent forces and to prevent other domestic communications or activities which might intentionally or unintentionally aid those rebel forces.

"I know many law-abiding Americans are troubled by certain restrictions on liberties we have enjoyed for generations. I join those people in their frustration, for I have spent a lifetime dedicated to the preservation of those freedoms. But I ask, were you forced to choose between a temporary restriction of some American rights and the absolute certainty of a great many American deaths, which would you choose? Which would anyone choose? We face the very real possibility that the full exercise of our constitutional rights may ultimately contribute to the permanent and bloody fracturing of our constitutional republic. I therefore call upon this generation of Americans to endure with me the terrible indignity of this temporary infringement upon our rights, so that in the coming years we and future generations may enjoy the freedom of our fully United States of America.

"Christmas is a time of peace. And so, in the spirit of peace, I hereby make the following offer. A bipartisan congressional coalition has agreed to grant me the authority to delay the implementation of the Federal Identification Card Act, pending possible amendments to the bill. I hereby invite the leadership of the state of Idaho, and other states with concerns about the bill, to abandon the tragedy of nullification and their futile bids for independence. Return to the negotiating table so that we can amend the Federal Identification Card Act in a compromise we can all live with.

"If Idaho is prepared to end this useless and costly fight and return to peaceful negotiations, I will grant blanket amnesty to all Idaho National Guard soldiers and other Idaho combatants. Because rebellion against the United States must be discouraged, the leadership of this rebellion must still be held accountable for the chaos they have caused, for the lives that have been lost due to their actions. However, I promise fair trials to Mr. Montaine, those members of the Idaho legislature who voted for nullification, and certain senior officers in the Idaho military. I also preemptively commute the sentence of death for those tried and found guilty of treason. To expedite these negotiations, and to allow Mr. Montaine and his associates to negotiate from a position in which they feel secure, I would like to ask the state of Idaho's leadership to allow a single unarmed helicopter carrying US Secretary of State Alex Clayton and his aides to safely land in Boise.

"In the spirit of peace and reconciliation, I make this generous offer in public. I await the state of Idaho's response, and I implore all the leaders of America to seize this opportunity so that we can restore peace to our beloved country. Thank you." •—⌁

K Dinnison: "Tactical deception"? Our freedoms die for a tactical deception?

about 8 hours ago   Reply - Shout Out

Patriot22: Great speech Pres Griffith! God Bless America!

about 8 hours ago   Reply - Shout Out

Chen: Griffith starts her speech by admitting to a lie, and then asks for Idaho's trust?

about 8 hours ago   Reply - Shout Out

---

the latest news from the Federal Idaho Reconstruction Authority. Tragedy struck today in Grangeville, Idaho, when rebel forces operating from the Nez Perce National Forest resorted to terrorist attacks similar to those used by Al Qaeda and the Taliban. Rebel insurgents launched a deadly rocket attack on an Army convoy full of food, medical supplies, and other humanitarian relief items. Grangeville, a north central Idaho city of three thousand people before the Idaho Crisis began, has been in desperate need of relief since rebel activities interrupted the free-flowing supply chain. Especially horrifying is the fact that this cowardly attack killed nine American soldiers and even destroyed Grangeville High School facilities, endangering the lives of innocent children.

In national news, Texas governor Rodney Percy has defied President Griffith's warning by signing his state's recently passed bill that would nullify the Federal Identification Card Act in Texas. In response, soldiers at Fort Hood, Fort Bliss, and Joint Base San Antonio, and airmen at Laughlin, Goodfellow, and Sheppard Air Force Bases have been placed on high alert. All soldiers and airmen in the Texas Army and Air National Guards have been ordered to report for

96

federal duty, with over 90 percent of Guard personnel in compliance. Units from the First Cavalry Division out of Fort Hood have been deployed across the state to protect National Guard installations and other critical facilities from possible rebel terrorist attacks.

United States military forces have triumphed recently along the north border of the rebel-controlled section of Idaho. Soldiers from the Tenth Mountain Division have made rapid progress, breaking up rebel positions along •—⋏

⋏—• In his Christmas address yesterday, Pope Michael made no secret of his concern over the troubles in Idaho, saying, quote, "The Idaho Crisis in America has become a civil war. This conflict has cost many good lives, but the potential for disruption of global markets and the greater violence that would bring now threatens the whole world. The message of the Christ child at Bethlehem is one of peace and mercy, and so I hope Catholics will join with people of all faiths in praying for a true, lasting end to this war. As an ally of the faithful everywhere, I offer my humble services as mediator, should the governments of the United States and of Idaho wish to resume peace talks," end quote. •—⋏

⋏—• You're listening to RIR, Republic of Idaho Radio. Idaho Army forces today dealt a setback to the US military in Grangeville, Idaho, when they destroyed an armed military convoy that was transporting weapons and ammunition in support of the illegal and immoral occupation of northern Idaho. This action was achieved with no loss of civilian life, a miraculous accomplishment considering United States forces are using schoolchildren as human shields, seizing high schools and even elementary schools for use as bases of operation. This act violates the treaty of the Fourth Geneva Convention by interfering with and even depriving children of their right to an education.

The Texas Senate has overcome an ongoing filibuster, and today Texas governor Rodney Percy has signed into law the nullification of the unconstitutional Federal Identification Card Act in the state of Texas. The Texas governor commented on this development in a speech earlier today, saying, "Texans are united in their opposition to the overreach of the federal government and to the Federal ID Card Act. Even as President Griffith claims to seek negotiation, she is abusing her power, expanding the definition of 'rebellion' within the Unity Act to include anyone who disagrees with her policies. This action exemplifies the way the federal government is moving closer and closer to totalitarian control. Texas will not stand for this. As commander in chief of the Texas military, I've activated the entire Texas State Guard, and have issued a counterorder to stop the federalization of Texas Army and Air National Guard personnel. Approximately 30 percent of Texas National Guard forces have reported for federal duty. The remaining National Guard soldiers are standing by as ordered. I abhor bloodshed, but if hostilities do break out, it will be the result of Texans defending themselves against federal attack. I'm asking President Griffith to not let that happen. Stand down the deployment of federal troops within the state of Texas. It's not too late to resolve our differences peacefully. Peace is the sincere desire of every Texan, but our history has proven our belief that peace without freedom is no peace at all, and like our ancestors at the Alamo, we will fight to the last man in defense of our liberty."

Public opinion in the United States continues to sway in favor of Idaho, with more and more protests calling for the immediate cessation of hostilities and the withdrawal of the United States *military from Idaho. Thousands of students have been arrested on charges of violating provisions of the Unity Act that prohibit, quote, "conspiracy to assist and promote rebellion," end quote. Civil rights groups are decrying these arrests as serious setbacks to the rights of Americans. Republic of Idaho Radio news.* •—⋏

CHAPTER
SEVEN

"This is the best Christmas present ever, even if it did come late," I said to Sweeney as we walked down the alley while the snow fell. The cold bit through my coat and the hat and scarf that hid my face from the Fed, but I still felt warm and free.

"Dude, I know. Happy New Year, right?" Sweeney said. "Just smell that fresh air! That dungeon smelled like . . ."

It smelled like death, and I was grateful that Sweeney didn't say so.

The Republic of Idaho Radio news had told us that President Montaine was considering Griffith's offer of negotiation. The process had stalled, though, since Montaine wanted his negotiator recognized as an ambassador, and the US State Department insisted they would only meet with a mediator. Citizens of Idaho were told to stay in the fight against the Fed until Montaine ordered us to stand down.

Kemp and Sparrow had gone on the first recon patrol, then Luchen and Herbokowitz took their turn. Each two-man team kept moving farther and farther out from the dungeon. It was hard to tell, since the Fed soldiers didn't all stand in one formation for counting, but we figured there weren't all that many of them stationed in Freedom Lake — just about one platoon, so almost forty soldiers. I guess our little town wasn't a big priority, or else, with troop cuts a few years back and two wars going on, the United States couldn't afford to send more guys. Either way, if we were careful, and if we could find some allies, we figured we had a decent chance of kicking these guys out of Freedom Lake.

Now me and Sweeney were on the biggest mission yet. We were supposed to casually walk by the Fed headquarters at the old cop shop and make mental note of its defenses and security setup.

"Hey," I said to Sweeney. "I know we're just supposed to scope out this one place, but do you think we should maybe take a really random route to throw off anyone who might be watching us? Like maybe instead of heading directly for the Fed HQ, we could loop around and go up Third Street." Sweeney didn't answer for a while, and the only sound was our boots crunching on the snow. "Hey, so how about it?"

Sweeney laughed. "Wright, are you serious?"

"What?"

"Oh, we're just going to casually stroll down JoBell's street, just to throw off the Fed." He laughed harder. "And TJ already told us that JoBell would just happen to be too, ahem, *sick* to go to school today. You're so pathetically transparent, man. Why don't you just ask me if you can visit her?"

I smiled. "Well, I saw her at Christmas, but we didn't really have a chance to talk, you know?"

"Yeah, I'm sure that's what you want to do. Talk."

"Well, can you blame a guy?" I said. "I swear I'm getting jealous down there, watching Sparrow and Luchen all cutesy on their side-by-side cots."

"Well, I was thinking of stopping to see Cassie Macer. She should be getting out of school in about an hour," said Sweeney. "You know we were getting really close before the invasion."

"Yeah. I wonder if she's moved on, though. Scored herself a real boyfriend since then."

Sweeney acted like a knife had been plunged into his heart, and he was trying to pull it out. "Women do not move on after a taste of Eric Sweeney's fine Asian loving. If you had heard her when we were —"

"Enough!"

"You're just jealous."

"You know I'm not."

"Hey!" someone whispered. I jumped and reached for my .45 hidden in the lining of my coat. "It's okay," said the voice. The woman who tended bar at the Bucking Bronc Bar and Grill was leaning out the back door, motioning for us to follow her inside. "Hurry!"

Sweeney shrugged and we went inside. The place was cold and dark, the opposite of the way it had been before the war. We followed the woman into a storage room in back.

"Can we help you, ma'am?" I asked.

"I know who you are, Danny," she said. She must have read the worried expression on my face because she hurried on. "I'm Sally. I own the place, for all the good it does me anymore." She shook her head. "Can't get any beer or anything with the Fed locking everything down. They put me out of business."

"I'm sorry to hear that," I said.

"We don't have any beer," said Sweeney.

Sally laughed and ran her fingers back through her curly sandy-blond hair. She was pretty the way some women in their thirties or forties could be. "You're fighting back against the occupation?"

"No, ma'am," I said. "That's dangerous and against the law. We love the United States."

She laughed again, unconvinced. "Well, if you ever get in trouble . . . If you need a place to hide . . ." She opened a hatch in the floor and started down the stairs into the basement, picking up a flashlight that hung from a nail on the wall.

Sweeney and me followed her again. It couldn't hurt. If she tried anything, it was two against one, and we were both armed. Besides, she seemed nice.

"This building's real old," she said. "Used to be heated by coal." She led us around the side of a huge metal tank and opened a big square iron door. "This boiler doesn't get used anymore. If you need a place to hide, pop in here. They'll never find you."

"Well, thank you, ma'am," I said.

Back upstairs she pulled a small loaf of bread from a cabinet. "I don't have much, but I want to help the resistance any way I can."

"You keep it," I said. The bread looked great, but Sally had lost her entire livelihood, and she was already risking everything to offer us a safe place. "We have supplies."

"We appreciate your help," Sweeney said. "Hope we never need it."

"We're all behind you, boys. You hang in there." She kind of rubbed us both on the back as she showed us out, and we said our goodbyes and hurried on our way.

We turned onto Third Street, only two blocks from JoBell's house. It had been a long shot, me getting on the duty rotation for a recon patrol the same day she was home from school. I wanted to run to her so bad, my legs almost shook.

"If I do go see Cassie," said Sweeney, "maybe I should grab a hot shower first. I can't imagine she'll want to . . . talk . . . if I'm sporting dungeon scent."

"Good idea," I said. "JoBell said she thought the Fed had given up on watching her house, but I think we better go around the block and sneak in the back, just in case they —"

Two Humvees rolled past us on the street. One gun turret sported a manned .50-cal, and the soldier in the other had an M307 grenade-launching machine gun. What kind of trouble did these jackwads expect to find in little Freedom Lake that they needed that kind of firepower? Hopefully, me and my guys would show them soon enough.

"Be cool. Just walk normal," I said.

"As opposed to duck-walking or doing the cha-cha slide?" Sweeney said quietly. "How do you think I'm walking?"

"At least they don't seem to be after us."

But maybe I'd spoke too soon, 'cause the Humvees' taillights flared when they were only a couple houses past us. Had they spotted me? How? I was wrapped up like a mummy with this scarf on. Were they on their way to JoBell's? I reached inside my coat toward my .45.

The Humvees pulled right into the Rourke family's front yard, setting up in a sort of V formation with their heavy guns pointed at the front door. If those guns opened up, they'd probably kill everyone in the house. Jill Rourke had graduated a couple years ago, so I didn't know her too well, but her father, Todd, had one or two little kids from a short second marriage. Mr. Rourke was a good guy, on the school board, and he'd coached little kids' flag football for as long as I could remember. What did the Fed want with him?

"Let's get out of here," Sweeney said.

"Hang on, I want to see —"

"Don't be stupid."

"If we just turn around right here, we'll really look suspicious," I said.

Todd Rourke came out onto his porch. "Can I help you?"

Soldiers had climbed out of the Humvees and set up a perimeter around the vehicles. One officer approached the porch. "I'm Major Alsovar, commander of the Reconstruction Forces for Freedom Lake. Mr. Rourke, we understand you've been doing some unauthorized driving. A neighbor who is interested in reducing rebel movements reported seeing you returning to your home in your pickup."

Mr. Rourke ran his hands through his hair. "I'm not a rebel. I'm loyal to —"

"I'm afraid we're going to have to impound your vehicle and search your home," said the major.

Mr. Rourke came down off the porch. When the soldiers readied their guns, he put his hands up. "Please. Please, I only drove to Coeur d'Alene to see my kids. Please, I haven't seen them for months. Comms don't work. I can't even call them. Search my house if you have to, but come on. I need my truck."

"You should have applied for a permit and filed a driving plan with my office." Alsovar turned to one of his sergeants. "Get the tow bar out. We'll haul his truck to the yard."

The sergeant nodded and opened the back hatch of the Humvee. Mr. Rourke ran up to him. "Please stop! Just hang on. We can work this out. Come on, guys!"

"Captain Peterson, arrest this man!" said Major Alsovar.

The captain looked from the major to Mr. Rourke. "Sir?"

"He's resisting federal instructions. Driving without authorization. He may be involved in insurgent activities. We'll take him to detention and find out."

"Sir, are you sure this is the right —"

"No! Please. I just wanted to see my kids!" Mr. Rourke started backing away.

Alsovar glared at the captain, then turned to another soldier. "Sergeant Dell, restrain that man now!"

"Yes, sir!" said the sergeant. He motioned to two specialists, and then the three of them were on Mr. Rourke. The specialists grabbed his arms, spun him around, and pushed him up against the side of one of the Humvees. Sergeant Dell gripped the back of his neck and slammed his face down on the hood.

"At ease, Sergeant!" Captain Peterson yelled as he took a zip tie from his pocket, pulled Mr. Rourke's hands back, and bound his wrists. "Do not abuse the prisoner. *Carefully* load him in the back of my Humvee."

When the soldiers lifted Mr. Rourke off the hood, blood ran from his nose and mouth.

"Let's start our search," said Major Alsovar as he marched up the stairs to the house.

"What are you doing?" A different sergeant with an Air Assault and Combat Infantryman Badge on his uniform stepped up to us with his M4 at the ready. My heart pounded as I realized that me and Sweeney had nearly stopped, watching these monsters beat an innocent man. "Nothing to see here," the sergeant said.

"Right." Sweeney grabbed my arm. "Sorry."

We did our best to look casual as we walked away. Instead of going up to JoBell's front door, we went to the end of the block, hooked a right, and came up the alley to the back of her place. We didn't want to draw any attention to her house if we didn't have to.

A high wooden fence protected JoBell's backyard, and since the gate was locked, we climbed up on a nearby garbage can before vaulting over. I slipped on the top of the fence and fell six feet to the snowy ground. When I sat up, a big white horse smile flashed in my face.

"What the hell?" Sweeney had dropped down next to me. He scrambled back and hit his head on the fence.

I laughed and patted the horse's face as she nuzzled me. "Hey, Lightning. What are you doing here?"

JoBell rushed out of the house toward us. She pushed Lightning aside and helped us both to our feet. "Never mind the horse," she said. "Get inside already." She pulled me through the back door into her kitchen. "They're telling the public you guys are dead, but they've been checking out your old houses, even my house again a couple times. You're one of the top people they're looking for."

I slid my hands to her waist. "You're looking pretty good for someone who's too sick to go to school."

She smiled. "Did you come here to take care of me?"

Becca came into the room. "You guys!" She ran and threw her arms around me. Then, keeping me close, she reached out for Sweeney and hugged him too. My eyes met JoBell's over Becca's head, and she gave me an apologetic look.

"You're sick too?" Sweeney asked Becca.

"Heck yes!" Becca said. "I wasn't going to miss this chance to see you two. But are we safe? Did you see what's going on down the street?"

Sweeney placed his M4 on the kitchen table and then jumped up to sit on the counter, until JoBell snapped her fingers and pointed down. He leaned against the counter instead. "When they drove past, we thought they were after us."

"What was going on?" JoBell asked.

"Mr. Rourke got caught driving without Fed permission," I said. "He only went to see his kids in Coeur d'Alene."

"And they're, what? Arresting him for that?" JoBell asked.

I took a glass from a cupboard and went to the sink to get some water. "Broke his nose first, but yeah. And they're taking his truck. Searching his house."

"That's illegal. Unconstitutional. This is all so wrong," JoBell said. "None of this should be happening! It's all getting way out of control."

"Yeah, war will do that sometimes," Becca said. "Anyway, I'm so happy to see you guys."

I sat on a chair at the kitchen table. "Did you know your horse is out back?"

"Becca is pretty much moving in," JoBell said.

"Becca and Lightning," I said.

Becca shrugged. "TJ finally brought word from my parents. They're safe and waiting it out in Oregon. It was lonely out there on the farm with just Lightning and me, and I had nothing to do with the livestock all sold. So I packed up some hay bales and the rest of the frozen beef I had. I loaded it onto our little buggy, and Lightning and I brought it here."

"You could have stayed at my place," Sweeney said. "The horse could have lived in my boathouse or something. Not like my parents will be using the house for a while." The Fed wasn't letting people return to Idaho until the crisis was over, so his parents were settling in down in Florida.

"Here I can hang out with JoBell and Mr. Linder," Becca said. "And Lightning does okay in the yard and the garage."

JoBell stepped up behind my chair, slipped my coat off, and began rubbing my shoulders. Her fingers melted warmth into me and I closed my eyes, pretending like the war never happened and everything was like it used to be.

Sweeney said, "We're supposed to be on a mission to walk past the old cop shop, see what the Fed has set up down there."

"That's pretty suicidal, isn't it?" Becca looked away from me. "You two hanging around Fed headquarters?"

"We aren't going to hang around," Sweeney said. "We're going to walk by and take a look. See how best to attack the place."

"I don't know if hitting that target is such a great idea," Becca said. "We heard on the news that Idaho and the Fed are talking again, that if they can get the ID card thing worked out, they might stop the war."

This was weird. Usually JoBell was the one telling us to be careful, telling us not to fight. Becca was so tough, me and her had kicked three guys' asses at the rodeo last fall when they tried to attack me.

"Montaine and the Idaho Congress have already declared independence," said Sweeney. "They're not going to turn themselves in and go to jail after we've come this far."

"Then everything that happens will be Montaine's fault, because if there's any chance of stopping or getting out of this mess, we should take it." JoBell's warm fingers massaged my shoulders and neck again. "Anyway, isn't *this* better than all that war junk?"

"Well, we thought we'd drop in, you know," Sweeney said. "I was actually going to kick it down the street to surprise Cassie Macer when she gets home from school. Think I could take a shower first? I haven't had a chance to clean up since the invasion."

JoBell didn't even look at him. "You know where the bathroom is. Towels in the closet. Maybe Becca can find you some clean clothes."

"Thanks," said Sweeney. He and Becca both headed for the stairs.

JoBell and I made out for the next ten minutes until the other two stomped down the steps really loud. JoBell got up off my lap but leaned over to whisper, "To be continued."

Sweeney had squeezed into one of JoBell's T-shirts, which read:

FREEDOM LAKE VOLLEYBALL

Try to beat our girls?
Don't go there, girlfriend!

"What?" Sweeney said when I laughed.

"So manly," I said.

Sweeney held his fists up and flexed. "My manliness isn't threatened by being a volleyball supporter. We never make a big deal out of the girls wearing football shirts. What's so wrong with me wearing this?"

JoBell shook her head. "If the war wasn't enough to tell me my world has gone totally crazy, now I'm agreeing with Eric Sweeney on feminist issues."

Sweeney smiled. "Thanks, kitten."

"I take it back."

"If we're going at all, we better hurry," Becca already had her coat off the peg by the door. "Nobody goes alone, remember?"

Sweeney grabbed his M4 from the kitchen counter. "And nobody goes unarmed. But what are you going to do while Cassie and I are hanging out?"

"Timmy and I will go for a walk or something. I'm a big girl. I can figure it out."

They left a moment later. When the door closed behind them, it was quiet in the kitchen. "Where's your dad?" I finally said.

"He's at work. Though what a lawyer does when the Fed is just making up our laws as they go, I have no idea. Still. We're all alone. Want to go upstairs to my room?" I stood up. JoBell leaned close, put her hands flat on my chest, and smiled. "Right after you take a shower."

CHAPTER
EIGHT

I'd been away from JoBell before. Basic training had been a whole nine weeks, and during that time we'd only been allowed comm calls twice. The rest of the time all we had were paper letters. She wrote me almost every day. Me? I was never too good at writing, so I wrote her once or twice a week. It had been agony missing her, especially alone at night in my rack in the barracks. Since the invasion, I'd been away from her for about half as long as basic, but it felt twice as bad. All that time in the dungeon worrying about her, missing her, and wondering what she was doing made that dingy prison even smaller.

Now, after I'd showered and rejoined JoBell, it was as if we hadn't seen each other in years. She yanked off my shirt, pushed me down onto her bed, and jumped on top of me. I pulled my .45 from under my belt and carefully placed it on her nightstand, next to her lamp and the framed photo of her and Becca. Then it was as if all the deadly dangers we'd been through lately, the whole damned world, fell away. I probably couldn't have stopped her if I wanted to, and I absolutely did not want her to stop.

She sat up, straddling me and moving her hips around as she slowly began to lift her shirt up and off. Her blond hair fell down past her shoulders and past her black lacy bra over her smooth white skin, and I had never seen anything more beautiful. Her eyes closed as I slowly slid my hands from her waist up toward her chest.

"I love you so much," I said to her. "I won't let anyone hurt you. You're my whole life. I've missed you."

"Shh." JoBell ran her fingers back through my hair and leaned forward to kiss me. "Baby, I'm right here. With you. I'm not going anywhere." She kissed me again. With her warm chest pressed against me, she spoke softly, her lips so close that they barely brushed mine. "I wanted to tell you something. . . . We've been dating for a long time, and at first I just felt lucky being the girl who got to ride around in that giant truck of yours. It was exciting. A lot of the girls talked about how hot you were, but you were all mine."

"Wait. What girls?"

JoBell sat up and pressed a finger to my lips. "Shh. So maybe at first this whole thing was kind of superficial. Maybe a lot of high school relationships are that way. But then you introduced me to your mom, and I learned about her . . . challenges, and I saw how much you loved her and took care of her."

My left hand ached as I thought of my mother, as I tried not to think about how I'd lost her.

JoBell continued. "I saw the sweet, loving, true Danny Wright under that tough cowboy image, and something inside me melted. And I loved you. That was one kind of love."

"What do you mean?" I asked.

"Danny, if you don't let me finish, I'm going to take back all the nice things I've been saying about you." She leaned forward and kissed my lips, tasting me before she kissed my neck and nibbled the bottom of my ear. "But even then, a part of me still worried that maybe you and I weren't meant for each other, that our goals for the future were too different. . . ."

Is that why she'd turned me down when I'd asked her to marry me a few months ago? What was she saying with all this?

"And then, in that dungeon, I smelled your rotten stink."

"What?" I said.

JoBell sat up straight again and laughed. "There I was, in this place where you were hiding for your life, and you smelled terrible," she said. "And there was nothing exciting at all down there, and you were not glamorous or sexy in any way." She kept her gaze locked on mine. "And I realized that I love you and will always love you. Because if it was good being with you at our lowest point, it will be so great being with you when this war is finally over."

Maybe this was the time. Maybe she'd changed her mind and was ready to say yes. But what kind of wedding could we have under this occupation? JoBell deserved something better than a quick, fake ceremony in the dungeon, and that was probably all I could give her for now.

After a moment, she brought my hand to her lips. She kissed my fingers and then sucked one into her mouth. I smiled. I'd loved everything JoBell had just said, but she was done talking and ready to play.

A door slammed downstairs. "You guys!" Becca shouted. "You guys, come on!"

"Hang on!" JoBell slid off me and scrambled toward the edge of the bed, ducking to grab her shirt.

JoBell's door flew open and Becca ran in. "Sweeney's in — oh —" She'd been crying, but now she froze in the doorway with wide eyes.

JoBell hurried to pull her shirt down. I rolled out of bed and grabbed my .45. "What's wrong?"

Becca held one hand to her chest and wiped her tears with the other. "The Feds stopped us for a random search. Eric shouted 'Scatter' and ran off, heading toward the high school. I went the other way. They went after him." She was almost out of breath when she finished.

I threw on my shirt and coat, stuffing my .45 into the lining. "Toward the high school?" I hurried to get my boots on.

Becca nodded.

"What are you going to do?" JoBell asked me.

I stood up and looked at her. "I'm going to get my best friend." I ran out of her room.

"I'm coming with you!" Becca yelled as she followed.

"You guys, wait!" JoBell rushed down the stairs after us. "What? Are you going on foot? We need a plan."

"No time for a plan," I said.

"We got Cal's motorcycle in the garage," Becca said.

"That'll do!" I shot out the door into the snowstorm and jumped down the three steps to the backyard. We pushed past Lightning and hurried through the side door into the detached garage.

JoBell followed us onto the porch. "Danny, Becca, hold up a second."

I hit the button on the wall to open the garage door, and then walked Cal's motorcycle around some hay bales before I mounted up. Becca climbed on behind me, wrapping her arms around my waist. I looked at my gorgeous girlfriend standing just inside the garage door. How long would it be until I could see her again? "I'll see you soon," I said to JoBell.

Then I kick-started the motorcycle, popped it in gear, and started to roll down the driveway. When I hit the street, I about waxed out right away. Put me in the rodeo ring on top of a raging bull, and I could ride with the best of them. On a motorcycle, I wasn't half as good, and riding a motorcycle down streets of fresh snow was pretty idiotic. I basically skidded my boots along on the ground like training wheels.

We passed a soldier walking along the sidewalk. He shouted something, starting to aim his M4. I didn't wait. Steering the bike with my left hand, I drew my .45 and fired three shots, dropping him in a pile of pink snow before he could bring his rifle to bear.

"Hold this," I said, handing Becca my gun so I could get to it faster if I needed it. "Where the hell is Sweeney?"

If we kept driving all over town, every Fed in the damned county would be on our ass before long. Machine gun fire sounded danger close, and I ducked down behind the handlebars without thinking. The bike slipped sideways, and I nearly dumped us on the street. Becca didn't scream or anything, just put her foot down and helped me right the bike.

The guns went off again, and we saw Sweeney sprinting across the street ahead. A Humvee was about thirty yards behind him, the gunner manning the .50-cal trying to line up a shot while Sweeney dodged around like in football. He rounded the back of the high school building, and I turned the other way to pick him up.

"Hurry!" Becca yelled.

I brought the bike to the back parking lot by the buses. Sweeney was still moving, but I knew he'd be running out of steam soon. The Humvee pulled up to the corner of the building.

I took my .45 out of Becca's hand, aimed, and fired three rounds at the Humvee. "Come on, jackwads! Come get me!"

The .50-cal gunner ducked for a second, then aimed. I whipped the bike behind a bus just before the machine gun unloaded. The windows above us blasted out, showering us with glass. I whipped the kickstand down on the bike and dismounted, running to the front of the bus and shooting off a few more rounds at the Fed. "Gotta keep them focused on us," I shouted back to Becca. "Let Sweeney get away." The bus lurched when bullets shredded its tires. I ran back to the bike. "I think we might be in serious trouble here," I said to Becca. "I'm sorry."

Becca grabbed the front of my coat and looked at me intensely, like she was mad at me or something. "There's something I have to do, Danny."

She pulled me close and kissed me. I was so surprised that I just stood there and let her.

A fresh round of machine gun fire finally snapped us to our senses and she backed away from me, looking into my eyes.

Sweeney commando-rolled under the bus. "Hi, guys. What's up?"

I helped Sweeney to his feet. "Let's go," I said. "Everybody on the bike."

"The second we come out from behind this bus, they'll light us up," Sweeney said. "And it's way too slippery out here to outrun them on the motorcycle. Mr. Cretis has the shop bay door open. It's a short gap." The school's temperature controls sucked, so in winter, lots of times the shop class got too hot and Mr. Cretis would raise the bay door four or five feet.

"The school's crawling with Fed," said Becca.

Sweeney held up his M4. "Too bad for the Fed."

"No, dude," I said. "We try to go through the school, and a lot of our people are gonna get hurt."

Another volley of machine gun fire went off. A few rounds ripped through our side of the bus.

"We're going to charge them," I said. "It's the only option we have left. Sweeney, you shoot for the gunner. I'll try to move around so they can't get a good shot. They won't be expecting us to head right at them, so the gunner won't be able to adjust his aim fast enough."

"We'll never make it," Sweeney said.

I shot him a sorry-but-we're-out-of-options look. I started the bike, and Sweeney squeezed onto the seat behind Becca. It was a tight fit.

"This is crazy, but I trust you," Becca said.

That trust might have been really misplaced. The odds were against us on this one, but the Feds were going to get tired of shooting at the bus and would be flanking us pretty soon.

"Here we go." I handed Becca my .45. But before I cranked the throttle, someone else started shooting. A scarf-masked shooter wearing a black armband was firing at the Fed from the roof.

"I don't know who the hell that is," I said, "but perfect timing." I cranked the throttle on the bike, bringing us sliding out around the back of the bus and toward the gun Hummer.

The guy on the roof of the school was a good shooter. One round tore through the gunner's throat. Another took off half his face. I sped up. "Sweeney, keep shooting at the Humvee," I shouted. "They can still drop a window and try shooting us that way."

The back passenger side door opened and one stupid soldier stepped out, leading with his rifle. Becca fired at least five rounds, taking care of him. The Fed driver tried swerving toward me, but he missed, and I gunned the bike past them and across the softball field out the back of the school yard, driving over a downed chain-link fence into the scrub brush. I cranked the bike up as fast as it would go, fishtailing through the deeper snow, heading off-road through people's yards. The Fed Humvee would have to take time turning around, and it couldn't squeeze through the tight areas we could.

"Where do we go from here?" Becca asked.

"We gotta dump the bike," I said.

"Cal will be pissed," Sweeney said.

"He can deal." I pulled the motorcycle into the woodshed in the Whilstens' backyard and shut it off. "It's like that time that party got busted at Brad Robinson's house."

"And we all ran like hell," Sweeney said.

"We grew up here," I said. "We know every fence, shed, and tree. We know every street and alley and where the barking dogs live. The Feds don't know shit. We head for the creek and then go for the secret tunnel into the dungeon. Becca, you —"

"I'm going to the dungeon with you. The Fed saw me with you on that bike. I'm a rebel now. I gotta hide."

"Oh, I'm so tired of running," Sweeney sighed. Then he sprinted away. Becca and I exchanged a look and then ran after him.

We moved even faster than we'd run after that busted party. One advantage to the Fed driving ban was that we could hear trouble coming any time there was engine noise. We darted through people's yards. Once, a gun Hummer drove by, and we crammed ourselves into the tiny playhouse in the Shiratoris' backyard again. It felt almost like home. After the Fed passed, we took off again, crossing two blocks before sprinting down an alley. At the sound of another engine, we dove over a wooden fence and landed in the snowy backyard at Samantha Monohan's place.

Sweeney found the gate and opened it. I led Becca right after him and then stopped.

A single Army specialist held us all at gunpoint, his M4 drawn and his finger on the trigger. The name tape on his uniform read MUELLER and he stood with a wide stance, the rifle's stock to his shoulder. He was so nervous, his rifle's barrel shook, but that wouldn't matter much at this range. Sweeney's rifle was slung from his shoulder and my .45 was in my jacket. This Fed had us.

I could charge him, take the bullet, and knock his rifle aside long enough for Sweeney to kill him and save Becca. Is that what was left? The suicide play? Or maybe if I went with him back to Fed HQ, he'd let my friends go.

"Specialist, do you know who we are?" I asked.

He tightened up on his weapon and aimed it at me. "Are you kidding me? Everybody knows who you are. Now what? I gotta shoot you?"

"No," Sweeney said. "Actually, we'd rather you didn't. It's all cool."

"You don't have to shoot," said Becca.

Tears were welling up in Mueller's eyes. "Eight months," he said quietly. "Man, I got eight months left in my contract. Just wanted the GI Bill so I could go to college. I thought, work commo in the Army, stick with the radios. Nice and safe, right?"

We didn't say anything, not sure what would happen next.

"A lot of guys are getting killed," said the specialist. "Snipers. IEDs. Some good guys." I said nothing, hoping he didn't know how many Fed soldiers I'd had to take out. "If I don't shoot, you people will kill me."

"No, no. We're just trying to get home," I said. "We got no problem with you."

Mueller's whole body shook now. That was bad news, since his finger was on the trigger. "I don't want to . . ."

"Hey, Specialist Mueller," Becca said. "It's okay. This is a tough situation. It's hard on all of us." She took a few steps toward him, but he backed up and aimed his rifle at her. Becca stopped and held up her hands. "I'm not going to hurt you. How old are you?"

"Twenty-three," he said.

"Not much older than me." Becca smiled. "I'm seventeen."

"Geez." The specialist shook his head. "You people are just kids." He slowly lowered his rifle. "You all get out of here."

Really? Was he going to let us go? We started taking cautious steps past him.

"But Wright?" he said. I stopped. "You tell your people, the insurgents, these Brotherhood guys or whatever. Tell them they gotta back off."

"The Brotherhood?" Sweeney asked.

"Just go!" Mueller yelled. "Before I change my mind."

Sweeney and Becca took off running, but I held back for a moment. "Thank you," I said. He jerked his head at me, and then I ran.

The three of us went back to the "run, hide, wait, run" routine until we made our way to the ravine. From there, we slid-tripped-ran along the creek. I shoved Becca into the tunnel first, then watched Sweeney go before I crawled in too. I hoped the snow would keep falling to cover our tracks. *Please, God,* I prayed. *Look after JoBell. Don't let them find us.*

CHAPTER
NINE

"What the hell were you thinking!?"

Less than two minutes after we got back with Becca, First Sergeant Herbokowitz had me and Sweeney locked up at the position of attention, his blade-hand inches from my nose.

"Private Wright, you seem to have the worst trouble following orders! You are always screwing up and escalating the situation!"

Sergeant Kemp sat on the table behind Herbokowitz. "It's risky going out there, Top. This could have happened to them in the first couple minutes of their patrol. I'd say we're lucky to get them back."

Herbokowitz did not turn around. "Sergeant Kemp, just because you're an NCO, don't think I won't PT you until you die!" He leaned even closer to me. "Why the hell did you bring your little girlfriend down here?"

Becca was crying on my cot in the narrow space between the storage shelves. "She's not my girlfriend, First Sergeant. She just kind of ended up —"

"I don't care if you're doing her or not! You know you can't be bringing any floozy off the —"

"Watch how you talk about her," I said. I didn't care if he outranked me or not. Becca was one of my best friends, and no way was I letting anyone insult her without a fight. "She's my friend, she's just been through a lot, and you will not disrespect her."

The first sergeant stared at me silently, red splotches flaring up on his neck and face. "Fine." He seemed to calm down a little. "You two fall out." Sweeney and I relaxed. "Everybody grab a weapon. If they followed you three clowns, we're in deep shit right now." He stepped closer to me for a moment, and I thought he meant to throw down. Instead he spoke quietly. "We'll figure this out. For now" — he jerked his thumb toward Becca — "go help her."

I started heading back to my cot to talk to Becca, but Sweeney grabbed my arm. "Dude, what about JoBell?" he said quietly. "She's home sick from school on the day we're seen running around? They're going to be asking her some questions, and they might not just let her go this time."

"I know," I whispered. "But what are we supposed to do? The whole town will be crawling with Feds on high alert."

"We can't just leave her out there."

"She's my girlfriend! Don't you think I —" I pulled Sweeney in closer. "Maybe TJ can find out how she's doing. Meantime, talk to Cal, real quiet-like. If she's in trouble, we'll sneak out or we'll fight everybody to get out. We'll go help her."

I tried to ignore the questioning looks from the others and went to the shadowy space between the supply shelves. Becca sat on my cot, leaning forward with her head between her knees, shaking with little quiet sobs. I stood next to her for a minute. She didn't seem to notice me.

"Care if I sit down?" I said. It was weird to ask that, since she was sitting on my sleeping bag. But then, a lot of weird had happened with Becca today. She shrugged.

I sat down next to her and noticed she wasn't only shaking from crying. She was shivering cold. Her jeans were soaking wet from our slippery run through the freezing creek. She was stuck with us now, and she didn't even have a change of socks with her. I reached into my rucksack for a pair of my sweatpants. They'd be big on her, but they were warm and clean and dry. I pulled my sleeping bag up over her shoulders and held it there with my arm around her. "Hey," I whispered. "You okay?"

She slowly sat up and looked at me. I wanted to wipe the tears from her cheeks. Maybe, in the past, I would have. But after we almost died together, after we kissed while we were being shot at — well, suddenly, all I could think about were her pretty eyes and her warm lips.

And JoBell. My JoBell was in a really bad position right now. What the hell was wrong with me?

"I'm sorry," Becca cried.

"It's okay," I said. "We're in this together."

"I shouldn't be crying like this. I'm supposed to be a soldier too." Her arm slid around behind my back and she leaned over and rested her head on my shoulder. "We all swore in. I thought I was ready. But I . . ." She shook her head against my arm. I could feel her wet tears through my sleeve. "I guess I'm not tough enough."

"What are you talking about?" I said. "You did great. You saved our lives."

"I . . . *killed* someone today, Danny. A Fed, yeah, but a *person*."

"I did too. You think I —"

"I never asked you about shooting that soldier in Spokane. I knew you were hurting. Maybe I should have talked to you about it. I should have been a better friend."

"What? No. You were — you've always been great."

"All I could think to do was cook food for you. Danny, how do we deal with this? How do we live with ourselves after what we've done?"

I gave her a little hug. "What you did, making sure I took time to eat, taking care of me when I drank too much — that stuff's important. That's what being a good friend is." I handed her the sweatpants. "So, you know, first, I got these. They're clean and everything. You should put them on so you don't freeze in those wet jeans." I would have gone around to the other side of the shelves to give her some privacy, but she was on her feet and taking down her jeans before I had a chance to move. Even though I turned away as soon as I knew what she was doing, I couldn't help but catch a flash of her panties.

"Thanks," she said. We sat back down and didn't say anything for a long time. After a while, Becca pulled the sleeping bag back over us. She looked down and rubbed her hands up and down her legs.

"Danny, I've imagined what it would be like to be under the blankets with you, wearing your clothes . . . kissing you . . . for a long time."

There it was. I kind of wish she hadn't brought up the kiss. We could have just chalked it up to a heat-of-the-moment reaction. Something we did because we were sure we were about to die. Her talking about it now brought the whole thing into the present. Made it real.

I decided to tell her the truth. "I don't know what to say. Everything was happening so fast. You really surprised me there."

"Really?"

"What?"

"Were you really surprised?" She put her hand on mine. "Couldn't you tell how I felt about you?"

Sometimes she had acted weird, like super friendly, but I always thought we were just friends. I mean, we were friends, but I thought . . . I didn't know what to think right then. "We've always been close," I said to Becca as she looked at me. "You're one of my best —"

"No!" she hissed. "I don't want to hear it."

"What do you mean?"

"You know what I mean."

124

She wanted to be more than friends. "Becca, you saved my life today. Again. Who knows how many times now? And you're really pretty. Beautiful. I'll admit it. But —"

"Don't say it."

"— I'm with JoBell." I could feel her shrink next to me. She started crying again. "I'm sorry, Becca, but I love her."

"And you don't feel anything for me?"

What was I supposed to say to that? I did feel something for Becca. Maybe a lot, and that was wrong. "I feel . . . It isn't fair to JoBell," I said.

"I know!" she said. "Don't you think I know that? She's my best friend. Do you have any idea how disgusted I've been with myself . . ." She was sobbing. "Falling in love with my best friend's boyfriend."

Becca Wells was in love with me? She couldn't be. "I don't know what you want me to —"

"Don't say anything. Just . . . We almost died today, Danny. We probably still will soon enough. I needed you to know how I felt. How I feel."

I'd grown up with Becca. We went to the same preschool, Sunday school, and confirmation. Before my dad died in the war, our parents got together to play cards and things. When I first started dating JoBell sophomore year, I'd gone to Becca for advice. Well, I'd talked to Sweeney too, but his advice was all about physical stuff, and that didn't come in handy until after JoBell and me had been dating for a long time. Even lately, Becca had helped me smooth things out with JoBell when she was mad at the Boise shooters, when she turned down my marriage proposal.

Damn, and Becca walked in on me and JoBell just today. That must have been hard on her.

"I'm sorry," I finally said.

"For what?"

"For not being able to say what you want me to say. Because I can't be what you want me to be."

She smiled sadly. "I want you to be *you*. And there's nothing to say. Part of me feels terrible for having told you this, for feeling this way. I mean, I love JoBell like a sister. It's all so complicated." She swept her hand around at the dungeon. "Everything is so complicated."

"About what you were saying, you know, about shooting. Killing. The right and wrong of it," I started. What was wrong with a world where I felt more comfortable talking about fighting and killing than I did talking about my feelings toward JoBell and Becca? What was wrong with *me*? "I haven't been able to make myself go back to church since Mom's funeral, and I haven't seen Chaplain Carmichael since before I went to get Mom out of Washington. 'Thou shall not kill.' I know that. But the Bible also has tons of wars in the Old Testament. All those Psalms about how God helps to overcome enemies." I hesitated. Was I making any sense at all? "I know that we did what we had to do to survive."

"But what makes our lives better or more valuable than the Federal soldiers'?" Becca asked. "Why should we get to live when a lot more of them died?"

"I don't . . . It's war, Becca. If you cut it by the numbers, think about how many Idahoans were killed when the Fed invaded."

"But I —"

"Or don't think about it at all. Maybe what we do is find something positive to focus on. For me, it's —" I was going to say "JoBell," but changed my mind. "It's you guys. My friends are the only family I got left now. And I force myself to remember what the Fed did to my mother. The anger helps."

I could tell Becca was fighting to keep from crying again. "I don't want to be angry all the time, Danny," she whispered. "I'll tough it out. For you, and for the other three too. Maybe someday this will all be over, and we'll be able to live in peace. Have fun together like we used to."

I squeezed her close and kissed her red-brown hair. "I hope so. I pray to God you're right."

A few hours later, Schmidty stood at the hatch above the stairs. "Strawberry jelly," he said.

"That some kind of code word?" I asked.

"Your best friend TJ stopped by to see if I could fix his old man's snowblower." Schmidty blew out a puff of smoke. I flipped him off for calling TJ my best friend. He went on, "He says he talked to JoBell, and she's allergic as hell to strawberries. Her old man had some nasty old strawberry jelly in the back of the fridge, had mold on it and everything. She ate half the jar before she vomited in a bucket next to her bed. By the time the Feds came to search the house, they found her with a nasty rash on her face and everywhere else, puke beside her, and looking sick as a dog. So they think she wasn't faking sick after all. She's off the hook."

I let out a relieved breath.

"She's a smart girl," Schmidty said. "Smarter than you. You all stay in there until shit cools down."

That night I wrapped up in a scratchy old Army field blanket on the floor at the foot of the cot, which I let Becca take. Like most nights, I lay there for hours in the dark, trying to remember better times, trying not to think of everything that had gone wrong. The guard shift changed three or four times while I both wished for and feared sleep.

Then I was back on Cal's bike, out in the snow, and Becca and Sweeney were gone. Four soldiers chased me down the street, and I kept trying to kick-start the stupid motor to get the bike to go. That was weird, because the engine was already running. The controls just felt sluggish, and the Feds were catching up. A bullet hit me in the shoulder and I screamed and sat up.

"Danny. Shh. Danny, you're okay." Becca's voice came from somewhere.

The thick dank smell of the dungeon hit me and I flopped back down on the floor, the nightmare over. I could feel my heartbeat throbbing in my neck and ears. My shirt stuck to my sweaty back.

"Are you awake?" Becca whispered.

"Yeah," I said.

She had her flashlight on, so I could see her put the cot pole on the floor. Good. She'd been smart enough not to get too close while trying to wake me. I took a deep breath to calm myself and shivered in the cold as I breathed out.

"You're okay now." Becca placed her warm hand on my shoulder. "Hey, you're sweating and freezing down there. You're going to get sick." She slipped her hands under my arms and tried to lift me. "Come on."

"No, thanks. I'm fine. You take the cot. I won't sleep anyway." I never knew if the sleeping nightmares were better or worse than the waking ones.

Becca leaned down from the cot until her breath was warm against my ear. "If you don't come warm up in this sleeping bag, then I'm going to stay awake with you. So please just do what I say so I can get some sleep tonight?"

"Fine. But what about you?"

She wriggled out of the bag and picked up my Army blanket. "You slide to the side, and I'll fit next to you."

I sighed and crawled into my old sleeping bag. Becca lay down on her side next to me on top of the bag and covered up with the blanket.

"You wanted to know how I deal with what I've done," I whispered. "With all the trouble I've caused, and the people I've had to kill? Well, I don't. At least . . ." I felt the tightness in my throat and was glad that it was so dark, so she wouldn't see my eyes welling up with tears. "If I'm not mad and I'm not numb, then . . . A lot of people are dead, Becca. Oh, God, I didn't want any of this to happen."

"Shh." Becca tightened the Army blanket over her shoulders. "Close your eyes." She propped herself up on an elbow and placed her fingertips on my temples, rubbing them in gentle circles.

"Becca, you don't have to do —"

"Shh. Breathe deep. Relax. You're safe now, Danny. Everything's okay." Her fingers slowly circled round and round. "Breathe deep and just float, like that day it was so hot and we all went tubing down the Freedom River. We stopped on that warm sandy beach, drank pop, and talked for hours. No problems. No worries. Be there with me right now."

Her soft fingers and warm whispers carried me away. In the morning, I found her next to me, and I'd had the first calm, dreamless sleep that I could remember in a long time.

✒—• listening to Federal Idaho Reconstruction Authority Radio. Major General Thane gave — Citizens of Idaho — inside his headquarters — for the initial broadcast — in Coeur d'Alene — ublic of Idaho Radio's new superstation on AM 1040 — eneral Thane •—✒

✒—• Greetings! Greetings! Fellow patriots from across the fruited plain! It's a great day for freedom-loving Americans and Idahoans everywhere. The Buzz Ellison Show is back on the air! The number to call if you want to be on the program today — if you're in an area where the United States government allows comm calls — is 1-800-555-INDY. That's 1-800-555-4639. It seems the United States shut down the old number that Buzz fans had been using for thirty years, since before people even had the old cell phones.

We're on the air coast-to-coast today despite the very best efforts of the United States government to crush freedom of speech. First, I must thank Republic of Idaho President James Montaine for making this possible. Then I must thank a whole secret network of people who have the courage to route this program to their stations. We're winning one for freedom today!

Folks, my pile of interesting things to talk about is through the roof. But I want you all to know that I am currently broadcasting on one of the most powerful radio transmitters in the world. The strongest commercial transmitter allowed in the United States broadcasts with fifty thousand watts. Republic of Idaho Radio, AM 1040 RIR, is on the air with five hundred thousand watts! You should have seen the efficiency, the dedication with which Idaho engineers and workers built this massive system. It's been almost two months since the federal government of the United States attacked Idaho and forced us to declare independence, and in that time, Idaho has built a network of broadcast cables that works basically as a giant antenna. If the United States destroys some of the transmitter network, there are redundant systems ready to continue getting the word out. That's the kind of progress that can be made when people are free from United States federal bureaucracy! Our broadcast engineers estimate that in clear weather, especially at night, people will be able to tune in to our programming throughout most of North America. So, to those politicians listening in Washington, DC, and especially to Laura Griffith, I think I speak for all the citizens of the Republic of Idaho when I say, "You can go to hell!"

Oh, I've been waiting for so long to say that, fellow patriots. And no FCC to slap me with a fine! Now we aren't just broadcasting loud. Our old affiliate stations in Texas, Florida, Vermont, Missouri, Iowa, and even — you'll never believe this — California are defying the United States government by broadcasting the Buzz Ellison Show. Those states have decided not to go along with the Unity Act's prohibition against any broadcasts the president happens to decide are "rebel communications." What's more is that some other broadcast networks have found a way to deliver their programming to RIR, because they don't believe it's constitutional to suppress freedom of the press. Look out, Laura! You're losing your grip on things.

Finally, I want to say this to all of you struggling under the United States' occupation of northern Idaho. We're here for you. The Fed has been able to disrupt our previous broadcasts, but they'll have a hell of a time blocking us now. We're here to connect you to your national capitol in Boise and to the rest of the world. God bless you, and God bless Idaho. I'm Buzz Ellison, back after some important information from the Republic of Idaho Department of Defense. •—⋀

⌁—• Hello, resistance radio! General Thane will be traveling with more security from now on. Our snipers tore up his convoy real good! Dozen dead Fed in Coeur d'Alene! Long live the Brotherhood! •—⌁

⌁—• From NPR news, this is Everything That Matters. *I'm David Benson. Today is a special program, as NPR is now broadcasting some of its programming to areas of Idaho, Montana, and the Pacific Northwest that it has not reached since Operation Unity began in November. President Griffith has backed off her initial threat to defund or even forcibly close down NPR production offices, saying, quote, "The federal government welcomes a more informed Idaho population and hopes that listeners united with the rest of America in their radio programming will understand the wisdom in uniting with their country in their actions and politics." The Republican leadership in the House, however, has pledged to call for a vote on a proposal to cut federal funding to NPR. Speaker of the House Nate Gregory of Virginia, an increasingly vocal opponent of the president, said, quote, "While many Republicans opposed Operation Unity, now that we are engaged in the conflict, the only acceptable outcome is victory. The Unity Act makes all rebel transmissions illegal. Allowing the restoration of anything like normal broadcasting in a rebel state is contrary to the spirit of our pursuit of unification," end quote. NPR's president, Kelly Darmon, made a rare public statement, explaining that even without the special arrangement with Idaho's new flagship radio station, NPR programming would have been recorded and smuggled into Idaho anyway.*

In Texas, federal troops are maintaining position while Texas State Guard forces appear to be making preparations for combat. Many speculate that President Griffith has withheld orders for military enforcement of the Federal Identification Card Act while she and a special bipartisan, federal congressional delegation negotiate with the Oklahoma state legislature in an attempt to persuade that body not to join Texas in voting for nullification of the act.

Despite several hundred arrests, rallies for peace continue in nearly every major American city, with dozens of organizations calling for an immediate cease-fire in Idaho. However, as NPR's Alicia Seeve reports, some criminal elements have taken advantage of these emotional situations to commit looting and violence. •⎯⋏

⋏⎯• Tonight, on the left, Sue Carlin. On the right, Jordan Lund. I'm Al Hudson, and this is Talk Fire on CNN. Sue, Jordan, thanks for joining us. We typically feature guests who represent a consistent Democratic or Republican perspective on the issues, but wouldn't you agree that — especially regarding the war in Idaho — those party perspectives aren't as clear as they once were? And what about President Griffith's proposal for negotiations? Are they a good idea? Do they have a chance of succeeding? Sue, we'll start with you."

"Thanks, Al. I think you're right. Mr. Lund and I were talking before the show, and I think he'd agree when I say the parties aren't as united in their opposition to each other as they have been in recent decades, especially after Jim Barnes agreed to become vice president."

"Exactly, Sue. Al, I think party affiliation is, in many cases, giving way to regional interests. With a real possibility of war in their own backyards, Americans are concerned about the economy, their jobs, their children, their lives. But since this show is usually about two opposing sides to an issue, I will say that personally, and I know many Republicans and more than a few Democrats agree with me, I think these negotiations with Montaine are a mistake. Griffith has given him an opportunity to stall, to prepare new defenses and train more soldiers so that —"

"But you don't know he's using this time to prepare for more war. For now, fighting in southern Idaho has backed off considerably. I do think President Griffith needs to set a time limit on these proceedings. And she needs to ignore Montaine's list of demands. He's calling for massive amounts of food and medical supplies, supposedly as a show of the president's good faith. I hate to sound harsh, but that's outrageous."

"Jordan, what do you think?"

"It is outrageous. These peace talks run the risk of putting us right back into the same standoff we were in before Operation Unity began. One thing Republicans understand better than Democrats is the importance of negotiating from a position of strength, with the potential for real negative consequences for the adversary always at hand."

"Democrats understand that concept just fine, except we know that what you've just described isn't negotiation, but intimidation."

"Fine, Sue. But while you quibble over semantics, people are dying. Maybe the time has come for a lot more intimidation. •⌐

⌐• several southern states are actively demanding the preservation of the union. And while the congressional leadership and the governors and senior state leadership of Georgia, Alabama, and Mississippi have been in a closed-door meeting for several hours now, we're told that they will soon be addressing the press.

And here they come, just the governors and senior senators taking seats behind the table as Representative John Lingham takes the podium. He is a Democrat from Georgia's Fifth Congressional District, which includes Atlanta, one of a handful of Democrats in the heavily Republican South, and chair of the Congressional Black Caucus."

"Good afternoon. To the members of the press and the members of the FBI: Thank you for joining us today in Atlanta. In my years of working for greater equality and prosperity for all Americans, I have become accustomed to the presence of law enforcement, and once again, I'm in a position to assure federal agents, and the government they represent, that my allies and I mean no harm. I have been in communication for the last few weeks and in meetings today with the Southern Coalition for Unity, which has elected me as its chair. While I am, perhaps, more experienced than some of my SCU Republican allies in helping to raise the voice of protest during times of war, today, instead of seeking an immediate end to hostilities, I am joining my fellow lawmakers in demanding a swift and decisive victory in Idaho.

"We do not believe that any productive gains can be made from negotiations between the federal government and the treasonous war criminal James Montaine. We do not believe the Idaho leadership will ever accept President Griffith's terms by surrendering themselves to federal prosecution. We hold that such negotiations only serve to give rebel insurgents in Idaho more time to improve defenses, build coalitions, and prepare for a longer, bloodier war. During discussions about the Federal ID Card Act, insurgent terrorists in northern Idaho continue to wound and kill American soldiers.

"I have dedicated my life to the pursuit of peace, and while President Griffith's desire for a peace settlement is admirable in spirit, it is flawed in execution. We have formed this political alliance because we are concerned about our sons and daughters being sent to a potentially prolonged conflict here on American soil. The Southern Coalition for Unity hereby strongly urges President

Griffith and her allies in the Senate and House of Representatives to discontinue Federal ID Card Act amendment proceedings, to end negotiations with the terrorist leadership of Idaho, and to immediately, completely, and swiftly prosecute the sort of total warfare in Idaho that will bring this conflict to an end and allow our southern soldiers to come home. The Idaho Crisis must end now, and we ask for the support of Americans everywhere in helping to ensure that it does. Thank you. ●—⁄⌐

CHAPTER
TEN

We stayed in the dungeon for the next two weeks. TJ made it down once a few days after our trouble outside the school. JoBell was okay, but the Fed was watching her house again.

"It's too risky for her out there," I said. "She should go into hiding. If not here, then somewhere."

"That's what I tried to tell her," TJ said. "I thought she was going to slap me. She's determined to stay out of this whole war, to live as normal a life as possible, I guess. But I don't know how much longer everybody else will. People are getting pissed. I've heard talk around school about people wanting to stage a walkout, a protest against the curfew and other stuff."

"That's stupid," said Sergeant Kemp. "The Fed will never stand for that. People could get hurt. You need to stop anything like that."

"Yeah," I said. "And if you step in and stop it, that might help keep the Fed from suspecting you."

TJ nodded, but I could see the fear in his eyes. All this dangerous sneaking was draining him.

I slapped him on the arm and he jumped a little. "Hang in there, man," I said. He nodded. "You're doing good."

We passed much of the time listening to the RIR and the Fed broadcasts. The Fed had mentioned a manhunt and reward for any information leading to the identification or arrest of the terrorist who had tried to attack Freedom Lake High School. They had to have figured out who was driving the motorcycle. We guessed that the Fed didn't want to let people know I was still alive.

The news described riots in Oakland and Detroit. Federal troops had been sent to clear out and tear down this giant tent city the homeless had built in Oakland. People who once had solid middle-class jobs had recently been forced to live in cars or scrap wood shacks, and then even those had been taken away. The trouble in Michigan set fire to blocks and blocks of abandoned houses and businesses. With all of the fighting and uncertainty, the value of the dollar was collapsing. That made everything more expensive, and with the added uncertainty in Texas, gas was expected to hit fifteen bucks a gallon by summer. People didn't even know whether they could afford to get to work. Many were mad at the president, saying she should either stop the war or finish it really fast. The whole country — well, *that* whole country, the United States, was falling apart.

At first, everybody in the dungeon was kind of pissed over having another person to squeeze into the already-cramped space, but it was hard not to like Becca. She liked to cook, and she worked some serious magic in our little kitchen. She broke into the MREs and started mixing up new dishes, like beef stew with cheese tortellini. She heated and buttered the shelf-stable bread and changed it from a chalky dead slab to something sort of good. Beyond that, Becca had a gift for listening, and for celebrating the best in whoever she talked to, so that just about everyone left a conversation with her feeling better about themselves. First Sergeant Herbokowitz was in charge, but Becca quickly became our caretaker.

Finally Herbokowitz started letting patrols go out again. We agreed that the M4s were too big to take out on recon runs, as they were too hard to hide. So we were breaking rule two until we could find other, smaller weapons. That left us with my .45 as the only handgun. I agreed to let the others use it, since I was banned from missions for a while. Sparrow and Luchen went first. Then Kemp and Crocker. We still wanted to make a move against the Fed and hit their headquarters at the old cop shop.

Finally, me and Sweeney and Cal were allowed to go topside. Since Schmidty had made plenty of tracks in the snow to and from the shop, we agreed it would be best to simply go out the front door when it was clear. Better that than making a trail out the back of the tunnel that would look suspicious. After fighting for at least ten minutes with the stupid latch on the door, the three of us got out of the dungeon.

The lights were on, but the shop was dead quiet. That was weird for the middle of the day. Schmidty had kept the place open this whole time. But where was he?

I thought about going right back downstairs, but I figured I'd take a very careful look around first, in case Schmidty was in trouble. I drew my .45 and almost shot the man as he came out of the front office. Schmidty stopped and stared at me a moment. "You gonna shoot me?" He reached into his front pocket for his pack of cigarettes.

"Sorry." I put the gun back in its holster.

Sweeney patted my back. "He's a little jumpy. We've been down there a long time."

"They finally let you out after that stunt you pulled at the school, huh?" Schmidty tapped the side of the pack, found it empty, crumpled it, and threw it over near the trash can.

"They're going to give us another chance at recon. Pretty soon, we're going to start hitting the Fed back," I said.

"How's business?" Cal said.

Schmidty flipped him off. "Go to hell." He braced a hand against his back as he sat down in his old dusty swivel chair, searching in a desk drawer, probably for more smokes. "Nobody allowed to drive. People couldn't bring in their cars even if they wanted to."

I looked around the empty shop. "Then why —"

"Someone has to be here to pretend like this place is open. If it's closed all the time and the Feds detect heat signs or something, they're gonna start to wonder, aren't they? Plus, if those sons of bitches come, I want to be here to distract them and warn you."

"Geez, Schmidty, you're a real hero of the resistance," Sweeney said.

Schmidty found a cigarette and pointed it at us. "I don't know anything about that shit, but if you boys are going out fighting, you better wise up. Not like last time. What were you thinking?"

I rubbed the back of my neck. "Kind of an emergency situation there."

"Just stay the hell away from the school now. Since your stunt, that place is a fortress. Whole fire teams guarding each door. Machine gun nests on the roof. It's a mess."

"Sure," I said. "No problem. Any other pointers?"

"Just this. If you are going to do something to stop the Fed, you better do it soon. They're getting set up for what looks like a damned long stay." Schmidty sat back in his chair and was about to light up. Then the rumble of an engine came from outside, followed by the sound of tires rolling over crunching snow and gravel.

"The Fed!" I hissed, pulling out my .45 and waving it toward the dungeon. "Go, go, go!"

In seconds, Cal and Sweeney were back by the closet, yanking the steel ring that would lift the hatch. Sweeney pulled, then knocked on the lid. "Hey!" he said quietly. "Open up."

"It's stuck," Sergeant Kemp said from beneath the metal. "Something's wrong with the lock. There's this one little piece of metal that's stuck behind . . ."

"The hell we gonna do?" Cal asked. "Give me a wrench or something. I'll split the Feds' damned skulls."

"A .45 and a wrench against rifles and machine guns?" Sweeney whispered. "See? This is why we should never break the rules. I tried to tell them, if you put the M4 under your coat kind of up —"

"Come on." I ran for the steel ladder to the loft above the office. The guys were right behind me, scrambling up the rungs through the metal tube cage near the top. We ducked behind a stack of three rolls of pink insulation just as we heard the front door open. There wasn't much between the dusty plywood loft floor and the Feds in the room down below. "Don't move," I whispered as quietly as I could. I prayed they hadn't already heard us.

The inside door of the office creaked. Several pairs of boots clunked on the concrete floor of the shop below.

"Still open for business, Mr. Schmidt?" said a voice with some kind of Hispanic accent. "Even when people are no longer allowed to drive?"

"Thanks to guys like you," Schmidty said with fire.

"Thanks to rebels like your partner, Daniel Christopher Wright."

It was so quiet then that I worried the Feds might hear my heartbeat thumping in my chest. The ghost of the wound in my left hand throbbed. Though it was cold up in the loft, a bead of sweat ran down from my temple.

I heard the flick-hiss of Schmidty's lighter. "You fellows need some work done on your Humvees?" The anger was gone from his voice. He had control of himself again. "Is that why you're here?"

"I am Major Federico Alsovar."

"I know who you are."

"What you may not know is that General Thane himself has assigned me to lead a special task force to locate and apprehend Daniel Wright. It seems a lot of rebels and their sympathizers have become rather fascinated with him — fist flags, 'We will give you a war' graffiti, and so forth. They feel sorry for the boy and his poor, dead mother."

I heard the sick squelchy rattle of someone hocking up a loogie, the splat as it hit the cement. "Well, congratulations on your new assignment, Mr. Alsovar," said Schmidty, "but you still haven't answered my question. Why are you here?"

"I am pretty sure you and I are going to wind up down at my headquarters, Mr. Schmidt. But let's keep up the appearance of following procedures. I will allow you the opportunity to be a patriot again, to serve your country, the United States, by helping me with my mission. Where is Daniel Wright?"

"Thought you people said he was dead."

"It's better for the morale of the nation that people think he's dead. Another of the president's 'tactical deceptions,' I'm afraid. But you and I both know he's alive," said Alsovar. "Where is he?"

"How the hell should I know?"

"You and his father were friends. Wright is half owner of this business. I think you know exactly where he is. I'm going to have my men search the premises."

Schmidty coughed. "You got a warrant?"

Major Alsovar laughed. "Under the Unity Act, soldiers operating on the basis of reasonable suspicion do not require warrants. Why? Do you have something to hide?"

"I just believe in the right to privacy, is all."

"Citizens of the United States enjoy a right to privacy. Rebels? Not so much."

"But you already searched this place!"

"Yes," said Alsovar. "But I think maybe the situation has changed. Perhaps my soldiers weren't careful enough when they were here before. Gentlemen, conduct your search."

"You can't do this!" Schmidty said. "This is private property!"

"Restrain him," said Alsovar calmly.

Schmidty grunted. "Get off me, you sons of bitches!"

That was it. No way was I letting these bastards take Schmidty in. I rose up a little to peek over the insulation, .45 in hand. Below, Schmidty cracked a Fed lieutenant in the nose with a quick hard jab. Blood splattered out in a circle from his fist. Another soldier came up from behind and swung the butt of his rifle at Schmidty, but he ducked under the blow and threw an elbow into the soldier's gut. I'd never seen the old guy move so fast.

"Come on, you shithead Feds!" Schmidty said. "You know who you're messing with? I done my time. Seen more combat than you!" The lieutenant had recovered enough to lunge at Schmidty again, but the old-timer dropped him with a right hook.

Major Alsovar calmly drew his nine mil and aimed it at Schmidty. "I am authorized to kill any insurgents who offer resistance."

I started to stand up. I'd shoot the major before I let him hurt Schmidty. But Schmidty was standing still while a sergeant major and a captain zip-tied his hands behind his back. Hands were on my shoulders. Sweeney and Cal pulled me back down to a crouch. "You can't take on all those guys," Sweeney whispered. The Feds started tugging Schmidty toward the front door.

"Come on!" I whispered. "We have to do something."

"Even if Wright was alive, you think you could use me as bait to bring him in?" Schmidty yelled. "He wasn't that damned stupid! He would never have risked himself for a washed-up old guy like me."

His act was a warning for me to stay out of sight. Or maybe he believed that's how I would choose to play it. He was wrong, though. I'd been forced to kill men to save my friends before. If I had to, I'd do it again.

The scuffle moved to the office below us. "He would never have risked letting you assholes arrest him! I taught him too well!"

"I'm classifying this whole place as a rebel installation," Alsovar shouted. "Turn it upside down. Impound any resources the rebels might find useful. The tools, the parts, everything."

I pressed my eyes against my fists. They'd arrested Schmidty. Now they were taking over the shop. They'd gone too far.

"Wright, pay attention," Sweeney whispered. "Someone's coming."

He was right. I heard the scrape of boots on the metal rungs of the ladder. This was it. Even if I'd wanted to obey Schmidty and stay hidden, I couldn't.

"What do we do?" Sweeney mouthed.

"We go out fighting," Cal whispered.

"With you all the way." I bumped fists with him and rolled onto my back, stuffing my .45 into the insulation so I could work the slide action to chamber a round without making too much noise.

Footsteps hit the wood next to us. I aimed my gun so I could handle the guy when he came around the insulation pile.

"Wait until I shoot," I mouthed to Cal. "Sweeney, you get his gun."

Cal nodded and moved into a three-point stance. He had his football game face on, ready to destroy.

The Fed rounded the corner with his rifle ready. I fired two rounds. One hit his chest plate, one went through his neck. Cal tackled him and Sweeney had his M4 in an instant.

"Let's take 'em out!" I shouted. Sweeney ran to the edge of the loft and fired four rounds into the shop. I joined him in time to see Alsovar duck into the office. I picked off the sergeant major with my .45. Sweeney had already wasted two lieutenants.

"Hurry, before they get away!" I climbed halfway down the ladder and then jumped the rest of the way to the floor. Cal skipped the ladder, lowered himself over the edge, and dropped. Sweeney was right behind him.

I holstered my .45 and picked up an M4 from one of the dead lieutenants. Cal took the rifle off the sergeant major. "Let's go get Schmidty!" I said.

"Wright, you okay?" Kemp shouted as he led Luchen, Sparrow, Bagley, and First Sergeant Herbokowitz out of the dungeon.

"Oh, *now* he gets the hatch open!" Sweeney said.

"Pack it up down there," I said. "We gotta move out!"

Cal was already in the office, opening up with his rifle through the front window.

Then the whole world exploded. Machine guns lit us up. Fist-sized holes burst open in the front bay doors. I dropped to the floor. Bagley screamed as a round took a bite out of his head. He was hit three more times before his body fell to the floor. The tool bench was shredded and sparks flew as rounds ate up the back wall. Herbokowitz's hip exploded and his leg flew off. I thought Sparrow'd been hit, but she started crawling back toward the dungeon hatch, covered in Herbokowitz.

"Cal!" I screamed. "Cal, get the hell out of there!" Most of the office was a giant window. He had to be dead. And we would be. There was no way out of this. *I'm sorry, JoBell,* I thought. *I tried. I love you so much.*

Sweeney wrapped his arms under mine and pulled me back toward the dungeon. "Move your ass, Wright!"

I came back to my senses and looked around. Everyone else had made it back downstairs. Sweeney would be there by now if he hadn't stopped for me. The Fed had Schmidty, had probably killed him, but there were people still alive to fight for. I'd never let them down again. All of these thoughts rushed through my brain in the time it took to crawl a single foot. Finally, I slid my way through puddles of blood and bits to plunge down the stairs into the dungeon headfirst.

"Danny!" Becca threw her arms around me.

I pulled away from her and nodded. "Get the guns! Luchen, grab the fifty-cal. Sparrow, you take his SAW. We'll go out the tunnel and flank them. Kill any soldier you see."

I wasn't the ranking soldier, but nobody wasted time with that shit. We moved fast, quick-crawling through the tunnel and flying out of the escape hole behind the slag heap next door like a swarm of pissed-off hornets. We could see the Fed from our new position at the side of the shop, but they hadn't noticed us yet.

"Spread out," Kemp said. "Don't give them a single area to target."

Luchen set up his .50-cal rifle behind a square piece of concrete sidewalk. Sparrow took cover behind a rock, getting the SAW ready. Kemp loaded a forty-millimeter grenade into his M320 on the bottom of his M4. Sweeney, Becca, and me readied our rifles.

"Danny?" Becca's whisper was shaky.

"You can do this," I said. "We gotta do this."

Becca nodded, and her face took on the same look of determination she wore when she and Lightning barrel-raced at the rodeo. She brought her rifle up and aimed at her target. I turned away, not wanting to watch that sweet, kind, beautiful girl I had known since we were both babies preparing to do something as terrible as kill.

Meanwhile, two Fed gun Hummers with big American flags flying from the radio antennas on the back opened up on the shop. Their guns fired an endless series of eight-round bursts, sending a shower of bullets ripping through the business that Schmidty and my father had built, destroying my dream.

I got ready to shoot. "Aim for the heavy gunners first! Let's waste the mother —"

I was cut off by the roar of our own gunfire as Luchen started shooting. One of their .50-cal gunners lost his head. The other jerked around in the turret as he was peppered by 5.56 from Sparrow's SAW. Six other soldiers were shredded before they even had time to shift fire on us or scramble for cover. Then our rounds were sparking off one of the armored Humvees as it started backing up.

"Don't let them go!" With the turret gunner dead, the Feds were all trapped in that armored truck with no way of taking a shot at me. I rolled over the top of the slag pile and high-stepped through the snow to the Fed vehicle. I dove up onto its hood, grabbing the big metal lift shackle ring and pulling myself face-to-face with Major Alsovar through the thick windshield glass.

I moved up to the roof, going for the gun turret to get inside the vehicle. The Humvee was on the street now, rolling away toward Main Street and the Feds' HQ. Alsovar picked up speed and then hit the brakes, probably trying to dump me onto the pavement. But I was ready, with a solid grip on the lip of the turret. I'd ditched my M4 along the way, but my .45 would be better in close quarters anyway.

I dropped headfirst — gun first — into the turret, firing rounds at the driver's seat. Alsovar was gone! Out the door. Schmidty coughed in the backseat. "Hold on," I said.

I pulled myself back up on top of the Humvee and swung my weapon around, aiming for the major. He ran for it, sprinting toward the steel cylinder grain bins of the Freedom Lake grain co-op.

"Alsovar!" I shot at him just as he ducked between the bins. "You hunting for me!? You better bring a whole hell of a lot more guys! This thing's just starting! I'm coming for you! I will *give* you a war!"

Two farmers slowly came out from around the side of a different bin with their hands up. One was holding an older comm, maybe shooting footage of me standing on the Humvee. I holstered my gun and whipped out my pocketknife, jumping onto the roof of the vehicle and bending its tall radio antenna down in front of me. Alsovar didn't like how the rebels were getting fired up about me? I'd make sure to give them a real show.

"Danny Wright? I can't believe you're alive," said the farmer without the comm. "The Fed's been saying you were killed in the border battle."

"The Fed lies." I cut the American flag on the Hummer's antenna loose in three hard slashes and dropped it to the ground. A few months ago, disrespecting that flag would have made me sick, but that was before America had betrayed me and my home. I held my aching left fist angled above my head the way I had the day the Fed killed my mom. This was the image that people were putting on posters and T-shirts, the one Alsovar was complaining about. I shouted my message loud and clear, right at the farmer's comm. "It's time to fight back. Rise up, Idaho!"

⌐• is why I wrote Lincoln the Dictator. *The man is revered for saving our democracy and freeing the slaves, and he did those great things, but history overlooks the fact that he ignored key freedoms essential to that democracy in order to do it. First, with no authorization from Congress, he ordered the blockade of the southern states. Then he single-handedly suspended the right of habeas corpus, which is the right of a prisoner to be brought before a judge —"*

"Dr. Lavinson, I'm sorry. I'm going to have to interrupt you there. NBC News has just received this video from an anonymous source who claims to have smuggled the footage out of Freedom Lake, Idaho. We're going to cut to that right now. Do we have . . . Is the video ready? Ladies and gentlemen, this is an NBC breaking news exclusive, and there it is. If you compare the photograph in the bottom right corner of your screen to the person firing from the roof of the Humvee, it's pretty clear. That's Daniel Wright, the teenage subject of so much controversy early in the Idaho Crisis. Wright was reported dead shortly after the beginning of the reconstruction of northern Idaho, but . . . And it's tough to make out the audio on this clip, but we believe he is taunting Major Federico Alsovar, commander of the FIRA in Wright's hometown of Freedom Lake. . . . There — we believe he just said, 'I will give you a war,' a sort of catchphrase, if you will, that Wright first used after his mother was killed by federal forces when he attempted to run the federal blockade. There you see Wright cutting down the American flag. Clearly, he is absolutely in league with the insurgency now. We're told this video was shot a matter of hours ago, recorded on an older digital video camera, and then smuggled into Washington where it could be sent to us via the Internet. Thus at this time, it appears Daniel Wright is still alive.

"So far, the White House has refused to comment on this development, but this would seem to prove that President Griffith's declaration of Wright's death was either in error or another 'tactical deception.' We're going to replay that video for you now, and we'll be joined by Idaho Crisis experts from the •—⅄

⅄—• Even if it turns out that the video is authentic and current and that it does show Daniel Wright, I really don't think it matters. Laura Griffith continues to call this the Idaho Crisis, but over five hundred American soldiers have been killed. The number of insurgents killed is unknown, but almost certainly higher. We need to face the fact that unless we act now, we will find ourselves in the middle of a full-blown second civil war. It's easy for the senators and representatives from the Southern Coalition for Unity to demand an escalation in the fighting, because the states they represent are far from Idaho, but many in California, Oregon, and Washington are worried about what will happen to our homes, to the sociopolitical and natural environments of the Pacific Northwest and the West Coast. We applaud President Griffith's efforts toward peace, and we hope James Montaine and the leadership of Idaho will take the steps necessary to end this conflict. •—⅄

⅄—• FriendStar and Shout Out are already buzzing with some important celebrity opinions on the newly released video that apparently shows Daniel Wright still alive and very much working with the insurgents. Chicago Bulls star point guard Ripley JeDaris shouts,

⅄—•
RipMan: Danny Wright is still alive! I'm no insurgent, but that kid has real guts. #StandWithWright

10 minutes ago   Reply - Shout Out
                                                      •—⅄

Kat Simpson, star of the teen vampire blockbuster Nightfall *shouts,*

KatSimpson: I hope the Daniel Wright video doesn't cause more violence. Like *Nightfall* shows, true love conquers all! #NightfallMovie #NightfallBooks

9 minutes ago   Reply - Shout Out

Moving words from some top celebrities. Maybe their example will inspire peace. •⌁

I drove Alsovar's ruined Humvee back to the shop.

"Wright, you okay!?" Sweeney yelled at me when I stepped out.

"Schmidty's in back," I said. "Cal?"

Sweeney shook his head. "Haven't had the chance to —"

"I'm fine!" Cal said, stepping over the bottom frame of the window. "Ears are ringing, and a couple pieces of glass cut the hell out of me, but I'm fine."

I laughed, offering a high five. Cal only held up his bleeding hand.

"Damn it, Wright. Every time you leave the dungeon, all hell breaks loose," Sparrow said. "If you'd just stay in hiding, we —"

"It's not my fault!" I said.

Crocker ran up to the Humvee with a huge box of food. "We should get out of here. The Fed could bring an air strike anytime."

"Where were you during the fight?" Sweeney asked.

Crocker had already stowed his box in the Humvee and was running back toward the shop. "Someone had to pack up the C4, the radios, and some food and blankets and stuff. Or do you want to rush out of here with nothing to live on?"

Sweeney followed him. "Maybe with another guy out here, we wouldn't have almost got —"

"Danny," Becca said quietly from over by the Humvee. "Hey, Danny, I think you need to come here."

"Hang on a second," I said. "We have to figure out —"

"Danny, never mind that shit." Schmidty's normal cracked voice sounded softer and more broken up than usual.

Becca held the back passenger Humvee door open. There were tears on her face.

Schmidty sat sideways with his legs hanging out of the vehicle. Blood ran down from a wound in his gut. Sparrow rushed up with a bandage, but he pushed her away. "No! Save that for someone who needs it."

"You need it," said Sparrow. "You've been shot."

"I know that, damn it! Now leave me alone!"

"I got this," I said to Sparrow and Becca, taking the bandage. "Help Crocker. We gotta move out."

"Yes, *Private*," said Sparrow, reminding me that she outranked me.

I ignored her. "Come on, Schmidty." I held the bandage up in front of him. "Let us take care of that for you."

"Alsovar already took care of me. Shot me right before you started to come down through the turret. You just . . ." He gritted his teeth against the pain. "Get me to my chair . . . in the shop, would ya?"

I wiped my eyes and nodded.

"Don't be a pussy," Schmidty growled. "We're trying to win a war here."

"Cal, help me," I said.

Cal and me groaned as we lifted the fat old man out of the Humvee. Sweeney joined us. With the bay doors shot up and useless, we walked Schmidty around to the front office window, crunching over the broken glass. It looked like a giant cheese grater had been taken to every surface. Junk, scraps, and blood littered the floor around the remains of Bagley, First Sergeant Herbokowitz, and the three Feds.

Schmidty grunted as we put him in his chair. Blood had soaked his belly and the crotch of his jeans, running down his thighs. "Cigarette." He coughed. My hands shook as I held out his pack of smokes. He took one and frowned at me. "Lighter, dumbass!" Cal put the lighter in his hand, and Schmidty lit up. He closed his eyes as he took a deep drag. Then he coughed again and wiped blood from his lips. "They said . . . smoking would kill me." He smiled. Cal and Sweeney and me tried to laugh.

Becca stepped up beside me and put her arm around my back. She was trying to look tough and avoid crying, but she wasn't very good at it. Neither was I.

"Come on, man," I said. "Let us help you. We'll get you to a doctor."

Schmidty shook his head. "Fed'll be waiting there to bring you in. You need to get your shit and find a new . . . place to hide."

"Guys," I said to Cal and Sweeney. "Get our stuff loaded in the Humvees."

"Right. Um . . . Goodbye, Schmidty," Sweeney said.

"Hey, moneybags," the old man said to him. "Basement at my house. Hidden real good. Bunch of cartons of smokes. Worth big in trade."

"Right," Sweeney said.

"But don't go there right away!" A fit of coughing shook him. "Damned Fed will be all over the place."

"Thanks." Sweeney nodded.

Schmidty waved my three friends away, and they went to help load the Humvees. "This ain't your fault, Danny. Don't blame —"

"I blame Alsovar," I said. "I blame the Fed."

He gave me a thumbs-up, the cigarette dangling from his mouth. ". . . never had any kids of my own . . ." His breath was getting shallow now. He pointed his cigarette around the building. "Sorry. I think the shop's a loss."

I looked back at the old man, my father's friend, my business partner. He deserved better than this. My eyes blurred, and I wiped my tears away.

"You gotta win this, Danny. Promise me."

"I promise." I squeezed the pistol grip of my .45. "And I'll get Alsovar too."

"Wright," Kemp called from outside. "Humvees are loaded. We can't stay here."

Schmidty brought his bloodstained cigarette to his lips with a shaky hand and took a long drag. "I got a buddy. He got a cabin, old converted barn . . . up on Silver Mountain. Shady Glen Road. Go there." He pointed at one of the dead officers on the floor. "Give me that bastard's nine mil. I'll stay here. Feds come back . . . I'll give 'em hell."

"Schmidty . . ." I couldn't help it. The sobs escaped me now. "I never thanked you. Never told you how much —"

"Would you get the hell out of here already!?"

"Yeah." I managed to smile. "You stay your regular old pissed-off self. Goodbye, Schmidty."

I left him there, bleeding out in his dusty old chair, watching over our ruined shop, ready to fight the Fed when they came. He would die as he lived, as a fighter.

"Schmidty?" Becca asked me when I took my place in the front passenger seat of one of the Humvees. Cal was ready to drive, and I didn't argue.

"On his own terms," I said. "Let's go." Becca turned away and looked out the window. I grabbed the radio handset, making up our call signs on the spot. "Rebel two, this is rebel one, over?"

"*Um, rebel one,*" said Kemp over the radio from the other Humvee. "*This is rebel two, go ahead, over.*"

"Two, this is one. Follow us. I got a plan, over."

"*One, two. That's a good copy.*"

"Cal," I said, "take us up to Sweeney's storage shed."

"The snowmobiles?" Sweeney asked.

"You got it." The Sweeney family had a whole extra building to house Sweeney's dad's 'vette, their four-wheeler, two Jet Skis, and four snowmobiles.

The radio squawked. "*Rebels on this frequency, be advised we are monitoring this channel and tracking the location of your vehicles. We are authorized to use deadly force to stop you. Surrender now if you want to live.*"

"Why would they bother warning us?" Sweeney asked. "Why not just sneak up and kill us?"

I shrugged. "Maybe they want prisoners for interrogation, or they'd prefer to take us without a fight. Either way, they ain't getting what they want."

"Just ignore them, dude," said Cal.

I held the handset to my head and keyed the transmit button. "Attention Fed assholes! You tracking us!? Fine! Come get us. I swear, I will kill every single one of you! You make sure you bring Major Alsovar along, because I got a special bullet just waiting for him. How copy *that*, shithead!? Rebel one, out."

I crawled back between the front seats, over the blood of the dead Fed gunner we'd tossed out before we left, and pulled myself up through the turret behind the .50-cal. If we were attacked, I'd at least be able to give them a fight. "Cal, speed up!"

"Fast as I can, man," Cal said.

Down the street, a man came out the front door of his house. I tensed up on the machine gun, ready to return fire if I needed to. "Yeah, Wright! Woo!" He waved the dark blue Idaho flag above his head. "Give 'em hell, Wright!"

In the past, I'd hated this kind of attention. All I'd ever wanted was to live my normal life. My truck, the shop, football, some country music with a little rodeo, my friends, Mom, and my JoBell were all I needed. Now the Fed had taken away almost all of that. There was only one thing left to do.

I held up my left fist to the man as we passed. "Fight back! The war is on!"

Sweeney was out of the Humvee almost before Cal brought us to a stop. I cleared the machine gun, pulled the two pins that held it on its mount, and put the gun and an ammo can on the edge of the roof so I could grab them from the ground.

"There's still some gas left in here!" Sweeney yelled from inside the shed. He filled up one snowmobile and then handed the can to Cal, who set about gassing up the other three. Sweeney hitched a sled behind his favorite snowmobile, a 1,000-cc Ski-Doo Grand Touring he liked to call the Silver Bullet.

"Come on, come on! Move it!" Luchen shouted.

When all four snowmobiles were running and out on the snow, everyone loaded food, ammo, radios, the two .50-cal machine guns, a couple extra M4s, and the C4 onto the sled.

"Hey, these guys were packing a bunch of 307 rounds. What should I do with them?" Crocker asked.

"Leave them. We don't have an M307, and I have an idea," Kemp said. "Wright, you know trucks, right?"

"Yeah, why?"

Kemp pulled four blocks of C4 from his rucksack. "Let's make sure the Fed can't use these Humvees against us anymore. Get a wire hooked up to the electrical ignition system. Three or four feet would be great. Then let's get these passenger-side seats off."

"Here." Sparrow popped the hood latch on her side as I did the same on mine. Then we raised the armored hood and I went right for the glow plug that started the diesel engine. I handed Sparrow my knife. "Get me some wire from the comm."

These Humvees were fitted with a system that allowed everyone in the vehicle to communicate via helmet radios. While Sparrow cut loose some wire, I struggled to pop the pain-in-the-ass latch that held the passenger-seat plate down. Finally, I pulled the seat away, exposing the two big batteries in the compartment below. Kemp took out the back passenger seat.

"Can I help?" Sweeney asked.

"You and Becca get those seats off the other Humvee," I said.

Sparrow came back with the wire. Kemp smiled at me. "Give me a .45 round and connect one end of that wire to the glow plug." I gave him a bullet and went to work. Luchen already had another wire for the other Humvee. Kemp pulled the free end of the wire through a conduit in the fire wall. Then in a few quick moves, he turned the bullet into an improvised blasting cap and primed a block of C4 with it.

"Luchen, Crocker, pull that battery up. Sparrow, stick this block and another on the floor under the battery. Make sure both blocks of C4 are pushed up tight together for continuity. Then, Sparrow, run a det cord line to the backseat. Use either end to prime one block under the front seat and one block in back. You know the knots. Put a chain of grenade rounds on top of them in back. Then close everything back up so the Feds don't know we did anything. Got it?"

"Roger, Sergeant!" Sparrow said.

"Luchen, Crocker, help her. Sweeney, Wright, Cal, Becca, help me rig up the other Humvee the same way. Move it, people!" Kemp said.

We worked very fast but perfectly in synch, everybody doing what they had to do. When a Fed started the engine, the electric ignition system would set off the improvised blasting cap, which would detonate the C4 blocks under the batteries. The batteries would fragment into a geyser of molten lead and battery acid, exploding all over the inside of the Humvee. At almost the same instant, the C4 under the backseat would explode, setting off the M307 grenade rounds.

"That ought to do it," said Kemp.

"Sucks to be the Fed," Cal said.

"Let's go!" said Sparrow.

We ran to the snowmobiles. Whatever supplies wouldn't fit in the sled we held in our laps.

"Schmidty said his friend had a cabin up on Silver Mountain," I said. "Shady Glen Road."

"Got it." Sweeney got on Silver Bullet, putting on a black helmet. "I know the trails around here better than anyone. We gotta move fast, so stay with me, and go exactly where I go."

"I kind of want to hang around and watch the Fed start those Humvees," said Luchen.

"Too late." Sweeney throttled up and slid ahead.

All four of Sweeney's snowmobiles could seat two, but there weren't enough helmets to go around, and out in that cold, zipping through the wind as the sun lowered in the west, the air bit deep. Sweeney led the way with Crocker on the back of his snowmobile. I followed with Becca behind me, her face pressed to my back to stay out of the wind. Sparrow drove behind me with Luchen holding on to her. Kemp brought up our tail with Cal riding backward, guarding our six with the SAW and more SAW ammo stolen from the Feds we'd just taken out.

Sweeney wasn't kidding. He made that snowmobile absolutely fly, sled and all. Up and up we moved, sliding along trails that would have been well-kept in peacetime. Now the snow was thick and powdery, getting deeper and deeper the higher up the mountain we went.

Sweeney led us around and around to make our trail too confusing to follow.

After a few minutes, a bright flash lit up the snow all around us. One second later another went off. The sound wave hit us two seconds after that. We all stopped to watch two fireballs roll up through the sky. Some unlucky Fed soldiers had started the Humvees, and the C4 had done its job.

"Got 'em!" Luchen shouted. Cal pumped his fist in the air.

Sweeney gunned his engine, leading us on up Silver Mountain. We drove on and on until my hands and legs were ice cold. I couldn't imagine what Becca was going through with no helmet or goggles.

Finally, Sweeney brought us to a halt in a clearing next to a steep, snowy slope. He shut off his engine and removed his helmet, and we all did the same. He motioned us all closer and pointed down the hill. "I'm pretty sure that Shady Glen Road is down below us. It's a two- or three-mile offshoot from the main road. I figured we didn't want to pull up right in front of the place. Feds might be all over the better-traveled streets."

"Right," said Kemp. "Now we got to get inside before we start to get frostbite."

"Anyone live at this place?" Cal asked.

I wiped my runny nose on my sleeve. "Schmidty didn't say. He just said his friend had a cabin up here, a converted barn."

"How do we do this?" Sparrow asked.

"Someone needs to stay up here with the gear," said Kemp. "Crocker, Sweeney, Luchen, Riccon, that's you. Crocker, guard the supplies. Luchen, you're a good shot. Cover us on overwatch with that fifty-cal rifle. Sweeney, you know the snowmobiles best. You stay with them. Four snowmobiles up here. Four people to bring them down to get us in case there's trouble."

"H-here." Crocker handed me a little Motorola hand radio. "We should assume the Feds are monitoring all channels. Try to keep radio silence. If you do have to use it, make short transmissions. The longer you keep the mike keyed, the easier it will be for the Fed to zero in on us."

"Right," I said. Our commo specialist might actually be getting the hang of this. "Good work, Crocker."

"Wright, Sparrow, Becca." Kemp shook his head. "Becca, you got a last name?"

"Wells. Becca Wells, um, Sergeant."

"Right," said Kemp. "Wright, Sparrow, Wells. Let's do this."

"Sergeant," I said. "Becca's never really been on an op like this. She hasn't been trained."

"I've done just fine so far," Becca said. "If Sergeant Kemp says I'm going, I'm going."

"It's your call, Wright," Kemp said, "if you think she's not ready."

"It is *not* your call! I'm coming with you!" She gave me a look that didn't leave a lot of room to argue.

"If you two are d-d-done with your lover's quarrel, I'd like to g-get down there and get inside," Sparrow said.

The four of us moved down the hill. With the snow up almost to our crotches, it was easiest just to dive and roll on top, dropping into the tree wells where the snow was shallow and we could use the evergreen trunks for cover. Sparrow slid down into the tree well right behind me. She was shivering and breathing heavy from the exercise.

"You okay?" I asked quietly.

"Oh yeah. I'm just great," she said. "Let's keep moving."

The place was easy enough to spot — a barn-style building with a garage and fireplace. Kemp and Becca tumbled down by us. "Doesn't look like anyone's there," Kemp said. "It's hard to tell, but the road hasn't been plowed. Let's get down there to make sure."

A short time later, we'd cased the place out. One end of the barn hadn't been converted to a cabin and remained fit for livestock, with two horse stalls, plenty of hay and straw, and even a small paddock outside. Becca looked hopefully at me, and I knew her mind was already turning over ways to bring Lightning up here. We moved around the place with our rifles at the ready, looking in the windows like some SWAT team from a cop show.

"It's empty," I said. "But there might be an alarm system. We should disable that before we try to break in."

Kemp looked up the snowy slope. "I wish we could radio the others, but we better save it for emergencies. Wells and I will go back up the hill. Wright, you and Sparrow see if you can find any alarm and get it shut off."

We looked around the outside, but couldn't find anything. "It's-s-s an old p-place. M-m-maybe there's no alarm," Sparrow said.

Maybe she was right. Or maybe there was an alarm, but no electricity up here. I stepped up to the locked back door with a crowbar I'd found in the generator shed. After a couple tries, all I could say about breaking open locked doors was that it looked a lot easier on TV than it was in real life.

"Give me that," Sparrow said. She slammed the crowbar into the door frame and threw her whole body weight against it. Wood cracked and splintered. She tried again, and the door finally popped open.

"By-the-book entrance?" I asked.

"Fine." She sighed.

I stood against the wall by the side of the door with the butt of my M4 pressed to my chest and the barrel pointed down at a forty-five-degree angle. Sparrow did the same behind me, so close that she'd feel me when I moved. "On three," I said.

"Roger."

I leaned back and counted out my forward movements. "One, two, *three*!" I ran into the room, leading with my rifle in a sweep to the right. Sparrow aimed her rifle around to the left. "Clear! Check high," I said. We pointed our rifles up to make sure the upper parts of the room were safe. It was all part of our room-clearing training, which the Army had made us drill over and over again.

By the time Sweeney and the guys had brought the snowmobiles down with our gear, Sparrow and I had cleared every room of the two-story, three-bedroom barn house. The place had a big, open stone fireplace in the living room and cast-iron wood stoves in the kitchen and one of the three upstairs bedrooms. Building a fire was a risk, but a heat signature in a residential place out in the woods like this wouldn't be as suspicious as one in a business like the shop, when it was supposed to be closed for the night. Besides, we were all so chilled that if we didn't get warmed up soon, we'd risk hypothermia.

A short time later, Cal and I had a fire going in the fireplace. Sparrow sat on the big stone hearth, shivering under a blanket I'd found in one of the bedrooms. Luchen rubbed her shoulders. Kemp lit a fire in the stove upstairs, where he stood watch with Luchen's .50-cal rifle near a big window that gave him a view of the road. Cal found some peroxide and bandages in a first-aid kit. He took care of his cuts from the attack on the shop.

We were safe for now, those of us who had survived. I went by myself into the third bedroom and shut the door behind me.

I was alone, with nobody else watching or listening to me. I didn't have to smell Luchen's farts. I didn't have to listen to Sparrow and Sweeney argue about some dumb thing. Finally, after all these weeks. Alone. I leaned back against the wall, closed my eyes, and slid down until I sat on the floor in the quiet.

Slowly my adrenaline died down and my body stopped shaking. The rush, the panic, the fight was over, and the thoughts and memories started flooding in. Herbokowitz . . . the way he'd been torn apart. Bagley, who'd been so scared for so long, shredded. The Feds I'd had to shoot. How many had we killed that day? I hated them. Yeah. But . . . in the moment, in the middle of the fight, the hate kept me going. Afterward, it was hard to keep the anger up. Some of the soldiers I'd killed had to have been like Specialist Mueller, who'd only wanted to go home, and who let me, Sweeney, and Becca go free after the school thing. Because of what we'd done today, the Army would be contacting more families, telling them they'd never see their loved ones ever again.

Then I thought of Schmidty, slowly bleeding out in the ruins of the shop. He'd started to tell me he'd never had a son of his own. He didn't have to say more. I knew what he meant. The Fed had killed him. Major Alsovar had killed him just to piss me off.

I rubbed my aching left hand. Well, fine. Alsovar had succeeded, but he had no idea the storm he'd brought on himself and the Fed. We were hidden up here for now, but soon enough, we'd bring a hellfire avalanche down the mountain.

⌁—• pending the notification of the deceased soldiers' families, but one thing is clear. Daniel Wright and his insurgent allies have resorted to Al Qaeda–style terrorist tactics, first in a deadly attack outside a school, and now by rigging an IED in two Army Humvees, killing innocent soldiers. That's why the FBI is issuing a substantial reward for information leading to the arrests of Private Daniel Wright, Calvin Riccon, Eric Sweeney, and Becca Wells, and Private First Class Henry Nelson, Specialist Shawna Sparrow, Private First Class Nick Luchen, Specialist William Danning, Specialist Anthony Crocker, and Sergeant Thomas Kemp. Anyone who wishes to help bring these terrorist insurgents to justice should contact the FBI via the number listed on the US government's Idaho Crisis resource site. •—⌁

⌁—• From ABC News, I'm Rick Calpis. President Griffith executed another in a series of unprecedented steps today when she announced that leave and passes have been indefinitely suspended for all officers and enlisted personnel in every branch of the military. The Department of Homeland Security has issued a National Terrorism Advisory System elevated alert for all military bases in the United States and imminent alerts for all bases in Texas and Oklahoma. The country has not been on this high a level of domestic military preparedness since the immediate aftermath of 9/11.

Despite larger signing bonuses and a near-record-high national unemployment rate, the US military is having difficulty filling recruitment quotas. Troop levels are up slightly from those after large Defense Department budget cuts several years ago, but Pentagon analysts warn that increased overseas and domestic deployments, coupled with the loss of some National Guard support, might reduce overall mission effectiveness.

In the wake of this report, congressional debate is set to begin next week on a bill to reinstate the draft for the first time since it was discontinued in 1973. The United States has required men from ages eighteen to twenty-five to register for selective service for decades, but this has remained a backup for an all-volunteer force. President Griffith says that in light of the current crisis, she is open to the possibility of draft reinstatement, but would also ask that the draft be expanded to include women.

In the Canadian Parliament, a discussion has begun over legislation designed to address Canada's increasing problem with American refugees. Debate was heated in the House of Commons today over a controversial proposal to deny entry to American citizens, even those claiming refugee status or seeking asylum. These proposals come in response to the thousands of US citizens crossing the border, many of them undocumented and unprepared for a longer stay in Canada. Supporters of these border-closing measures emphasize that such restrictions would not constitute a trade embargo or any other diplomatic barrier. The White House was unavailable for comment.

According to recent surveys, religious practice in America has reached levels unheard of in many years. Churches, synagogues, mosques, and other places of worship are all seeing sharp surges in regular attendance. Almost all religious leaders cite fear and uncertainty regarding the Idaho Crisis as a significant contributing factor behind the increase. You're listening to ABC News. •—ᴧ

ᴧ—• Broadcasting with five hundred thousand watts, AM 1040 Republic of Idaho Radio, RIR. In Idaho news, President Montaine attended the graduation ceremony for nearly ten thousand soldiers, including just over three thousand women, the first class of troops to complete training after the president invoked the militia clause in December. Most of the soldiers will serve in the Idaho infantry and other combat units, but about eight hundred soldiers, a large proportion of whom are conscientious objectors or unfit for combat operations, will serve in various support capacities. President Montaine, after expressing his pleasure at an estimated 97 percent compliance rate with the enlistment requirement, said this in his address."

"It has been said that those who came of age during the Great Depression of the 1930s and who went on to win World War II are the Greatest Generation. But I'm here to tell you today, as president of the Republic of Idaho and your commander in chief, that you are the greatest generation that any country has ever known. You are the revolutionaries of the new Republic of Idaho, facing a powerful enemy who wishes to rob us all of our freedom. Your efforts in the coming months will be spoken of with reverence in our history books for generations to come. Soldiers of the Republic of Idaho, I salute you! •—⋀

⋀—• Welcome back to Viewpoints. Ladies, have you seen the latest . . . absolute garbage coming from Montaine? I think I'll call him Mudstain. Anyway, Mudstain has the audacity to compare his terrorist thugs to the men and women who won World War II! Were the handful of National Guard soldiers who murdered twelve people in Boise at the start of all this better than those who liberated France? Better than the Tuskegee Airmen who fought Nazis in the air and then discrimination at home?"

"That's a great point, Belinda. And you know all of us women here on Viewpoints are Laura Griffith's number one supporters. I always say, 'She's our gal!' But I also want to say, 'Madame President, if you're watching this . . . Hello. Montaine is playing you with these peace talks. He doesn't care about the ID Card Act anymore. He's stalling to keep you off his back, so he can get his army built up.'"

"Jubilee, while I agree with you about Mudstain, I think the president has a plan. She was on the show several times when she was a senator and I can tell you, nobody plays Laura Griffith. •—⋀

CHAPTER
TWELVE

"You sleep at all?" Cal spoke quietly as he and Becca joined me the next morning in the bedroom we'd named the guard tower.

"I swear, I never sleep." I turned around and sat on the heavy wooden table on which we'd set up one of our new .50-cal machine guns. We'd need to bolt the tripod to the table and the table to the floor if we didn't want the weapon's recoil to knock the whole thing over, but it would do for a last-stand-at-the-Alamo-type weapon. I squeezed my dry eyes shut. "I'm so fried."

"You should have come got me. I would have helped you sleep," Becca said.

Cal looked at me like *What is* that *all about?* I shrugged him off. I wasn't about to get into it. Besides, I hadn't wanted to sleep. I would've dreamed of Schmidty bleeding out or of Herbokowitz or Bagley getting shot. It was better to stay awake.

Cal looked out the window at the gray morning and fresh snow falling on the empty, unplowed road below. "It's already after seven. You were supposed to wake me up to relieve you. You been on guard duty since you took over for Kemp?"

I nodded. Sweeney slipped into the room, being careful not to spill either of the two cups he carried. "Hey, guys. Wright, I made you what I hope is coffee." He handed me one of the mugs. "Sorry, Cal, Becca. I didn't know you were up. Wright's been awake all night, and I could only carry two. You'll have to get your own."

My faded mug read SEATTLE SEAHAWKS 2014 SUPER BOWL CHAMPIONS.

I held it up to take in the smell, trying to remember the last time I'd had coffee. "Where did you get this?"

"Found it way in the back of one of the cabinets in the kitchen. We're long past the 'best if used by' date on the coffee, but . . ."

"Come on, Cal. I'll make you some," Becca said. "And I better figure out what else this place has for food or supplies. Get the kitchen ready." Cal slid down off the table and followed her out.

"Pretty wicked machine gun," Sweeney said after the other two left. "Good position here."

"I hope we never have to use it," I said. "Not up here, anyway. If the Fed get this close, we're in deep shit."

Sweeney was quiet for a moment. "Don't take this the wrong way," he said. "You hate talking about this, but hear me out for a second. I know you felt terrible about having to shoot that staff sergeant in Spokane when we were trying to get your mom back home." He took a sip of coffee. "You had to do it. It was him or us. It was horrible, but I also secretly thought it was kind of badass. I've played a ton of *Call of Duty*. Always thought it was so realistic or whatever. Then I saw you do the real thing."

"That was nothing like a stupid video game," I said.

"I know. That's what I'm trying to tell you, man," said Sweeney. "I know we had to shoot those Feds at the school, at the shop. And if we had to go through that again, I'd do it the same way." He steadied his cup with his other hand. "But this stuff is nothing like the movies or the video games. It's not only that we're actually in danger or that we could be killed any second. It's —" His voice tightened up.

I took a drink. The coffee tasted a bit like soap. "The bodies are real. You can see them. The blood gets on you, and that smell doesn't wash out right away. Real dead people don't just disappear like on the games."

"Yeah. And now I've killed those real people," Sweeney said, his voice shaking. "I've killed a *lot* of real people. They had parents and brothers and girlfriends or whatever. So I wanted to talk to you in private. I know this is a war and everything. But . . . how do I . . ."

How did he live with himself or get past the nightmares? How did he balance a lifetime of hearing stuff like "Thou shall not kill" with the need to stay alive and to protect his friends and family? How did he deal with the increasing uncertainty that the need for the few of us to survive was greater than the right of so many others to live?

"I don't know," I said. "I guess I try not to think about it. Focus on what we have to do."

I finally looked at Sweeney. Most of the time, he was smooth and confident, like one of those action heroes in the movies who gets all the girls. He always seemed to have an answer for everything, but now he looked really lost.

I patted him on the shoulder, careful not to hit him hard enough to make him spill his coffee. "Hey. You did what you had to do. And, when I froze up in the shop . . . Well, thanks for getting me out of there."

"With you all the way." Sweeney smiled a little. Then he took a drink. "Ugh, who am I kidding? This coffee tastes like ass."

I laughed. "It really does, dude."

Cal came back into the room. "If you two are done making out or whatever you're doing up here, everybody's awake. Kemp wants us down by the fireplace."

Sweeney flipped Cal off. "You go," he said to me. "I need to be . . . I'll keep watch."

A fire roared in the fireplace in the living room, and Becca patted an empty place beside her on the couch. I sat down, and after so long in the dungeon with nothing but metal folding chairs and Army cots, I felt like I was floating on a cloud. I struggled to keep my eyes open.

Luchen sat in a faded old recliner with Sparrow on the armrest. She was eating cheese tortellini from an MRE food pouch. Cal dragged a kitchen chair in, turned it around backward, and sat with his legs spread around the back. Crocker was on the stone hearth. Kemp stood in the middle of us all.

"Before we talk about anything else, I want to . . ." He let out a long breath. "I want to remember the people we lost yesterday. What can I even say? I . . . I'm sorry. I'm not so good . . . They never trained us for this." He laughed sadly. Sparrow snorted and leaned against Luchen. "I didn't know Bagley that well," Kemp continued. "I know he could be tough to get along with, but you have to give him credit for being brave enough to jump into all this with almost no training."

"He just wanted to go home," Becca said. "Maybe if we'd found a way to make that happen . . ." She leaned over and put her head in her hands. "And we just left them there on the floor."

"Wasn't like there was time for a funeral," said Luchen.

"Scott Herbokowitz was the best first sergeant I ever served," said Sergeant Kemp. "He could be a bit rough sometimes, but he —"

"He cut out the bullshit," said Luchen.

"Right." Kemp paced in front of the fireplace a couple times. "So I guess I'm in charge." He looked at all of us as if checking that we agreed. "And the question is, what do we do next?"

"We need to send someone into town to see how the Fed has reacted to yesterday," Becca said. "But mostly to let TJ and JoBell and Cal's dad know we're still alive."

"Enough with the endless recon mission," Luchen said. "I want to stick it to the Fed for a change."

"Normally, I'd say that's impossible," Sparrow responded, "but since we've proven that hiding doesn't work either, I suppose we might as well try."

"Hiding didn't work in the dungeon because we kept going around town planning for a fight," Becca said. "It was too small and nasty to stay down there. Now we have plenty of space. A lot more privacy. Maybe if we just stayed here and waited it all out, we could —"

"You guys are the ones who ruined everything by getting into a firefight with the Fed at the school." Sparrow pointed at me and Becca. "You brought them down on us!"

I winced a little at that. I'm not gonna lie. I kind of agreed with her.

Sergeant Kemp sat down on the base of the stone fireplace. "Wright, what do you think?"

I knew JoBell would say I should sit out the fight. I looked at the tired faces around me and thought of how rattled Sweeney was. Then I thought of the people the Fed had killed. "We need some downtime before we hit back," I said. "And we need to get set up out here. Then we can figure out what to do next."

"I agree wholeheartedly that we should wait a while," said Crocker in his nasally voice. Luchen grabbed a food pouch from Sparrow's MRE bag, holding it up to her as if to ask if he could have it. She shrugged and he opened it up. Crocker continued, "The Fed will be looking for us all over Freedom Lake. Maybe after a week or two it will be safe."

"Two weeks?" Pieces of dry poundcake burst from Luchen's mouth. "Oh, hell no! I ain't sitting on my ass for two more weeks."

"Hey, at least you *can* sit on your ass now," Cal said.

"Damned right." Luchen wiggled his butt around in the chair just to show he could. "But if we do have to make a trip into town, to get supplies or send word to Mommy and Daddy, well, Wright is the Fed's most wanted, and some of you are not too far down the list. I could go instead. They're not looking for me like they're looking for him."

"Makes sense," Cal said. "We could give him directions to TJ's, pass along word that way."

"I'm not going to sit and do nothing," I said.

"Right," said Kemp. "There will be plenty for you to do up here. We'll prepare some defenses and recon the area, looking for escape routes and more supplies. Maybe there are more abandoned cabins with stuff we can use."

"And then we attack the Fed," said Cal.

"Can I say something?" Crocker said.

"What's up?" I said.

Crocker wouldn't meet our eyes. "Before we launch any attacks, I think we should get our radios set up."

Cal snorted. "I know you're scared, but we're in a war here," he said.

"Cal, listen to him," Becca said.

Crocker nodded to Becca. "I'm not saying we shouldn't fight, but if we don't do it smart, we're going to get killed, and we won't be able to fight real great then, will we?"

Cal wasn't backing down. "What good is a radio going to —"

"Maybe I am scared!" Crocker shouted. "Okay? And if you guys aren't, then you're stupid. Winning wars isn't just about being brave or running around shooting people. It takes good strategy. Planning! And for that you need good communication. Right now we have none! Zero! We're clueless on our own, and we have basically no information. But, if we get our radios set up, if I can get some help rigging a really good antenna, maybe we can make contact with other resistance cells in the area. Maybe we can intercept some Fed transmissions, if any of them are dumb enough to be using unencrypted radios. Better yet, if we can contact Idaho, we might be able to call up an air strike to hit the Feds, instead of rushing around risking our own lives."

Here was short, lumpy, totally out-of-shape Specialist Crocker shouting down Cal Riccon, two hundred and twenty pounds of pure muscle. Cal stared at him with his big arms folded. "So you're saying we should get the radios hooked up?" He shrugged. "Okay."

We'd had a class on commo in basic training. "If you start trying to call people on the radio, won't the Fed be able to locate you?" I said.

"I'd just listen at first," Crocker said. "Maybe try some very short transmissions. I think it would be worth it."

In the end, we agreed to make commo a priority, and then we all went to work.

Sweeney took Luchen and Sparrow on one snowmobile to drop the two of them off within walking range of Freedom Lake. The rest of us started preparing our new base. We got the electrical generator in the shed running and charged our comms, in case Idaho ever figured out how to make the Internet work for someone besides the Fed. On scouting runs to the three cabins that we'd seen on our lane, we found more shelf-stable food, a couple axes and other tools, and, best of all, a shortwave radio kit, complete with antenna. Crocker was so excited about the radio, he about shit his pants.

Then Becca, Kemp, Cal, and I drove two snowmobiles along the side of the road, but back far enough in the woods so nobody would see our tracks. After about a mile, our lane came to a T intersection at a larger road that had been recently plowed. If only the Fed were driving, that meant this road was trouble.

We'd brought some extra wood down on the snowmobile sled,

and Kemp and I stacked it up to make a small, two-man fort. A piece of plywood formed the roof, and then we buried the whole thing in snow, except for one front window facing the intersection. We set up our second .50-cal machine gun on its tripod in this igloo. If the Fed turned up our lane, the guards on this position could light them up and then bug out on the snowmobile. The guards would be cold out here, but at least we'd have advance warning of any attack.

Best of all, though, later in the day, we fired up the gasoline-powered water heater, and after a while we all had our first hot showers in weeks. I was the last to wash up and the water was cooling down a bit by my turn, but it was still incredible to get clean.

Later that day, I heard the sound of an engine approaching from the woods. Cal was covering the guard tower and Kemp and Crocker were on duty in the igloo. I picked up my M4 and ran for the stairs. "I think we got company! Cal, be ready on that machine gun. Becca, grab a rifle. Let's go!"

We rushed outside and took up positions behind tree trunks, only to see Sweeney slide in from a different path than he'd taken before, with Sparrow riding behind him.

"Where's Luchen?" I asked as soon as they stopped.

"Oh, he's coming," Sparrow said.

Sweeney laughed, and Sparrow elbowed him. "Sorry," Sweeney said, "but it is kind of funny."

"What's funny?" I said. We were missing someone. What could possibly be funny about that?

Sparrow finally relaxed her seemingly permanent scowl. "Wait till you see."

"Come on! Damn it! Would you . . . Go. Giddyup, horse. Go!" Luchen's voice came from somewhere off in the woods. "No. You can eat later. I swear, I'll get you a carrot. Do you eat carrots?"

Sweeney and me laughed. Becca stood still with her mouth open and tears welling in her eyes. "Eric?" she said, almost in a whisper. "Is that . . ."

Sweeney smiled. "We got your horse back, baby."

Becca threw herself at Sweeney, hugged him around the shoulders, and kissed his cheek. "Oh thank you, thank you, thank you!"

Sweeney laughed. "If I'd known that it just took a horse to get some action from you, I'd have bought you a whole herd by now."

Becca laughed and kissed him again, then went to hug Sparrow. "You are totally my new best friend!" Becca said.

"Yeah." Sparrow leaned away, lightly patting her on the back. "Yeah. Okay. All right."

Becca actually jumped up and down when she finally saw Luchen guiding Lightning up the trail. Actually, "guiding" might have been a stretch. It was more like Lightning had decided to take her time following Sweeney, and Luchen did his best to manage. The stirrups on the saddle were way too short for him, so both of his feet hung loose. He tried kicking the horse's flank a couple times to make her go faster, but she completely ignored him, pausing to nibble a bit of shrubbery.

"Horse! That's an order! I'm so serious, horse. You have to go faster. I think there's like a whole bag of sugar at the cabin. Horses like sugar, right? Really. Whole bag."

Becca laughed with tears in her eyes. "You *guys*. I can't believe it. I worried I'd never . . ." She took a couple steps forward, reaching out to her old friend. "Come here, Lightning. Come here, we have a nice warm stall for you and a paddock where you can run around." She wiped her eyes. "You'll be safe and happy here."

Lightning whinnied and picked up the pace when she heard Becca. Luchen leaned forward. "Finally, it decides to move." As

Becca and Lightning greeted each other, he struggled to climb down out of the saddle, slipping and falling on his ass in the process.

"That stupid . . . I swear it tried to piss me off on purpose," Luchen grumbled as he stood. " 'Bout ready to shoot that —"

Becca kept one arm around Lightning's neck and reached out with the other to pull Luchen into a big hug. "Thank you so so so much for bringing her back to me."

Luchen tried to hold back a grin. "Yeah, well. The trick was getting her out of town. TJ found us some old guy he knew to ride it to the edge of town. I guess soldiers stopped him twice, but since there's no rule against riding horses and the man flashed them his federal ID card, they had to let him go. When he was finally sure he wasn't being followed, he brought the horse out to the woods and tied it to a tree out there." He shrugged. "After that, it would have been easy, except the horse would hardly go."

We needed that happy reunion. That and the chance for everybody to get cleaned up let us end the day with a desperately needed glimmer of hope.

⌁• If you can hear me on this shortwave radio . . . We hit the Fed patrol right outside of Kamiah. Dynamite took out both Strykers. We shot up the five-ton trucks. Long live Idaho! •⌁

⌁• CBS Radio News, I'm Harvey Kennison. Secretary of Education Manuel Mendoza issued a statement today warning that unless changes are made, this could go down in history as America's 'lost school year.' Due to high energy prices, an unstable supply chain, a massive domestic refugee problem, and violence, record numbers of American school-age children are being homeschooled or receiving no education at all. Here's Secretary Mendoza."

"Some districts have had to reduce to a four-day or even a three-day school week. Those districts have tried to make up the time in lost teacher contact hours via the Internet, but student participation is sporadic, and there have been challenges with Internet interruptions due to security concerns. Other parents who fear violence are keeping their kids at home for 'homeschooling,' but with two working parents, there is often too little or insufficiently rigorous instruction. On behalf of the United States Department of Education, I would like to assure parents that our schools are safe, and encourage everyone to make sure their children get the best education possible. If something doesn't change, we risk raising the least-educated generation in decades. Such an outcome would be a catastrophic setback, not only for the personal development of millions of American youth, but for the civil and economic life of the American people. •⌁

⌁• Every time the Fed sends a patrol to Moyie Springs out of their HQ at Bonners Ferry, we tear 'em up. Twelve dead Feds this last time. Rise up, Idaho! •⌁

⟋─• This is going out to all my fellow citizens of Idaho listening to their shortwave radios tonight. Me and my guys are out here around East Hope. We're set up at cabins and secret bases all up in these mountains. Feds come looking for us, we keep picking them off one by one, and then moving so they can't find us. Today we nailed a whole Fed convoy! You should have seen it. •─⟋

⟋─• Calling East Hope! Break transmission! Don't stay on so long, over! •─⟋

⟋─• Convoy had two armored gun Hummers and four cargo trucks. We'd already weakened the supports on the Route 200 bridge north of town, but then we set up fertilizer bombs underneath. When the convoy was on the bridge, BOOM! We took them all out. Blew 'em up and dumped the bits of bridge and Fed into Lake Pend Oreille. Only the lead Humvee made it across. We blocked the road with an old pickup truck, and then attacked the Hummer from both sides of the road. Wait a minute. Guys, you hear . . . Like a roar. Oh no! Get out of here! •─⟋

THIRTEEN

"The Fed commander in Wallace, Idaho, is dead. Sniper got him. Long live Idaho!"

"Did you hear that?" Crocker shouted from his radio desk up in the guard tower. We'd set him up there so he could monitor the radio and keep secondary watch on the road at the same time. "That's the third strike this week!"

We went up to hear the details. "You'll never believe what else happened," he said. "One attack was just south of Coeur d'Alene. We captured two M142 HIMARS trucks."

"High mars?" Becca asked. I'd never heard of it either.

"High Mobility . . . Artillery Rocket System," said Kemp. "Pretty serious weapons. Not used very often, and then mostly in Iran and Pakistan."

Crocker nodded. "They were probably going to be used against Idaho forces in the mountains near White Bird. But a ton of resistance fighters took out the Fed, stole the trucks, and drove them off somewhere!"

"Whoa. Some guys got rockets now?" Cal said. "Wish we had some. Be so badass."

"It's too bad we couldn't get those things turned over to the actual Idaho military," I said. "They could use them."

Crocker scratched his belly. "Someone also radioed to say they've taken an M777 Howitzer and a bunch of M795 rounds. The Howitzer is a field artillery weapon, a big cannon," he said to Becca. "The

M795 is a 155-millimeter high-explosive round. It weighs about a hundred pounds and has over twenty pounds of TNT."

"Sounds like a seriously nasty weapon," I said. "I wouldn't want to be downrange of that thing."

"From the little bits and pieces I've heard on shortwave, the Fed blockade line along the border with free Idaho is stacked with even more weapons than the one that surrounded the state before the war."

"I think the Fed's getting ready for another big attack on southern Idaho," Kemp said. "They're going to level everything until there's no resistance."

I went to stoke the fire in the woodstove, shifting things around with the poker. Would President Griffith really order an attack that would level and burn everything? So far, it seemed like she'd tried to hold back a little. She hadn't simply destroyed the state in order to force it to obey the Fed.

"With Texas and maybe Oklahoma on the edge of fighting, the Fed might be willing to be a lot tougher on Idaho to get this over with," said Becca. "Stop the rebellion here, stop the civil war in its tracks."

Kemp nodded. "The last time states were in rebellion, back in the Civil War, the Union Army destroyed everything it could. Burned whole cities to the ground."

"We're not alone," I said. "We gotta find the others in the resistance. Maybe if we work together, we can slow down the enemy until Idaho can figure out what to do."

Luchen moved to stand behind the .50-cal. "I'm tired of getting our asses beat."

"No shit," Cal said. "We're running out of time. If we don't fight, the Fed's gonna kill us all."

"Remember TJ told us that the Fed supplies are coming across the border from Washington?" Luchen said. "Right through our old checkpoint on the state line. That must be the shortest route for them or something."

"It might be a good idea to shut that road down," said Sparrow. We all nodded slowly.

"We have to do this smart," said Kemp. "But if the Fed is bringing traitor bait over the mountain, I think we can close the road fairly simply."

"But if we shut down that road and stop the convoys, won't we prevent a lot of innocent people from getting food and stuff?" Becca asked. "I hate that the only way for people to get anything is through the Fed, but if that's how it is, maybe it wouldn't be so great to stop them."

"I hear what you're saying, Becca," said Sweeney, "but I don't see that we have a choice. The Fed also has to be bringing ammo and weapons on that convoy."

"But how do we stop them? Set off charges to cave in the tunnel up on the mountain?" Luchen asked.

Kemp shook his head. "That's reinforced concrete supporting a tunnel carved out of solid rock. They built that tunnel to last, and we don't have close to enough explosives to bring it down. I'm thinking we wait until the next Fed convoy rolls through, and then we use fougasse."

"Fougasse?" Becca said.

"A sort of homemade napalm."

"Sergeant, how do you know all this?" Sparrow asked.

"Yeah, first rigging the Humvees to explode, now this fougasse stuff," said Luchen. "I don't remember any of that from combat engineer school."

"One of my buddies in our unit who's deployed to Iran right now is a sapper, and he learned just about everything there is to know about explosives at the Sapper Leader Course. We used to talk about this stuff at annual training in the summer."

"You think this fool's gas will stop a whole convoy?" said Cal.

"Fougasse," said Kemp. "And yeah. If we do this right, they don't have a chance."

Sweeney shrugged. "Then it's settled. Let's do it."

"Right," said Kemp. "Luchen, Cal, we found a bunch more cold-weather gear in the closet. Why don't you both get suited up for the cold and then go down to the igloo to keep watch there. Luchen, you know the fifty-cal, right?"

"The Ma Deuce is like a beautiful woman." Luchen closed his eyes and held his hands out in front of him like he was feeling up some girl. "I know all her sweet spots and . . ." He opened his eyes and saw Sparrow shaking her head. "I know the gun, Sergeant," he said quietly.

Kemp smiled. "Good. Show Cal how to load it, unload it, cock it, functions check, and everything."

"Can we shoot something?" Luchen asked.

"Nick, no," said Sparrow. "Think about it. You'd be wasting ammo and giving away our position."

Kemp tried to keep from laughing. "Right. So, suit up and take care of all that without firing. Crocker, stay on the radio. Sweeney and Wells can help you if you need it. They'll keep watch on the machine gun. Sparrow, Wright, you're with me."

Out in the generator shed, Kemp started me cranking a hand pump to empty the rest of a fifty-gallon gasoline barrel into the electrical generator. After the barrel was empty and we'd wiped it out and even lit the remaining gas on fire to dry it, we placed a wad of steel wool on the bottom of the barrel. On top of that we taped down one block of primed C4, running the det cord from that block out of the barrel. Next, we pumped diesel from a second barrel into the one we were rigging.

"So long, hot showers," Sparrow said.

Kemp sent me inside to grab all the soap powder in the cabin. I found some in the laundry room and more in the kitchen under the sink.

"Mix the soap into the gas. We want it pretty thick," said Kemp. "The soap will act as a binding agent and will help stick the burning fuel to everything. The C4 will heat the steel wool to ignite the mixture just as it's blasted out of the barrel."

When the barrel was full, we sealed the lid back on and ran the det cord from the C4 three times around the top. "These det cord wraps will cut the lid off just as the ignited mixture is flying out," Kemp said. "We gotta find a truck somewhere. Then we haul this baby and park the truck in the tunnel, using a brick or something to tilt the barrel at about a forty-five-degree angle. When the Fed convoy rolls through, they'll have to stop because the truck will be blocking the road. Then, when the fougasse explodes, the soldiers and their vehicles will be burned up. The oxygen will be sucked out of the tunnel, suffocating anyone who survives the burns."

"Geez," Sparrow said. "Are we sure we want to do this?"

The Fed had taken my life, killed my friends, and murdered my mother, but even I had to think about what we were proposing to do.

"It'll stop the convoy and block up the tunnel. The Fed will take forever to clear the road," Kemp said.

It would leave burned corpses everywhere too. It would rob people of their loved ones. I remembered what me and Sweeney had talked about that morning in the guard tower. Then I looked at the scar on my left hand. The Fed hadn't worried too much about right and wrong when they killed my mother or the other guys in my Army squad. This was a war, and the rules were win or die.

"We'll use this to hit the next Fed convoy," I said. "Burn the bastards."

"I wish I'd been able to work with Lightning more this fall. With everything that's happened, she hasn't been able to stretch her legs and get exercise for months." Later that day, Becca was brushing Lightning down while I shoveled manure out of the stall into a wheelbarrow. "I mean, I know there probably won't be any rodeos come summer, but Lightning gets restless if she doesn't get to work out."

"She wants a workout? Have her muck her own stall," I said.

Becca made like she was trying to kick me, and though her foot came up about two feet short, I still acted like I'd taken a hard shot to the gut. I groaned, bent over, and fell back onto a bale of straw.

"He deserves it, doesn't he, Lightning?" Becca said.

I stayed on my back on the bale. The prickliness of the straw in the dusty barn and even the smell of the manure tugged me back toward simpler times. "Remember when we first learned to ride? That little pony your parents bought you named —"

"Trigger!" Becca laughed. "And you cried and cried when your dad first put you on him."

"I did not!" I'd kind of blocked that part of the memory out, and I wasn't about to admit to it now.

"Did too!"

"How could you possibly remember? We were like five."

"I remember everything as if it were yesterday." Becca sat down on the bale next to me. "I tried to explain how Trigger was nice, but you were so scared he'd bite you. You had no trouble in the mutton-busting event at the rodeo — you rode that sheep longer than anyone else. But when our parents decided you were ready for all four feet of big, bad Trigger, you panicked."

"Yeah, well, I figured out riding eventually, and when you messed up and fell and skinned your knee, who came and carried you back to the house while you cried?"

"You did," Becca said quietly. "You kept saying everything would be okay, that you'd take care of me."

"Exactly." I sat up. "And I always will."

She took a deep breath, and her eyes were a mix of emotions. There were the ones I feared and even worried that I was starting to share. But there was also something else, a dark cast of anxiety, like she used to get before a tough test in biology class. Now it ran deeper, and when she reached over to take my hand, I knew it was for comfort and not romance.

I closed my eyes. I'd go back to the dungeon in a second if it meant that Bagley, Herbokowitz, and Schmidty could be alive again, but since we'd moved to this mountain cabin, I often took time to simply enjoy being alone, or mostly alone. "If I make it out of this war alive, I'm going to disappear," I said. "Find a cabin like this one, even a trailer on the bank of a river somewhere. Just fade away. Just sleep. For the rest of my life."

She gave my hand a squeeze. "Not *if*, Danny." Her voice shook as she spoke. "When. We'll make it through this."

I squeezed her hand back. "You're worried about this attack. I am too. And I meant what I said. I will take care of you."

Becca remained silent for a moment. "Great," she said. "You can start by hauling out that wheelbarrow of manure." She chucked a dried horse apple at me.

"Hey!" I laughed, catching the grassy ball of shit and whipping it back at her. "I'm going, sicko." We both stood up, and I left the warmth in the barn, pushing the wheelbarrow with its heavy load.

* * *

The next day, I smashed the side window of a truck with my hammer. It had snowed all through the night, and probably would again later in the day. The end of January bit into our spines with a paralyzing cold.

"C-come on, man, w-would you hurry up?" Cal said. "If the Fed drives by, we're toast."

"At least toast would be warm." I opened the door and leaned in to get at the wires down below the steering column. The only truck we could find up here was a beat-up late 2000s Ford F-150 with a FOR SALE sign. It sat way out in front of a cabin about half a mile down the main road from Shady Glen. Snow covered the top of it and icicles hung from its bottom like stalactites in some old forgotten cave, so we'd had to dig it out to get even this far. This road had been plowed, we thought, so the Fed could run supplies up to an outpost they were establishing at Silver Sunset Resort on a different part of the mountain. To get into the truck, we'd tracked all over and messed up all the snow. There was no way soldiers would pass by on the road without thinking something was up. With any luck, by the time they noticed, we'd be long gone.

Thanks to everything I'd learned from Schmidty, hot-wiring the truck was easy. I cut and stripped a little insulation off the end of the accessory and engine wires. Then I did the same with the end of the crank wire. "There's no guarantee this thing would start even if we had the keys. It's so damned cold." I started cutting the insulation off the end of what I hoped was the power wire. "It would help if I had the right tools. Working with this bayonet really sucks."

Cal opened the passenger door, put his AR15 on the seat, and leaned over to look more closely at what I was doing. "You need help?"

"I need you to keep watch so some damned Feds or the owner of this truck don't jump our asses."

"Okay, okay. Just if you can —"

"Hurry," I said. "I know. I about got it, I think." If the wire I'd just stripped was the power wire, the truck would start to turn over as soon as it touched the other three wires that I'd twisted together. "Let's hope this works." I made the contact and the engine started turning over. It was a low rumble, though. She was cold. Careful to keep the wires touching, I pushed down on the gas pedal. "Come on, baby! Fire up!"

With a short whine and a strained *vroom*, the engine started.

"Yeah! You got it, buddy! Let's roll." Cal climbed up into the truck.

I finished twisting the wires together and climbed in behind the wheel, resting my head on the top of the steering wheel for a moment. The only thing I'd ever stolen was a small, twenty-five-cent pack of three SweeTarts from the checkout lane at the grocery store when I was about five. When Dad saw that I had them, he drove me back to the store and forced me to apologize to old man Travers, who owned the place. I was shaking and crying, but I apologized, and I never stole anything after that day. Not until after everything fell apart at Boise.

"You okay, man?" Cal asked.

I picked my head up off the steering wheel and laughed for a second at my own stupidity. How could I be bothered by stealing a truck after I'd killed so many people? What kind of person had I become? My bad hand ached, and I looked out the windshield at a world blurred by frost.

I put the truck in gear and drove out of the yard, spinning out a little in the snow, then hooked a left down the main road, heading toward the rendezvous point. "They better have the fougasse there waiting for us."

"Relax. Sweeney's all over this plan. You know he'll get it done."

The plan was kind of idiotic. So many things could go wrong. Sweeney's job was to drive Silver Bullet through the woods, towing the fougasse barrel in the sled, with Luchen standing right behind it to make sure the weapon stayed upright. Kemp, Becca, and Sparrow would drive down with them. That way, we'd have enough empty seats on the snowmobiles when we needed to get the hell out of there.

I stopped the truck right by a rocky outcropping. Kemp and Sparrow rushed out onto the road with their M4s drawn. Kemp checked that I was driving, and then he and Sparrow spread out and took a knee, scanning the road and woods. We were already out in the open and in trouble if the Fed saw us, so there was no use trying to hide our weapons, and we might as well set up good security.

Sweeney drove his snowmobile to the tailgate of the truck, and Cal jumped out to help Sweeney and Luchen lift the heavy fougasse barrel up into the bed. They were straining so much that I put the truck in park and ran back to help them. When the drum was loaded, I slammed the tailgate closed and hurried to get back behind the wheel. Cal hopped in back to steady the weapon.

I went as fast as possible without spinning out on the slick roads. By the time I finally pulled up to the tunnel, everybody else in our group was supposed to be up on the ridge keeping watch. I drove into the tunnel and started what felt like a sixty-point turn so I could get the pickup's ass end pointed west, where the convoy would be coming from. TJ had told us that the Fed supply convoy rolled in most Saturdays in the late afternoon, maybe about seventeen hundred. We figured that meant they'd roll through the tunnel about fifteen minutes before. We had about twenty minutes to spare, if they came today. We might be camped out here for a while.

Finally I stopped the truck and shut off the engine. There wasn't much fuel left in the pickup's gas tank, and I didn't want to waste it by leaving the thing idling. The more gas in the pickup, the bigger the explosion.

Now me and Cal did the rest of our job, dropping the tailgate and tilting the fougasse at about a forty-five-degree angle. Cal was stronger, so he held the barrel while I slid a brick under one side.

"This is a perfect spot," Cal said. "Around the curve so they won't see the truck until it's too late, and with the pickup parked right in the middle like this, they'll have to stop."

Kemp would be coming down from the ridge to set the time fuse and light the thing. Me and Cal jogged out of our end of the tunnel and started climbing up to join our team on the ridge.

"Abort! Abort! Abort!" Kemp's voice came on my little Motorola radio. *"They're early! They're one minute out! Get out of there!"*

I radioed back. "Roger. Stand by."

Cal swore. "Great job keeping watch, guys," he said.

"Kemp and everybody must have just got up there," I said. "Stay here!" I sprinted back into the tunnel, heading for the pickup. I couldn't let all our effort go to waste.

"I'm coming with you!" Cal ran right behind me.

"You don't know nothing about time fuse," I said.

"What's to know? Light it and run!"

When I made it to the pickup, I could hear the Fed trucks coming through the long tunnel. I whipped out my bayonet to cut the time fuse. There were a bunch of black tick marks spaced a few inches apart on the thick plastic rope-type thing. Each segment was supposed to be one minute's burn, but Kemp had told me it wasn't exact. A combat engineer would cut off one segment, light it, and check how long that segment took to burn. He'd then know how much fuse to use. I didn't have time for a test. I cut the fuse down so it wouldn't even burn through a whole segment before the blasting cap set it all off. We had less than a minute.

"Oh shit! Lighter! I don't got no —"

"Truck lighter!" Cal tossed me the little silver pop-out truck lighter. I burned the hell out of my hands catching it.

"Get out of here!" I shouted. "I'm right behind you!" I could see the light from the convoy's headlights coming around the bend. Cal took off running. I held the red-hot coils of the truck lighter to the fuse. I'd never lit time fuse before. Smoke started rising from the end, and the fuse hissed. I pulled the lighter away. We had a good burn.

"Wright! Get out of there!" Cal yelled.

I jumped from the truck and sprinted even faster than I would on my most desperate touchdown run. A few shots went off, and rounds sparked against the wall.

Then a sound like a kettledrum blasted a second before my eardrums were punched out and my chest crushed. The light from the fire lit up the little bit of tunnel still ahead of me. A wall of heat hit my back, and I stupidly looked back to see if I was burning.

A pure white-hot spinning eye of flame held me in its gaze. The front grille of the pickup looked like the exposed teeth of a burning skull, and the truck's back end was shredded like a frayed rope. Behind it, flames covered every surface of the Stryker fighting vehicle that had led the convoy. Its tires had melted, sticking it in place. The five-ton truck behind that had stopped as well, its canvas tarp gone and supplies in back burned. Over the roar of the fire, I heard the agonized shrieks of dozens of people. Combat troops assigned to kill me and anyone else in the Idaho Army, yeah, but also truck drivers and supply specialists. Guys like Specialist Mueller. All burning. A soldier screamed and dropped down out of the passenger side, her uniform and skin shredding as her hair melted and burned. She tried to roll on the ground, but that too was covered in flames.

I finally broke away and tried to run again, but my chest ached like I'd run the Army two-mile test. I gasped. Ground wobbled.

Mouth dry. Eyes itched. Gripped throat. Tried suck air. Feet wood. Fell . . .

Pain in my cheek. "Wright!" A gray-black shape. "Wright! Come on, buddy!"

I sucked in as deep a breath as I could, but coughed. I felt like I'd been smoking nonstop for three days straight. "Wa-ter." My blurred vision cleared. Cal looked down at me. His face was bright red.

"Here, buddy." He handed me a clump of snow. "Eat this."

I crammed the snow in my mouth and pushed it around on my tongue to melt it. The cool water at the back of my throat gave me life when I thought there was none. I ate more snow.

"You passed out," Cal said. "No air in there. I went in to get you. Had to hold my breath. It was like walking into an oven." He smiled. "You got a little cooked. No eyebrows. Worst sunburn I ever seen."

I hurt everywhere. "The others?"

Becca crouched down next to me and put her hands on my chest. "Two trucks backed out of the tunnel. We had to shoot them up. Everybody else is unloading the useful stuff from the backs of them."

"What'd we get?" I asked.

Cal smiled. "Explosives, ammo, and food. Everything an army needs for a war."

I sat up and looked around. Cal had pulled me out of the tunnel and off the road into the snow. "The fire?"

"It burned out in a few minutes," said Becca as she rubbed my back. "I don't think it could get enough air."

"Neither could the Feds, or the engines of their trucks. We torched up three five-tons. One of them was a ways away from our pickup and wasn't burned that bad. I think its engine shut down from no air. The soldiers in it suffocated."

Becca wrinkled her nose and turned away, but Cal told the whole story with the same kind of excitement that he might have when talking about a great football game.

"That's how I would have died if you hadn't pulled me out of there," I said.

Cal smiled, stood, and held out his hand to help me up. "Got you covered, buddy."

I let him help me, glad I could still walk. Thick black smoke still rolled out of the tunnel, and then the smell hit me — a mix of gasoline and summer barbecue. I thought of the soldier falling out of her truck, helpless to do anything but watch the skin burn from her bones until her eyes melted away or she died. My stomach heaved and I bent over to puke, but I had nothing in me, so I just retched until my face was hot and tears were in my eyes.

Becca patted my back. "Danny, we have to get out of here."

I gripped her arm to steady myself, nodded, and stood upright. "Let's go."

"Dude, you should check out the tunnel first, though," Cal said. "The Feds in the Stryker must have gotten their hatch unlocked, but that's about it. I finally got it pried open with a crowbar. Those dudes weren't burned at all, but cooked alive. Their skin was all juicy and split open —"

"Cal!" Becca looked at him.

"What?" He shrugged.

"Let's just move out," I said, before they could start fighting.

We met up with Kemp, who said only, "Glad to see you're okay." He was trailing a line of shock tube while Sparrow and Luchen crammed C4 charges into the walls at the mouth of the Fed end of the tunnel. "We found a combat engineer's treasure chest on one truck. C4, TNT, det cord, time fuse, shock tube. You name it." He plugged the end of the shock tube into an M81 detonator. "I think I can rig this so if any Feds come up and try to move any of these wrecks, they'll pull the pin on one of these detonators and set off more nasty explosives. We'll never get the tunnel collapsed, but it'll take them even longer to clear it."

I nodded, suddenly dead tired. We finished setting up the booby traps and took off on our snowmobiles, loaded up with as many Fed supplies as we could carry.

FOURTEEN

"Riccon, get a fire going," Kemp said as we came into the cabin.

Crocker ran down the stairs to meet us. "How did it go? Is everyone okay? I have some bandages and things ready in case —"

Sergeant Kemp frowned. "Specialist Crocker! Have you abandoned your post?"

"Um, well, I . . . Just for a second. I mean —"

"Get on that radio and put the call out! Fed convoy destroyed in Freedom Lake!"

"Yes, Sergeant!" Crocker ran back upstairs to his shortwave radio.

Cal slapped a high five with Luchen as they cheered. Even Sparrow smiled. Sweeney put his arm around me. "I'm not sure if what you did was really brave or really stupid, but great job. I'm glad you're okay."

We all joined Crocker in the tower to watch him send the message. "Fed convoy destroyed on Silver Mountain. We torched 'em!"

"Nice shooting, rebels." "Rise up, Idaho!" "We'll give them a war!" People from who knew where answered us. If we still had the Internet, we would have had a high star rating for this FriendStar post.

That night, our group celebrated our first victory with an ancient bottle of some nasty whiskey stuff called Drambuie, which Becca had found during her kitchen inventory. I had one shot, then I put my coat on and went to the door. "I'll set up the machine gun and take first watch in the igloo."

Cal knocked back a shot of the liquor. "Wright, come on! We're celebrating! You gotta party with us. Some of this might help your eyebrows grow back."

I couldn't get in the party spirit. My hot skin kept pulling my mind back to that fire. Those screams. I forced a smile. "Another time, maybe." Becca slipped her snowmobile suit back on. I elbowed her. "Hey, you should stay and have fun if you want."

She zipped up the suit and then mashed a big knitted stocking hat down on her head. "Rule number one."

"Nobody goes alone." I nodded.

A few minutes later we had the .50-cal machine gun set up on its tripod in the igloo. It was a dark, snowy night, and cold, but the wood and snow walls would shield us from the storm and keep us at least a little warmer than we would be just sitting out here exposed.

"We should have built the walls higher in this thing," I said to Becca, tilting my head to the side under the low ceiling.

She was laying down over on the side away from the machine gun. "You want to fix it?"

"Not right now," I said. "I'm kind of fried after the attack."

She shrugged. There was enough space between her and the tripod for me to lie down as well, and there'd be nothing wrong with trying to make myself a little less miserably uncomfortable out here. I told myself it wasn't like we were laying down naked in my bed or something. We were both wearing about six layers that we'd found at nearby cabins to try to stay warm. I rolled onto my side next to her.

"How long are we on duty for?" she asked after a while.

"Don't know. Long as they party. Maybe longer if they get real wasted." I looked out the window at the intersection of the main road and ours. The wind was picking up. If the road snowed over, the Fed would probably come plow it again. Hopefully, they'd stay off our road.

We didn't say anything for a long time. "I don't get . . ."

"Don't get what?" Becca asked after a moment.

"Nothing."

She elbowed me. "Come on. You can say anything to me. You know that."

I looked at her, trying to ignore how cute she looked in that red stocking cap with the little puffball on top. "I don't get how they can party. Back in football, we used to always say we were going to kill the other team. Or we'd win a game and celebrate afterward, talking about how we'd killed them. But we never really . . ." I bit my lip for a second. "It's like, I hate the Fed. I do. I want them out of Idaho more than anyone. And I know we gotta do, you know, these terrible things to beat them. I fantasize about seeing all these Fed soldiers out in the field getting all shot up until the rest of them run away and leave us alone."

I took a deep breath. "Still, when I see their faces . . . They're soldiers, yeah, but they're still people. They ain't all maniacs like Alsovar. Not even all infantry. Today we killed . . . people who probably thought they were joining the Army just as a job, or to pay for college. I can't forget the screams and all the bodies from that tunnel fire." I thought of the purple-black burned meat left on the bones of their arms and legs, their exposed skulls. I was shaking now, but not just from the cold. "I can't stop thinking about how many we left dead on the ground in that tunnel." I clenched my fists. "Then I get mad at the Fed all over again. We wouldn't have to be doing attacks and shit if they'd just leave us alone!" I pressed my forehead to the snow. "Now I'm blaming them for *me* killing them? I can't figure out what to think."

Becca didn't answer right away. She was always a good listener.

"Maybe I'm not supposed to think or feel anything, you know? Maybe I'm supposed to be all 'mission first' and the hell with everything else. Am I a weak soldier?"

Becca moved closer to me and pressed up against my side. "Danny, you could never be weak. What you're thinking, feeling . . . It has to be normal, right? You *should* feel bad about —"

"But sometimes I like it. Well, almost. Not like I *like* it, but sometimes when we're taking out the Fed, I feel good, like I'm glad there's some justice or that I'm getting revenge or whatever. And I think sometimes I love the feeling of power that comes from handling all our badass guns, the adrenaline rush of the fight. What kind of sicko thinks that way?" I looked up at her. "What the hell is happening to me, Becca? I think like, even if I survive this war, I'm dying inside."

"Hey." Becca put her gloved hand on my arm. "Hey, Danny, no." She took her glove off and touched my face. Her hand felt so soft and warm. "This is hard on all of us. The fact that you can recognize those feelings, the fact that they bother you, is proof that you're no psycho. This is so hard for you, it bothers you so much, because you *do* have a soul, and you *are* a good person." Her fingers caressed my cheek and I closed my eyes. "And you're so brave, and so kind." She had leaned close to me, and when she spoke again, I could feel the warmth of her breath on my skin. "And we're here for you. I'm here for you, Danny."

I opened my eyes and saw her shaking a little. Was she shivering from the cold or because we were so close? I put my arm over her to try to warm her, but I didn't stop looking into her eyes.

I don't know how it happened, who made the first move, but we were kissing. Our lips parted and we shared breath and held each other close. In this world where everything had gone wrong, shot through by gunfire, somehow in that moment, being with Becca felt very right.

Our team wanted to maintain the momentum and morale on our side, to keep the enemy off-balance with no time to recover. So three days later, me, Cal, Becca, and Luchen crouched in the attic in Samantha Monohan's grandma's old house. Mrs. Monohan had moved to an apartment in Spokane when the federal blockade started, leaving a nice, furnished two-story house with a big attic. TJ had asked Samantha if some "friends of his" could use the place.

I was looking out the window at our target across the street when I felt Becca's hand on my shoulder.

"Are you all set?" she asked quietly.

I stepped away from her touch. I'd kind of been avoiding her since our time in the igloo, telling myself that I needed to stay focused on our mission, that I couldn't afford any distractions. While that was true, I also hated like hell that I had made the idea of us as a couple stronger in her mind, and maybe stronger in my own too.

"You okay?" she asked when I didn't say anything.

"I'm fine," I said. "But I need you to cover the door. Rule number three. Always post a guard."

A pained look passed through her eyes. "Yeah," she said. "Fine."

"Hey, you guys, check *this* out!" Cal came out from behind a stack of dusty boxes and trunks, pulling a saber from its scabbard. "An old calvary sword!"

I laughed. "I think you mean cavalry."

Cal gave me his usual openmouthed stare. "What's the difference?"

"Calvary is the name of the hill where they crucified Jesus," said Becca. She paced back to the stairs that led down from the attic. Luchen's job was to hide out on the ground floor to prevent any Feds from sneaking up on us or cutting off our escape. Becca was the backup in case the Feds found another way up or if they took Luchen out without us knowing. "Now put that back, Cal. It's probably been in the Monohan family for generations."

"Hell no! This is war, and I need me a sword."

Becca looked to me, but I shrugged. "It could come in handy," I said. "But right now, Cal, I need you over here, ready with the SAW." I'd found a wristwatch in our cabin, and I checked it now. "Six thirty. They should be lighting the place up now."

"I'm still not sure this is right. Mary Beth is nice," Becca said.

"We've been over this," I said. "Her father works with the Fed. Her dead uncle's house is fair game."

"Shh, someone's coming!" Becca whispered. She took a knee at the side of the door, keeping her M4 pointed down the stairs. I grasped my own rifle, and took a position standing, pressed behind Becca. Sweeney walked up to the base of the stairs, saw our weapons, and froze. Becca and me relaxed.

"Luchen's doing a bang-up job guarding the ground floor," I said when Sweeney had joined us in the attic.

"He's got it covered," said Sweeney. "He about shot me before he realized it was me sneaking in through the back door. Anyway, Operation Wet Blanket is a success. Kemp and Sparrow told me to tell you the torch is lit."

"Now we just wait," I said. We'd had TJ pass the word to some people we could trust — guys from the old football team, mostly. They were supposed to keep eyes on the Fed's vehicles, and then, at six twenty, they'd dump water into Fed fuel tanks. At six thirty the house across the street would start to burn. Skylar Grenke's dad was on the Freedom Lake Volunteer Fire Department. Skylar promised that his dad would make sure the guys in the fire department weren't around to volunteer for this fight. The Fed would have to either let the house burn and risk all the houses nearby, or they'd have to send soldiers to drive the fire trucks themselves. When they showed up, conveniently without many armored vehicles, they'd have very little protection, and we'd start shooting them from the window. Sparrow and Kemp were in the attic of another abandoned place several houses down across the alley. They had the .50-cal rifle, and that thing would tear up anyone, body armor or not, from over a thousand meters away.

"Is that fire?" Cal asked. "I thought I saw a flash."

"Well, put that saber down and pay attention," I said.

"Saber?"

"Sword," Sweeney said as he crept up to the window with his M4. "Nice piece, though."

Across the street, orange light flashed from a living room window. "Oh yeah," I said. "She's lit." Smoke began to roll out from somewhere around the side of the building. "Get ready."

The light in the living room got brighter and brighter. The tan vinyl siding on the front of the house began to melt. More and more smoke billowed out. Finally, the town fire whistle went off. Still, nobody came, and the house burned.

"What if the regular fire department shows up?" Becca asked.

"TJ was very clear with Skylar," Sweeney said. "He told him that any firefighter who showed up would risk being shot."

"Hope you can trust that guy," Luchen said.

"Grenke's an idiot," I said. "But he's loyal. He'll get the word out."

Red-and-white flames slashed through the walls and began to roar from the side of the house. Smoke and fire had invaded the second floor. We waited. Finally, two Fed Humvees showed up. Four soldiers dismounted from each, leaving someone behind to man both of their machine guns on top.

"Is that all they're bringing?" Cal readied the SAW. "Maybe they're gonna let it burn down."

The snow on the roof had steamed off and a few flames began to lick up through the shingles. Some downstairs windows shattered.

"Wait." I eased down the barrel of the SAW. "They'd never bring only eight guys for a fire this big. Wait until we got more targets."

Finally, we heard sirens. Minutes later, all three Freedom Lake fire trucks rolled onto the scene, all covered in soldiers in full combat gear. Skylar's dad climbed out of the first truck and started barking orders, pointing at the fire hydrant and hoses.

"Grenke a traitor?" Sweeney asked.

Skylar's dad was frantic, trying to get the Feds to get the hoses running. Had he sold us out? A Fed pulled a nine mil and aimed it at Skylar's dad, yelling something. Mr. Grenke put his hands up and shrugged, then pointed out some of the control valves on one of the trucks. Whatever he'd said seemed to satisfy the Fed, and Mr. Grenke looked around the neighborhood nervously.

"No, he's cool," I said. "They're forcing him to help them fight the fire. He's no sellout." There had to be at least forty or fifty soldiers down there. "Get ready," I said. "Sweeney, hit the Humvee gunner on our left. Cal, you take out the one on our right. Becca, watch for returned fire. I'm going for that son of a bitch who was pointing a gun at Skylar's dad. I shoot first." I picked up my little Motorola radio and hit the transmit button to call Sparrow and Kemp. "Don't hit the civilian. The civvy is not a target."

"*Roger*," Sparrow radioed back.

I aimed through the glass, but the glare was messing up my shot, so I grabbed Cal's new saber and used it to pry the old window open. It swung up, and then I hung the frame on a hook on the wall. "Welcome to the Fed shooting gallery," I said.

I caught a concerned look from Becca and remembered our conversation about war and killing. She gave an encouraging nod. *Focus, Wright. Mission first.* I fell back on my training, aiming at Nine Mil Soldier, controlling my breathing, and easing on the trigger. The Fed seemed to drop at the same second my rifle fired. Sweeney and Cal cut loose. Mr. Grenke dove into the snow, sliding under a fire truck.

"Go! Get 'em all!" I fired again. Again. Two soldiers fell.

"Suck it, Feds!" Cal shouted. He fired a series of quick bursts, raining showers of bullets all over the field below.

Sweeney let off a shot. "Damn. Missed."

Two rounds hit the outside of the attic. I spotted two Feds set up by the front fender of one of the fire trucks. They had to be able to see us perfectly in the firelight. But I had a clear line of sight on them too, and the next time one popped up, I put a round through his face.

"We gotta think about getting out of here!" Becca yelled.

Around the side of the house across the street a Fed's lower body ripped away from his chest, arms, and head in a shower of blood. Kemp's .50-cal. A soldier tried running toward one of the Humvees, probably going for the machine gun there. I put a round through his thigh, shook my head, and put another into his skull.

We rained down hundreds more bullets for another minute until the last of them was dead. "Mr. Grenke, you okay?" I called. Skylar's dad crawled out from under a fire truck and gave a thumbs-up. I slammed the window shut. "Time to bail! Let's go!"

We rushed down the stairs and out to the yard behind the house. Then hot pops of gunshots went off and we all hit the ground. Some Feds were firing from behind a backyard fence across the alley. I fired four rounds. Luchen, Sweeney, and Becca shot too. "Alpha, this is bravo," I said into the little Motorola radio. "RTB! We'll catch up!" With them heading back to base, I focused on returning fire. When I'd emptied my rifle's magazine, I rolled onto my side to pull another one from my pocket. Where was our machine gun? "Cal, let 'em have it!" But Cal was gone. I slammed a full mag into my rifle, rolled back onto my stomach, and fired. We had no cover. Our only chance was to continue the suppressive fire to keep those soldiers from jumping up and killing us.

"Your boy left us!" Luchen yelled with his cheek fixed to the stock of his M4. He squeezed off one round after another.

"Oh shit, oh shit, oh shit," I said. We'd run out of bullets soon, and more Fed soldiers had to be on their way. "Cal, where the hell are you!?"

Sweeney had switched to Cal's SAW, stabilizing it on its bipod and shooting in three- or four-round bursts. "I'm almost out," he shouted.

I pointed to a white toolshed in another yard. "I'll cover you guys! Get behind that shed!"

"I can shoot on the move," Sweeney answered. "You come too!"

"Okay, get ready." I fired more and more, hoping some of my rounds would cut through the fence and take some of those assholes down. Sweeney and Becca rose to their knees, getting ready to move.

Then across the alley, Cal hurdled the fence right into the nest of Feds. "Wanna hurt my friends!?" He swung his stolen sword down, twisting his whole body, and blood sprayed the white snow on a tree nearby. He pivoted and whipped the bloody blade around again. "I'll kill you all!" More blood splattered up over the fence, and a shrill scream echoed through the neighborhood. "You leave 'em alone! Die, asshole!" Cal slashed down at the soldiers behind the fence again and again.

"Cal!" Becca yelled.

He kept hacking. "Not so tough now, are you!? Huh? Come on!"

Becca ran toward the crimson-stained fence. "Cal! Calvin Riccon! Stop!" I followed her. When Becca looked over the fence, her eyes went wide and she gagged, holding up a hand to stop me. I stayed back. "Cal, you got 'em! Let's get out of here."

When Cal turned to us, his face was unrecognizable, his bulky shoulders heaving. Blood ran down his cheeks and dripped from his nose and chin.

"Cal?" I asked. Could he even hear me?

Cal found a small clean spot on his coat and wiped his sword mostly clean. "Ain't none of them gonna hurt my friends." His boot thudded like an ax on wood as he kicked something on the ground. "I'll kill them *all* first!"

"Cal!" I shouted.

He shook his head and seemed to recognize me for the first time. Then he sheathed his sword in the scabbard hanging from his belt and reached down to pick up a blood-soaked M4 and a couple full mags of ammo. The five of us sprinted down the alley, away from the tower of fire and smoke behind us.

"Follow me," I said. Sally had offered us a hiding place at the Bucking Bronc. We had to move fast if we were going to make it.

We rounded the corner into another alley, and Luchen slipped on a patch of ice, landing on his ass. "I'm good," he groaned. Becca helped him up.

"Wright!" someone hissed from a garage nearby. My rifle was at the ready in a second, but I lowered it when I saw Coach Shiratori. "Follow me. You all have to hide."

"Yes, Coach," Cal said, following him immediately.

"Cal, we can't bring Coach into this," I said. "They're going to be after us, and he doesn't deserve to —"

Coach glared at me. "Now, Wright!"

Moments later, we were rushing down the stairs into Shiratori's basement. "Daddy?" A little girl's voice came down the stairs.

He looked up. "Stay up there! In fact, go to your room and play. I'll be there in just a little bit. Go find your mom and you two play in your room." He let out a shaky breath and tossed a dingy old towel to Cal. "Mr. Riccon, you're getting blood all over. Clean yourself up."

"Wow, Mr. Shiratori." Becca slowly turned around, taking in the main basement room. From the floor to the ceiling, every wall was covered in shelves filled with paper books. "So many books."

He shrugged. "I have a big storage closet in a back room down here. You all can hide there until things calm down and you can sneak off to wherever you go."

"Thanks for helping, Coach." Cal wiped blood from his face. "You're a real patriot. Like George Washington, but for Idaho."

Shiratori stopped as he opened the door to the back room. "I'm doing this to keep my former students alive, not for Idaho."

"Come on, Mr. Shiratori," Sweeney said. "The Republic of Idaho needs good guys like you."

"Yeah, you almost sound like a Fed traitor," said Cal.

I moved to put my hand on Cal's arm to tell him to go easy on Coach, but I stopped when I saw all the blood on his sleeves.

"Yeah, I like America, Mr. Riccon. Are you going to burn my house down now?"

"What? No, but Coach —"

"Was the United States of America really so bad?" Shiratori asked. "Water, roads, electricity, and plenty of food all the time. Was there a war in your backyard in the United States? Look at you, Mr. Riccon, all covered in blood. What happened to the powerhouse football player I knew? The biggest worry on all of your minds should be your schoolwork and basketball games and the Valentine's Day dance. Now what do you have? You're lucky to be alive, and who knows how much longer you'll live, if you keep this up."

"The Fed attacked us," I said quietly. "We have a right to defend our —"

"Were you defending yourselves when you killed all those soldiers up on Silver Mountain? Which, by the way, destroyed Freedom Lake's food ration, so now I'm down to one meal a day just so my daughter can get enough to eat. And I'm not the only one in town going hungry. Were you firing in self-defense today?"

"I'm sorry you ain't got quite as much food, Coach, but it's been tough for us too. Because of the *Fed*. Anyway, it's too late for all this," said Cal. "We're in the Idaho Army now. This is the revolution."

"Okay, say hell freezes over and Idaho somehow wins. What happens then?" He sounded like he was lecturing. I missed the tapping of his Stick of Power on the classroom tiles. "A lot of people here in the Northwest have been prepping for a war with the federal government for years. Certain groups have been inviting like-minded people to this region, stockpiling weapons and getting ready for a war just like this, in their own little self-sufficient villages and compounds. Some of them are neo-Nazi, white supremacist groups. Some are basically terrorists or wannabe terrorists."

"It ain't like that, Coach," said Cal. "Don't go playing the race card. There are a lot of people who just want their freedom. Not everybody fighting for Idaho is some weird racist or whatever."

"Of course not. But you can bet that plenty of the people on your side have belonged to these sick and dangerous groups for years, and now some of their dreams are starting to come true. And even putting that issue aside, how do you know this government in Boise will be any better than the one in Washington, DC? Over a hundred years ago, some revolutionaries in Russia had this idea that everybody should be equal. They threw out the tsar and the old government, and what they got instead was the Soviet Union, an evil empire that murdered millions. Even this government you're fighting now was once fought for by revolutionaries."

Now Mr. Shiratori was way off. I folded my arms. "The Founding Fathers never intended for the federal government to be so powerful and run every bit of our lives."

"That's what the Soviet leader Stalin always said about anyone he put to death — that they were traitors to the intent of the
revolution."

"President Montaine isn't Stalin," Sweeney said.

"You don't know who he is." Shiratori opened the dark closet in
the back room and pushed some boxes aside. "You don't even know
who's really in charge anymore. Could be General McNabb. Could
be anybody. Tyrants always use fear and uncertainty to rise to power
in times of chaos. Over and over in history, revolutionaries turn
around only to realize, too late, that they've made themselves slaves
to a worse government than the one they'd fought to overthrow." The
five of us found places to sit behind the pile of boxes in the closet.
"Rest. I'll come and get you when it's a little safer. And please, for
your own sakes, take some time to think about finding a way to leave
this war behind, while you still can."

He closed the door, leaving us there in the cold dark.

⌁—• *FIRA News continues. I'm Army Staff Sergeant Hinkelthorn. Tragedy struck last night in Freedom Lake, Idaho, when terrorist insurgents resorted to arson, setting fire to a civilian house and endangering an entire neighborhood in an apparent attempt to lure United States soldiers to the scene. Eighteen soldiers were murdered while they fought to extinguish the blaze. The house was completely destroyed and a small adjacent structure was damaged by the fire. Local reconstruction authorities are still investigating possible insurgent accomplices among Freedom Lake residents.*

FIRA officials in Smelterville report almost total compliance with reconstruction regulations, with over 95 percent of citizens there signing up for the federal identification cards. Ration distribution in the small mining town has brought a standard of living unheard of since James Montaine's criminal regime forced the late President Rodriguez to halt the flow of food and other supplies into the state. One Smelterville resident was nearly in tears as she watched the trucks roll into town to distribute food. "It's like Christmas," she said. "Thank you so much. Now I can finally make sure my kids are getting fed. •—⌁

⌁—• *From ABC News, I'm Tara Albron. Only moments after the legislatures of New Hampshire, Vermont, and Maine voted to officially declare themselves neutral in the national conflict, the governors of those three states activated their entire National Guard forces. Their first orders to their troops? Stand down. Here's New Hampshire Governor Madeline Hanson: "The soldiers and airmen of the New Hampshire, Vermont, and Maine National Guards enlisted to protect their states and their country. Many of them have contacted me and other elected representatives, expressing fears about the federal government forcing them to fight against other Americans. Our actions today will prevent that grievous step and protect our* enlisted men and women. We support the United States and the federal government, and while we encourage reform to the Federal ID Card Act, we do not support nullification. What we demand is peace, and we will not allow New England soldiers or New England resources to be used in a destructive and counterproductive war against United States citizens, even those who claim to live in the so-called Republic of Idaho. I know I speak for the other governors, legislators, and people of the New England Peace Alliance when I call for other states to follow our lead in doing whatever they can to stop this needless bloodshed." No comment from the White House on these developments.

Five people were killed and dozens injured after a peace rally on the Florida State University campus went terribly wrong. What began as a demonstration calling for a cease-fire in Idaho quickly escalated into mob disorder before ending in tragedy. Some students attempted to resist arrest, and shortly after that, shots were fired. It is unclear who fired first or why, but Florida officials are asking for calm pending a full investigation.

Pressure is growing in Congress for a change to the status of 952 Idaho Army National Guard soldiers who have been pulled from their service in Iran and reassigned to correctional facilities in Fort Leavenworth, Kansas. Colonel Brent Hayes, special officer in charge of these Idaho Guard detainees: "I've spoken to the president. She and I are in agreement, and I've made it very clear to the Army corrections specialists in charge of running the facility that the Idaho Guardsmen stationed here are guilty of no crime. They are not prisoners, but simply soldiers who are staying at this facility on a temporary basis. They are being well paid, and every possible effort has been made to ensure that these honorable soldiers are as comfortable as possible. They are, however, trained soldiers, and they cannot be allowed to return to their homes in

Idaho, where they might strengthen the rebel cause." A number of veterans groups as well as Amnesty International continue to press Congress to order their release. You're listening to ABC News. •—⋏

⋏—• South Korean Prime Minister Jung Park reassured the United States and the United Nations today that South Korean military forces are capable of withstanding any possible future aggression from North Korea, and after over fifty years, the majority of American military forces are withdrawing from the Korean peninsula. In Seoul, at a ceremony to mark the historic transition, Prime Minister Park also offered military and humanitarian aid to assist the United States with its quote, "domestic challenges." White House Spokesperson Kelsey Santos says the president appreciates South Korea's generous offer and will take it under advisement. Meanwhile, while there are no signs of increased military activity in North Korea, the North Korean supreme leader has ordered his citizens to celebrate what he is calling "a historic victory." •—⋏

⋏—• The world's most powerful superstation, broadcasting with five hundred thousand watts of freedom. AM 1040, RIR."

"Greetings! Greetings, fellow patriots! You're listening to the one, the only Buzz Ellison! In peacetime or wartime, freedom-loving people everywhere tune in to the Buzz man, a shining beacon of truth! If comms are functioning in your area, the number to call if you want to be on the program today is 1-800-555-INDY. That's 1-800-555-4639.

"You know, I've been getting some criticism lately, and . . . Believe me, I'm used to dealing with criticism, particularly from liberals who have a political and financial interest in stopping me from getting the truth out to the world. But these days, I'm facing accusations that I've lost my credibility, that I'm just a propaganda mouthpiece for President Montaine. I've also heard from listeners who are outraged by these accusations, who are rushing to my defense. And I appreciate the support, but folks, this is nothing new! This is the same old, tattered, yellowed page from the liberal playbook. These are the same people who said I wouldn't have much of a show when Obama finally, finally left office. People say I don't have much of a show here in the Republic of Idaho where we're at last free of partisan bickering. But those people don't understand that the Buzz Ellison Show has never been about one man, never about one politician, and never about one political party. It's not even about me! This show is about the solid, unfailing principles of conservatism. That's what brings us together, folks, our love of freedom. Our desire to live without the United States federal government watching us all the time, telling us every single thing we can and cannot do, say, or think.

"So now liberals want to discredit me, say I'm reading President Montaine's script? I will tell you that in general I do support Montaine. I think history will justifiably remember him as a hero, a modern George Washington. But I will also tell you, I'm a little pissed at him right now. In fact, I'm mad as hell, because this effort to negotiate with Lazy Laura Griffith over the Federal Spy Card Act is an utter crock of shit! And it stinks of deceit. Laura is never going to make good on her side of the bargain. She's never going to pardon Idaho soldiers, citizens, or people like me, who have the audacity to go on the air and call that woman the lying bitch that she is! Woo! I love true freedom of speech without the FCC threatening me with fines! And Montaine should fight to keep that freedom, not make a deal with that liar. •—⌒

⌒—• THANK YOU FOR VISITING THE OFFICIAL WEBSITE OF THE ANTI-DRAFT COALITION. The Anti-Draft Coalition is a growing organization determined to resist all efforts to reinstate the draft that would force civilians into military service in the United States.

We believe that the draft has no place in a civilized modern society, and that forcing someone into military service violates the Thirteenth Amendment, which prohibits slavery.

While we may ally with anti-war groups in pursuit of our goal to resist reinstating the draft, we do not oppose necessary wars.

We advocate maintaining a strong, all-volunteer force and demand Congress return our armed forces to the level of troops we enjoyed in the first decade of this century.

We believe that our once-adequate all-volunteer military has been reduced to a level that renders it ineffective for dealing with modern challenges, and that by reversing these cuts, the so-called need for a draft could be avoided entirely. •—✓

FIFTEEN

Later that first day in Shiratori's basement, I bent the one-person-at-a-time rule and followed Cal to the bathroom.

"What? You gonna hold my hand?" Cal said when I slipped in and closed the door behind us. "Seriously, man, I'd rather be alone." He leaned over the sink and looked at himself in the mirror. Dried blood was caked on his face, in his hair, and on his clothes. He laughed. "Damned Feds made a mess all over me."

"Yeah. Hey, buddy. I wanted to talk to you about that."

He frowned and looked at me in the mirror as he turned on the water and let it warm up. "I know. You're pissed that I wasn't covering on machine gun. But I thought I could save the ammo when my sword would do the job just as well."

How could I say what I needed to talk to Cal about when I couldn't even straighten out my own thoughts about the whole thing? I hated the Fed. But Cal had been out of control. "I'm worried about you," I said. Whatever had happened in his head while he stabbed and slashed those Feds hadn't been good for him. I understood a little of how he must have been feeling. Could I snap and go all animal the way he had?

Cal scrubbed his face. "I'm fine. By the time they saw me, they didn't have a chance."

"I know. You got 'em. But Cal, maybe you shouldn't use the sword anymore."

"What are you talking about? That sword is badass. Sharp as hell."

I sat down on the toilet lid. "I mean, maybe it's not right. Maybe it's too cruel."

Cal leaned over and dipped his whole head under the faucet. The water in the sink went orange-brown. When he stood up, the water ran down his face and dripped on his sweatshirt. "You don't think I should have killed them?"

"No, you did what you had to do," I said. Cal wouldn't really listen if he thought I was bashing him. Maybe I could get through to him if I made this about tactics. "We were all shooting them to stop them. But shooting them, killing them as quick as we can . . . It's, like, more humane. Slashing them with the sword makes them suffer more." Cal reached for a towel on the rack, but I snatched it away from him. "You didn't get all the blood off."

"Who gives a shit how they die? Dead is dead." Cal went back to scrubbing. He used a squirt from the hand soap dispenser.

"But there are rules, and I'm worried about —"

"And don't you want these bastards to hurt after all they done to you?" He turned to me, the top of his head still under the stream from the faucet and soapy water running over his face. He blinked against it in his eyes. "We gotta stick it to 'em. Show them we ain't messing around."

"I'm worried about you, Cal. You know, I worry that if we get too deep into this, the violence, the killing, that maybe we won't come back out."

Cal grabbed the towel and dried off, even though bits of dried blood still clung in the folds of his ears and a little around his eyes. "Really, Wright. I'm okay."

"Just promise me you'll take it easy. Necessary targets only, and then take them out quickly and professionally. Like soldiers. Not animals."

Cal shook his head and laughed a little. "Yeah. Sure."

"I'm serious."

"Okay, buddy. I know. I'll do my best."

I waited there silently, trying to figure out what to say to get through to him. I knew he didn't get my point, but he was agreeing with me, so what could I do? Call him a liar?

Cal lifted a leg a little and ripped a big fart. "Now will you get the hell out of here so I can take a dump?"

That was more like the Cal I had grown up with. I laughed a little as I walked out, but my smile was a cheap cover for my worry about my friend.

We spent the next four days in Shiratori's closet. It was a little like being back in the dungeon. He brought us food and a flashlight, and we could sneak out to the basement bathroom. But other than that, there was nothing to do and not much room. I tried my best not to get close to Becca.

Then one day the door swung open, blinding us in the light. I reached for my rifle in case this was the Fed.

"Come on," Mr. Shiratori said. "Time for you all to go. Hurry up."

There was an edge of panic in his voice. "What's up, Coach?" I asked.

"Nothing. Just, well, an Army truck full of supplies for civilians broke down on Main Street, and there's trouble brewing with people trying to get food."

"Sounds dangerous," Becca said. "How many people are there?"

"A lot. A whole bunch of kids who always think they're invincible, but dozens of adults too," said Shiratori. "While the soldiers are distracted with this, you all can make your move."

I stood up. "We'll go, but Coach, those people gotta get out of there. The Fed won't put up with that kind of disturbance for long."

"I know!" Shiratori yelled. "I'll get people to go home. Just move it."

One cold thought whispered through my mind. "Coach, is JoBell at this thing?" Shiratori turned away from me. "Shit. She *is* there!"

He spun back to face me. "I think she's trying to talk people into leaving, but . . . don't worry about it. I'll handle it. This is your chance. Everything will be fine."

"I have to make sure she's safe," I said.

"Yeah. We take care of our own," said Cal.

"Wright, more and more soldiers are moving down there. It's probably over by now. If not, then it is absolutely not safe for you to be there."

"He's right, Danny," said Becca. "I'm worried about JoBell too, but we can't go there. Mr. Shiratori can help her."

"Wright?" Sweeney asked.

Damn it. I had to get my head on straight. This was a war, and people's lives were on the line. "Thanks for helping us, Coach." I picked up my rifle and pulled back the charging handle to ready it for action. "Let's go."

"Wright! I mean it. Don't go downtown." Shiratori called out as we left his house, but we were already headed that way.

"Danny, this is stupid," Becca said.

"We'll stay far back, out of the way, and only get involved if shit falls apart," I said.

"Wright, I'm kind of with Becca on this one," said Luchen. "Odds of getting spotted and in trouble are real bad on this."

I stopped. "Fine! If you all want to bug out, then go!"

"Hell no," said Cal.

"I'm with you," said Sweeney.

"We're going to need to get out of here. There's no way Kemp and the others left our snowmobiles out in the woods for this long.

Luchen, Becca, get back to the rally point where we were supposed to pick up our sleds." I ignored the hurt look in Becca's eyes as I handed my radio to Luchen. "Don't key the mike for long. Call Kemp and Crocker and tell them to bring some snowmobiles to get us out of here. We'll be there as soon as we're sure the situation is cool."

"Danny," Becca started.

I patted her arm. "Seriously, Becca. We'll need you two to provide cover in case we're followed on the way back. See you at the rally point."

About ten minutes later, me, Sweeney, and Cal had used a dumpster and wooden pallet to climb up on the flat roof of the post office. The roof had a two-foot wall around its edge, which provided ideal cover. Shouts and chants came from down the street. We crawled up to the front of the building and peeked over.

"Must be half the school out there," Sweeney said.

A mob of just about everyone we'd grown up with had surrounded a bunch of soldiers on an Army five-ton truck loaded with food supplies. Dylan Burns's dad pushed past a soldier to slip around the side. He pulled away with a cardboard case of MREs, and the roar from the crowd got louder. One soldier fell down, and seven or eight people reached the back tailgate. Newly arrived Feds were taking position at the edge of the street.

"This is just like Boise," I whispered. The soldiers had formed a circle of death around the riot all over again. Except now I saw JoBell, in the middle of it all, waving her arms and trying to get people to calm down.

"No," I whispered. "No, no, no."

"What do we do?" Cal asked.

I didn't have a clue. If the Fed messed this up as bad as we did in Boise . . . I wanted to run into the circle, grab JoBell, and get her the hell out of there. But the Fed would light me up, and probably everybody else with me, as soon as they saw me. Maybe we shouldn't have come down here. My hand throbbed like someone had spiked a nail through it. It was going to go to shit again, be my fault all over again.

We waited a long time while the crowd yelled and soldiers tried to keep people away from their truck. How long were the Fed going to let this go on?

"Hey, check it," Cal finally said, pointing to the roof of the hardware store down the street from us. Two uniformed Fed snipers were setting up positions, watching through high-powered scopes and scanning the whole area. Same thing on the roof of the Fed HQ in the old cop shop and the abandoned thrift store across the street. We watched for another fifteen or twenty minutes as more and more Feds took up positions.

I remembered rule number three. "Sweeney, cover our six. Make sure some sniper doesn't come up behind us."

An armored Humvee drove up from the Fed HQ and stopped about a dozen feet from the protest. Major Alsovar got out and surveyed the scene with his hands on his hips. I tightened my grip on the rifle. "I could shoot that bastard right now," I breathed.

Then Coach Shiratori climbed out from the other side of the Humvee, holding a powered megaphone. "What the hell?" I said.

"Geez, Coach. Work with the Fed much?" Cal said quietly.

Alsovar nodded to Shiratori, and Coach took a couple steps forward, holding the megaphone to his mouth. *"All right, listen up! I know you're hungry. I know times are tough. I've talked to Major Alsovar about this, and he says that if insurgent activity dies down, meaning if it is safe enough, we'll get more food convoys so we won't be in this position. But for any of that to happen, we have to cooperate and let these soldiers do their jobs. We need order so they can get this food to the distribution point without anyone getting hurt. We have to work together. Right now, in the interest of safety and secu-rity, these kinds of assemblies are not allowed."*

Some people in the crowd started to boo.

"He's right! We should go home!" JoBell shouted.

"It's not up to him what we do!" someone yelled from the crowd.

"Come on, guys!" JoBell tried again. "We need to break up this crowd."

How could she be this dumb? Alsovar wasn't playing around. He wouldn't put up with this mob. Worse than that, why was she out there saying exactly what he would have wanted her to say?

"No, it's not up to Major Alsovar!" Coach said. *"It's up to President Griffith —"* Now the crowd drowned him out with their shouts and booing. *"Up to President Griffith and the United States Congress. Please, for your own safety, you have to —"*

His words were lost in the roar from the crowd. I ducked down behind the wall. "Guys, what the hell are we gonna do?"

"I don't like this, man," Cal said.

A gunshot blasted through the air. I peeked over the edge of the roof and saw Alsovar holding a nine mil above his head. The protes-tors had all dropped to the snow-packed street. The major reached a hand out to Shiratori without taking his eyes off the crowd. Shiratori handed over the megaphone, and the major spoke through it to the group.

"This assembly is in violation of the Unity Act. I do not care what you think of this law. I myself have no opinions about it. But I will do my duty to obey it and to stop the insurgency in and around Freedom Lake. I am authorized to use all methods, up to and includ-ing the use of deadly force, to stop or prevent any activities that might bring aid and comfort to the rebel insurgency, or that might encourage insurrection in the future. My duty does not require that I provide you with any warning, but because so many of you are

young, and because above all I value peace and unity, I have allowed your voices to be heard. I have allowed a trusted teacher and coach to politely encourage you to obey the law and return to your homes.

"*But I will not play games. I have fourteen more rounds in this gun, and I will not miss at this range.*" Some of the Fed soldiers looked at one another, tensing up on their weapons. Maybe they weren't as comfortable with threatening civilian kids as this sicko Alsovar. "*You have sixty seconds to stand up, put your hands on top of your heads, and begin walking home. If you do not, I will shoot fourteen of you, one at a time. Then I will reload and shoot another fifteen. Which of you will die first?*"

"Get out of there," I whispered to JoBell, to everyone. But I was ready with my rifle. If Alsovar fired, I'd take him out.

The crowd looked confused, mumbling to each other. A couple girls were crying.

Alsovar pointed his gun at the crowd. "*Forty-five seconds!*"

They all stood up now and put their hands on top of their heads. Even JoBell did as the man said. I let out a little breath of relief as the crowd silently began to break up. Most of them walked down Main Street away from Major Alsovar. The soldiers in the circle opened up on that side to allow the group to walk through.

"Okay," Cal said. "This is all cool. I think we can bail now."

The two of us ducked down again and started crawling back across the roof toward Sweeney.

Three gunshots went off. Screams came from down below. More shots.

"What the hell!?" I crouched-ran to the edge of the roof and caught a glimpse of the major diving into his Humvee. The bodies bleeding on the ground were Feds. Coach Shiratori was kneeling, his arms covering his head. Someone down the street was shooting at the Fed. Other resistance fighters? Everyone from school ran in all directions. Some Feds fled while others returned fire. I caught a look at some of the resistance shooters. A few wore black armbands. One or two raised their left fists up over their heads the way I had the day Mom had been killed.

Tucker Blake was running like hell when he took a round to the back. It bent him backward almost in half and he fell. I saw a sniper aiming in the direction of the fleeing crowd.

"The Feds are shooting our guys!" I aimed my rifle at the rooftop snipers and dropped one with a bullet through the neck. Sweeney and Cal were at my side, opening fire on the Fed. The other hardware store rooftop sniper tried to turn and draw a bead on me, but I hit him once in his chest plate and again in his unprotected lower gut.

"Wright! They hit Jo!" Cal yelled.

I turned and saw blood gush between JoBell's fingers as her hand pressed to her side. She fell to the snowy street.

I screamed. Then I swung my legs over the side of the roof and dropped down into the snow. While Cal and Sweeney opened fire on Fed soldiers all over the whole area, I ran out and slid to my knees next to JoBell.

"Jo! Jo!" I rolled her onto her back. "Hey, talk to me! Come on!"

She opened her eyes and smiled. "Hey, babe."

"Thank God! Come on." I slipped an arm under her shoulders and helped her to sit up. "Damn." Any second we would be shot. A soldier was sighting us with his rifle, but someone shot him in the back. I tried to lift JoBell, but she winced in pain. I yanked off her scarf and set to work tying it around her body to stop the bleeding. *Oh, God, don't let the wound be deep. Please, God, take me instead. Please don't let JoBell die.* "Cal! Cal! Sweeney, I need some help!"

Someone was running up to me. I almost shot him, but at the last second I saw it was Cal. Sweeney was right behind him. Cal shoved me aside, almost knocking me down. "This is gonna hurt, Jo!" He grabbed her by one arm, lifted her to a sitting position, then hoisted her up over his shoulder as easily as he might carry a tackling dummy in football practice. He looked like a pissed-off bull in the arena. He held his AR15 in one hand with the stock under his arm and fired six rounds downrange at the Fed. "Let's go!"

Sweeney and me ran after Cal, but even though he had JoBell over his shoulder, a rifle in his hand, and his sword dangling at his side, we could hardly keep up with him. More shots went off behind us. Any second now, I'd take the bullet that would end me. Would I even feel it? I hadn't had the chance to say goodbye to JoBell. To anyone.

Cal turned the corner and cut through some yards to the next block. The sound of engines rumbled after us. They were coming in Humvees. They'd open up with machine guns and that would be it.

Then three snowmobiles whipped around the corner. Kemp drove the lead. "Get on! Let's move!"

Luchen pulled up next to him. "This snowmobile's the biggest! Put her on here!" Cal put JoBell down behind Luchen and climbed on with them. Kemp moved out of the way so Sweeney could drive Silver Bullet, and I got on behind Sparrow.

"Follow me!" Sweeney yelled. "The way we're going, it's full throttle or you're dead!" He sped off just as a Fed Humvee fishtailed around the corner. Luchen followed Sweeney, slapping the side of his snowmobile like it was a horse he was trying to speed up.

Sparrow took off, and I twisted in my seat to fire at the Humvee's turret gunner. It was an awkward-as-hell way to shoot. Sweeney tore through the streets and backyards toward the creek. His snowmobile hit a steep snowy embankment and launched into the air.

"Oh shit!" Luchen yelled. "We're too heavy! Ain't gonna make it!"

"Just gun it, Luchen!" Cal yelled.

"Hold her down!" In the next instant they hit the bump and were in the air. Cal held JoBell tight as they slammed down on the other side of the creek.

The *crack-crack-crack-crack-crack* of a .50-cal machine gun fired behind us. Limbs fell from the trees around the stream. We wouldn't last with those guys shooting us.

"Speed up, Sparrow!" I turned and fired back again. We hit something, and I reached for the rear handle. I missed. Then my world was cold snow and ice as I face-planted and slid to a stop.

"Wright!" Sparrow screamed as her snowmobile hit the bump and jumped the stream.

"Oh shit!" I stumbled up, ran for cover behind a tree, and fired blindly toward the turret gunner. When they pulled up, all those soldiers would dismount and it would be me against a whole firing line.

"Danny!" Becca's voice came from behind me. She rode Lightning at full gallop toward the creek. Leaning low in the saddle and holding the saddle horn with her left hand, she held her M4 with her right, the stock wedged in her armpit. Lightning whinnied as she leapt across the creek and Becca fired wildly. I'm not gonna lie. It was kind of awesome.

That horse would be dead in seconds if I didn't make a move. With the turret gunner distracted, I ran out from behind my tree, heading straight for him, firing at least ten rounds on the way. The turret soldier slumped over his machine gun. Becca never stopped shooting, keeping the Feds pinned inside their vehicle. She slowed Lightning long enough for me to use her stirrup to climb up behind her. It was a tight fit with my ass up on the back of the saddle, but it would have to do.

"Something we stole from that convoy." Becca whipped out a grenade. She kicked Lightning and we rode straight at the Humvee. Then she pulled the pin and chucked the grenade down the turret as we rode by. Two seconds later, an explosion painted the inside of the Humvee windows red.

"Geez, Becca —"

"Hold on!" Becca yelled. She patted Lightning's neck. "Come on. One more time, girl. We're almost there. Ha!" She kicked the horse and Lightning sped up to a full gallop.

"You can't ride her this hard on the snow. If she slips by the creek —"

"She won't slip. The trees have kept most of the snow off the ground there." She spoke to Lightning again. "Come on, girl." To me, she added, "Lightning won't let you down. Neither will I."

I held Becca and my rifle tight as the horse made the jump, slipping just a little as she landed. Becca didn't let Lightning slow down much as she caught up with the snowmobiles. We sped on as the sun dipped behind Silver Mountain, twisting around again and again to throw off the Fed as we headed back to base.

SIXTEEN

"Ain't *nobody* gonna hurt my friends!" Cal paced back and forth in the upstairs bedroom where we'd put JoBell. He'd ditched his coat and kept running his hands back through his hair, flexing his giant biceps until they looked like they'd rip his T-shirt. "They come after you guys again, I'll kill 'em." He swung his fist hard in a low punch that smashed through the bedroom wall.

"Damn, that's three-quarter-inch drywall," Sweeney whispered to me.

Becca put her hands on Cal's shoulders. "Cal, honey, this isn't helping. You're okay. She's okay."

Cal pulled his hand out of the wall, flexing his fingers as white flakes fell around them. "I mean it. I'll shoot 'em all up again." He finally sat down on the bed next to JoBell. He wiped his eyes as he looked down at her. "Dad always on the road. My brother Jimmy in and out of juvie. You guys are all I got. I ain't losing you. You be okay, Jo. You be okay." He looked up. "No shit. That goes for all y'all."

"Cal." JoBell reached up and touched the big guy's face. "I'm all right. Just . . . Not now, okay. I need to get . . . to a hospital."

"You were at an illegal protest or riot or whatever, Jo," said Sweeney.

"I was trying to get people to leave," she said.

"But think about it," Sweeney said. "You were there. The Feds were attacked. And your boyfriend, America's most wanted, was there as well. If you go to a hospital, they'll think that's all a little too convenient. They'll arrest you, and this time they won't let you go."

"You don't . . . know that," JoBell groaned.

"We can't take the risk," said Becca. "Anyway, there's not really a good way to get you to a hospital right now."

Kemp and Sparrow came into the room, Sparrow carrying a proper white sterile bandage and the little that was left of that bottle of Drambuie.

"Riccon, Sweeney, Wells," said Kemp. "I need you three to grab a rifle and stand guard. We need to be extra careful in case the Fed were able to track us."

"Come on, Cal," Becca said. She and Sweeney both put their arms around the big guy and led him out of the room.

"Crocker's been covering the radio," said Kemp. "Shortwave bursts. Someone talking about the Brotherhood attacking the Fed at that protest."

"Idiots," I said. "Who the hell are these Brotherhood guys?"

"I don't know," Kemp said. "But they're getting a lot more active."

"They could have at least waited until all the protestors were clear."

Sparrow had a flashlight pointed at JoBell's wound. "Can we hold off on that political shit until we get this taken care of?" She leaned down to JoBell's side and looked carefully. "It didn't cut her deep. Might have buzzed a rib a little." To me she added, "What do you want to do? We could stitch it up, but we also stitched up Danning and . . ." I wished she hadn't mentioned him. She shook the bottle around. "Maybe it's better to sterilize the wound, bandage it up, and hope for the best."

Tears welled up in JoBell's eyes. "Come on, guys. I need a real doctor."

"The only real doctors are with the Fed." Sparrow raised her eyebrows. "Is that where you want to go?"

JoBell stared Sparrow down. "I am *not* working with them."

"Didn't say you were," Sparrow said. "Interesting that you did. Now are we going to do this or not?"

I looked to JoBell, who bit her lip and nodded at me. "Okay," I said.

"You two are gonna need to hold her down," Sparrow said. Kemp held her legs while I pinned down her upper arms.

"You'll be okay, Jo," I said. "It won't be so bad."

Sparrow took the cap off the bottle of liquor. Was that a little smile creeping onto her face? "Actually, JoBell, this is going to hurt a lot." She lowered the bottle near the bloody slash in JoBell's flesh and dumped on the booze.

JoBell screamed and arched her back, struggling against me and Kemp. She shook her head and then smashed it back hard into her pillow as she cried. Before Sparrow was done, JoBell had passed out.

"What? What?" Cal shouted, pounding up the stairs. I stopped him at the bedroom door. Sparrow was applying a clean bandage to JoBell's wound.

"It's okay, buddy. She's alive. She's resting. She's going to be fine." I looked at my girlfriend and prayed that I was right. I met Sparrow's eyes as she stood up from the side of the bed. "Thank you, Specialist, for helping with this, and for coming to get me today."

She shrugged. "I didn't do anything, since you couldn't hold on to the sled. You really ought to be thanking the cowgirl. She's the one who saved you." She knocked back a swig of Drambuie and walked past me, grabbing Cal by the shirt and pulling him out of the room.

The door closed behind them, and I carefully crawled into bed next to JoBell. She woke up a few hours later. "Danny?" she said sleepily.

"I'm so glad you're okay," I whispered to her. "So glad we're together again." I kissed the top of her head, and we lay like that in silence. Nothing more needed to be said.

The next couple days were relatively peaceful. JoBell looked a lot better, and besides guard duty and a little working out, we took some time to rest. Luchen contacted TJ, who promised to let Mr. Linder know his daughter was safe. That helped JoBell relax. We made a rule that she'd never be alone, that we'd pull shifts so someone would always be with her. Becca took the most shifts.

"Bad news," Sweeney said the following Tuesday night. "The tracks on the Silver Bullet are busted. No place to get replacement parts. Three snowmobiles left, and we have barely enough gas to run two of them."

Him and me were taking turns on the hand pump to fill the snowmobiles for future missions. I was the one cranking the lever this time. "You've lost a snowmobile. Your dad's Corvette, Jet Skis, and four-wheeler were probably destroyed when we exploded those two Fed Humvees. Who knows where your Mustang is. Doesn't it bother you that you've lost so much stuff?"

Sweeney lay down on the seat of Silver Bullet. "If you'd asked me that question last year, I would have said hell to the yeah. But life is different now. Now all that stuff that seemed so important just seems like . . . stuff." He laughed. "Don't know if my old man will see it that way, though. He's lost a fortune, and he was even interrogated by the FBI in Florida once or twice, but compared to what we've been up against, those are just kind of minor inconveniences. Basically he left his son in the middle of a war zone while he takes an extended vacation in Florida."

I stopped cranking the pump for a second. "You know that wasn't his choice, right? He'd be back here in a second if he could."

"Intellectually, I understand that. But it doesn't feel right, you know?"

"No, I don't know," I said. "I'm an orphan, remember?"

"Shit. Sorry, dude." Nobody spoke for a while, and the only sound was the squeak of the pump as I cranked it. Sweeney took a big breath. "Speaking of feelings. You want to tell me what's up with you and Becca?"

I kept cranking the pump like everything was normal. "What do you mean?"

"Dude, seriously? You think I can't tell something is going on between you two? First, I'm the Great Asian Lovemaster. Second, I've been friends with the two of you for as long as I can remember. I've had the sense that she was into you for a while, like before this whole war even started, and you two got closer for a bit. Then suddenly you hardly talk to each other and there's a high level of weirdness. So do you want to tell me what's up, or are you going to leave it to my substantial imagination?"

I sighed, stopped cranking the fuel pump, and told him about the kiss under fire and making out in the igloo. "So now what? I'm in one of those dumb love triangles like from those *Nightfall* books?"

"Hmm," said Sweeney. "So is JoBell the vampire, and Becca the werewolf? I'm hoping Becca is the werewolf because in the movies the werewolf's shirt always comes off in the first three minutes, and Becca's got better —"

"I'm serious," I said. "This sucks."

He sat up. "I know you're serious. I think that's part of your problem. You're way too serious. Dude, nobody dates just one person his whole life."

"I'm not like you," I said. "I can't get with a million different girls."

"You could if you wanted to. You were a popular guy. But my point is, you're seventeen and you've only ever dated one girl. You already asked her to marry you. If you do get married, aren't you ever going to wonder what it would be like to at least hold another girl's hand? To kiss a different girl?" I started to say something, but Sweeney shook his head. "Becca's great. She's beautiful and really nice. And now you've been through life-and-death situations together. That's only going to bring you closer."

I leaned toward Sweeney and spoke quietly. "I cheated on my girlfriend, I hurt Becca, and I feel terrible about it. Can't you understand that?"

"Yeah," said Sweeney. "I get it. You made a mistake, and now you can move on."

"But I still feel like . . ." I didn't know how to explain the way I felt about Becca. "It's not right to have feelings like this for two girls. That makes me such an asshole."

"It makes you human, dude. How are you supposed to control your emotions? Go ahead. Tell yourself to stop being attracted to Becca, to stop caring for her. Did it work? Hell no. You can't turn these things on and off like a switch."

"I shouldn't have kissed Becca," I said. "Okay, maybe when we thought we were going to die next to that bus, because it's a goodbye kiss or whatever, but not after that."

"Well, if you're not going to give Becca a serious chance to be your girlfriend, then yeah, you're right. You shouldn't make out anymore. She's a really great girl, dude. Don't hurt her."

I nodded and started cranking the fuel pump again. "I don't know how you do it, man. All those girls."

"Seriously? I really envy what you and JoBell have. You have someone to be with you, someone to support you through this whole mess."

I thought about it, and I'm not gonna lie, but Becca had really been the one who had helped me through this war the most. I wasn't about to bring that up now, though.

Sweeney looked down. "I wish I had something good like that. Something real." He smiled at me. "So you kissed Becca. If that's the only mistake you ever make in your relationship with JoBell, you're heading for greatness. Just, you know, be cool with Becca. This awkwardness is driving me nuts."

A couple days later, with everybody else busy or sleeping off guard duty, Becca asked me to help her with Lightning, so the two of us went to the stable in the late afternoon. For about the thousandth time, I petted that horse and thanked her for saving my life. Shoveling her manure was still a stinky job, but I didn't mind it as much. Plus it gave me something to do so I could avoid talking about what I knew me and Becca needed to talk about.

"How long are you going to be weird with me?" Becca said after a few minutes.

I stopped working. So much for not talking about it. "What?"

"How long are you going to keep ignoring me?"

I stood the shovel on end in the manure and pulled the hood of my sweatshirt a little tighter. It was one thing to talk about this with Sweeney, but a lot harder to get into with Becca. "I haven't been ignoring you."

She pushed my hood aside a little so that I could see her close to me, even though it was dark. "We used to have fun taking care of Lightning. Now, when you're not with JoBell, you spend as much time on guard duty and as far away from me as you can."

"I do not."

"Don't lie to me, Danny." She rubbed her purple butterfly hair clip.

"I . . ." What did she want me to say?

Becca turned away from me and rested her head on Lightning's, rubbing the horse's neck. I was about to go back to shoveling when I heard her sniffle and saw her wipe her eye.

"Are you crying?"

"No," she whispered evenly.

"We shouldn't have done that, you know, together. In the igloo."

"Wasn't I good enough for you?" She sounded bitter. "Am I not a good kisser?"

"What? Becca, no. It's not that. I mean, you were great. Or, it was good. It felt good." I sighed. What the hell was wrong with me? I couldn't be telling her how much I enjoyed our mistake. "Becca, I have a girlfriend. Wounded in the upstairs bedroom. JoBell? Remember?"

"And you feel bad for betraying her?" I wasn't thinking of a word like "betray," but I figured it sounded about right. "Did you ever think that maybe I feel bad about it too? She's my best friend."

I guess I hadn't thought about it that way. I'd only been thinking about how much I screwed up, how I'd betrayed my JoBell. And I loved JoBell. I'd been terrified I was going to lose her.

But in the dungeon, and all through this war, Becca had helped me remember I was human. She gave me hope that some of my soul might actually survive this. And I'm not gonna lie, kissing her had made me realize that, wrong or right, there was a warm place inside me for her too. I had to admit that I had feelings for the girl, something more than just friendship. I laughed a little.

"What's funny?"

I reached over and squeezed her forearm. "Everything. Well, not you feeling bad about JoBell and all that, and me too, but us. Here we are, in the middle of a war, taking care of a horse you just jumped commando-style over the creek to save my life, and we're talking about feelings and stuff like we're back in high school, trying to figure out who we're going to take to prom."

Becca chuckled too. "It is a little nuts, but I'm serious, Danny. We have to work this out."

"I know," I said.

"You regret what we did?"

"I . . ." How could I explain to Becca what I barely understood myself? "If we lived in a different world, I wouldn't. If I'd never been going out with JoBell. Because you're great, Becca. I wish you could live a normal life and all, but I'm also glad you're here, because I swear you're the only thing keeping me sane right now. So thanks for that."

"You don't have to thank me. You know I'd do anything for you." I tried not to think of how much "anything" could be. She reached over and squeezed my hand. "Can I just ask, do you feel anything for me? Anything more than just friends?"

I sighed. "Come on. You know I can't answer that."

"Why not? It's a simple question."

"It is not a simple question. And the answer would be unfair to both you and JoBell."

She smiled. "I think I understand. What if we just agree that it didn't happen? That we never kissed or anything?"

"I feel like that wouldn't be fair to you, though," I said. "I don't want you to think I was just using you. That it didn't mean anything."

"But it also can't mean anything, can it?" said Becca. "We can't hurt JoBell."

"I love her," I said.

"So do I."

"You and me can remember that it happened," I said. "It can't happen again, but we can remember it as a good thing between the two of us."

"But nobody else will ever know," Becca said.

Nobody but Sweeney, and I knew I could trust him. "Right," I said.

She nodded. "But can we at least go back to being friends? Can we stop acting like I'm the principal, and you're the kid who just got caught cutting class?"

I slapped her shoulder and laughed quietly. "You got it."

After chores, I washed up using water heated on the stove and then went upstairs to see JoBell, stopping outside the open door to the bedroom.

"Probably . . . twelve," Sweeney said. "No, wait. Thirteen . . . *Four*teen. But are you counting girls I've just made out with? Because then it's gonna be like, well . . . Are you also counting girls I've only kissed? 'Cause that'd be like —"

"Eric." JoBell coughed. Her voice shook. "Don't you feel bad at all? You can't even remember how many girls you've been with. You could never give me all their names."

"Not all of them *told* me their names."

Becca stepped up close behind me. "I can't believe him sometimes," she whispered.

"I think they're trying to have a private conversation," I whispered back.

"Do guys really want that?" Becca asked. "To get with as many girls as they can?"

"No, not all guys. I'm not even sure Sweeney wants that anymore." I inched away from Becca, feeling awkward in all kinds of ways. "For a lot of guys, it's about love. They're just trying to find that one perfect girl, you know?"

Becca sighed. "I wish I could find a guy like that."

"You will," I said. "I have no doubt in my mind."

She smiled sadly.

"And hey," Sweeney continued inside the room. His voice had changed, getting more serious. "I know the two of us are always arguing, and you don't take me very seriously. Maybe that's because I haven't taken much of anything seriously in my whole life. I never needed to. But when you got shot, I was so scared. I thought we were going to lose you. I couldn't handle that, JoJo."

I knocked on the door, and Becca and I went in. "Hey, JoBell, how you feeling?" I said.

JoBell put on a smile and offered a thumbs-up. "Good, I guess."

Sweeney looked at me like *No, she's not*, and I noticed the sheen of sweat on her forehead and above her upper lip. Becca kept on her own smile and went around to the other side of the bed. "I'm just going to check that bandage. No big deal. Lie real still now." She pulled the bandage back a little and looked at JoBell's wound. "Healing up," she said cheerily. But I could see the worry in her eyes.

"I don't feel so good," JoBell said. "Dizzy."

"Oh, no problem," Becca said. "Danny and I will get you something to make you feel better."

JoBell smiled and squeezed Becca's hand.

Guilt twisted inside me as I watched the two of them together, but Becca pulled me away from those thoughts and the room.

Sweeney joined us in the hallway. "Something's wrong with her," he said.

Becca closed the bedroom door and brought the two of us closer to her. "She's faking like she's better than she is," she whispered. "I think she's really sick. Like you said Danning was."

"What are you talking about?" I whispered back. "She's fine. She's talking and joking. She's not close to as bad as Will was. We're keeping the wound clean."

Sweeney looked at the bedroom door. "I don't know, dude. Danning seemed pretty much okay for a while there close to the end too."

Becca looked at me hard. "She's running a fever, and that wound is all purple and black."

"What can we do about it? I can't get her down to the hospital in Coeur d'Alene. And even if I did, we'd all end up arrested." I pressed my hands to my face. Was that my choice now? The only way she could live was by getting medical treatment in Fed prison? "She's going to be fine."

"The wound is infected, Danny. I've seen this before, like when a cow gets a bad cut on a barbed wire fence or something and we don't get to it for a long time. Without some serious antibiotics, the cow can die from it."

"Then why don't you take her to the veterinarian . . ." My voice trailed off as I realized that wasn't a bad idea. "Shit." Our eyes met and I almost hugged Becca, but stopped myself. "You say the vet has antibiotics?"

Becca nodded with a smile. "They have everything. They even do surgeries at the clinic. A lot of that stuff has to work on humans too, right?" she whispered. "But how will we get the medical supplies? We don't have any money."

"We might have to go the IOU route," I said.

I went back into JoBell's room and pressed my hand to her forehead. She was damp with sweat and burning with fever, just like Danning had been. *Oh, God, please help her to hold on.* I couldn't let her die. I'd promised to protect her. And I was done breaking those kinds of promises.

CHAPTER

SEVENTEEN

I thought we'd just bust into the vet clinic and take all the medicine we could, but Becca insisted we talk to the doctor first. "She's nice," Becca said. "She's helped out Lightning plenty of times, and anyway, we won't have any idea what to get, so we might as well ask her."

We snuck down to the vet's house outside of town early the next morning. Dr. Randall, a tall slender woman in her early thirties, twirled a strand of her long dark hair around her finger as she leaned back against the washing machine in her basement. "I'm afraid I can't just give you the medicine and other things you need," she said. She looked at me. "If the Army found out I'd given away medical supplies, especially some of the controlled substances, especially to wanted fugitives, I'd be in a lot of trouble."

That was exactly what I worried she'd say. "Dr. Randall, I'm sorry about this, but we need —"

She held her hand up. "Please. Call me Nicole. So here's what you need to do. Break into the clinic, and tear the place up good. Bust the cash register open. Try to crack open the vault. The antibiotics you need are in the cupboard in the back above my desk. It's to the left of the wall where I've hung photos of my husband and our kids. Look for penicillin or amoxicillin. They'll be labeled just like that. Maybe grab the ceftiofur. You should stay away from the sulfa-trimethoprin. Humans are often dangerously allergic to that. To the right of the desk is a green file cabinet. The bottom drawer is locked."

"You got a key?" I asked.

"I'm the only one who keeps a key for that drawer. If it's unlocked, they'll know I was involved. It's a basic file cabinet. Just use a crowbar. In that drawer you'll find the pain meds. Morphine. Even better, hydromorphone. You have to be careful with that stuff, though. If you give her too much, she'll OD. No more than four to six milligrams every two hours, or less." She sighed. "On the wall to the left of the desk you'll find cupboards with clear bags full of saline to replenish fluids. There's also tubing, bandages. All that stuff's good for people too."

"Right." I started moving toward the door.

"Oh! And get some stuff to clean the wounds. Just grab some iodine. It's really important to keep wounds and everything clean and disinfected."

"Dr. Randall, why are you doing all this?" Becca asked.

She shrugged. "Thanks to the blockade, everybody has slaughtered most of their livestock. All I see anymore are a few dogs and cats. I took an oath to help. I'm not going to limit that oath to *only* animals, and I'm not going to hoard medicines that I no longer have much use for while people die."

I smiled at Dr. Randall. "Thanks. I won't forget this." She nodded. "But you should probably forget that you saw us here today."

Dr. Randall reached out, and I shook her hand. "Take care of your girlfriend," she said. "Watch out for yourselves."

"We will," Becca said. "Thanks, Doctor. Um, sorry, Nicole."

With that, we left the veterinarian's house and headed to the clinic in Freedom Lake. We approached it from behind, making our way down the alley to one of those heavy steel doors with a serious lock and a narrow window in the upper right corner. The door wouldn't budge. After some searching up and down the alley, I found an old rusted piece of rebar. The window was reinforced with that chicken wire stuff, but I attacked it, and in about five fast hits, I'd busted a hole big enough to reach through. I popped the deadbolt and the lock in the knob, and then we were in.

"Let's hope nobody comes down the alley and sees the window," I said, leading Becca inside.

"And that there's no alarm system."

I flipped a switch on the wall, but nothing happened. "Doubt it. No power."

"Great." Becca passed by me into a big, dark room. "Should have brought a flashlight." She vanished through a door into the next room. "Come on, Danny. This is it."

I followed her into an office where a pass-through offered a view of the front desk and waiting room near the entrance. A lot more light came in through the big front window. Becca already had the cupboard near the desk open. "Bingo!" She held small white boxes up to the light. "Penicillin. Amoxicillin." She laughed. "Tons of it! I'll get all this stuff. You bust that locked bottom drawer open. There'll be plastic bags out front at the counter. I'll get a couple to carry this stuff in."

I looked at the bottom drawer, trying to figure out how to break into it. Dr. Randall had said I should use a crowbar, which would have been good advice if I had a crowbar. I spun the piece of rebar in my hand. If I hit that drawer really hard, I might be able to bend it enough to get the bar in there and pry it open. Or I could just shoot the lock.

"Danny, hide!" Becca hissed. "The Fed is here! They've seen me. I'm gonna pretend I belong here."

"Damn it," I whispered. I stayed crouched down below the window between the office and the waiting room with my .45 drawn. Dr. Nicole had sold us out! Now we were stuck in a dangerous game.

There was a knock on the door. I heard Becca take a deep breath and open it. "Can I help you?" she said.

"Good morning, ma'am. I'm Private Olsen. Sorry to barge in on you like this before you're open for the day, but there's something wrong with my platoon's dog. He's been throwing up and he's really lethargic. My platoon sergeant sent my squad to get him checked out. They're back in the Humvee."

A whole squad was out there? I looked at my .45. It wasn't close to enough ammo or firepower to take out a whole squad. Damn it! I should have been keeping closer watch. At least Dr. Randall hadn't turned us in. What were we supposed to do now? If that dog had my scent, or if it was one of those pissed-off attack animals who went crazy if he heard a weird sound — say someone hiding on the other side of the wall — getting out of this might get real complicated.

"Well, I'm only a vet technician," said Becca. "I just come in early to clean up and take care of the animals. That's why my clothes are so dirty already." She laughed. "Dr. Randall will be here in, oh, maybe an hour, maybe later. I'll call her and let her know about your dog. We're always eager to help the troops!"

"You have an authorized comm?" said the private.

"No!" Becca laughed again. "'Calling' . . . You know what I mean. Sometimes I forget!" She laughed more. I hoped she wasn't overdoing it. "So where you from?"

"Me? Nebraska, ma'am. Tiny little prairie town called Wymore."

"Oh, please stop with that 'ma'am' stuff. You're making me feel old. I'm only seventeen."

"Seventeen, huh?" He sounded disappointed.

"How old are you?"

"Nineteen."

She was totally flirting with this Fed prick. And I knew she was just trying to make this guy relax so they'd leave us alone, and Becca could flirt with whoever she wanted, but I found myself wanting to blast this guy.

"But I'll be eighteen April 13," she said shyly.

The private laughed. "That's coming right up."

"But it feels so far away. I want to be eighteen so I can date older guys. Because I just broke up with my boyfriend. Can you believe he said he had to break up with me because I wanted too much . . . you know?"

"Seriously?" The private sounded like he was choking on the word. "Wow," he said. "I'd never get tired of . . . I mean, well, that's none of my business. I'm not saying that we'd . . ."

She giggled. "Private, relax. I'm glad he broke up with me. It was tough having a boyfriend with all these studs in uniform around town. But with these stupid rebels messing everything up, now I probably won't get any birthday presents."

"Well, I . . . you know . . . I wouldn't be too sure of that. You say you're eighteen on April 13? I wouldn't be surprised if you get more gifts than any girl in the whole reconstruction zone."

Becca giggled a little more. "So do you want to bring the dog back when the doctor's here, or should I just put him in one of our kennels for later?"

"Right! The dog. Could you take him now? He actually threw up in the Humvee. Sergeant was real mad about that."

"Oh, poor puppy! Well, don't you worry, Private Olsen —"

"Ben. That's my name. You can call me Ben."

"Ben. Well, like I said, Dr. Randall will be in after an hour or two, probably closer to two. Come on back then."

"Wait. What's *your* name?"

"My name?" She laughed again, and I heard a note of panic in it. "You want to know *my* name?"

After such a perfect performance, now Becca was stalling out?

"Emily," she said. "But *you* can call me Em, if you want to."

"Right. Em. I'll be back in an hour?"

"Two hours."

"Two hours. Roger that."

"I'll be waiting." Becca held out the last word all sexy and teasing. Finally I heard the front door close and lock. But I stayed down just in case the private was gazing in at Becca through the front window.

"Okay, you can come out now," Becca said as she led the dog on a leash toward the kennels in the back. "They're gone."

"Are you sure *Ben* isn't hanging around getting you some flowers or something?" I teased.

"Shut it," she called. Metal clanged on metal and she came back. "That little show was a lot easier than shooting him, wasn't it? I swear, guys can be so dumb."

I bent over and slammed the rebar into the front of the controlled substances drawer. "I think you really liked him."

She kicked me in the butt. "He *was* kind of cute."

We took what we needed and made it look like a robbery, but knowing how much Dr. Randall had helped us, we did as little damage as we had to. Then we headed to where we'd hidden our snowmobile and rushed away with the medicine that would save JoBell.

As soon as we got back, we gave JoBell a white amoxicillin pill, because we knew it was an antibiotic and it was clear how she should take it. The penicillin was liquid. Should we squirt it on the wound, have her drink it, run it through an IV? Who knew? After giving her the pill, we cleaned the wound, first with just water and then with iodine.

"Okay," Sparrow said to JoBell. "We're going to give you a tiny bit of morphine now, and when that's kicked in, we'll close this wound up." She popped a syringe into the bottle of clear liquid and drew a very small dosage. "And I mean tiny," she whispered. "I've never messed with this stuff, but I know you gotta be careful. Two milligrams, and we'll see how you do."

She wrapped one of those giant rubber bands around JoBell's arm and pushed the needle into a vein. We waited about five minutes, but when nothing happened, Sparrow added two more. JoBell still wasn't numb, so she gave her a final milligram.

"Are you guysh gonna *do* thish or are you *not*?" JoBell finally said, with obvious trouble focusing her eyes.

"I think she's ready." Sparrow laughed.

"I'll do it," I said. "I can do it." I scrubbed my hands and dipped a needle and thread in iodine, then gritted my teeth as I started to sew her up. JoBell didn't even flinch.

"Are you shewing me?" she asked.

"No," I said. Why worry her? "Relax. We're just cleaning you up and getting a new bandage." I kept going, trying not to think about pushing and pulling a needle and thread through my girlfriend. I'd done this before with some of the other wounded people, and treating it like sewing two pieces of cloth together worked a lot better. "I'm not sure I'm getting these stitches close enough."

Sparrow kept a flashlight beamed on the brown, iodine-slathered wound. "Yeah, try to get them a little smaller, I think. She's going to have one hell of a scar."

JoBell closed her eyes and her head slumped to the side.

"Is she okay? How much morphine did you give her?" I said.

Sparrow checked her breathing and then her pulse. "I think she just fell asleep. And I only gave her five milligrams. She'll be good. If her fever and swelling doesn't start to go down, we can hit her again with the antibiotic. I didn't want to overdo it on that either."

I finished stitching her up and cut the thread with iodine-covered scissors. "Can she overdose on that . . . what was it called?"

"Amoxicillin. And how the hell should I know?" Sparrow said. "I'm not a doctor. We're winging all of this with shit you stole from a vet, remember. We just gotta be careful and hope for the best."

I nodded to her, wiping my hands on a rag and taking my place on the bed next to JoBell. "Thanks for all your help, Sparrow."

Sparrow shrugged and left the room, leaving me alone with JoBell and my prayers that what we'd done for her would be enough.

〜• *You've worked hard to care for your loved ones. You bought insurance in case of unexpected tragedy. But in these uncertain times, are you sure you've provided for the safety and protection of your family? In the event of the loss of electricity, clean drinking water, a safe and reliable food supply, or even breathable air due to natural disasters or war, how can you improve the odds that your family will survive? Go to www.survivethetimes.com. At www.survivethetimes.com, we don't simply offer you lifesaving products, we also connect you to a one-on-one consultation with your personal survival advisor. Your advisor will be a trained survival specialist who will consider you and your family's unique needs. Shelf-stable food, water and air purification systems, protection from radiation, and more — you can find it all at www.survivethetimes.com, so that you and your family will weather any trouble in comfort and style. www.survivethetimes.com. Make plans to protect your loved ones. Before it's too late.* •〜

〜• *Both sides in this idiotic war (and let's face it, this isn't just an "Idaho Crisis" — this is the Second American Civil War) would like to downplay the loss of life, claiming to be oh so humane in their killing. I think it is important to tell the truth, not only to honor the dead, but in the hope that representing the horror of war in human terms might help us prevent a further escalation of this war. That's why I started this blog, which I'm calling* The Last Full Measure, *a title taken from a line in President Lincoln's Gettysburg Address during the first* Civil War.

Please note that the list below contains soldiers and combatants only. Civilian deaths are not included, so the total number of dead is much higher. Also, since casualty lists are not being publicly released, please send me a private message to report a confirmed death as a direct result of this war. However, IN ORDER TO REDUCE DUPLICATION,

FEDERAL: TOTAL: 967	IDAHO COMBATANTS: TOTAL: 1,258
SSG Jason Kirklin	2LT Chad McFee
SPC Alfredo Gamboa	SSG Shane Donshel
SGT Marcelo Lozano	TSgt Isaiah Krieger
PFC Tim Fisk	1LT Jay Vinson
TSgt Amy Quick	SSG Ron Torres
2LT Wes Kerns	PFC Jay Robertson
SrA Carlos Rojas	SGT Ken Hyde
CPT Yolanda Knight	CPL Thad Jamison
SPC Breann Dowd	SPC Will Danning
SSG Phil Unger	PFC Henry Nelson
Scroll down for more . . .	*Scroll down for more . . .*

⌁—• *Warning! You are about to enter the Truth Zone. Here comes . . . The O'Malley Hour!*

Good evening. I'm Bruce O'Malley. Our talking points tonight: The Islam Society of the United States is complaining about discrimination and backlash against American Muslims after people blame Islam for the Idaho Crisis and other problems in America. To be sure, nobody should blame any particular religion for our current difficulties, but leave it to a quote unquote "victim group" to exploit this whole situation for their own publicity. They should be ashamed of themselves. •—⌁

⌁—• *A spokesman for the Brady Center to Prevent Gun Violence said today that significant blame for nearly three thousand deaths related to the Idaho Crisis lies in the fact that too great a portion of the civilian population is armed with weapons that are more power-*

ful than civilians ought to be allowed to own. The National Rifle Association countered, saying that the situation in Idaho is a perfect example of why the Second Amendment rights of Americans must not be trampled by gun control legislation. •—⌁

⌁—• Welcome to Armed Forces Network News. I'm Tech Sergeant Beth Mullen. Special session debate on nullification of the Federal ID Card Act in the Oklahoma House of Representatives began today, and a vote could take place as early as two weeks from now, with most experts predicting passage. Chaotic protests continue on the Oklahoma capitol grounds, but federal agents and Oklahoma City police seem to be keeping the situation under control for now. Some appear to be protesting the passage of nullification, fearing the federal government's response, while others are cutting up or burning their federal ID cards. Many protestors are armed in accordance with Oklahoma's open carry weapons permit law. President Griffith says that she is monitoring the situation and hopes that, quote, "foolish and illegal nullification legislation does not lead to another tragedy such as the one in Boise last year," end quote.

Citing an urgent need for more pilots, the president announced today that the curriculum at the Air Force Academy would be accelerated. Cadets will focus exclusively on pilot training and be commissioned as officers after just eighteen months. They will return to the academy to complete their four-year curriculum and earn their degrees once the pilot shortage has abated. •—⌁

CHAPTER
EIGHTEEN

"Griffith's not going to wait until this governor chick in Oklahoma makes her move," Sparrow said.

Sweeney and Becca were in the igloo, JoBell was sleeping comfortably and recovering thanks to the medicine we'd gotten her almost two weeks ago, and Crocker was monitoring the radio and keeping watch in the tower. The rest of us had gathered around the kitchen table, eating leftover MRE casserole. I was glad that JoBell wasn't with us to hear Sparrow call the governor of Oklahoma "this governor chick."

"Every day Crocker is hearing stuff on the radio about the Fed buildup around southern Idaho," I said.

"Yeah," Cal said. "I guess from Fairchild Air Force Base all the way to Coeur d'Alene, it's like one big Fed convoy. They fly stuff into the base and then ship it thirty miles over the border into Idaho. They're gonna kill us all."

"Then what do we do?" Kemp asked.

Luchen took a drink of what he called "choco-wawa." Since we didn't have milk, he mixed Nesquik chocolate powder into regular tap water. "We can keep launching these little attacks, but they ain't gonna do much. We need to kick the Feds' asses right out of town, and for that, we're gonna need a hell of a lot more guys."

"Yeah," Sparrow said. "We need to find these Brotherhood people and work with them."

"Those guys almost got JoBell killed," I said. "Do we really want to work with people stupid enough to launch an attack when all those civilians were still in the area?"

"Says the guy who got into a firefight outside his own high school," Sparrow said.

My chair scraped the linoleum as I stood up. "I didn't have any choice!"

"Whoa, calm down, Wright," said Sergeant Kemp. "Idiots or not, we have to find the Brotherhood so that at the very least we can make sure we're not in their line of fire the next time they launch a strike."

"How do we do that?" Cal dumped a teaspoon of Nesquik into his mouth and tried to chew it. Unable to speak with all that dry powder in his mouth, he frantically motioned to Luchen, who shrugged and passed him his glass of choco-wawa. After a drink, Cal said, "It ain't like we can just go around town calling out, 'Here Brotherhood, Brotherhood, Brotherhood.'"

"Well," said Kemp. "At least we know they're against the Fed. Maybe if we can pull off a few more big attacks, we'll get their attention and they'll find us. And speaking of big attacks, I have an idea for a nasty one that might really throw the local Feds off."

"More sapper stuff?" Sparrow asked.

Sergeant Kemp smiled. "Sometimes it's great to be a combat engineer."

That night I was scheduled for the late shift on igloo duty, so I joined JoBell in her bedroom with the hope of getting a little sleep before going out to freeze with the machine gun. But when she rolled to face me and her lips met mine, I knew sleep was the last thing on my girlfriend's mind. She'd been complaining for the last couple days that she was well enough to get up, but we'd all begged her to take it easy a little longer to make sure her body had completely fought off the infection. We didn't want to take any chances after the way we'd lost Danning.

Now she moaned and ran her fingers through my hair as she kissed me harder. I slid my hands down her back and squeezed her ass as she moved up on top of me. Her long blond hair fell down around her face, hiding my view of everything but her, so that across the universe there was only the two of us. She sat up, grinding over my hips as she slipped off her shirt, and then looked down at me, her warm hands pressed to my chest.

"Feeling better?" I asked.

She smiled. "I'm about to make it all feel *so* much better."

The last time we'd been together, back in JoBell's room, felt like a lifetime ago. I reached up, meaning to pick up where we left off and take care of that bra.

But I stopped when my fingers found the bright pink jagged scar on her left side. I'd seen it before, but I'd always focused on it clinically, like the wound was something on my truck that needed to be fixed. Now it looked more like part of JoBell, a mark against her intense beauty, a reminder that I'd almost lost her. I slid my hand away from the scar. "Sorry," I whispered. "Did I hurt you?"

She stopped her gentle grinding on me and leaned forward to look into my eyes, moving my hand back up to touch her wound. "No, Danny," she said. "You saved me."

"I was so scared of losing you," I said to her. "I didn't know what I'd do without you. You gotta promise me you'll stay away from protests and riots and things like that."

She leaned forward, pressing herself to my body. "Danny." She kissed me. "How do you think I felt every time you went on one of your missions? I never knew when you'd be doing what. A Fed convoy is hit up on Silver Mountain? A burning house sniper attack?

Were you there? Were you safe? It got to be where I had to focus on my schoolwork, regurgitating federal propaganda, just to keep my mind on something besides worrying and wondering if you were dead or alive." Her eyes welled with tears.

"Hey." I wrapped my arms around her as she laid her head on my chest. "Hey, I'm fine."

"Yeah, for now," she cried. "But how long can your luck hold out? How long until Cal comes back with your dead body? Or worse, nobody will come back, and I'll never find out what happened to *any* of you."

"Jo," I whispered. "I know you've never been a supporter of Montaine or of this war, but —"

"No!" JoBell slid off me so she was lying on her good side, propped up on her elbow. "It's not about the war. Not anymore. I don't care who is right or wrong. It's about *you*, Danny. It's about us." Her soft hand caressed my face. When she spoke next, it was in a low near-whisper. "Do you still have that ring you tried to give me once?"

I sat up and slid away from her. "Yes. Always. But don't mess with me."

She smiled and wiped her eyes. "I'm not messing with you, babe. I'd love to wear your ring." She lowered her gaze. "If you still want me."

"Of course . . . Of course I want you, JoBell. But, what about . . . When I asked you to marry me, you said we were too young. And you were worried about college —"

JoBell laughed sadly. "Danny, nobody's going to college. The whole country is falling apart. We'll be lucky to stay alive. Anyway, if marriage is all about going through hard times together, show me a couple who has been through more than us." She locked her gaze with me. "What I want now, more than anything, is to go somewhere safe and just be with you, be your wife."

I rolled out of the bed and sprinted to the guard tower room where I kept my rucksack.

Crocker looked up from his radio. "Is there a problem?"

I grabbed the quarter-karat engagement ring from my ruck and hurried back without answering. Dropping to the floor on both knees, I held the ring up to her. "JoBell Marie Linder, I love you more than anything. Will you marry me?"

She moved to the edge of the bed and held out her hand so I could slip the ring on her finger. "You know I will," she said.

She pulled me up to her, and we kissed, long, hot, and deep. JoBell only winced a little bit from her tender scar when we fell back onto the bed. "You've just made me the happiest guy in the whole stupid world," I said. "You've got a seriously smart strategy to trick me out of the war."

"I'm not tricking you, Danny." JoBell pushed some hair away from my eyes. "This is something I've been thinking about for a while. Everything that's happened has only helped me make up my mind. And just like, married or not, you'll never make me do anything I don't want to do, I'm not going to force you to do anything you don't want. So if you want to keep fighting the Fed, go for it." She kissed me. "Or we could find some place to hide away and be together, start our lives together."

Close to her ear, feeling her heat, I whispered, "The guys just planned another attack. They're counting on me. But after this one, I'm out. After that, it's just you and me."

JoBell attacked me then, and kept her promise to make it feel good.

A few hours later, I asked Becca to join me in the guard tower. Crocker saw me and Becca come in. "Wright, do you mind if I ask about the nature of the urgency that brought you running in here a few —"

"I'll take over the watch, Specialist," I said. "Can I have the room?"

Crocker stood up and stretched. "Well, I suppose I could use a break." He headed toward the door. "Becca, is there any of your latest MRE casserole down in the fridge? You know I could really go for some of —"

I closed the door to shut him out. Becca smiled. "That was a little rude. Something must be up." We kept the room pretty dark at night so we could see out the window better and so nobody outside could spot the machine gun we had up here. Faint moonlight shined in just enough so we could see each other, standing at opposite ends of the room. "Are you okay?"

I'd charged into gun battles, but I swear sharing my news with Becca was a million times harder. "Becca, I gotta tell you something. Figured I should tell you before I let the others know."

She shrugged. "Okay?"

I let out a breath. There was no way to make this easier. The truth was the truth. "JoBell and I are engaged."

All traces of amusement dropped out of her face and she grabbed the back of the chair at the radio station.

"Tried to get supplies through the Fed lines surrounding Lewiston to help the resistance heroes still holding that city, but we got turned back. We'll keep trying. Idaho rising."

The radio transmission snapped Becca out of her empty stare. She nodded and found her smile again. "I'm happy for you, Danny. For both of you." She took a step back and wiped her eyes.

"You good?" I asked.

"Are you kidding?" She held out her arms and we hugged. "Two of my best friends will be marrying each other. It's my duty to be happy. I'm so excited." She stepped back from me. "Surprised. But excited." I searched her eyes. Was that a trace of sadness there? Maybe. I didn't figure I should say anything about it. She made a little punch to my shoulder. "Really, Danny. I'll . . . find a way to be okay. Thanks for telling me like this."

Becca Wells was easily one of the coolest people I'd ever met. "Thank *you*," I said.

"But what are we just standing around for!" She grabbed my arm and pulled me out of the room. "Come on! We have to tell everyone the news!"

Everybody was really happy when we told them about the engagement. JoBell had to beg Cal to stop swinging us around and put us down. The rest congratulated us less physically. Even Sparrow managed a smile and a "Congratulations."

We unfroze an old, store-bought pie that we'd been saving, and we toasted with orange juice from that canned concentrate stuff. It turned out to be one of the best nights we'd had in a very long time. The guys were in such a good mood that I didn't have the heart to tell them the next mission would be my last.

NINETEEN

The next day, we set up one of our nastiest attacks yet. The Feds were building a second level of their Hesco barrier wall around their cop shop HQ on Main Street to protect everybody near the building. A ring of infantry soldiers formed a security perimeter to guard the guys building the barrier. They even had a machine gun nest on the abandoned thrift shop across the street from their HQ. Altogether, there were probably over twenty-five Fed soldiers in one place — a perfect target for an attack.

In the alley behind the thrift shop, Sparrow and me crawled between the brick wall and an old dumpster until I made it to the basement window. I kicked what was left of the glass out of the window well and slipped into the dank basement. Sparrow handed me a heavy roll of barbed wire before she crawled down there with me. The two of us worked our way toward the front of the building.

The old hard-core adrenaline rush came back as I heard footsteps on the floor above us. Dust and grit fell down through the floorboards. My toe hit a paint can or something that rattled away into the dark.

"Watch it!" Sparrow hissed.

"Sorry," I whispered.

Finally we reached the busted-out window at the front of the building. The wind outside was blowing icy cold, but sweat had formed a damp layer under my coat and jeans. "There's about twenty seconds of time fuse on this thing," Sparrow whispered. "It's supposed to go off before they can see it and have time to react."

We'd packed several pounds of C4 into the hollow space at the center of the roll of barbed wire. When the time fuse burned down and set off the blasting cap, it would detonate the C4 and scatter bits of barbed wire everywhere — the nastiest antipersonnel bomb ever made. It was another idea from Kemp's old sapper buddy.

Twenty-five more dead, I thought. Almost an entire platoon. That would put a dent in Fed forces in Freedom Lake. It would mean a lot to beg God's forgiveness for. But then that would be it. I'd get out of the fight and spend the rest of my life with JoBell. *One more mission.*

"I'll need your help pushing the wire out there," I said.

"You got it," she said. "As soon as we get it out, hit the dirt and plug your ears. This will be loud as hell."

I nodded, and we positioned the roll of barbed wire on the ground outside the window. Sparrow lit the fuse. "Now!" We pushed it, but it hit a bump and didn't roll far. *Eighteen, seventeen, sixteen . . .* Sparrow was on the ground. "Wright, get down!"

"Hang on! It's just gonna kill us this way," I whispered. *Thirteen, twelve . . .* I tried to shove the wire roll with my rifle's buttstock, but the weapon's magazine caught on something.

"Hey, what's that?" someone said out in the street.

Nine, eight . . .

"Wright!" Sparrow hissed. I pushed hard on the wire. This time the bundle cleared the bump and rolled away.

Six, five . . .

I dropped to the floor and plugged my ears.

Four, three . . .

The air all around us shook like the whole world had exploded. Dust and grit fell down on us. I could hear screams from outside, but to my jacked-up ears, everything sounded garbled, like when some-one talked through a fan. We didn't wait around, but ran back the way we came. I was the first one up and out of the back window, checking the lane and looking up toward the roof. All clear.

In seconds, I'd crossed the alley to the back door of the Bucking Bronc. I waited in the doorway, shifting my aim right and left to cover the alley until Sparrow was clear of the thrift shop basement and had joined me in the bar. We closed and locked the door behind us, then crawled through the building so that nobody would see us out the front window. I reached the basement hatch first and opened it for Sparrow, who looked at me like *Are you sure this is a good idea?*

I knew what she meant. I wasn't crazy about basements anymore either. But Sally had offered us a perfect shelter, and the Fed would expect us to be running away. The last place they'd look is right by the kill zone. I opened the little door in the giant metal tank that Sally had shown me. Sparrow and I squeezed through the small open-ing into the dusty, dark space. We'd staged blankets, CamelBaks for water, and a couple MREs there, and we settled in to wait a couple days and let things cool down outside.

"You were a little off on the time fuse," I joked quietly.

Sparrow only kicked me.

I tried to get comfortable in the total darkness, shifting around on my blanket. My hand brushed against Sparrow.

"Watch it!" she hissed.

"Sorry," I said. I gave up on comfort and just lay there. The faint sounds of shouts and sirens filtered in from outside. I prayed they wouldn't find us.

We waited for hours that seemed like days. We were supposed to stay until things calmed down outside, but how would we know the time was right to try to leave? How could we maintain our sanity sit-ting here doing absolutely nothing?

"So you're engaged," Sparrow finally said.

"Yeah," I said.

"How does Becca feel about that?"

"Good. She congratulated us and everything."

Sparrow snorted. "Those weren't tears of joy in her eyes."

"What are you talking about?" I said.

"Oh, please," said Sparrow. "You two have a . . . thing going."

"Yeah. We're friends. Been friends since we were born, basically."

"You're very defensive about it. And you're a bad liar."

"Okay, well, what's up with you and Luchen?"

"We have sex sometimes. At least I can be honest about it."

I'd never met a girl more direct than Sparrow. "I, um . . . wow. Back on border guard duty, I thought you said Luchen would never touch you."

"It gets lonely in the Army, and when you spend all your time living and working with someone who likes you, sometimes things happen. And I said that stuff about not touching before our country fell apart and I became convinced that we're going to die any day. But you're dodging the question."

We'd just set off a deadly bomb, and Sparrow wanted to talk about relationships? "I wasn't lying. Me and Becca are good friends."

"Right," she said. "Nothing more?"

"I have a girlfriend. A fiancée."

"And while she was in town for so long, you and Becca —"

"Nothing! Just friends."

"Whatever," said Sparrow. "I've seen the way she looks at you."

Why wouldn't she let this drop? Worse, if she thought something had been going on between me and Becca, what did everyone else think?

The quiet settled in again. "Specialist?" I said. "You're not going to die. We're going to get through this."

She laughed softly. "I actually believed your lie about Becca more."

"Don't move! Let me see your hands!"

I woke up into blinding white light. Hands gripped my arms and my back scraped against the metal lip of the hatch as someone dragged me out of the boiler. "Let go of me, asshole!" I shouted. A rifle butt slammed into my gut and I gasped for air.

"Let me go! Don't touch me!" Sparrow screamed.

I tried to get up to help her, but hands were all over me, pushing me onto my stomach. The cold pressure of a gun barrel pressed into the flesh at the base of my skull. A heavy knee rammed against my spine. They yanked my arms back and cinched a plastic zip tie tight around my wrists, digging into my skin. Then they left me on the ground.

"All right, all right, I'm not . . . Get a good feel, pervert?" Sparrow said. She shrieked. "Aaah! Shit! Wright!"

"Hang on! I'll get us out of this!" I turned my body toward where our attackers stood. "Leave her alone! I swear, I'll kill you all!"

"Gag him and bag him," said a deep voice with just a trace of an accent. Alsovar. "The girl too."

A wad of gritty cloth was shoved in my mouth and then tied in place by a rope or something. I heard Sparrow screaming into a rag too. I caught one last look of her terrified wide eyes before a black bag was pushed down over my head and everything went dark.

They lifted me up to my feet. I kicked out to the front, but I connected with nothing. A firm grip seized control of my head through the bag. "Good. Fight back, Danny. The more you resist, the more excuse I have to leave bruises on you," Alsovar said. Then he let me go and shouted, "The prisoner is resisting!" A boot crunched down on the back of my leg, dropping me so that I slammed down hard on my knees, and then on my shoulder and head. My brain sloshed around inside my aching skull. "Pick him up!" Searing pain throbbed from both the front and back of my knee, like someone had stabbed right through my leg. My foot felt puffy, detached, like it was made of wood instead of part of my body.

They hauled me up the stairs and out of the bar. I heard the sound of a running engine. Then they crammed me and Sparrow, both of us shouting against our gags, into a vehicle seat and we rolled out.

"Should I radio this in, sir? Let them know we have him?"

"No," Alsovar said. "You will mention this to no one."

"But, sir, General Thane will want to know we caught him. You're probably looking at a promotion at the very least. The president herself will be —"

"Lieutenant, you will discuss this with no one." Alsovar yelled louder, "The same goes for you, Sergeant. If you follow my instructions exactly, promotions are coming for both of you, but if we turn Wright over now, we'll lose a chance for valuable intel about the local insurgents. Because, gentlemen, we just caught their ringleader. He's the key to taking out the rest of them. And we have to break these damned insurgents soon, before we lose any more of our people. Do you men understand me?"

"Yes, sir!" the other two said at once.

My world became a blur of noises, voices, and hands pulling and shoving me along, out of the vehicle and into a building. Finally I was pushed down into a hard chair, my arms freshly zip-tied to the back. Nothing remained but the throbbing in my knee, my pounding heart, and the sound of my breath through my nose. I couldn't even hear Sparrow anymore. I leaned my head back, hoping to rest it on the back of my chair, but instead it just kind of dangled there.

Just like I'd be dangling from a rope soon enough. All that I'd done. All that people had sacrificed for me. The people I'd hurt and killed. My whole life had been destroyed since the Battle of Boise, but I'd held on. Held on to . . . what? Hope, I guess. I'd dreamed of a day when the war would be over and we'd be safe and free. JoBell and I would have a place together. Sweeney, Cal, and Becca would live nearby. Now none of that would happen. It would all end like this. The Fed had me. I was a dead man.

TWENTY

I sat on that hard chair with that oily rag that tasted like ashes in my mouth, barely able to breathe, for hours. I probably would have fallen asleep if not for the pain in my knee, the swelling bruise on my head, and the way the zip ties cut off circulation so I couldn't feel my hands. I couldn't even get out of the chair. They'd zip-tied my hands to the back.

If they were going to kill me, I wish they'd hurry it up. The cloth had been crammed so far into my mouth that even while I pressed on it with my tongue, every couple minutes it would make my chest tighten up and my throat lurch like I was about to puke. This made tears well up in my eyes. If I did throw up, I'd probably choke to death on my own vomit.

I closed my eyes — not that it mattered, since this damned bag blacked out all the light. I hoped the barbed wire bomb had killed a bunch of Feds. I hoped they'd died slowly, bleeding out while they screamed. I hope it cut into their knees. Took their hands off.

But no. We'd used a big bomb. At least six pounds of C4. We'd killed them fast. We didn't torture people like these sick shits were doing to me.

JoBell. I let you down. Oh, God, I'm sorry, baby. I tried. I should have tried harder. I should have got out earlier like you wanted. JoBell! If they had me, how long until they found everyone else? Until they found her? Tied her up like this. Felt her up like they did Sparrow. I couldn't protect her anymore!

I pulled against my restraints. "Ye fufsh he ooo fe ooo!" I tried to threaten them through the cloth. But after a few seconds, I thought, *Get yourself together, Wright.* This was only the beginning. They didn't have JoBell. They didn't know shit. As long as I kept my mouth shut, it would stay that way. They could do what they wanted to me. They'd never hurt my friends or JoBell.

The bag flew off my head, and I found myself in a plain, windowless, white cement room, half the size of a classroom. A cold blade cut the rope that held the gag in my mouth, and finally the cloth was taken out. A long string of drool trailed the rag, and the man wiped it on my face. My lips and jaw ached so much that it hurt to close my mouth. When I forced it shut, my jaw didn't seem to line up right, like the feeling I'd get when a tooth had been knocked crooked in the rodeo.

"Sorry to keep you waiting, Danny." Major Alsovar sat down in a chair across the table from me. "Remember me? Your old buddy Major Alsovar? What was it you said to me after you murdered my men at your shop?" He leaned across the table. "Oh yes. You were coming for me? I should bring more guys? Two soldiers, Danny. That's all it took to bring you and your insurgent whore in." He sat back and smiled. "What's that thing you do? Gets the insurgents all riled up?" He held his fist at an angle above his head. "Arrrrrr! I'll give you a war." He laughed. "How much of a war do you think you'll give me while you're tied to that chair?"

"Private Daniel Christopher Wright. 492 55 7114."

Alsovar clapped his hands together slowly three times. "Oh, very good. You remember your training from when you used to be a soldier. From before you broke your oath and betrayed your country."

I was still a soldier, and I hadn't betrayed anyone. I wouldn't betray Idaho and my friends by telling him anything more than my rank, name, and serial number, like the regulations said.

"Do you know . . . I've served in the United States Army for seventeen years. This is my fifth war. I've been in combat in Afghanistan, Syria, Pakistan, Iran, and now this mess. I have experience, whereas you have nothing but" — his eyes went wide — "delusions. So let me explain something to you. You're trying to follow the procedures of the Geneva Conventions, the treaty that provides us with" — he made air quotes with his fingers — " 'rules' for prisoners of war. But your little rebellion hasn't been recognized by even *one* nation in the whole world. Not even by your terrorist pals in Iran or Pakistan. Certainly not by the United States. So Idaho hasn't signed the Geneva Conventions, and the rules do not apply. Even better for me, under the conditions set forth by the Unity Act, officers and other field commanders are allowed to use all reasonable means to stop rebel activity, including deadly force." He slapped the table. "So don't hold out hope for a lawyer. Don't be expecting the president to come take you to some big trial.

"Now listen very carefully. I'll tell you an important secret." He leaned across the table and whispered, "*Nobody* knows you are here."

The major stood up and walked a slow circle around the featureless room, his boots clomping on the cement in the silence. He probably wanted me to act all scared, especially as he made his way behind me. I stared straight ahead. When Alsovar came around to the other side of the table from me again, he stood still for a moment. Then he quickly reached down for something out of sight.

He slapped a pair of dog tags down on the table, both colored red-brown with dried blood, one of them twisted and mangled somehow. "This was just about all that was left of Captain Rosado after your attack the other day." I turned my head away. "No!" Alsovar marched around to my side of the table, grabbed my head, and forced me to look. "You open your eyes and look at what you did, or I'll cut your eyelids off! This is what your little barbed wire terrorist attack did to him! This tag was embedded in his flesh. I had to rip it out of him!" He swung me and the whole chair forward, crashed my face against the table, and pushed me upright again. He shouted the rest close to my ear as though he'd bite it off. "He was my best friend! Saved my ass way back in Syria and again in Iran! I especially requested him for the task force to find you, and now he's DEAD!"

He spun me on my chair to face him. "He had a wife and two daughters." Alsovar wound back his fist and decked me hard in the face. The chair flew back and my head hit the floor. Little black dots danced in my vision, and I screamed in pain at having my full weight on the chair crush my hands beneath the back.

Seconds later, he hauled me upright. I spat blood in his face. "Come on and untie me, pussy. I'll show you how much of a war I'll give you. Big tough war hero fights a man who's tied to a chair?"

"This isn't a fight, boy. I'm going to break you." He shrugged. "First, I need information from you that will save the lives of my soldiers. More than that, I'm going to have fun getting justice for my friend and all the other good soldiers you've killed. I'm going to *enjoy* breaking you. Then I'm going to kill you and that insurgent bitch and dump your bodies in the basement of that bar where I found you. The bartender knew where you were hiding. She wanted the reward money. I'll just tell everyone that when we went down to check out the tip, little Danny Wright tried to kill us, so I had to take action to defend my men. Then, using the information you're going to provide me, I'll wipe out the rest of the insurgency and restore freedom and peace to Idaho." He smiled. "They'll probably give me a medal for it."

He picked up the dog tags and slipped their chain over his head, tucking them under his uniform shirt. Then he shoved the bag back over my head. The door slammed. A second later, the lights shut off, and I was plunged into total darkness.

At least the gag was left out of my mouth. But my wrists and shoulders throbbed in pain from being tied up and mashed under the chair earlier. Blood ran from my nose down into my mouth. I spat into the bag.

"You gotta forget the pain," I whispered to myself. "It's going to hurt a lot more. But then it will be over." All I had to do was stay quiet and wait to die.

I'd been close to death many times since August. But before, I'd always had a chance, been on a chase or in a shoot-out or something. Now none of my friends knew where I was. Even if they did, I was probably too well guarded for them to stage a rescue. Death was a certainty. Major Alsovar would kill me. This asshole who had killed First Sergeant Herbokowitz, Bagley, and Schmidty had beaten me.

For a moment, that thought made me want to try again to break loose from my restraints. But then I relaxed. If I was going to die, I didn't want to go to God full of anger and rage. I didn't want to bring the war with me when I saw Mom again in Heaven. If God would let me into Heaven. I'd killed so many people.

Maybe my torture and death was some kind of payback. *Oh, God, please forgive me. I'm so sorry. Please help me to stay silent through this. Don't let me tell them anything that could hurt my friends. Please help Sparrow, wherever she is. Be with us both. Amen.*

Hours later, the door opened, and there was a flurry of activity. My chair was moved and, I thought, bolted to the floor. The zip ties were removed from my wrists, but my arms were handcuffed to the chair at my sides. The door opened and closed many times. Whatever they were doing, they were taking their time.

A mechanical buzz started up. Then another. A moment later I felt a wave of heat.

A soldier removed the bag from my head, walked out of the room, and slammed the door. I blinked my eyes against the fierce bright light shining on me from the other end of the room. Squinting, I saw two large space heaters on the floor. They both must have been running full blast, because this room was warming up quick.

A tough jolt knocked my whole body. It felt like it came from inside me.

"Could you feel that, Wright?" Major Alsovar's voice droned through a speaker somewhere. The sharp spasm rocked me again. I looked down at the chains that held my arms to the chair. An electric wire ran down the length of each chain, connected to some kind of shock emitter on my wrists. *"Yeah, I think you felt that."*

So they were going to cook me alive in here and torture me with electric shock. I smiled, turning my face away from the sunlamps. I'd been zapped by electric fences in cattle pastures that had way more charge than that shock. Such a tiny jolt would never get me to talk.

Alsovar came into the room a moment later with two men. One was a soldier with what I thought was a captain's insignia. It was hard to tell in the blinding light. The other wore a white lab coat. A doctor?

The doctor went behind me as the other two watched. I could hear him rattling around with something back there. Then I felt a cold cloth rubbing the pit opposite my elbow. He was going to inject me with something. I shook my arm around to stop him. Alsovar nodded at the captain, who walked over and held my arm in place against the side of the chair. The doctor duct-taped my upper arm to the chair so I couldn't move it. Then the needle went in, and he started an IV.

"Hold his head back at a forty-degree angle," the doctor said quietly.

The captain leaned over me, putting his arm around my head and forcing me to tilt it back. "If you stop struggling, this won't be as bad," he whispered in my ear.

The doctor stepped in front of me with a clear plastic tube, wrapping it around his finger several times. Then he unwound the tube and dipped the end into something that looked like a ketchup packet, only when he brought it out, the end of the tube was covered in a clear gel.

"What the hell is that for?" I shouted. "Get off me!" I tried to shake my head to stop them as the doctor brought the tube closer.

"This will be much more comfortable if you don't move," the doctor said. To the captain he added, "Keep him still." The doctor pushed the tube into my nose. I felt it working its way toward the back of my throat like a giant booger. If I moved, it would probably tear something. "Give him the water," said the doctor. The captain held a water bottle with a straw to my mouth. "You must drink this," the doctor said to me. "It is important that you swallow to help the tube go in."

I didn't want it in me at all, but this guy wasn't about to pull it back out. I gagged as the tube went down. I swallowed the water again and again as the doctor kept pushing the thing up my nose. Finally, he stopped, but only after he'd shoved at least a foot of tube into me. A piece of tape held it in place on my nose.

"What's this for?" I asked, just to see if I could still talk.

Nobody answered me. They left me alone in the sweltering heat and blinding bright light.

TWENTY-ONE

"Idaho, Ida . . . ho," I whispered what I could remember of our new national anthem. "Land where . . . fffreedom lovers go. We . . . we will . . ." What was the next line? Why couldn't I remember it? I should have remembered.

A shock woke me. I'd figured out the game. The electricity wasn't to torture me. They wanted to keep me awake.

The doctor and the captain came in a couple times. Like days apart. Not days. Could it be days? There weren't any days anymore. No days. No nights. They changed my IV bag. Once, the doctor gagged from the smell that surrounded me. I laughed at that. Smell had gone away for me after a while. They must have been feeding me through the IV or the tube in my nose, because I hadn't had any food the whole time.

"Hello, Danny, I trust you're feeling rested." Major Alsovar stood in front of me. "Ugh." He waved his hand in front of his face. "You smell absolutely horrible."

"Go to hell," I said.

"But Danny, we're already there! In a hell that you have created for yourself, first by shooting up those people in Boise —"

"An accident! Didn't mean to. I only shot once."

"And then by participating in a rebellion against your own country. Where were you and your fellow insurgents hiding? What is your base of operations?"

So bright in here. I couldn't even look this asshole in the eye. "Won't tell you nothing."

"Yes, you will."

"If I tell, you'll *kill* them!"

"Danny, I'm going to have them dim the lights in here for a while. It's tough on my eyes. I can't imagine what it's been like for you." He called out, "Captain, kill the floodlights."

The sun across the room went out. I felt like I'd gone blind again. I blinked, but couldn't shake the blue-green afterimage.

"Your vision might clear eventually, Danny," said the major. "Where is your insurgent base of operations? Where can I find your accomplices?"

"Don't know. They moved when you captured me, you dumb shit."

"They probably did move. But I want their old base, then. And where do you think they would have gone after they left your old base?"

"I tell you, I might as well kill them."

"No, Danny. If you tell me how to find them, you'll be saving them."

"Bullshit!"

"Danny, Idaho is out of time. The president has been making the military hold back in Idaho because she didn't want any more casualties than were absolutely necessary. And I don't know, but maybe she really did hope negotiations with that criminal Montaine would work out. Liberals always have to at least appear as if they're working for peace, right? I think the main reason she ordered us to go easy on Idaho is because she's still trying to negotiate with Oklahoma, trying to convince them to obey the law and reject nullification of the Federal ID Card Act. She wants to keep your little rebellion local."

"I don't care about ID cards," I said. "Tired of damned ID cards."

"You know, there you and I are in total agreement. I think the federal ID card is a terrible idea. But the difference between you and me is that I choose to follow the law and honor the duty I'm sworn to obey."

"Diff'rence is I'll . . . kick your ass, you unchain me."

"When diplomacy fails with Oklahoma, the president will have nothing left to lose. Danny, whatever you think of me, you know that I have military experience. Trust me. Nothing can hold back the attack that is coming. When it is over, whatever is left in the ruins of what was once Idaho will be back under the control of the United States, where it belongs."

"So we're all dead anyway? What's it matter? Why should I help you?"

"Because if you give me names of insurgents, even the names of people who maybe aren't quite insurgents but have helped you, if you make it easy for me to find them, then I can quickly and carefully arrest them. If they are in my custody, they will live. If they are out there, Danny, then even if they aren't insurgents, they will probably be killed when the attack comes."

"I ain't gonna let you bring in my friends to torture them like you done me!"

"Then they'll all die. Anyway, I am only making it difficult for you, Danny, because you killed my friends, and because I need information from you. If you tell me what I need to know, this would all end. Believe me, it takes a lot of effort to keep up this level of discomfort for you. A hundred and twenty degrees. All that light. Someone watching around the clock to make sure you stay awake. Tell me the names of the insurgents. Tell me where to find them. You don't have to say it to my face. Just say it out loud. We're recording everything you say and do in this room." He walked over to the door, but stopped with his hand on the knob. "Oh, and Danny, this . . ." He waved his hand around the room at the heaters. The spotlight. My chains. "This isn't the torture. The torture hasn't even started yet."

He went out, and the steel door slammed behind him. The sun burst into light in front of me again.

TWENTY-TWO

"Wake up!" A hand cracked across my cheek. "Wake up, Danny!" I put my head up and opened my eyes. The white brick room spun around me. Had I fallen asleep? The major stood almost at the position of attention. "No more sleep games, Danny. No more bright light and heat. You stink. I think it's time we gave you a bath."

I didn't know how much sleep Alsovar had given me, but whatever I got allowed me to fully wake up for the first time in a long time. I was still a little dizzy and out of it, but at least I knew where I was and I wasn't hallucinating anymore. Unless this was all a hallucination.

The captain, whose name tape read PETERSON, carried in a decline bench that looked a lot like the one we used for lifting weights in school, but this one had nasty restraints for my arms, ankles, and head. The doctor pulled out my IV and then removed the tape for the tube in my nose. "I'm going to remove this tube. You need to take a deep breath and hold it."

I did as he said, and my eyes watered as he pulled the tube out of my nose in one smooth motion. Snot and a little blood came out of my nostrils and ran down my lips, but I couldn't do anything about it. The captain and the doctor unlocked the handcuffs, and I tried to attack them, but after sitting in the same position for so long, my limbs felt welded in place. They grabbed my shoulders, and Peterson yanked my left arm up behind my back to control me.

Major Alsovar nodded. "Strip him."

"Sir?" Peterson asked.

"Take his damned clothes off, Captain."

The captain shifted his weight. "That isn't necessary for the procedure —"

"Do it!"

"I'll hold him," said Peterson. "Doctor, you strip him."

I relaxed my legs and dropped in the captain's grip. The pain bit my shoulder and elbow as my arm was wrenched up, but when Peterson tried to lift me, I jumped, pushing with my legs with everything I had. At the same time I jerked my head back, nailing Peterson in the face.

He lost his grip. I sprinted the seven feet to Alsovar before he could reach for his sidearm and took him down hard, my shoulder slamming into his crotch. "I'll kill you!" I had him on his back and jabbed my fist straight up, catching him under his chin. He screamed as he bit his tongue or lip. I cranked back my fist and brought it down on his nose with a good crunch so it broke. Blood splattered everywhere. I wound my fist back to punch him again, trying to hit him again and again until he died.

But the other two men grabbed my arms and dragged me onto the bench. "Let me go! Come on and fight me!" I shouted. A strap latched down on my head. My wrists were buckled in next. Then my pants and underwear were taken off and each ankle was locked up. After that the doctor cut off my shirt.

Alsovar loomed over me, his blood dripping on my face. "You'll pay for that, you little shit."

"Little?" I said. "I've been tortured for days, and I still kicked your ass. That what they teach you at officer candidate school —"

"I graduated from West Point!"

"Teach you at West Point to be a giant pussy? Come on, let me up. Let's settle this like men."

The doctor leaned over to examine Alsovar's crooked nose, but the major pushed his hand away. "Sir, that's broken," said the doctor. "We need to set it."

Alsovar glared at me. "When I come back, I'm going to make you suffer."

A punch to my ribs woke me up. Alsovar stared down at me, his nose already swollen. "You will tell me the names of your fellow insurgents. You will tell me the location of your old base. You will tell me the probable location of their new base."

I spat at him, but he moved away in time. "I'll tell you shit. So do whatever you're gonna do."

Major Alsovar smiled and held a white cloth in my field of view. "What I'm going to do, Danny, is put this over your face. Then I'm going to pour water over it."

That was it? Was it supposed to bother me that my face got wet? Was his plan to use really cold water or something? It would take a lot more than that to break me.

I watched the cloth come down over my face, and I lay there for a long time as my breath heated up the air in my little enclosed world. He must have been trying to freak me out, to let me stew in my fear. It wouldn't work. "You going to actually —"

Water hit my face. Some went up my nose. I coughed. I tried to breathe, but the cloth just got sucked to my face, and it was like slurping a drink of water. Only no water came into my mouth. Nothing did. No air. I couldn't breathe. I tried to kick my legs. Turn my head. I spat at the cloth, and that gained me a little space. A tiny sip of air. More water in my nose. I sputtered. Chest burning. Every muscle tight, trying to get free.

The water stream stopped and I gasped. The wet cloth got sucked to my face again when I inhaled.

Alsovar laughed softly. His voice sounded deep, quiet, and crisp next to my ear. "See how this works, tough guy? I can keep this up all day. Can you? I can assign my men to keep this up for weeks. Months."

"I won't talk," I said.

"Good," said Alsovar.

The water stream splashed my airway closed again. He must have turned up the pressure this time, because I got nothing but a trickle up my nose. I closed my mouth and did my best to hold my breath, but the water up my nose made me gag and cough. After a cough, my first instinct was to breathe, but that was impossible. I yanked at the restraints as hard as I could. Did anything to move. The water continued. Chest burned. Throat closed up. Face puffed. Dizzy. *Oh God!*

Water stopped. Gasped for air. Choked and coughed on water.

Water again. *No! No air!*

A bug. No, a black speck. Trailed by white light. A bunch of them swirled around under the wet cloth as my heart throbbed in my ears. Coughed and sucked for breath, getting barely enough. Then the water hit again. Chest burned. Arms and legs tingled.

So dizzy. I hacked hard against the water in my throat. Tried to suck air. *Almost there, Danny. This is the end. Mom, I'll see you soon.*

"How's that feeling, Danny?" Alsovar asked. The cloth was lifted off my mouth. I hocked water as hard as I could and breathed. I frantically sucked air. So wonderful to breathe.

"Go ahead and kill me," I said. "I'm not afraid of drowning. I'm ready to die. I won't tell you anything."

"Oh, be patient, Danny. I'll kill you. I promise. But you see, I have a lot of experience with this enhanced interrogation technique, this waterboarding, as they call it. We used to use it all the time in what they called the 'war on terror.' Even when the practice was officially banned . . . Well, sometimes in war, my men and I were far from command, and we needed information quickly. It only takes two or three guys to interrogate a prisoner like this, and afterward, we'd all agree that it never happened. We'd have our information that would help save the lives of our soldiers. The world would have one less insurgent scumbag. And command would never have to know or worry about it. Everybody wins. Well, except the insurgent scumbag.

"You see, I know your fear of drowning isn't what will make you talk. I have the doctor here to make sure you don't die. He'll restart your heart if it stops. Instead, I'm going to put you into the gray space, that state of mind somewhere between active consciousness and death. I'm going to speak directly to your subconscious, where you have no secrets. In this way, I'll learn everything I need to know from you. I'll understand you better than you do. And you will have no conscious memory of speaking to me. I'll find out the identities and location of all your insurgent friends. Then, you are right, Danny. I *am* going to kill them all."

The cloth went down over my mouth and the water poured on and I held my breath as long as I could. I could tell him something. If I told him only the location of the barn cabin. That wouldn't help him. And it would buy me time. A little more time to breathe. When my mouth finally burst open to breathe . . . No air. Couldn't turn head. Couldn't move —

Pressing on my chest. The doctor above me. I coughed water hard, and something else, snot or blood, came with it. Alsovar stood at the edge of my vision. The doctor turned to the major. "He's back. If his heart fails again, I don't know if I'll be able to restart it."

"He's going to tell me what I want to know! This little maggot is at the heart of the insurgency, and I *will* break him."

"Yes, sir, but he can't tell you anything if he's dead," said Peterson. "Maybe if we gave him a break. We've tried the stick. Maybe if we offered —"

I was hauled roughly across the room and buckled back into my chair. I sat there naked as the lights and heater were turned back on. The doctor started the IV again.

Captain Peterson leaned toward me while he adjusted my chains. "I'm sorry this is happening to you," he whispered close to my ear. "Try to hold on."

Try to hold on? What the hell did that mean? I dropped my head back. Why wouldn't they just let me die? Seconds later, an electric shock woke me up again. Why did he say hold on? Why would he say that? Whisper it.

I thought about that for a long, long time. I'd never been so tired in my life, but I could still think things through. I wasn't losing my mind. Yet.

CHAPTER
TWENTY-THREE

A jolt woke me. "They still even alive out there?" I smiled. "Maybe they's dead. Maybe Swee —" I realized I was talking out loud. I shook my head, shook myself around in my chair against the handcuffs. *Shut up, Wright! You damn near gave Sweeney away.* Or did they already have him, know about him? Just couldn't talk. Not at all.

No end. No sleep. Sit. Exist. So many shocks. What if they never let me go? What if they kept this up forever? They could. Sweat caked my body. The doctor and captain came sometimes to check my blood and change my IV. New feeding tube. I asked them, "How long? What day is this?" They never said nothing. This wasn't gonna end.

"Oh, God, I need to sleep."

"If you say the names of your fellow Idaho soldiers. Say where they used to live. Say where the Idaho soldiers are now. Then you can go to sleep, Danny."

I forced my head up. Squinted my eyes in the glare. Who said that? Nobody in the room. "God? Why won't you help me?"

"Just say anything, Danny. You've been in this room for days. Your friends have moved on to another location by now. It won't hurt to tell them about the old place. Where was your old base?"

What? "Aren't you God? Don't you *know*?" God would already know. Unless . . . "You ain't God! Alsovar, you son of a bitch! I'm not telling you nothing! Stop trying to trick me!"

* * *

Shocks woke me up. If I shut down. Just . . . If I sleep and can't wake up. Will the shocks . . . just fry me? What if . . . if Alsovar was right. "They aren't there no more. Leavin' no clues." If I said it. 'Bout the cabin. Would he really let me sleep? Really?

Another shock. I jerked awake. Dizziness wouldn't stop. *"Danny, Shawna Sparrow already told us the names of your friends. It's over now, Danny. Time to sleep. She already gave you up. You might as well tell us about your old base. About where you think they've gone."*

"Sparrow! She told you? She . . ."

"She's already sleeping comfortably on a nice, soft bed. She gets to sleep whenever she wants. No handcuffs. Nice, cool room. She had steak and eggs for breakfast. You could too, if you'd just tell us where you think your friends are. Tell us the location of your old base."

"Seriously? A bed?"

"Where was your old base? That's an easy one, Danny."

I thought about it. We had ham and eggs in the morning sometimes when we were guarding the border. She'd take my ham. Me her eggs. "Sparrow don't like eggs! She won't eat 'em! You damned liar! Ha! Ha! Alsovar, you bastard! I win again! 'n if she *was* telling you stuff . . . If she told you all that. Names. You wouldn't need me to tell you nothing."

My head drooped but I shook off the sleep. "Why don't you come fight me, Alsopussy? Unchain me." I shrugged. "I'm tired. Okay. I am. I *admit* it. But you . . . you give me a fair fight. I'll whoop your ass."

Not givin' in. Never gave in before.

So much time. Heat. Doctor, captain checked blood. Changed IV stuff. Many times. Many shocks. Sing me some Hank McGrew.

"When I was a . . . a country boy down on the farm
I never knew nothing that could do so much harm
As that blue-eyed girl who lived down the lane
She loved . . . she loved tractors, and huntin', and . . . huntin',
And me all the same."

Another shock hit me. "What? Don'tcha like Hank McGrew?"

Me and Becca were on guard duty back in the igloo, only it wasn't cold. "You'd think a snow fort would be really cold." I turned to Becca. She was naked. "What are you doing?"

"It's about to get a whole lot hotter in here, Danny." She leaned forward and kissed me, so deep and so sweet. I wanted to slide my arms around her back, to feel her soft skin, but I couldn't. She backed away from me and I opened my eyes.

JoBell was lying there, with her long blond hair. "What's the matter? Don't you want me, Danny?"

"I love you." I smiled. "I love you." I wanted to say her name, but for some reason didn't think I should. "I will always love you."

"Danny, who is your leader? Who is your best friend in your team? Who do you love? Who will you always love?"

"I love . . . It's so hard to know? I guess I love them both. What's the right thing to do?" Wait, this was Alsovar. How long had I been asleep? What had I told him? "No! I won't tell you. You lose, Major. You can't beat me. I'll never break."

Door opened. Three Fed assholes. "Okay, Danny," said the major. "The doctor thinks your heart is in good-enough shape. It's bath time again."

What? "The hell you talkin' 'bout?"

Doctor removed my feeding tube and IV. Then the chains were gone. I tried to fight, but they had me on the table. The decline bench. Strapped in. Waterboarding!

"No! Hey! Come on! No, we don't gotta do this again!" I wouldn't last. I'd wanted to talk last time. I'd been close to talking lately. "No! You bastards! Let me up!"

Alsovar's voice was low and close to me. "Where is your old base?" Water splashed right next to my face. I could hear it. Feel it. "Last chance, Wright."

I could tell him about the cabin. It wouldn't hurt nobody. They'd be long gone by now. And he probably knew everybody on my team. He knew all the Idaho Guardsmen who hadn't shown up for Fed duty. He probably knew all about my friends. Only JoBell. He didn't know nothing about JoBell.

"Okay." Alsovar sighed. "Have it your way. Let's get the cloth on you."

A damp cloth was draped over my face. My heart pounded. Ached in my chest. The doctor had said it was strong enough. Really? *Boom. Boom.* Then a cracking sound.

"What the hell is that?" Alsovar said. An alarm shrieked. I thought it was an alarm. The screaming could be going on in my head. "Keep the prisoner here. I'll be right back."

Blinded under the wet cloth, I heard the door slam. A moment later it opened again. "Insurgents. It's an attack! Doctor, get to your med station. We'll have casualties. Captain Peterson, with me." The door closed again.

The cloth was taken away. Captain Peterson leaned over me. "Don't fight me. Don't yell." He unbuckled the restraints from my legs. "Your pants and underwear are over there on the floor. Wait here until the time is right."

Was this a dream? That subconscious stuff Alsovar had talked about? Peterson tapped my face. "Hey. Hey. Look at me." I forced myself to focus on the captain's eyes. "Private Wright. Your friends are coming for you. Be ready." He released the strap that held my head. Then he freed my arms and ran to the door. "Wait here until it's time. This is your last chance if you want to live." Then he vanished.

TWENTY-FOUR

I put on my underwear and jeans, but my shirt had been cut off me, and they'd taken my boots. How did he even expect me to finish dressing? More shouts and explosions went off outside. But since I'd been locked in this room, I'd heard gunshots. The gunfights I'd been in had become dreams, but the dreams didn't stop when I was awake. And I was always awake in this damned place.

And *wait here*? What the hell was he talking about? I didn't want to be here. My legs wobbled like a newborn calf's as I walked to the door. That was as far as I'd walked in how long? "Let me out of here, you bastards," I said quietly. I turned and yanked the doorknob. Fell back on my ass. The door thudded closed. It was unlocked! I could go. My sore muscles fought as I struggled to my feet. I opened the door and peeked out into an empty hallway with a cement floor and cinder block walls. Gunfire went off somewhere close, and I backed into the room fast.

I needed a weapon. What had they left me in the room? A rubber hose hooked up to a spigot on the wall. Weak at best. Tubing, some bandages, and some syringes. Not much help in a fight. I shuffled around through a pile on top of the little table that had been behind me for so long. The light glinted off the sharp blade of a scalpel. I picked it up.

Alsovar. This is for you.

The door burst open and I spun around, slashing out with my new blade. TJ stood in the door frame. He wrinkled his nose. "Oh no."

I frowned. How could TJ be here? This had to be a trick. Another of Alsovar's games.

"Wright, come on. Let's go!" The image of TJ motioned with his M4.

"Are you even real!?"

"Real? What? The hell you talking about?" He moved toward me, reaching out to grab me. "It's me — TJ. We've come to get you out of here, but we gotta move now."

"How did you figure out his name?" Had I broke? Had Alsovar accessed my gray zone, tapped my brain or something? I could finally see the camera where they'd mounted it behind the huge spotlight. "How did you learn his name!? I never told you nothing!"

TJ looked from me to the camera and back again with his mouth open. Then he frowned, turned, and shot the camera. "I'm not the Fed, Danny. Would the Fed shoot their own camera? If they did that, they couldn't watch you. Come on. I know you hate my guts, but you gotta trust me. JoBell's waiting."

This could be a trick. A camera was easily replaced. But Alsovar had said there was an attack. Captain Peterson said people were coming for me. "Travis?" I felt tears starting up. I dropped to my knees.

"Hey." TJ ducked down under my arm, wrapping his arm behind my back and picking me up. "It's me, buddy. Whatever these bastards did to you, it's over. We're going."

"Going home?"

He checked up and down the hallway as he led me out of the room. "Yeah, we're going home."

"Shopper, this is pickup. Where the hell are you!? Over."

I pulled away from TJ and crouched to the floor, looking all around. "Alsovar must have cameras everywhere."

"Danny, it's my radio." TJ keyed the mike on a little Motorola. "Pickup, this is shopper. I have the package, but he's, um, kind of got a problem. They messed him up good. He's not quite lucid. Not moving very fast. Over."

"*Shopper, pickup.*" It was a different voice this time. A girl's voice. JoBell? "*Use your old football rivalry.*"

TJ radioed back. "I don't know if that's a good idea. He's got a scalpel."

"*Just do it! We're taking shots here.*"

"I heard what she said. You aren't going to trick me," I said.

"I know," TJ said. "That was JoBell's worst idea ever. There's no football rivalry when you barely played this year." He tried to pull me down the hall.

"I did better than you!"

"Yeah, but then you quit. I was getting better, and I'm faster, so it's probably good for you the season was cancelled."

"This is a lamer trick than the Feds would try to use on me," I said.

We were almost to the stairwell at the end of the hall. The sound of gunfire roared outside. TJ shrugged. "It's not a trick. You're just not as fast as I am."

"Go to hell, TJ!" Trick or not, I could outrun that jackwad. We raced up the stairs. Three Feds ran into the stairwell from the hallway on the first floor, but bullets cut through their chests, arms, and necks. TJ slung his rifle so he could pick up two of the Feds' weapons.

"Wright!" Sweeney stood on the first landing with a smoking M4. TJ handed one rifle to me and another to Sparrow, who leaned against the wall behind Sweeney. She looked pale, her hair had been buzzed off, and her eyes were ringed with dark circles. She wore Fed MCUs with a bloody hole over the heart and no shoes.

"I'm okay, Danny," Sparrow said.

Sweeney pointed out the door. "We go out and run like hell to the plane. Then you two sit back and let us handle the rest." Sparrow looked down at her bare feet. "Sorry," Sweeney said. "If you run fast enough, maybe the snow won't be so bad."

"Plane?" I asked.

"No time to explain," TJ said. "Sweeney, you lead. Wright and Sparrow go in the middle, try to protect our side. I'll bring up the rear."

Sweeney took his position by the door. He gave me a light punch on the arm. "You ready for this, dude?" Was this really happening? "Wright! With me all the way?" I nodded. He shoved open the door. "Go, go, go!"

We ran out into an open snowy field past a sign that read SILVER LODGE. We were at Silver Sunset Resort. They'd turned the ski resort into a base? The roar of heavy machine guns echoed down the mountain from the summit of the ski slope. Bullets rained on the base village, shredding the three lodges and pinning down the Feds there. A big chain-link fence ran about three hundred yards down the slope from the lodges. A fierce firefight was going on by the gate they'd built across the access road. How many people were involved in this attack?

The snow froze my feet until I ran on numb, wooden pegs. I would have given anything for a shirt or shoes.

"Pickup, this is exit," Luchen's voice said over TJ's radio.

"Exit, this is pickup. Go ahead, over."

"Pickup, exit. We got a problem. They found us. We're set to blow the fence, but we're trapped down in the vehicle ditch. Y'all want to hurry with the package?"

TJ keyed the mike on his radio. "Exit and pickup, this is shopper. Package is moving. Hang in there."

"How are we —" I started to ask about the escape plan when up ahead I saw the old red-and-white seaplane that Cal's boss owned, the one that gave rides to tourists on Freedom Lake. The plane had no wheels, only big, long cylinder floats. I guess they could skid to a stop on deep snow as easily as they could on water.

We were within thirty feet of the plane when Cal hopped out of the copilot seat, aiming an AR15 up the hill. He took a couple shots at someone up by the lodges. "Come on! Get in." When we'd covered the last distance, Sweeney opened the back door. JoBell leaned out and beckoned to us. She was so beautiful, and right there. How could this be happening?

Sparrow reached the hatch first, but she didn't have the strength to climb up into the plane. I laced my fingers together so she could use my hands as a stirrup, then followed her into the bench seat in the back, where we sat close together to try to keep warm. JoBell slid in beside me and wrapped her arms around me.

"Remember way back when you said I shouldn't take the lake job 'cause it didn't pay enough?" Cal settled in the copilot seat and slipped on some ridiculous mirrored sunglasses. "Well, today it's gonna save your life. You remember my boss, Lee."

Cal's boss down at the lake, Lee Brooks, was gripping the controls tight. "Um, I'm glad you're okay, Danny," he said. "You better strap in."

Sweeney and TJ scrambled to each of the two middle seats and fastened their seat belts. JoBell buckled me in. She tried to reach around me to do the same for Sparrow, but Sparrow knocked her hand away.

"Okay." Lee pushed up on a red-handled lever in the middle of his controls. "Throttle up." He patted the console. "Come on, baby. We're going downhill. Nice slick snow. Just like the lake. You can do it."

The seaplane sped up, sliding down the hill toward the Fed fence.

JoBell keyed the mike on her Motorola. "Exit, this is pickup. We have the package. Clear our way. Over."

"Pickup, this is exit. Do you have . . . both of them? Over."

JoBell radioed back. "Roger that, exit. We have them both. She's safe."

"Well, safe is kind of a shaky term here," Sweeney said.

Sparrow silently took my hand. She stared straight ahead, tears welling in her eyes.

The plane began to bump up and down on the snow. We were two hundred yards from the fence. "I was right," said Cal's boss. "We won't make it with that fence in the way."

"Exit, pickup," JoBell radioed. "Status report?"

"Pickup. This is Luchen. We got a problem. Feds are all over. Two of my men are dead. It's just me and a couple of Brotherhood guys in this anti-vehicle ditch next to the fence. We can't make it out. I'm gonna blow it anyway. Danger close."

Sparrow sat up straight and squeezed my hand hard. "No! No, wait, what? No! JoBell, you tell him . . . Give me the radio. Give me the radio! You tell him to get his dumb ass out of there."

Tears ran down JoBell's face. "I can't, Sparrow. He's got the mike keyed."

"Pickup, this is Luchen. Tell Shawna . . . Tell her I said . . . It's worth it. For her. She's worth it. This is Private First Class Luchen. Out."

A white flash popped at the base of one fence post ahead of us. A half second later, snow, fire, and dirt blasted out in all directions.

"No! Noooo! Luchen, no!" Sparrow tried to get out of her seat, but I held her back. She slapped at my arms, screamed, shrieked like a cat. She shook around on the bench, and I held on to her. She beat my back. "Luchen, noooooooo!"

"Come on, baby, fly!" Lee Brooks pulled back on the control stick. Finally, the plane rose up off the ground. Three feet up. We passed the smoldering pit where Luchen had blown the fence. A couple bullets cracked against the side of the plane. Five feet up. Twelve. Twenty. Fifty.

"We're up," Lee said, finally smiling.

"Yes!" Cal said. I could tell he wanted to shout, to celebrate, but he stayed quiet. The only sound was the drone of the engine and Sparrow's sobs as she buried her head in my shoulder and cried.

"I tried so hard to protect him," Sparrow sobbed into my chest. "They did . . . The things they did to me . . ." She sat up and looked at me with wide eyes. "But I never broke, Danny. I didn't tell them anything. I protected him." The tears came again. "And for what?"

I squeezed Sparrow close. "We're safe now, Shawna. Luchen wanted you to be safe." I turned to the others. "Where are we going?"

"Freedom Lake," Lee said.

"You sure you know how to get there?" I asked.

"Giant watery lake of water?" Lee ran his hand back through his graying hair. "The one I take off and land on a thousand times every summer? Yeah, I think I got it."

Sparrow leaned away from me, resting her head on the wall of the cabin.

JoBell smiled at me sadly. "I'm so glad you're . . ." She frowned. "We've got company!"

I looked out the back window. An Apache attack helicopter was closing in on us. "Go, Mr. Brooks! Floor it!"

"It's not a car, Danny. I have her throttled up. JoBell, call the recovery teams. Tell them we're going to recovery two. Tell them we're gonna need help!"

JoBell keyed the mike. "All recovery teams, all recovery teams.

This is pickup. We're going to recovery two. An attack helicopter is following us."

"It's on our six," Cal said. "You're supposed to say 'on our six.'"

"Shut up, Cal!" JoBell said. "Recovery teams, how copy? Over."

"Pickup, this is recovery two. We're ready. Rolling Runway is in motion. You're go with the plan. We got you covered. Over."

"There's only one way I know to pick up speed." Lee pushed the yoke forward and the plane slid into a dive. We hurtled toward Freedom Lake.

I tensed up in my seat. It felt like we were coming in too sharp. The seaplane always came down at a nice gentle angle when landing with tourists in the summer.

"You got this, boss," Cal said.

Lee said nothing. He banked the plane hard to the right as red-hot blips of tracer fire flew by on our left, splashing into the water below. He pulled back on the yoke and kept us in the air only a few feet above the lake. "River's over there." He guided the plane over the river, right up the valley created by the blur of trees on either side of us. We flew by the Abandoned Highway of Love, coming up on the steel trusses of Party Bridge.

"Oh shit," Lee said as he dipped the plane.

I flew forward in my seat belt as we touched down briefly on the surface of the river. Water sprayed out to either side of us while we shot under the bridge, then Lee pulled up and the plane climbed again. I looked out the back window as two pickups rolled out onto the bridge. About half a dozen people in the back of each truck opened fire with at least four .50-cal machine guns and two AT4 rocket launchers.

But they weren't shooting at us. Sparks lit up the hull of the Apache, and smoke began spraying from one of its engines. It spun sideways and then seemed to try to turn away before its power gave out. It crashed hard into the river fifty yards shy of the bridge, bursting into flames.

"They got it!" I said. "Back to the lake?"

"The Fed is going to be all over the lake," Cal said. "We have a different plan."

"On snow?" I asked.

"Just enjoy the ride, Danny," Lee said. "And pray."

Brooks brought the plane out over Highway 41. "There it is," he said. "Right on time." A big pickup pulling a flatbed trailer rolled along on the road below. Lee eased back on the red throttle lever, and I felt the plane lose a little power. He brought the aircraft down. Sweat ran down his face.

"Cross wire," JoBell said.

"Shit," said Lee. He pushed the yoke forward and ducked the plane under the wires. The floats had to be inches from the pavement. Good thing there was a ban on driving, I thought. Oncoming traffic would really mess this up.

Lee pulled up just a few feet. The truck and trailer in front of us braked, so that we came up right over the trailer. "Gotta match the truck's speed exactly," he said quietly. "Then we can drop it on the trailer and kill the engine. Ready with those chains, boys." A few moments passed. "I'm going to put it down. Hold on. Jesus, please," he whispered.

"Amen," said JoBell.

Lee pushed the yoke forward and the plane dropped, bumping a little hard on the trailer. He pulled the throttle lever all the way down and killed the engine.

"Slow down, slow down!" JoBell shouted over the radio.

Sweeney and TJ hurried to open the back doors, climbing down onto the trailer.

"What are you doing?" I called to them, hugging myself against the blast of cold air from the open door. I hated being an outsider to the plan. Everyone knew what to do but me. TJ and Sweeney hooked up some chains to hold the floats down, cranking them tight with a ratchet. Once they climbed back into the plane, the truck turned off the main highway onto a paved county road, then onto a dirt lane back into the woods.

Lee Brooks relaxed in his seat and wiped his sweaty forehead. "I've never tried that before. Just saw some videos about it online once."

Cal slapped his arm. "Relax, boss. You did it. It's over. We made it."

I looked at Sparrow, curled up in her corner, trying to hide from the world.

"Not all of us," she said.

EMILY MUNSLEY ★ ★ ★ ☆

Come on, Oklahoma, do the right thing. Don't vote to nullify!

IT'S ALL IN YOUR HANDS NOW, OKLAHOMA. SAVE THE UNITED STATES OF AMERICA.

★ ★ ★ ☆ This Post's Star Average 4.05   [Star Rate][Comment]   33 minutes ago

JOANNA RINKS ★ ★ ★ ☆ ☆

If the US Congress won't repeal this unconstitutional law, then the states have no choice but to outlaw it themselves. Idaho, Texas, and now soon Oklahoma! Down with the Federal ID Card Act!

★ ★ ☆ ☆ ☆ This Comment's Star Average 2.13   [Star Rate]   27 minutes ago

BENJAMIN SHULTZ ★ ★ ★ ★ ☆

Nullification isn't the answer, but clearly the ID Card Act isn't working. Write to your representatives and demand that Congress repeal it!

★ ★ ★ ★ ☆ This Comment's Star Average 4.25   [Star Rate]   25 minutes ago

TAMMY PAULSON ★ ★ ★ ★ ★

Nullification. Repeal. Whatever happens, we must demand peace. Not victory. Not the defeat of our enemies. Peace. Now.

★ ★ ★ ★ ☆ This Comment's Star Average 4.56   [Star Rate]   14 minutes ago

Before the truck that hauled our plane stopped, I was already losing the battle to keep my eyes open. My head felt like it was moving even when it wasn't moving. I woke up enough to climb down out of the plane onto the trailer. Someone draped a scratchy but warm wool Army blanket over my shoulders, and I quickly took in my surroundings.

The truck had pulled into a big pole barn. A kitchen setup occupied the end of the building opposite the big bay door. A row of six double bunks ran along one side wall with a cast-iron wood furnace in the middle. A black T-shirt with the emblem of my bleeding fist and the words WE WILL GIVE YOU A WAR hung on the wall above the furnace. On the other side of the truck was a huge green cannon. Several pallets were stacked high with what had to be stolen ammunition. On the wall opposite the bunks, a big rack stored rifles, shotguns, and handguns of various kinds. Above that, hanging in the center of the wall up by the ceiling, was an enormous black flag with the simple silhouette of a white eagle in the center.

"What is this place?" I said. "Who are all these people?" Now that I thought about it, there was no way the attack on the ski lodge base had been carried out by my group alone. Again I had my doubts about whether any of this was real.

Four men, each with different rifles slung over their shoulders, got out of the pickup that had pulled us here. They smiled and clapped. "It's good to see you again, Mr. Wright," one of the men said. "It was a real honor to help get you out of there. Name's Jake

Rickingson — don't know if you remember me." We shook hands and he smiled. "Mr. Crow told me you might not like talking about this, and I'm sorry if it bothers you, but you've really been an inspiration to us all. The way you've stood up to the Fed since all this began — it showed us that anything is possible. Gave us the chance we been waiting for." He finally stopped shaking my hand and took a step back, still grinning.

"Mr. Crow?" I asked. "Sheriff Nathan Crow?"

JoBell slipped her arm around me, and I jumped at her touch. "A lot's happened while you've been away, Danny."

"What day is it?" I asked.

Sweeney looked up from the comm he'd been tapping and swiping away on. How did he get his comm working again? "Dude, it's March 15."

"What?" March 15? I leaned back against the trailer and stared down at my dirty bare feet. The Feds caught us on . . . what? February 25? Maybe the day after? It was hard to tell in that hiding place. I looked up at the others. "The bartender! Sally. She sold us out! Don't trust her."

A big bearded man nodded. "Don't worry about that."

"March 15," I whispered. "I only slept . . ." I had no idea how long Alsovar had let me sleep. "Maybe a few hours. Maybe only minutes." JoBell squeezed me closer. I turned to face her. "What is this place? Where's Becca? Sergeant Kemp?"

"You have a lot of questions, Danny." Nathan Crow smiled as he came around the back of the trailer. "Jake, why don't you and the men work on mission recovery? Help the wounded, clean the weapons, and increase the guard at the perimeter just in case someone was followed."

"You got it," Jake said. Lee Brooks shook my hand and patted Cal on the back before he left the building with Jake and the other men. Only Crow, Sweeney, Cal, JoBell, TJ, and me were left, plus Sparrow, who was still in the back of the plane.

Crow shook my hand. "I'm glad to see you again, Danny, but truthfully, you don't look so good. I have no idea what the Fed did to you, but you've obviously had a rough time." He sat down on the trailer and patted a spot next to him. When I sat down, he went on, "I know you must be tired, but we have a lot to do and not much time to do it."

"Mr. Crow," said JoBell. "He's been awake for like nineteen days straight. Maybe he can get a little sleep before we start on everything else?"

"They've had you awake this whole time?" Crow said.

I looked at him, gripping the edge of the trailer. "Had me chained to a chair. Kept shocking me. Kept asking me questions." I sat up straight. "I didn't tell 'em nothing. Kept everybody safe."

"I'm sorry," Crow said. "I can't imagine what you must have just gone through. Thanks for holding out. Yeah, everything else will have to wait. You want to eat first? Get a shower? Or would you rather —"

"I want to sleep," I said. "Please. Can't even think."

Crow stood up. "There's a little house next to this barn. I can set you up in a nice quiet bedroom in there. How'd that be?"

"That sounds great," I said.

"I'll get Sparrow," Sweeney said, heading back toward the trailer. I stared down at my feet.

A few seconds later we heard a scream. "Don't touch me!" Sparrow shouted.

Sweeney stepped out of the plane and shrugged. "All I did was tell her she could get some rest, that she's safe here."

JoBell stood up. "You want me to talk to her?"

"Naw," I said. "I got this." I climbed up on the trailer and into the plane. "Hey, Sparrow?" I said quietly. "Shawna?"

She turned and looked at me, tears in her eyes. "It should have been me," she said. "He was wrong. I wasn't worth him dying for. How's that a fair trade?"

"I don't think it works like that." I sat down next to her.

"It should," she said. "I should have died in that hellhole and Luchen, that dopey . . . He should still be alive."

"I get how you feel," I said. "But he wanted you to live. That's what he chose. So you have to take care of yourself. For him, you know?"

"I'm so tired, Danny. So dirty. What they did . . ." Tears ran down her cheeks. "I couldn't stop it. I wasn't strong enough." She leaned over and put her arms around me, crying on my chest. "I should have been stronger. Smarter. I shouldn't have let them capture us. I should have made our group choose a different target. Made us find a better place to hide after the bombing. Wright, what am I gonna do?"

"By the numbers, Specialist." I struggled to focus, talking as much to myself as to her. "One step at a time. We'll drink some water. We'll sleep. Make ourselves mission-capable again. There's this house next door. We can sleep there."

"I don't think I have . . . that I can . . . even make it there," she whispered.

"Neither do I," I said. "Come on. We'll make it together."

Me and Sparrow climbed down out of the plane and off the trailer. With our arms draped over each other's shoulders, we slowly followed Crow toward a door in the back of the barn. Cal reached out a hand to help Sparrow, but she pulled away from him. Me and her made our painful barefoot walk through the snow across a clearing in a grove of evergreens to a little house nearby.

Crow gave Sparrow the queen-sized bed in the master bedroom, and I had a smaller bed in a side room. I was out probably five minutes after I hit the mattress, but woke again a few minutes later as Sparrow crawled into bed next to me. She was asleep before I had the chance to ask what she was doing, but I didn't really need to ask. We lay there back-to-back, protecting each other even in our sleep.

My gas mask was malfunctioning. I couldn't pull a full breath, and water kept going up my nose. The mob of people around the capitol building in Boise had all taken up the chant, screaming, "Tell us the names of the insurgents! Where's the insurgent base? Where are they hiding?!" Major Alsovar pushed through the crowd, flanked by Captain Peterson and Staff Sergeant Kirklin. They started shooting at me, and I returned fire. Kirklin dropped dead again, but Alsovar and Peterson got away.

Luchen stood near me, holding a little green M81 detonator rigged to a barbed wire bomb. His voice came from a speaker somewhere. *"This is Private First Class Luchen. Out."* The barbed wire bomb leveled the crowd, but somehow my armor saved me. I took off my cracked, useless gas mask and could finally breathe. I walked out among all the dead. The redheaded protestor girl from the Battle of Boise. Kirklin. So many Feds I'd shot in and around Freedom Lake. Body parts everywhere.

Someone grabbed my arm from behind. I swung my fist around to take him out. "Aaaaaaaaaaaarrgh! Get off me! I won't tell you shit!"

"Danny! Danny, it's me. It's JoBell. You're okay. Danny, you're safe now. It was all a nightmare. You were having a bad dream."

I was lying in a bed in a dark room. JoBell stood beside me, holding her hands out in front of her. My body was covered with a sheen of sweat and my head spun. "Where am I?" I said.

"We're safe in the Brotherhood compound," JoBell said. "You looked like you were having such a bad nightmare, I had to wake you up."

Someone groaned and shifted position in bed next to me. Sparrow, with her hair all buzzed off, fluffed her pillow and settled back down. I looked from JoBell to Sparrow and back again. Had something just happened with the three of us, but I was too out of it to remember? No, I decided. I would have remembered *that*. Plus, Sparrow only slept here by me because she was freaked out. They might have messed her up even more than they did me.

I rubbed my hand over my face and looked around my bed for a knife or a gun. This was the first night I'd slept unarmed in a very long time. I must have been completely fried if I could have gone to sleep while so vulnerable. "Yeah, don't wake me up out of a nightmare again," I said to JoBell. "Or else poke me with a stick or something. I could have hurt you." She looked scared, so I reached out and squeezed her hand. "It's good to see you," I said quietly. "I thought I'd never . . . I guess I didn't do such a great job of getting out of the war."

JoBell sat on the side of the bed and ran her fingers back through my hair again and again. I closed my eyes and soaked in the warmth of her touch. "I hate this war," she whispered. "But when you were overdue for checking in, and we figured out you'd probably been captured . . ."

She leaned over me and put her head on my chest. I wrapped my arms around her and breathed deep. If only the world would go away, leave us alone, and let me hold her here like this forever.

"I thought I'd die, Danny. I thought I'd lost you. I had to join the fight — TJ too — especially after we found out you were still alive, that they had you in that cell. I was freaked. We all were. Becca would hardly eat or sleep." I looked sharply at her when she mentioned Becca. What did JoBell know? She looked up, smiled, and squeezed me. "I'm so glad to have you back."

"Don't you dare start messing around on the bed right next to me," Sparrow said flatly.

JoBell laughed and sat up. "Oh my gosh, I thought you were asleep," she whispered. "Sorry."

"I'll just go to the other room," Sparrow said.

"No, no," I said. "You're settled in here. Stay." I threw the covers off, turned, and sat up with my feet on the floor. "We'll go." JoBell and I stood, but before I could take one step, Sparrow grabbed my wrist and locked eyes with me. "Don't worry," I said. "We'll be right in the next room." JoBell picked up the M4 that she'd leaned against the wall, and I took it from her to show Sparrow. "We got you covered."

Sparrow frowned and flipped over to face away from us. "I don't care where you go." She pulled the blanket up over her head.

"What time is it?" I asked JoBell when we'd reached the big main room of the house. Everything was dark outside. "How long have I been out?"

She checked her comm. "It's 3:17 in the morning. You've been asleep for about fifteen hours."

"I've never slept so deep. I hardly even dreamed for once."

"Well, you should sleep some more. Unless you're hungry. Dr. Strauss said something about your electrolytes or potassium or something being all out of alignment."

I went into the kitchen. Under the dim light above the stove, a big steel pot of coffee steamed on the burner. "Dr. Strauss?"

"Major Dr. Strauss of the Idaho Army. President Montaine sent him up here to make sure you and Sparrow are okay and to help with the wounded."

I pulled a paper coffee cup from a plastic sleeve and ladled a drink for myself. My group had been in contact with President Montaine? A lot had changed in nineteen days. Now I was completely out of touch. The coffee burned my hand, and I had to slide a second cup around the first for insulation.

"You okay, Danny?" JoBell said as I walked silently to the living room window, looking out into the dark.

"Maybe this window should be boarded up." I shook my head. I couldn't even look out a window without worrying about being shot. Always on guard and ready for a fight. Always expecting to die. That was life now. "I didn't want this for you," I said. "The war, I mean. I thought I did. Or maybe I wanted you to accept me being in it. But you deserve something better than this, JoBell. And we'd agreed to get out."

"Like I said, I had to help them rescue you. I'm not some helpless glass princess who can't take care of herself and —"

I waved her off. "I know. I know. It's not that. It's just —" I rubbed my throbbing wrist.

"Besides," JoBell said, touching my back. "The situation has changed."

"How?"

She sighed. "We should all sit down together and talk it out. But for now, remember that someday, somehow, this will all be over. This will all be behind us and —"

"I don't think it will ever be behind me." I choked out the words, fighting to hold back my tears. "You don't know. . . . You weren't in that room. I don't think I'm ever going to be able to move past this war. Even if I survive it, I don't think it will ever be behind me."

JoBell pulled me into a hug. "I'm so sorry. I know it's tough, but we're here for you. I'm here for you."

"I don't want you here for this. I don't want what's happening to me to happen to you."

"Oh, sorry," said Sergeant Kemp. He'd come into the room without our noticing. "I didn't mean to interrupt."

JoBell turned around and faced the sergeant, keeping her arm around me. He smiled and held up a little thermos. "I'm sergeant of the guard tonight. Gotta keep everyone awake. Bring coffee to the troops. It's good to see you, Wright. Glad we could get you out of there." He looked down. "Sorry about Luchen."

"Yeah," I said. "Me too. But who are these troops? What the hell is going on here?" I was grateful for Kemp's interruption in my talk with JoBell. Even though I wanted us out of the war, I knew my words wouldn't make any difference. There was no escape. And I couldn't handle any more serious conversation. "Whose house is this? Who are all these other guys? I mean, they must have helped you attack the resort."

"If you're awake, we should go talk to Nathan Crow," said Kemp. "He said to come get him the moment you were up."

"Wait a minute," I said. "Sergeant, you're taking orders from a civilian now? Come on. We're our own unit."

Kemp shrugged. "It's the new Idaho Army. President Montaine made Crow an officer. Besides, it's way better working with these guys in the Brotherhood than being on the run by ourselves. That kind of ended up in disaster, right?"

"The Brotherhood?" I asked. "Those other resistance guys we've been hearing about on the radio? The ones who botched the job on Main Street and almost got JoBell killed?"

Kemp frowned. "Well, Crow said that the guys who started shooting got chewed out. They were supposed to wait until all the civilians were clear."

I guess I could understand messing up by shooting at the wrong time. "But you're in contact with President Montaine?" I shook my head. "I mean, you must be if he sent a doctor."

Kemp smiled. "We really should go talk to Crow."

"Sergeant," said JoBell. "He's been through hell and barely had a chance to rest. Can't we let him sleep a little longer?"

"Thanks, JoBell, but I'm good," I said. Anyway, I didn't want to have to go through any more nightmares. "The war waits for no one."

"Welcome to the Brotherhood of the White Eagle," Crow said as he sat down with us at the kitchen table. His police uniform had disappeared, replaced by simple jeans and a gray sweatshirt.

"I thought this was the Idaho Army," I said. Then, remembering that Kemp had said President Montaine had made him an officer, I added, "Sir."

"Please, call me Nathan. And yes, this is the Idaho Army, but we've been fighting on our own for so long that we've become accustomed to a certain informality. You might say the Brotherhood is a special unit within the Idaho Army."

What kind of name was "The Brotherhood of the White Eagle"? I hoped this wasn't one of those Nazi white supremacist groups or the Ku Klux Klan or whatever. Some parts of Idaho, especially around here, had a real problem with those psychos. Last year, this kid who went to our school for a while started giving Sweeney shit for being Asian. He tried calling him something that I couldn't understand because I dropped his ass with one punch. Another time, a couple of douche bags who had graduated a few years before us started following Sweeney and me when we were in the Beast like they were going to jump us. I drove onto a back road. Those guys parked behind us, and me and Sweeney pulled those idiots out of their little pussy Buick and beat them down hard. We were cool about it. We let them get back up if they still wanted to fight, but then we crushed them again. By the fourth or fifth time they stayed down. No racist assholes bothered us after that.

"I know what you're thinking." Crow brought me back to the moment. "I can tell by the look on your face. And JoBell had the same idea. But you can relax about that. The white eagle doesn't mean white supremacy. In fact, the Brotherhood recently stopped a bunch of skinheads who were shaking families down for food and fuel. No, we chose the eagle as the symbol for our organization because the legend goes that one of the first battles of the American Revolution stirred up a bunch of eagles that had been nesting nearby. They flew above the field and screeched the way eagles do. Some of the patriots said the eagles were calling out for freedom. That's what the Brotherhood is all about, a call for freedom from the United States federal government, which has expanded its power well beyond what the Constitution allows. At first we were only a small fraternity, a political group who tried to encourage people to vote for politicians who supported our views. Since the Idaho Crisis, more and more people have joined us, and eventually we determined that the United States is a lost cause. We're now committed to Idaho and Northwest independence. And we won't rest until every last occupying Fed soldier is dead or driven from our home." Crow smiled. "But I know you agree with that, right, Danny? You don't need this speech. You figured all this out the hard way, before the rest of us got into gear."

"How many are in this Brotherhood?" I asked.

"It's difficult to say. Since the war began, we've organized into a sort of military outfit, but we keep units separated. You know, that way if one of us is captured —"

"He can't rat out the others. I get it."

"Not that any of my guys would talk, but . . . Well, I guess the Fed can be pretty rough on you." Yeah, I knew something about that. Crow sat up straighter. "Anyway, they call me an officer, a general. But that's not like all the stuck-up, spit-polished elitism of the US military's officer corps. It's just a term for the sake of organization. There are other generals, but I don't know how many or what their names are. A grand general commands us. Among the officers, the truly trusted, the Brotherhood of the White Eagle has maybe hundreds. Among our ranks, thousands, and we're adding more all the time. The more the Fed cracks down, the more people join us. What's really great is that the Brotherhood is everywhere. We have people working in city and county government, law enforcement, even active-duty military positions. It's taken us years, even decades, to get to this point, but the organization is really coming together."

"Enough people to get me and Specialist Sparrow out of that prison," I said. "Thanks for coming to get me."

"Well, President Montaine gave me a direct order, but more than that, I owe your old man." This wasn't the first time Crow had mentioned his friendship with my father. Had Dad been a part of the Brotherhood? I wondered. Why hadn't he ever told me? Crow continued, "And we are all indebted to you for giving us this chance to stand up to the Fed. I'm only sorry that we lost so many. Sorry we lost your friend PFC Luchen." He stared down at his coffee. " 'For greater love hath no man than this, that a man lay down his life for his friends.' Nick Luchen went out a hero. And we won't forget him."

JoBell rubbed my back. "Or the five soldiers of the Brotherhood who also died to take that section of the fence down."

Crow nodded. "We lost seventeen men in all."

Seventeen? Seventeen of our people had died fighting the Fed at the Silver Sunset Resort? And who knew how many Fed soldiers had died trying to stop them? All of that just to release me and Sparrow?

No. As much as I hated to admit it, Sparrow had only been a bonus. President Montaine wanted me released so I could do more of that "We will give you a war" stuff. Back when this all started, when President Rodriguez demanded the investigation or arrest of the Battle of Boise shooters, I had thought about turning Montaine's offer of protection down. I doubted if I was worth all the trouble, the division and chaos, but I'd held out hope that people would find a way to work it all out peacefully. Now I wondered, if I had turned myself in back then, would all these people have died?

"Seventeen. How is that possible?" I whispered.

"Well, the first phase of the attack had the element of surprise," said Crow. "The Fed had set up antiaircraft machine guns at the top of the ski slopes, just inside a wire perimeter. We took those quietly. Your Sergeant Kemp led that assault and did a great job. His team turned the guns on the ski lodge and any Feds they could take out. Their job was to keep the Fed pinned down so your friend's boss could bring in the seaplane."

"We argued about using that plane for hours when we were planning it all," said JoBell. "People thought landing on the snow would crush the floats, but Mr. Brooks insisted it would work."

"At the same time, a whole platoon of Brotherhood soldiers attacked the main gate. We got inside, took out the guard shack, destroyed some tactical vehicles, and snatched some ammo."

"But Mr. Brooks had worried they wouldn't have a long-enough runway inside the fence," JoBell said. "Luchen led a small team to set off a charge and create a hole in the fence. We figured with the antiaircraft guns firing and the attack near the main gate, the Fed would be too distracted to worry about checking an out-of-the-way part of the perimeter fence." She rubbed the back of my neck. "We were wrong. I still can hardly believe what he did."

"But how did you know where me and Sparrow were?"

Crow sipped his coffee. "We received an anonymous tip from someone who claimed to be working inside. Someone who called himself Spartacus."

I sat up in my chair. "You staged a raid based on what some Fed said? What the hell were you thinking!?"

Crow laughed a little. "We were thinking the same thing you're thinking right now. Don't believe them. Don't trust them."

"But Danny," JoBell whispered. "The contact said you were mumbling about making out in the igloo and how it would be better in the bedroom and they wouldn't hear you in the guard tower. Nobody would know those silly place names except you."

I'd talked about making out in the igloo? What else had I said? I watched JoBell's face to see if she was upset, if she knew about what Becca and I had done, but she seemed fine.

"Which means that the contact was at least telling the truth that they had captured you alive," said Crow. "And it was clear that if you were still alive, you were dangerously close to telling them a lot of stuff that could hurt the cause."

"I didn't break!" I said. "I didn't tell them anything." It bothered me that Crow and especially JoBell thought I'd been about to give up. They had a point, though. I must have mumbled a few things. But who would have passed that information along to the Brotherhood, though? As far as I could tell, nobody even knew I was there except Alsovar, the doctor, and Captain Peterson.

"Babe, nobody is accusing you of anything," said JoBell.

I shook my head. I couldn't get my mind around what had happened, couldn't sort out what had been real and what had been hallucination. How had I gotten out of my cell? Peterson? No, TJ. Right? "Nobody. Nobody but Sparrow knows what it was like in there. What Alsovar did to us, and I'm not going to listen to people saying that —"

"You want a chance to get back at Major Alsovar?" Nathan Crow asked.

"What?"

"Do you hate him?" He locked eyes with me. "Do you want to get back at him for what he did to you and your friend?"

311

"Mr. Crow, this war isn't about revenge," JoBell said. "We're only trying to get them to leave us alone."

Crow didn't look away. "Fine. What if I said President Montaine wants you to help with a plan that will prevent Alsovar from doing to others what he did to you?"

JoBell nodded. "See, that's different. It's about doing what we have to to save lives. To prevent more atrocities. That's the kind of mind-set we need to hold on to."

I understood the point JoBell was trying to make, and I was glad she felt that way, that she hadn't lost so much of what made her wonderful that she'd given up on ideas like that. But I'm not gonna lie. I did want payback.

"I want revenge," Sparrow said from behind us. She leaned against the side of the archway that separated the kitchen from the living room and ran her hand back over her scalp. "I'm going to make that bastard hurt. I'm going to kill him for what he did to me. And for Luchen."

I gave Sparrow an understanding look, squeezed JoBell's hand, and then fixed my gaze on Crow again. "Let's do it. I'm in."

CHAPTER
TWENTY-SIX

"Wright!" Crocker spun away from a video game on an antique computer and jumped up out of his swivel chair. JoBell, Kemp, and Crow had led me to an upper room in the back of the pole barn, where, from the looks of things, Crocker was running the commo center. He had an ASIP III radio and what looked like his shortwave set up, along with the game. "Good morning, sir," he said to Crow. He smiled at me. "It's good to see you're okay. Feeling better?"

A shower, a breakfast, a clean change of clothes, and a cup of coffee had injected new life into me and helped me focus on something besides that horrible, hot, and sleepless room. That, and Crow's promise of revenge. "I'm okay."

A voice came on the radio. *"Alpha base, this is talon, three five two. Over."*

"Oh, hang on," Crocker said. He picked up a radio handset. "Talon, three five two, this is alpha base. Go ahead. Over."

"Alpha base, talon three five two. We're moving that load of M240 rounds. I'm hearing a different story on this from different people. Did you want those moved to charlie base or delta base? Over."

"Damn it. If I knew that sergeant's name, I'd find him and kick his ass." Crow stepped up to Crocker's radio and computer table. "You have the file pulled up there, Specialist?"

"Hang on a minute, sir." Crocker keyed the mike. "Talon three five two. Wait one. Over." He worked the mouse, opening folders and keying in passwords, running the antique computer like a pro. A spreadsheet came on-screen.

Crow ran his finger down a list of figures. "What's the lot number? Let's make sure they have the right shipment."

Crocker called the unit back and got the number. Crow checked it off the list. "Come on, guys." He grabbed the mike. "Talon three five two, this is talon actual. That shipment is not going to a base. Transport that ammo to firing position charlie forty-seven. How copy? Over."

"Talon actual. This is three five two. Roger. That's a good copy. Talon three five two, out."

"You got the radios working?" I asked.

Crocker picked up a metal device that was about four inches square and an inch thick. He petted it like a kitten. "When the Idaho Army sent operatives to link up with the Brotherhood, they gave them this Communication Security Encryption Protocol device. A COMSEP."

"Okay?" I said.

"It contains a bunch of codes. When it's connected to the radio, it encrypts the transmissions the same as every other radio that has been synched to those codes. It also makes our radio change frequencies over a hundred times per second at exactly the same rate as other radios on the network change. Protected this way, we're able to talk safely with any radio that's on the net and in range. We can communicate with just about all our bases and with Idaho Army operatives in the area."

"But tell him the best part." Sweeney came into the room. He unplugged his comm from a charging station by the computer.

Crocker shrugged. "The Idaho Army has configured this COMSEP to reprogram the Internet protocols on COMMPADS. Our comms are back online."

"And all charged up," Sweeney said as his comm turned on. "Good morning, Trixie."

"*Ooooooh, Eric.*" Digi-Trixie's naked body squirmed around in the lower right corner of his screen. "*Good morning, baby. You left me charging up when we should have spent the night together.*"

Crow shot an annoyed look at Sweeney. JoBell rolled her eyes and said, "Trixie, calm down, put your clothes back on, and become Hot Librarian Trixie. No. Just become . . . normal."

A simple brown dress instantly appeared on the digital-woman. "*She's jealous of what we have, Eric.*"

Sweeney put on a sad act. "JoBell made me add her to the voice control so she could boss Trixie around." He smiled at me. "How you feeling, buddy?"

"Better," I said.

"Private Sweeney, do you have somewhere to be?" Crow asked.

Sweeney's energy dimmed a little. "Oh, sure. I'm on guard duty in an hour, but I just wanted to check the news first."

"Check it somewhere else," said Crow.

"Right. Sorry." Sweeney headed down the stairs.

Crow smiled. "If we're not careful, we get too many people hanging out up here, and then we can't get anything done." He put his hand on my shoulder for a moment. "And what we have to do is really important."

JoBell squeezed my hand. "I'll get out of the way."

"No, stay," I said.

Crow nodded to Crocker, who handed me my old comm. "We made sure to grab this old thing before we abandoned the cabin." He plugged in the COMSEP and tapped a button on its screen. After a minute or so, the status bar showed 100 percent, and Crocker unplugged the little black box. "Should be go," Crocker said.

I nodded at him.

"Well, let's try this thing." I held my comm up. "Hank, you there?"

"Right here, buddy! My stars, it's been a month of Sundays since we've talked. I've released a new rootin' tootin' single since the last time you've been on. Would you like to hear it?"

Crow handed me a slip of paper with a comm number. "President Montaine is waiting to hear from you."

I let out a breath. "I guess I should have been expecting that. Hank, I need to make a video call."

"Well, yippee ki yay, let's have the number!" I gave it to him.

A flat, deep computer voice picked up. *"Enter code now."* Crow handed a different slip of paper to me and I read a series of numbers and letters from that. *"Authenticating. Please stand by."*

I waited for at least ten minutes. Crocker started telling me about his part in the attack on the ski lodge. Crow had wanted him to stay behind to monitor the radios, but he'd insisted on being on the mountaintop machine gun team.

"Thanks, Crocker. Thanks for coming to get me. I wish —"

"Private Wright?"

I snapped my attention back to my comm. President Montaine smiled on screen. When I'd vid-talked with him before, he'd been at his desk or at a podium in the governor's mansion. All I could see behind him now was a gray cinder-block wall. I said, "It's good to see you again, Mr. President."

Montaine smiled even wider. *"Are you kidding me? It's good to see you. When the United States reported you dead, we were crushed. Then we saw you alive on that video and realized you'd survived the invasion. We had a little party that night. Emphasis on little. Everything is in short supply."*

"It's been rough, Mr. President."

He looked down. "*I know. I am sorry for so much suffering on both sides. Idaho has lost too many good soldiers and airmen. I swear to God, Private, I'll never forget their sacrifice. And I'm sorry we couldn't hold the north. Sorry you've all had to live under United States occupation. Sorry . . . for what they just put you through.*"

"I'm okay," I said. Would everyone treat me like one of Mom's old fragile ceramic horse knickknacks for the rest of my life? I nodded at the former sheriff, who sat on a metal folding chair with one leg crossed over his knee. "Nathan Crow says there's a way I can get . . . justice?"

"*I'm glad you brought that up.*" Montaine leaned toward the camera. "*Private, we're running out of time. The United States is planning a massive attack any day. We believe they haven't hit us full strength since their failure to take southern Idaho because President Griffith wants to make a show of trying to negotiate a peace settlement with me. She's also holding out hope that Oklahoma governor Martha Fergus will veto Oklahoma's nullification bill. As soon as Governor Fergus signs the bill into law and President Griffith has nothing to lose, the US military will hit Idaho and probably Texas and Oklahoma pretty hard.*"

That was what Alsovar had said as well. "Mr. President, what chance do we have against all that?"

"*A good chance. Because we're going to make our move first with plenty of surprises they aren't counting on. We'll throw them off-balance and seize the advantage. That's where I need your help, Private Wright.*"

"Sir?"

"*Like I said before, for better or worse, you've become a symbol of our hope. You're an inspiration to all of us who are fighting for our freedom, fighting for our right to exist. The people of Idaho are* motivated by your struggle. We share it. And so, at the right moment, I want you to deliver a live address to all of our allies. You'll tell Idaho to rise up and fight back."

My cheeks felt hot. "Um, Mr. President, I'll follow orders, but I don't think I'm the right guy to make some speech. I'm just a private."

The president folded his hands in front of him. *"Private, I don't think you realize how close we were to losing this whole thing a few months ago. Fed forces were pushing on almost all our borders. They were beginning to make headway, especially on the northern front up by White Bird. Morale was at an all-time low. Then we saw that video, the one with you screaming back in defiance of the United States. We played it across all the networks we were building here in Idaho. Everything changed. Our forces fought back harder. Even our pilots had more success stopping Fed flybys. People rally around you, Private Wright. Right now, a lot of folks are unsure about joining this fight. They see you as one of them, someone who lives the way they do, but stands up against the United States just the same. You inspire them. Hell, you inspire me."*

I held up my hands. "Okay, okay. Um, Mr. President, could you please stop with all that kind of talk?" Then I realized what I'd just said. Since my life had been twisted inside out at the Battle of Boise, I'd talked to the governor of my state probably more than any other private in the history of the National Guard. But I still couldn't give orders to the president. "Um, sir. Respectfully."

President Montaine roared a big bear of a laugh. *"Yes, sir, Private, sir."* He saluted me. *"Relax, Private Wright. If you've met the Brotherhood, you know that in this war, we tolerate a little more informality."*

"Still, I shouldn't talk to the president like that."

"Well, I haven't been the president long. So how about it? Will you give the word to start the final fight against the United States?"

"I'll do whatever you tell me to do, Mr. President, but . . . I never did too good on my speeches in English class. Best I ever got was a C."

"That's no problem, Private. As long as you can remember to use the code phrase, 'We will give them a war. Rise up. Rise up. Rise up.' That's the phrase that will set everything in motion. Once you say that, we're on our way to victory."

"But how will me saying a few words make any difference in —"

"We're not relying on inspiration alone. We have a strategy. I've been working with Governor Fergus in Oklahoma and Governor Percy of Texas as well as the leadership of a couple other states. Your speech will be the signal for our allies around the country to begin a surprise counteroffensive against the United States. Our plan is for you to give the signal at zero six hundred hours the morning after the Oklahoma Senate passes nullification. After that, the United States will never be the same. Mr. Crow will have more instructions about how to make that transmission. I'm asking you to trust me like you did before. We're all in this together. Can I count on you?"

"I'll do the best I can, Mr. President."

"That's all any of us can do. That's what you've been doing since this whole thing started. And the thing is, Private Wright, your best is pretty damn good."

"What should we do when the fight begins? We were hitting some convoys here and there, I mean, before me and Specialist Sparrow were captured. I've been kind of out of the loop since then."

President Montaine nodded. "I'm sending classified orders to your inbox. The code to access them will be the same one you used to call me. The file will give your team instructions. In the meantime, work with Mr. Crow and his Brotherhood. *They're organized and ready for the fight.*"

"Roger that, Mr. President."

"*Zero six hundred the morning after the Oklahoma nullification bill passes. Just talk about why you're fighting against the United States and why people should join you. Then give the code phrase. Be ready. It's time to win this war. President Montaine, out.*"

The image of Montaine vanished, replaced by an image of a gold, snow-capped mountain with sunbeams shining behind it, enclosed in a circle with the words IDAHO! OUR LIVES FOR THEE written on a ribbon near the bottom. The circle floated in the center of a field of dark blue.

"Hank," I said. "Open my inbox."

"*You bet, partner. Woo-wie! You got friends in high places. Urgent message from President Montaine. How'd you like to watch my latest music video while you —*"

"Shut up, Hank," I said. Maybe it was time to get a new digi-assistant. Maybe a digi-soldier or something. I looked up at Crow, Crocker, and JoBell. "We better start getting ready."

The next three days were full of tense preparation. I slept through most of that first day, only interrupted by nightmares two or three times. After that, my friends and I helped the Brotherhood distribute ammo, loaded up magazines for our own weapons, and went over our plan for the coming fight.

The night before the mission was one of those warm mid-March evenings that come along sometimes. In the old days, nights like these would tease me, reminding me that the end of the school year was just around the corner. Now my friends and I were out back behind the pole barn on an old, broke-down, mid-seventies Ford pickup, eating MREs for supper. Sweeney and Becca sat on top of the cab. TJ and Cal sat on opposite bed walls. JoBell and I stood, using the tailgate as a table. It might have been any old back-road party, except we didn't have any beer and we were all carrying assault rifles.

"Man, I hate politics," Cal said. "I hate watching the news all the time, waiting to see if the Oklahoma Senate is going to outlaw the ID card. I mean, what if they don't pass it? What do we do then?"

"Cal, they're going to pass it." JoBell opened her heated packet of beef stew. "They have enough votes. They're just drawing out the debate while Montaine and his allies get ready."

Cal drew his sword and looked it over. The blade shined in the fading sunlight. He wore that thing all the time. "I wish they'd hurry up. I'm ready to stick it to those bastards."

TJ squeezed cheese from a packet onto his cracker. It came out all oily. "Gross. What the hell?"

"You gotta squish up the packet first to get it mixed right," I said.

TJ shrugged and pushed a lock of greasy brown hair out of his face. "Crow says this is it. They think they can kick the US military out of Idaho."

"Doesn't seem possible," said Sweeney.

"On our own, maybe not," JoBell said. "But he says when the time comes, the Fed will have too much else to deal with. They won't be able to hold on to Idaho. With the war here and overseas, the US military is spread too thin, and if they have to also cover Texas and Oklahoma . . . Well, Idaho's not the most valuable state they could lose." JoBell said all that with the same fire in her voice she used to have about staying out of the war. Had she changed her mind because of what Alsovar had done to me? Funny, after all this time hoping JoBell would understand why I had to fight for Idaho, even hoping that she'd join us, I now wished she wouldn't.

"But it isn't like the war will be over," I said.

"No," said JoBell. "But the Fed won't want to spend a lot of resources trying to keep control of little places like Freedom Lake."

I decided that was a good enough introduction for something I wanted to say. "Guys, there's something I've been meaning to tell you," I said. "On the night before the barbed wire bomb attack . . ." I took my fiancée's hand. "The night me and JoBell got engaged, I made the decision . . . *we* made the decision to get out of the war."

"What?" Cal said.

"What are you talking about?" asked Sweeney.

"So you're not with us for this fight?" TJ said. "The whole plan starts with you."

"And why the hell would you want to chicken out now?" Cal asked. "We're right on the edge of winning."

"Guys, give him a chance to explain," Becca said. She looked a little sad somehow, but held out a hand, inviting me to continue.

I nodded at Becca. "I was going to do the barbed wire bomb and then find someplace safe to go and hide and wait out the war. JoBell's been wanting me to get out for a long time, and when she was shot, I was so scared of losing her, I realized what's really important. JoBell, and you guys."

"Yeah, well, Jo didn't seem that out of the war when we attacked the ski lodge to save your ass," Cal said.

JoBell dropped her spoon on the tailgate. "I was going to save my boyfr — my future *husband*, Cal!"

Becca looked away. Sweeney patted her back.

"Yeah, but what about now?" Cal asked her. "You been planning on going on this op. Can we even count on you? Are you in this or not?"

Maybe this was my chance to deal with one thing that had been bothering me since I got out of Alsovar's cell. "She's not. JoBell, I think you should stay behind on this one."

"What? I can handle myself," JoBell said. "I'm not afraid."

"It's not that," I said. "And you *should* be afraid, by the way. I just . . . If this is going to be our last battle, you might as well stay out of it."

"I've seen Crow's photos of the Fed military buildup," JoBell said. "They're about to launch another serious attack. If we can get them out of Idaho, I think it will ultimately save lives. One last push, and then we can find some peace."

"But won't we be helping make the war worse?" Becca said. "Won't a lot more people die?"

JoBell pushed her hair back. "The war is going to escalate anyway. The attack is coming no matter what we do. Our only chance of survival is to do this mission."

Cal stood up in the bed of the truck. "The war ain't gonna be over after tomorrow! We push them out of the state — I mean country, we still got a war on our hands! You can't just quit, Wright. This is bullshit!"

"Yeah, Wright," said Sweeney. "This might have been something to bring up *after* the mission."

Cal pointed at me. His shoulders heaved with every deep breath. "Ever since Boise, we've been with you all the way —"

"That's my point!" I said. "I don't want JoBell or any of you risking your lives for me anymore. One last hit. We take out Alsovar, and then we gotta get out of this."

"It ain't about you, Danny! You dumb shit! I'm doing this for all of us, for my future kids. So we can be free and shit! Damn it! I can't believe you don't want to at least get back at these bastards for what they did to you!"

Becca put her hand on Cal's arm. "Hey, come on. Calm down."

"No, you calm down! I ain't listening to any more of this bullshit. Danny, a while back you was saying how we gotta be humane to the

Fed. Don't take 'em out with my sword. Then they locked you in a room and tortured you. Almost killed you." Cal jumped down off the truck. "Who knows what they did to Sparrow. She won't talk about it. But you can bet those filthy sons of bitches got off on it! You still think we should be so nice? Still think there's rules to all of this? I can't believe you're quitting. This is bullshit!" He started walking past me. I tried to stop him from leaving, but he slammed both hands into my chest and knocked me on my ass. "Go to hell! Should've left you in that cell!"

"Cal!" Becca yelled.

But he'd stormed off. Sparrow came out of the wood line, her M4 slung from her shoulder. "You know this is still a secret rebel military base. You want to shut the hell up before the Fed hears us?"

"Sorry," Becca said.

JoBell reached to help me up, but I waved her away and stayed on the ground. Nobody said anything for a moment.

"Well," TJ said. "That could have gone better."

✓—• *with the worldwide coverage of ABC News."*

"Good evening. I'm Dale Acosta, and this . . . is Night Time. *A nation on the brink. And this time we're not talking about a civil war in the Middle East, but about the desperate situation right here in America. As we reported a few months ago, the governors of Vermont, Maine, and New Hampshire formed the New England Peace Alliance, activating their National Guard units and ordering them to disregard any federal orders that might send them into combat against other Americans, including the people of Idaho. Then President Griffith federalized every Reserve unit in the military, and when NEPA soldiers and airmen refused to comply with the federal activation, the president cut all funding and began the immediate disarmament of all New England Reserve components, effectively disbanding the National Guard and Reserve forces of three states. Now the states of Massachusetts, Connecticut, and Rhode Island have committed to NEPA as well. Joining us live via satellite from several secure locations are the governors of the New England Peace Alliance states, Dennis Milam of Connecticut, Preston Loomis of Maine, Doug Palmer of Massachusetts, Madeline Hanson of New Hampshire, Leonard Cahill of Rhode Island, and Parker Shoemaker of Vermont. Welcome, all.*

"Governors, I'll get right to it. The law is pretty clear that the president has the authority to activate National Guard units for the purposes of stopping rebellion in the United States. Isn't the refusal to allow New England National Guard forces to activate really an act of rebellion in itself? Governor Milam of Connecticut, you have your hand up."

"That's a good question, Dale. As you know, Connecticut was late in joining NEPA precisely because our people were concerned that it was some kind of rebel organization. However, we did not want to put our National Guard soldiers in the position where they

would be required to fight Americans. The order to help in the fight against other Americans is the only order we sought to counter-mand. That's why federal forces are meeting with no resistance as they seize weapons, ammunition, and equipment from armories and airfields across New England."

"And Dale, if I may, in the state of Maine, about 30 percent of Guardsmen did volunteer to answer the president's call to federal duty. I'm told that figure is pretty consistent across New England. We certainly did not stop them."

"Governor Cahill?"

"Thanks, Dale. The men and women of the Rhode Island National Guard didn't sign up to kill Americans. They enlisted to pro-tect Americans. The New England Peace Alliance is only trying to protect our soldiers. Nothing more, and certainly nothing less."

"Joining us now via satellite from Washington is Vice President Jim Barnes, formerly the senior representative from New Hampshire. Mr. Vice President, you have defended NEPA's position. Doesn't that represent a split from President Griffith?"

"It's not a split at all, Dale. Look, the fine governors you have on the show tonight have expressed valid concerns on behalf of their constituents. Now President Griffith and I are really the only two leaders in the country working together across party lines, except for the leadership of the New England Peace Alliance. Together the governors, the president, and I came up with this temporary solu-tion, redistributing combat assets from New England to where they are needed, while still leaving the National Guard in the New England states prepared and equipped to handle natural disasters or other problems."

"Excuse me, Mr. Vice President, but you've been a supporter of a tougher war on the Idaho rebels. Doesn't this peace plan repre-sent a total one-eighty from your previous position?"

"The redistribution of combat assets from New England is only one part of an aggressive solution to the present problem. A lot of the other components of that solution are classified, but what's important to remember is that the people of America, certainly the people of New England, are demanding peace and leadership, and I aim to provide them with both. •—⋏

Texas Infantry: Fighting Idaho rebels. But if my home state is attacked, me and other Texans in my unit will abandon our posts. #TexasTrue

50 minutes ago   Reply - Shout Out

•—⋏

Steel Rain: Texas Infantry, you shouldn't post that kind of thing online. The government is watching everything.

45 minutes ago   Reply - Shout Out

•—⋏

Texas Infantry: I'm not afraid to take a stand. I've seen what is happening in Idaho. I won't let it happen to my home and family. #TexasTrue

43 minutes ago   Reply - Shout Out

•—⋏

⋏—• *I'm Teresa Bradley for KGWN Cheyenne Action Eye News, about ten minutes south of Cheyenne at the Wyoming-Colorado border. Ever since the late President Rodriguez enacted a blockade against Idaho nine months ago, federal military personnel have been restricted from entering our state, but they have been allowed to freely move to and from F. E. Warren Air Force Base near Cheyenne. However, traffic heading into the base has recently increased dramatically, with large military convoys coming north out of Colorado. This possibly confirms a recent leak from White*

House insiders that President Griffith is tired of requesting that Montana and Wyoming allow troops to enter the state, and she may be preparing to force the issue. I want to see if our KGWN cameras can get a look at this. As you can see, Wyoming Highway Patrol and National Guard personnel are assembling on this service road beside the interstate and in this nearby RV lot. There appear to be armored personnel carriers and armored Humvees with machine guns massing on the Wyoming side."

"Excuse me, ma'am, but I'm going to have to ask you to shut down your camera and vacate the area."

"Have we done something wrong, officer? Can you tell us why all these Wyoming soldiers and police officers have gathered here? Are they preparing to forcibly close the Wyoming border to all federal troops?"

"Ma'am, we need you to move along. We're here to protect you from Idaho rebels."

"Idaho rebels? Idaho is hundreds of miles away, clear on the other side of the state. That's completely ridiculous."

"Ma'am, that's all I can tell you."

"Well, no help from Wyoming Highway Patrol, but a potentially dangerous situation on the Colorado-Wyoming border. Teresa Bradley, KGWN News. •⎯ᴧ⎯

⎯ᴧ⎯• The police have arrested everyone down by the Columbia River who are trying to film this. Smashing comms right on the street. So I'm in big trouble if I get caught, but people got to see this. Something is happening. You can see this huge ship, like a battleship or something — I mean, not a battleship, but this sucker isn't a pleasure boat, those are some serious guns — four of these ships, just rolling upstream past Portland. If I zoom in . . . there it is. LCS 1, USS Freedom. LCS 3, USS Fort Worth. LCS 5, USS Milwaukee.

The last one . . . LCS 7 . . . I think . . . USS Detroit. *I heard that Idaho had scuttled some barges upriver so the Fed couldn't get through, but maybe those have been cleared out, or maybe these ships are going to shoot them out. Look at the size of those forward guns. I don't know . . . If you're watching this, stay away from the river. There's trouble on the Columbia.* •––ᴧ–

––ᴧ–• in the CNN Idaho Crisis Situation Room. Nothing has been confirmed, but we are getting reports from anonymous sources that some federal soldiers in Idaho who posted shouts sympathetic to Texas opposition have been relieved of duty and confined. The White House has not commented on these reports, but •––ᴧ–

AMY DILL-HIETZ ★ ★ ★ ★ ★

Four of these Littoral Combat Ships just rolled past The Dalles, Oregon. I found this picture on the web. The rebels holding out in Lewiston don't have a chance.

★ ★ ★ ★ ☆ This Post's Star Average 4.75   [Star Rate][Comment]   15 minutes ago

Varen Johansen ★ ★ ★ ☆

Federal tanks, Stryker fighting vehicles, armored gun Hummers, and a hell of a lot of troops are staging in Bushnell, Nebraska, less than 15 minutes from Wyoming. The town has been evacuated "due to safety concerns." They won't say what those safety concerns are, but it's clear. There getting ready to roll into Wyoming. Next stop, Cheyenne. If your in Cheyenne, you should get the hell out of there. They're coming soon.

★ ★ ★ ☆ ☆ This Comment's Star Average 3.13   [Star Rate]   10 minutes ago

Alexandria Paulson ★ ☆ ☆ ☆ ☆

Varen buddy you can't be posting stuff like this. About SOldiers and where there at. I had a friend who was doing that. His comm and all his screens shut off. The internet company said his account was temperarily suspended for security concerns cause of the Unity Act.

★ ★ ★ ☆ ☆ This Comment's Star Average 3.13   [Star Rate]   7 minutes ago

⌁—• *CBS News live coverage of the Oklahoma Senate action continues. I'm Simon Pentler. Federal officials attempting to enforce Unity Act prohibitions against so-called dangerous public assemblies are struggling tonight with rallies in full force all over Oklahoma City and around the country. The nation's military and law enforcement communities are on high alert. Republican delays on voting on this bill mysteriously evaporated yesterday. Now the debate is over, and the Oklahoma Senate has come to the moment of decision. President Griffith has made it clear that the federal government will not tolerate any further nullification of federal laws at the state level, and many speculate she has not ordered military enforcement of the Federal ID Card Act in Texas, which passed a law to nullify the act over a month ago, in hopes of being able to peaceably persuade Oklahoma not to follow suit. Bear in mind, of course, that if the Oklahoma Senate passes this nullification bill, Governor Martha Fergus still has the final say as to whether or not it becomes* law. Governor Fergus has said only that she will consider the bill carefully based on its own merits, regardless of, quote, "federal intimidation tactics," end quote. Many have speculated that her choice of words might be an indication that — hold on. Yes.

Ladies and gentlemen, the last vote is in. It is a tie! The vote is twenty-four in favor of nullification and twenty-four against. The outcome is much less along partisan lines than had been anticipated. Twenty of the state's thirty-six Republican senators voted in favor of nullification, joined by four of the state's twelve Democrats. Eight Democrats opposed the bill, along with sixteen Republicans. Oklahoma law now requires the lieutenant governor to vote to break the tie. Lieutenant Governor Toby Lenthin is in the Oklahoma Senate chamber tonight. He is expected to — wait a minute.

And there it is. One of the longest special sessions in the history of the Oklahoma legislature is over. Lieutenant Governor Lenthin has voted in favor of nullification. Under Oklahoma law, Governor Fergus has five days to veto the bill. If she signs the bill or allows the five days to pass without her signature, Oklahoma will join Texas and Idaho in open defiance of the federal government. And now those senators who were opposed to the bill are walking out of the chamber together, singing a rather mournful rendition of "America the Beautiful," on their way out to the capitol grounds to join anti-nullification protestors there.

As there is no comment from Governor Fergus at this hour, we welcome to the CBS newsroom an expert in states' rights issues and constitutional law. Dr. Hernando •⎯⋏⎯

⎯⋏⎯• WE INTERRUPT ALL BROADCASTS AND TRANSMISSIONS FOR AN IMPORTANT MESSAGE. LIVE FROM THE OVAL OFFICE, HERE IS PRESIDENT GRIFFITH."

"More than a hundred and forty years ago, our ancestors brought to an end the bloodiest war this continent had ever known, and, as Abraham Lincoln said, we as a people resolved at that time that government of the people, by the people, for the people should not perish from the earth.

"We now stand on the brink of a second terrible civil war, testing whether the rule of law and its accompanying general welfare and domestic tranquility — whether the United States of America itself — can long endure. As many of you know, the decision as to whether or not Oklahoma obeys the United States Constitution by respecting the Supremacy Clause now rests entirely with Oklahoma governor Martha Fergus.

"I want to be perfectly clear. Nullification is illegal, and if the governor signs the nullification bill, the full power of the United States military will be brought to bear in order to make sure federal law is carried out in both Texas and Oklahoma. Personally, I abhor violence and value peace above almost everything else. However, as president, it is my duty to carry out the laws set forth by the US Constitution and by the Congress, and, if necessary, I will order the most overwhelming military force in order to perform that duty.

"Many of you might be wondering why there is so much disagreement over something as seemingly simple as an identification card. Certainly, it does not seem as if blood should be spilt for the enforcement of such a law. But what is at issue is something far more important than an ID card. We cannot, under any circumstances, allow states to decide for themselves which federal laws must be obeyed and which can be disregarded. If states are allowed to disregard the Federal ID Card Act today, then what would stop them from tomorrow deciding to withhold all nationally beneficial federal revenue? What would stop states from disregarding federal laws that provide for the equal treatment of all its citizens? Our very unity as a country, the form and function of this nation, is necessarily predicated on the establishment of constitutional federal authority over state governments.

"And now, I would like to make a personal appeal directly to Oklahoma governor Martha Fergus. Governor Fergus, you have said that you will carefully consider this nullification bill regardless of federal intimidation tactics. I assure you, the federal government does not wish to intimidate you or anyone else. Instead, I am begging you, Governor Fergus, to please think carefully about the implications of your decisions. Just as you would not tolerate a county in Oklahoma blatantly disregarding a law you had signed, I cannot allow states to willfully disobey laws passed by the United States government. Governor Martha Fergus, the fate of the nation lies in your hands. I ask you, leader to leader, person to person, to please save us all from chaos and anarchy. Please save our democracy.

"People of Oklahoma, my fellow Americans, I ask you to prevent disunity and violence. Oppose nullification. Contact your elected officials and representatives to demand that they oppose nullification. I opened my message tonight by quoting from President Lincoln's Gettysburg Address, and there are no better words to close. 'Let us highly resolve to be dedicated to that unfinished work that our honored dead have so far fought for. Let us be dedicated to the great task remaining before us, that those who gave the last full measure of devotion shall not have died in vain, that the United States of America will live on. •⟿

⟿•————————————————————————————————

NatureLois: Griffith. You're no Lincoln.

1 day ago   Reply - Shout Out
——
                                                                    •⟿

D_Thompson09: Hey Griffith, remember what happened to Lincoln!

about 8 hours ago   Reply - Shout Out

M Hawker74: @D_Thompson09 I thought she sounded great! Inspiring. #UnityAct

about 8 hours ago   Reply - Shout Out

CHAPTER

TWENTY-SEVEN

At zero four thirty on the day of my mission, I walked through the dark morning along the perimeter trail around alpha base. Even though I hadn't been posted to guard duty, I'd still been out there all night, and my hand ached from squeezing the grip of my rifle.

Had the world been normal as recently as last summer? Now we were about to go into combat again. One of my best friends hated me. And by the end of the day, a lot of people would be dead. Everything had gone to shit, and I was pretty sure it was about to hit an industrial-sized fan.

"Thunder," a voice challenged me from out of the shadows.

"Badger." I quickly gave the password. It was JoBell. She was one of the very few who could have made it this close to me through the woods without making a sound, even while carrying that thirty-pound monster rifle she'd been practicing with.

She joined me on the trail and kissed me. "What are you doing out here?" she said. "Nobody goes —"

"Nobody goes alone. I know rule number one," I said. "But I spent some time visiting Lightning in the horse barn, and guards are posted about every thirty yards. I haven't been alone all night." JoBell slid her arm around me. Her warmth pushed away the night's chill. "Except for Alsovar's hell chamber, I haven't been alone much since this war began."

JoBell started to move away from me. "Sorry. Do you want me to go?"

There was playfulness in her voice, but I pulled her close anyway. "No. I meant what I said back then about wanting to spend my whole life with you. But I'd like us to be alone together, not just to mess around." I laughed a little. "I mean, I *like* messing around with you, but more than that, not to have to be on duty all the time. Not to have to live with strangers."

"I understand," she said.

"But even if we could be together, have our own place, and no more of this damned war, even if we win . . . JoBell, what kind of life are we going to have? What's left for us? My shop is shot to hell. You didn't get to finish high school. All your plans —"

She kissed me. No quick peck. No comforting consolation prize. She devoured me, sucking my breath and soul and any tiny idea of resistance. Good thing my rifle had a shoulder strap. I let it hang while I wrapped my arms around my girl, while my hands slid up under her coat and sweatshirt. She gasped against their cold until her warmth melted the ice in my fingers. "Danny, all my plans are nothing without you." She took a step back, taking hold of my hands. "We get through this. Together. For now, that's all that matters." JoBell dropped my hands and held up the rifle she had slung from her shoulder. "See, I learned something while you were locked up. If I can't live without you, I have to get active in protecting you. I have to help you through this one last fight."

We walked hand in hand along the trail in silence for a while, and it felt like old times. Except for the guns. Always the guns. They brought on a weird mix of feelings. I knew we needed them, and if I was totally honest with myself, I'd have to admit that a part of me liked the power I felt when I carried a gun. But they ruined everything, and often I was just so tired of always having them around. "Remember when we used to go —"

"For those long walks? Yeah. Way back when we were first dating." She squeezed my hand.

"On the railroad tracks," I said. "For miles out of town."

"We talked about everything. I told you about my mom and her damned dentist before anybody knew she was leaving us for him. You listened to me like no one else ever had."

"You were . . . You *are* interesting to listen to."

"I began to fall in love with you on those walks, Danny."

"Thunder." A man spoke from down the trail. The next guard.

"Badger," I said. Silence fell as we walked past him. He sat on a stump with a SAW resting on a bipod on a little dirt berm in front of him.

"I think I fell in love with you the first time we danced together," I said to JoBell when we'd cleared the guard. "Freshman homecoming."

"What? No way," she said. "The first dance?"

"The third song of our first dance. I still remember you standing there in front of me wearing that silver dress and the corsage I bought you."

"The silly pin-on one that you picked out instead of one I could wear on my wrist." She smiled.

I laughed a little. "Yeah, it was so hard to pin on your dress. I was so afraid of poking you with the pin."

"And of my father."

"Yeah. And there wasn't all that much fabric at the top of that dress. But we worked it out. And you were an angel on that dance floor. Hank McGrew's 'Cowgirl Lasso My Heart' started playing, and I didn't even have to ask you to dance." I put my arms around her right then on the trail.

JoBell leaned her head on my chest. "Mmm. I remember." She started us swaying.

"What are you doing?" I asked.

She kissed me and looked into my eyes. "Dancing with you."

For a few minutes the whole world left us again. The memory of old songs carried us along as we pressed our bodies together, sharing our warmth, and slowly turned, like we were hanging there, floating in space.

Then our slung rifles clicked together. The sound yanked me back to my world at war. A thousand worries ripped through my mind right then, little movie clips of all the ways JoBell could get hurt or worse. But she was the best shooter I'd ever met, and she'd already saved me during our escape from the ski lodge. I had to trust her.

The sky was just beginning to lighten. I looked at her, all bundled up against the cold, with her blond hair pulled back in a rough ponytail. She had just rolled out of bed before the toughest test of our lives, not all dolled up like for prom or something. Still, my JoBell was dazzlingly beautiful. "I love you," I said.

"I love you more," she answered.

"Thunder." Becca's voice came from behind the trees.

"Badger," JoBell and I said together.

Becca timidly stepped out onto the trail, almost as cautious as a doe in hunting season. She approached us, armed with a battered M4, the ugly opposite of her purple butterfly hair clip. "Hey, Jo," she said in a near whisper. "Danny."

JoBell put her arm around her, rubbing her back to keep her warm. "Hey, baby. What are you doing out here so early?"

"Hardly slept all night," Becca said. "It's almost time anyway."

I sighed. "A part of me wishes it could be simpler, that I could just take out Alsovar and the local Fed. If I do this, launch this big nationwide action, a lot of people are going to die."

"A lot of people are going to die anyway," JoBell said. "This fight is going to happen with or without us. It's better if we strike first and get it over with. Then maybe fewer people will get hurt."

"Or the right people will be saved," said Becca. "'Cause I made up my mind, if it's us or them, I'm saving you guys."

In the morning gray, I could just make out that look of determination in Becca's eyes, the same expression she had riding Lightning around barrels at the rodeo. Becca and JoBell had both joined the fight completely, and I knew that meant a certain light had gone out inside them. The commandment, the old moral certainty that we'd learned in school and church about the absolute evil of killing, had no place in what we would have to do that day.

A twig snapped out in the woods. The three of us crouched down and readied our weapons. Another stick broke. The rustle in the shadows grew louder as someone moved closer.

"Thunder." I spoke quietly, but my voice sliced the silence like a knife.

"Wright, is that you?"

The three of us looked at each other. "Cal," we said together.

"Badger, I guess," Sweeney said, following Cal onto the trail. "Though following this ox through the woods, I don't think we really need to bother with the password stuff."

"Good thing we don't gotta mess around in the woods today." Cal wore jeans and a plain black sweatshirt. He was carrying the M240 Bravo machine gun, his sword hanging from his belt. Draped with belts of ammo, he looked like one of those mercenary guys from some action hero movie.

"Hey, Wright . . ." Cal's boot scraped the ground. "Hey. You know."

Becca wrapped Cal in a big hug, leaning her head on his chest and looking at me. "Cal's sorry for getting so mad at you last night."

The big guy shrugged. "I get what you were saying. I just . . ."

"It's cool, dude," I said. Cal and I had argued before. What friends hadn't? But we never stayed mad for long.

Cal coughed and nodded toward JoBell's .50-cal rifle. "How you holding up with that big thing?"

"There's nothing I can't hit with this baby."

I bit my lip. It wasn't "things" she'd be shooting at today.

"It's five a.m. TJ, Sparrow, and Kemp have the vehicle up and running. We gotta get going," said Sweeney. The war had taken away the smooth-talking ladies' man, leaving this sharp-looking Asian kid dressed all in black, carrying an M4 with a nine mil in a leg holster.

"I wish there was some way I could get you guys out of this," I said. "Give you back your normal lives somehow."

"We're with you all the way, brother," Cal said. He strummed his M240 like a guitar.

"Yeah, dude," Sweeney said. "No matter how you think this all went down, we got into it together. Long as we got each other's backs, we'll always come out on top."

Becca and JoBell nodded in agreement.

A lot of people were going to die today. And I would do my damnedest to make sure most of the bodies belonged to the enemy.

Back at the house, Sergeant Kemp, Specialist Sparrow, and TJ met us out front by a Humvee that the Brotherhood had stolen from the Fed. A year ago, I would have wished TJ wasn't coming along, but the guy had really done an awesome job throughout the war. He'd risked his ass by staying in the civilian world with the Fed everywhere, moving information and building a network of resistance. Today he would put that network to use. I was glad to have him on my team.

Crow marched across the gravel lot toward the house, all business. "Sergeant Kemp, is your team ready for Operation Flashpoint?"

"Roger that," said the sergeant.

"Private Wright?"

"We're up, but I still think it's weird they're naming the whole operation after us."

Crow smiled. "It's not named after you. You're just kicking it off, so we might as well give you the call sign. If you're ready, I'll call in the perimeter guard." He smoothed his mustache. "We're going to need every man."

"And woman," JoBell said.

Crow ignored her. "My unit will be in position for phase two by the time you give the signal."

"Roger that," I said.

"Let's squeeze into the clown car, then," said Sergeant Kemp.

This time Kemp had picked Cal for our driver. He climbed in behind the wheel, placing his M240 in the little flat space to his right. Kemp went around to the co-driver seat up front. The rest of my team moved into their places. TJ was assigned to the dinky SAW in the gun turret. Sparrow squeezed in next to him to man the turret's .50-cal.

She grabbed my arm and stopped me before I took my seat. "Listen. I know we both want Alsovar dead. The first one who sees him, shoots him. That's it. No heroics. No speeches. No extra risk. It won't do any good to die before we can take him out."

"Yes, Specialist," I said. She started toward the Humvee. "Sparrow?" She stopped and faced me. "Are you sure you're okay?" I said.

"No." She narrowed her eyes.

I nodded, and the two of us took our positions in the armored Humvee, heading back into the war.

✓—• All Idaho units, all Idaho units. This is rattlesnake two two. Rattlesnake two two is go to execute firing sequence. Rattlesnake two two, out. •—✓

✓—• As you can see, Tom, the scuttled barges that have sealed off the Columbia/Snake River corridor for months are nearly cleared. Soon this portion of the river will be navigable again, allowing these four warships to continue upstream to Lewiston, Idaho, a city held by insurgents but completely surrounded by US military forces since they entered northern Idaho back in November. Each of these ships is equipped with a fifty-seven-millimeter gun firing thirteen-pound shells, four fifty-caliber heavy machine guns, two thirty-millimeter chain guns, a surface-to-air missile system, a rocket launcher, and two well-armed helicopters. All of that, in addition to possibly a hundred troops on each ship, will present a serious challenge for rebels holding out in Lewiston, Idaho. •—✓

✓—• from an antique computer I found in the basement of the Royal Oak Public Library in Detroit. I couldn't use my comm or a screen at my house to make this recording for fear of being branded a rebel by the Unity Act. But I'm not a rebel. None of us in the Videos for Peace Campaign are rebels. We only want a cease-fire. This video campaign is a virtual peace rally that doesn't break the law against large meetings. I'm asking you. We're all begging the leaders of this country to please stop the fighting. This isn't about politics. It's about saving our society for future generations. •—✓

✓—• All units, all units, this is talon five one. In position. Target in sight. Talon five one, out. •—✓

⌐—• It's 8:47 a.m. here in New York. Thanks for joining us on NBC's Every Day. At the top of the hour, we'll be joined by chef Wynn Haverly, who will show us some ways to make our food budget stretch further — an important skill as the national unrest has created food shortages in a number of cities. But first, leading our news this morning, the country waits with bated breath as Oklahoma governor Martha Fergus is still behind closed doors, trying to decide whether to sign her state's nullification bill. After President Griffith's address to the nation last night and with reports of military movement around the country, many worry that Governor Fergus's signing of the bill would result in the Idaho conflict expanding to other parts of the nation. For more on that, we go to •—⌐

TWENTY-EIGHT

When we reached our destination, TJ left to implement his part of the plan, Sparrow stayed in the turret, and Kemp moved behind the wheel of the parked Humvee. The rest of us made our way up the freezing cold steel lattice of one of the legs of the Freedom Lake water tower. I led the way with JoBell just below me. Next came Sweeney, Becca, and then Cal.

Sweeney and I had climbed the water tower once before, on a bet the summer after sophomore year. A couple of guys had put down fifty bucks, saying that we'd chicken out or get busted before we made it to the little ledge that circled the base of the big water tank. After we climbed all the way up there, ran around the tower a couple times, took a few pics with our comms, and came back down, the guys refused to pay us. They changed their minds after we kicked their asses. Now we were climbing this stupid thing again to kick some Fed ass instead.

The lattice bars were slanted, and that meant my feet were always wedged in the sharp point at the bottom of a diamond shape. The real freaky part was up near the top where I had to switch from the lattice to a rinky-dink ladder that shook and rattled a little as I crawled up to the platform. When I'd made it up there, I stayed low to the steel floor and away from the edge to keep out of sight. Our target was on the other side of the tank, but who knew when a Fed patrol might look up and see us? This mission was crazy dangerous. JoBell handed up the huge .50-cal rifle. I'd offered to sling that heavy thing over my shoulder for the climb, but she'd insisted on carrying it and four ten-round magazines. She lay down where I pointed as I helped Sweeney up.

"Just like old times, right, buddy?" He sounded jokey but looked totally serious. He leaned against the steel wall of the tank, powering up his comm. Becca made it up next, her M4 hung over her back like Sweeney's. She crouched down and powered up my comm. I looked down the hatch. Cal hadn't even reached the ladder yet.

"Come on, Cal," I hissed. "We're gonna be late. This ain't Mr. Hornschlager's chemistry class. We can't miss our time hack."

Cal didn't answer. Sweat rolled down his pale face and he bit his lip, climbing the lattice with shaking hands. The M240 was dangling from his shoulder by its strap.

"Hank, answer me quietly. What time is it?" I asked.

"You're out on the range early, partner. It's 5:51 in the morning. How'd you like to hear a little wake-up music?"

"Hank, you ask me to listen to one more song, I swear I'll shoot you."

"Ouch. Somebody woke up on the wrong side of the saddle."

"Cal! Move your ass!" I said.

He was even slower on the ladder. "Wright, are you sure this thing will even hold my weight?"

"I'm looking at the bolts right now," I said. "They're fine. You're fine. But you have to hurry."

Finally, he was close enough that Sweeney and I could help him up to the platform.

"5:55," Becca whispered. "Let's get in position."

Our mission had three parts. First, we had to broadcast a good dramatic show to signal the start of the larger mission against the Fed. Then we'd fire down on Alsovar's little Main Street base from about the only vantage point we could get. Finally, Sweeney needed a clear view of the Fed outpost for what he had to do.

"Sweeney, you all set?" I asked.

He stared at his comm, carefully and slowly swiping his fingers on the screen. "I never played a video game like this before," he said. "But I've taken control of the drone from our friends in Boise. It's about two minutes to the ski lodge, and the drone is packing two Hellfire missiles. One will blast a hole in the mountaintop fence to let our guys in. The other will take out the guard shack at the main entrance. After the missiles go off, I'll have the drone here in about thirty seconds."

"Good luck." I went to the others.

JoBell was lying down in the prone with the .50-cal rifle resting on its bipod. She had an awesome new scope for it. The Brotherhood guys said it was one of the best optics available. She looked so comfortable, so professional, set up there to kill. I hated that it had to be this way.

Cal set his machine gun up on its own bipod, his spare belts of ammo at the ready. "Remember, Cal," I said. "Hold down the trigger while you say, 'Die, bastards, die.' Then let up a second before you fire again. That way you won't overheat your barrel." Concentration had replaced his fear. He gave a thumbs-up and took aim.

"We're all set, Danny," said Becca. "I have the uplink, so we can broadcast your message whenever you're ready. Four minutes to go. Should we do this?"

I stood up by the steel railing. Major Alsovar's cop shop was three blocks behind me down below, its American flag fluttering in the breeze.

"Roll it," I said to Becca. She tapped the screen and then pointed the comm at me. I took a deep breath. *God, please give me the right words.* "I am Private Daniel Wright, a soldier in the Army of the Republic of Idaho. President Montaine has asked me to speak to you today about the United States. I used to be a proud soldier in the

Idaho National Guard, under the command of both Governor James Montaine and President Rodriguez. I loved my state, and I loved my country just as much." I felt the anger build up when I thought of all they'd taken from me. "Then the United States Army started coming after me. They killed my mother. They locked me in a room and tortured me and my friend. They've tortured all of us, keeping us trapped in our own homes, not allowing us to go anywhere or do anything. We're supposed to have rights. We're supposed to be free. But you show me a place in the entire United States where our rights aren't being spit on. No freedom of speech. No freedom of assembly or movement. The Unity Act turns our whole Bill of Rights into a list of wrongs. That's why Idaho had to break free."

I squeezed my hands into fists. An explosion rocked the distance. Then another. Sweeney had fired his two Hellfire missiles. He'd have the drone here in half a minute.

"Enough! United States Army, go back where you came from and leave us alone! We're not doing things your way anymore. We will not back down. We will not give up. We will never surrender. Some people call this the Idaho Crisis, but we haven't even started." I held my left fist up at an angle above my head. "Rise up, Idaho! People everywhere, rise up and fight. We will give them a war! Rise up! Rise up! Rise up!"

I screamed the last part to be heard over the shriek of the incoming aircraft. A huge blast thundered behind me. I could see the light shining off the water tower and the back of my comm in Becca's hands, but I didn't turn around to see the explosion. Instead, I glared at the camera.

"Cut! We're clear!" Becca slipped the comm into her pocket. I spun to check out the explosion at last. Sweeney had put the drone through the giant fuel tank in the Fed HQ, and the place was now a hellish mess of fire.

The loud crack of gunfire pierced my eardrums. Two more shots. "Here they come!" JoBell fired three more shots.

"Roof of the thrift shop!" Cal rained a shower of bullets down on the Fed guards who tried to shoot us. "Waste 'em!"

"There's the Brotherhood!" I said. Men with black armbands rushed up Main Street, storming the front gate of the cop shop.

A couple rounds hit the water tank a few feet away, and freezing cold streams of water sprayed out. "Let's get out of here," I said. "This is a bad position. We're going to get hit, or we'll hit the Brotherhood." I shoved Becca back toward the ladder. "JoBell, you're next. Cal will cover us."

"He's not accurate," she yelled. "You guys go. I'm right behind you." She fired off the rest of the rounds in her magazine and switched it out for another. Then she sighted the last Fed on the thrift shop roof across the street from the burning HQ. In one trigger squeeze, she ripped his head off his shoulders.

"Cal, get out of here!" I grabbed his shirt and pulled him up. He slung his machine gun and ammo. "Careful. Hot barrel."

I dropped down next to JoBell and started picking off targets as they tried to flee the fire bowl made by the Hesco barriers that surrounded the cop shop. My scope wasn't as powerful as hers, but I could see plenty good from this range. I put a round dead center mass on one soldier and dropped him on his back. His chest plate must have saved him, because he started to get up. I put a second round through his crotch. Blood burst everywhere as he screamed.

Then I caught a glimpse of Alsovar, climbing over the top of the Hesco barrier farthest from the fire. I had seconds. Aim. Fire! "Damn!" I must have jerked the trigger too hard, pulled off my shot. "Come on, JoBell. We gotta go. Alsovar's getting away!"

We both rolled to our feet and ran back toward the ladder. I could see and hear shots ringing out all over. At least four different Fed Humvees across town were up in flames. TJ had done his job coordinating the homemade bomb attacks. Guns had been distributed to people we could trust, and they'd set up sniper positions everywhere. With my call, all of Freedom Lake had become an endless series of death traps for the Fed.

I followed JoBell down the leg of the water tower as fast as I could, nearly slipping off the cold steel a couple times. As I reached the ground, a low, dull roar was building up in the distance, getting louder and louder as something came closer.

Sparrow, still in the turret of our Humvee, pointed the .50-cal as high as it would go. An F-22 whipped past overhead and then seemed to bank left for a second before cutting back hard to the right. Another jet, maybe an F-35, dove for it from a lot higher up. Smoke puffed out from under the F-35. The F-22 ripped in half, exploding into a ball of flames as one of its engines and part of its wing spun away. The F-35 vanished in the distance seconds later.

"Danny, come on!" JoBell leaned out the backseat of the Humvee.

"Get down!" Sparrow cranked her body to rotate the turret and aim the .50-cal right at me. I hit the dirt as she opened up, then rolled to see what she was shooting at. A Fed squad had moved into position behind some dumpsters and other junk at the back of the city water pump house. Fed bullets hit the ground about six feet away as I crawled as fast as I could toward our Humvee. I'd never been so exposed under fire. If Sparrow hadn't spotted them and started shooting, I'd be full of holes. Instead, two soldiers became pulp as she sprayed them.

I saw the long barrel of JoBell's .50-cal rifle poke out the window of the Humvee. Sparrow let up for a second, and as the Feds popped up to take advantage of the break in suppressive fire, JoBell picked them off. Then Sparrow opened up again, and I crouched-ran for the vehicle.

"They're toast! Forget 'em," I yelled. I jumped in the backseat while Cal sat behind the wheel. With everyone loaded up, he hit the gas.

✓—• I sign this nullification bill, outlawing the Federal Identification Card Act in the state of Oklahoma, not as an act of rebellion against the United States, but as a desperate request for the federal government to reconsider its inflexible and overbearing intrusion into our lives. The days of the federal government exercising the sole power of determining which of its own laws are constitutional and which of the states' laws are not, have come to an end. In order to achieve peace, we must seek a new form of cooperation and compromise. To reach that goal, I ask President Griffith to offer an immediate and unconditional cease-fire to allow for negotiations to resolve the current crisis. But make no mistake. If she does not desire peace, we in Oklahoma are prepared to defend ourselves. •—✓

✓—• People of Montana, I address you this morning not only as your leader, but also as a fellow citizen of this great state, on the most important matter facing our people since our state Constitution was ratified in 1889. That document declares as our very first right that all political power is vested in and derived from the people and is instituted for their good. The second right we are promised is that we the people of Montana have the exclusive right of governing ourselves as a free, sovereign, and independent state, that the people may alter or abolish the constitution and form of government whenever they deem it necessary. As our state constitution does not provide a procedure whereby our present form of government may be abolished, and as federal military aggression in our region presents an unacceptable danger, I have consulted with members of the Montana state legislature and with the leadership of the Montana Air and Army National Guards. By a majority vote and with the help of Montana's military, we have determined that as of seven o'clock this morning, Montana is a free and independent nation, severing all political ties with the United States of America, and willing to defend the sovereignty of our home. I am now Interim President Stan Brenner until such time as presidential elections can be held.

"My message to the people of Montana is simple. We are unshackled, free from constant federal interference and control in our lives. Free from being spied on by a paranoid security agency determined to trample our rights. Free from massive federal debt. Free to chart our own peaceful and prosperous future here in our great land. Many of you are afraid, but you need not be. You will be protected. A plan is in place to assure our future peace, productivity, and wealth.

"My message to President Griffith and the United States is also simple. We have no quarrel with you, unless you wish to fight us. If we are attacked, we will have no mercy, and we will fight to the last man. Montana has signed a mutual defense pact with the Republic of Idaho and the nation of Wyoming, which declared its own independence moments ago. We will fight to free our sister nations from your tyranny. Leave our countries in peace, and we will leave you in peace.

"At this time I join with President Michael Major of Wyoming in issuing this solemn promise to President Griffith and people around the world. We have no desire to use or possess the nuclear weapons that the government of the United States has deployed in our countries. We will grant permission for unarmed United States aircraft to enter our airspace for the purposes of securing nuclear missile silos. The United States is allowed one platoon-sized element to occupy each of those facilities. Upon application for permission, the United States will be allowed flights to rotate and resupply those soldiers. However, any redeployment of those soldiers to other locations within our sovereign countries will be considered an act of war.

"I ask the United States to allow Montana to peacefully leave the union, but no one should mistake our desire for peace as a lack of resolve to fight if necessary. Thank you. God bless Montana, a new nation! •—⌁

⌁—• This is live footage! My producers — geez, that was a big explosion — my producers are telling me to get out of the area, but as you can see, the US military line north of White Bird in Idaho is taking massive fire, even as they are unleashing an equally power-ful barrage on Idaho forces dug into the mountains. Full air-to-air combat. This is total war, ladies and gentlemen. I'm going to con-tinue bringing you the footage as long as I can. •—⌁

⌁—• Again, we cannot confirm this information at this time, but we believe that at least part of Fort Hood, Texas, an enormous military installation about halfway between Austin and Waco, is under insurgent control. There were five explosions on the base earlier, and now we're hearing massive gunfire from all around the area. We do not know if these insurgents are Texas National Guard, armed civilians, or a combination of both. We cannot stress enough that viewers should stay indoors and well away from the Fort Hood area. •—⌁

⌁—• Attention Idaho rebels occupying the city of Lewiston. I am Commander Mitchell Jenson, commanding officer of the USS Freedom and the fleet of four Littoral Combat Ships in your port. Each of these state-of-the-art ships is armed with extraordinary firepower. Several United States Army artillery units are stand-ing by with heavy cannons across the Snake River in Clarkston, Washington. United States Army armor and infantry units com-pletely surround all land approaches to the city. You are hopelessly *outmanned and outgunned. My voice is being relayed to you to deliver the following message: Surrender. Surrender immediately and you will be treated humanely. You have forty-five minutes to disarm yourselves and report to the Marine officers standing by on your docks. If I do not see a sufficient number of rebel insurgents surrendering by that time, I will order my gun batteries to open fire and completely destroy the city of Lewiston. There will be no further warnings.* •—ᴧ

ᴧ—• *of the several large fires burning in Cheyenne, Wyoming. The fierce fighting that was taking place there moments ago is now over, as Wyoming National Guard and armed civilian forces are fleeing the city. The US military seems to be completely in control of the capital, which is now almost certainly under martial law.* •—ᴧ

ᴧ—• *Forces out of Oklahoma City have apparently seized most of Fort Sill. It is not safe for our reporters to get too close to that military base, but casualties are expected to be high. Oklahoma residents are advised to take shelter. This is a sad day in Oklahoma.* •—ᴧ

TWENTY-NINE

My whole war so far had been about running away. The Fed had hunted me, tortured me, and messed with my dreams, probably since the FBI had chased us from the school last fall. Now, with the local Fed headquarters in ruins, I felt recharged. We were on offense now. I had the ball and wanted to run with it.

"Texas has declared independence too!" Sergeant Kemp called out as he listened to what was coming across his radio. "Crocker's working overtime putting out the news." He listened again. "Six Stryker fighting vehicles moving north on Highway 41. Everybody check your weapons. Get your ammo squared away. Anybody need any? I got six mags of five-five-six up here."

"Hey, partner, you got . . . a voice call from T . . . J. He's marked it emergency," Digi-Hank said.

That couldn't be good. "Put it on speaker, Hank."

"You got it, buddy."

"What do you got, TJ?"

"Danny, you gotta help us. We're in deep shit here!" TJ screamed in pure panic. I could hardly hear him over the sound of gunfire. *"We're outside the high school. We tried to kick the Fed out, but we got pinned down in the parking lot. Then two Strykers and a gun Hummer pulled up out in the street. We're using cars for cover, but we're low on ammo and —"*

"TJ, who you got there with you?" I yelled.

"*Chase Draper and his older brother, Dylan Burns, Brad Robinson and his dad, Randy Huff, plus two of his cousins —*"

"Shit, they got half the football team," said Cal.

"*You gotta help us or we'll be dead in minutes. Mr. Morgan is already hurt pretty bad.*"

"Principal Morgan?" Becca said.

"TJ, we're on the way," I said. "Hold on. Just fire in quick bursts to save ammo."

"Wright, we're supposed to go help Crow," Kemp said.

"This is my town, Sergeant," I said. "These are our people."

"Even Mr. Morgan?" Cal asked.

"Yeah, some of them are jackwads, but they're still our people. Get us to the school, Cal."

"But we can't take out two Strykers," said Kemp.

"Hank, give me an emergency voice call to President Montaine," I said.

"*You got . . . it pal. Whoops . . . The system . . . delays due to . . . high volume.*"

"Kemp, give me the radio!" When Kemp offered me the handset, I keyed up and shouted, "Alpha base, this is flashpoint. Crocker, answer right now. Over."

"*Flashpoint, alpha base. Go. Over.*"

"Base, you get me through to Montaine. Tell whoever answers that if I don't get the president right now, everybody in Freedom Lake is dead. Do it now!"

Crocker didn't answer. *Please, God, let him get through.* We were four blocks from the school and closing fast.

After what felt like hours Crocker finally radioed back. "*Flashpoint, alpha. I have the president. What message? Over.*"

"I need an air strike on two Strykers at the high school five minutes ago!"

"Roger. Wait one."

"I can't wait one, alpha!"

But Crocker only made us wait for like one city block. *"Flashpoint, be advised, F-35 is already in the area and inbound your location. ETA imminent."*

"Roger that. Out."

When we were a block away from the school, we could see the firefight and hear the thunder of the bullets, with the Feds firing from all directions at a circle of cars in the lot. The roar of an incoming jet built up in the distance.

"Hank, emergency voice call TJ on speakers," I said.

"Danny?" said TJ.

"TJ, get everybody over by that green pickup and get down right now!"

Two blasts zapped out of the sky. One second the Strykers threatened our friends. The next, the two enemy fighting vehicles were fireballs.

"Sparrow, get the turret on the Hummer. Cal, get us in there."

"Cal, what are you doing!?" Kemp shouted.

Cal floored the Humvee right between the two burning Strykers. Sparrow kept shooting. Our Humvee charged out into the open field between the school and the parking lot. Fed soldiers tried to get out of the way, but Cal cranked the wheel and ran them down. Sparrow sprayed the Fed gunners on the school roof with .50-cal rounds. Most of the soldiers had already been shot before Cal made his second pass.

When Cal finally stopped in the middle of the parking lot, the remaining Fed soldiers were coming out of the school with their hands in the air.

"They giving up?" Cal said. "Must be scared now that we got air support."

I leaned forward and hit Kemp's arm. "Well, Sergeant. I think you're the ranking soldier here."

Kemp nodded nervously, grabbed his M4, and exited the vehicle. I followed right behind him with my rifle. TJ and the others were approaching. "TJ, all you guys set up a security perimeter. Make sure no Feds can surprise us."

TJ nodded and the ragtag group that had tried to take back our school circled up.

"You want me to help with security?" Cal asked, holding up his M240.

"No, buddy," I said. "Come with us. We're going to enjoy this."

Sergeant Kemp kept his rifle at the ready, silently looking over the surrendered soldiers. "Who is your ranking officer?" he asked.

A second lieutenant stepped forward from the formation. He turned to his men and locked up. "Group. Atten-*tion.*" The Feds all stood up straight. The lieutenant did an about-face and looked at Sergeant Kemp. He saluted. Kemp returned it.

"I'm Sergeant Kemp, Republic of Idaho Army. Do you have any more soldiers inside, Lieutenant?"

"No, Sergeant. We had more soldiers, but many have been reassigned to the mountain base. We're on a skeleton crew here."

The whole screwed-up world had just flipped upside down again. An officer never saluted an enlisted first, never sucked up like this.

Kemp nodded. "Lieutenant, you and your men will be searched for weapons. Your hands will be zip-tied behind your backs. You will be secured in . . ." He hesitated.

"The boys' locker room?" Mr. Morgan limped up, holding a bloody bandage to his thigh.

I shrugged. "Can you lock those doors?" I asked him.

The principal pulled his keys from his pocket and smiled as he jingled them.

"And all entrances to the locker room will be under armed guard at all times," said Kemp. "You and your men and women will be treated as proper prisoners of war, except that I cannot afford to separate you by gender right now. If any of you attempt to flee or resist, you will be killed. Do you understand these instructions?"

"Yes, Sergeant," said the lieutenant.

"Issue the proper orders to your soldiers," Kemp said.

The lieutenant saluted again. Kemp returned the salute. Then we set about zip-tying the Feds before TJ and his crew locked them up.

Mr. Morgan limped over to me as we were getting back into our Humvee. "Daniel, thank you for your help. We were in trouble there." I nodded. What do you say when the principal you've always knocked heads with was suddenly being nice to you? After he'd been wounded in war with you? "The Army left food, bottled water, and limited medical supplies here. We have plenty of room in the gym and in the classrooms. We'll secure the school. Send the wounded here. This can be Freedom Lake's hospital for now."

I nodded. "You got it, Mr. Morgan."

TJ slapped my arm. "I'll stay here and help."

Cal had moved to the driver's seat, so I hurried to the back.

"Right, let's go," said Sergeant Kemp. "We gotta get up the mountain to help Crow."

⌐▪ *This is a CBS News Special Report. From the CBS newsroom, here's Simon Pentler."*

"You'll have to excuse me, ladies and gentlemen, but if ever there were a time for tears, that time has come. And when you hear the news that is coming in from around the country, you might be inclined to tears as well.

"At this hour, it has to be said: The United States of America has begun its second civil war. Moments after forces in Idaho and some other parts of the country broadcast a live video featuring controversial Idaho soldier Daniel Wright, the states of Montana, Wyoming, and Texas joined Idaho in seceding from the union. Fighting has erupted all over Texas as rebels in that state attempt to seize control of Army and Air Force bases near San Antonio, Waco, and El Paso. Highways and freeways are completely jammed with vehicles full of people fleeing the fighting and with military convoys rushing from other parts of the country to fortify those bases. This aerial footage from our affiliate KWTX in Waco shows that many civilians have abandoned the roads altogether, so that even the medians and shoulders are full of cars.

"We have confirmation that Oklahoma governor Martha Fergus has moved to a secret secure location and that Oklahoma National Guard and armed civilian forces have seized at least large portions of Fort Sill. Rumors run rampant about that situation, and right now the only thing that is known about Oklahoma is that a tremendous amount of fighting is going on across the state.

"The self-proclaimed presidents of both Wyoming and Montana have made assurances that they have no intentions of using the considerable nuclear missile arsenals that are deployed in their states, but despite these claims, thousands, perhaps tens of thousands, of people are fleeing major cities all across America. In the New York area, Interstate 95, the New Jersey Turnpike, and most

other major roadways leading out of the city are at a complete standstill, with many abandoned vehicles only compounding the problem. Police trying to maintain order are completely overwhelmed. More and more reports of riots and looting are coming in faster than we can possibly relay them to you. Um . . . the president, that is, the real president, President Laura Griffith, has just ordered all commercial flights grounded. If you are receiving this broadcast, please try to remain calm. Take shelter and remain indoors. Do not attempt to •⎯〉

〉⎯• Idaho, Idaho
Land where freedom lovers go . . . •⎯〉

〉⎯• Because we are closer to the critical information that our viewers need, we here at KREM 2 News in Spokane and eastern Washington are going to hold off on switching to the CBS national newsroom. We have reports of fierce and deadly fighting, not only just across the border in Idaho but all across Spokane and at Fairchild Air Force Base as well. We have unconfirmed reports that some members of Spokane law enforcement may be working with the insurgents.

"If you're just joining us, we cannot stress this enough: Remain indoors. Do not even attempt to go out to secure food or supplies. Our reporters tell us that most grocery stores have been overrun and their shelves are bare, while dozens of people have been shot attempting to secure supplies. Every hospital in the area has asked us to inform you that they are completely full and only accepting patients with immediately life-threatening wounds or injuries. All others will be turned away. So it's important . . . We're now getting a report of a fire that has broken out at Deaconess Hospital. Most streets downtown are at a complete standstill. State and local police have tried to close I-90 to all but military, law enforcement, and emergency response traffic, but their blockades at the on-ramps have failed at several locations, and traffic on the interstate is complete lawless chaos.

"Oh my word! What is . . . Is everyone okay? Ladies and gentle-men, that shaking of the image you just witnessed was the result of an enormous explosion. It sounded very close. What? And now I'm getting the order from our producer to evacuate. Is there a fire? Steve? Is the building burning? No. I'm staying. You guys going to . . . Ladies and gentlemen, we're going to stay on the air here as long as we can, to get you the latest information. •—⋏

⋏—• CNN has just learned that the Department of Defense has confirmed rumors that President Laura Griffith's son, Second Lieutenant Douglas Griffith, is missing and presumed dead after his F-22 fighter jet was shot down in a firefight in the skies above Idaho. He was twenty-three years old and recently commissioned from the Air Force Academy. Unfortunately one loss among many, but certainly this is deeply painful for the president. •—⋏

⋏—• From fertile plains to mountains tall
Brothers, sisters one and all . . . •—⋏

⋏—• This is Commander Jenson, USS Freedom. All stations, all sta-tions. Fire code delta, uniform, bravo, one, seven, alpha foxtrot. Commence firing sequences at will. Fire, fire, fire! •—⋏

⋏—• CITIZENS OF THE UNITED STATES, PLEASE STAND BY FOR A TOTAL BROADCAST FROM THE PRESIDENT OF THE UNITED STATES, LAURA GRIFFITH."

"Good morning. In order to ensure that the functions of our government continue without interruption, my staff and I are conducting necessary business from our offices on Air Force One. Our Air Force pilots assure me that most parts of America today would have enjoyed clear skies. However, as March 21 dawned, sunny skies were soon replaced by ominous clouds of thick black smoke rising from the fires in Texas and Oklahoma, Montana, Wyoming, and Idaho.

"The material losses for both sides in terms of military assets, damaged infrastructure, or destroyed civilian property are estimated to be in the hundreds of millions, while the human cost of even the first hours of this war is beyond measure. Thousands of our fellow Americans have already been killed. The victims of this war are soldiers, sailors, Marines, and airmen. The victims are also civilians: doctors, teachers, tradespeople, secretaries, businessmen and women, beloved family, friends and neighbors, daughters and . . . sons.

"Unless we decide to make immediate and drastic changes, this dire situation will only worsen. This particular aircraft has served as Air Force One for several United States presidents, and wherever it has flown, it has stood as a symbol of peace and hope. Today, I extend that hope for peace across America. Having no desire to be the last president of the United States, I ask the leadership of Idaho, Montana, Wyoming, Texas, and Oklahoma to stand down the military forces under your command. In exchange, I repeat my offer for a full, free pardon for all soldiers, officers, and civilian combatants in rebel states. And I promise a fair trial and comfortable, humane treatment for rebel state political leaders. We must act now, today, in order to preserve tomorrow.

"Historians will title this tragic period of American history the Second American Civil War, but the end of this sad chapter has not *yet been written. We, the authors of our own story, together will determine what happens next. Working with one another toward peace, we can yet secure for ourselves, our children, and our children's children a happy and hopeful future.* •⌁

⌁• *Idaho, Idaho*
Light of hope in darkness glow . . . •⌁

⌁• *Ladies and gentlemen, those sounds you might be hearing in the background are gunshots and screams coming from inside the KREM 2 News building. My coanchor Grace Spicer has taken cover. I'm going to stay on the air as long as . . . Who are you people!? Ladies and gentlemen, there are armed —"*

"Take it easy, Rex. We ain't gonna hurt you. Step aside. Is that camera rolling?"

"I will not allow terrorist thugs to use this station to make threats or —"

"We're rolling, Lieutenant."

"People of eastern Washington, I'm Lieutenant Ron Meyers, a soldier of the Brotherhood of the White Eagle. We're a militia group working with the Republic of Idaho and the countries of Montana and Wyoming. We've been getting ready for this day for years. Thanks to all of our hard fighting, what's left of Fairchild Air Force Base outside of Spokane is now ours. We have taken over all military stuff at the Yakima Training Center. Interstate 90's been destroyed at Snoqualmie Pass, and all other passes through the mountains are closed to the United States. Everything east of Washington's western mountain range is now a part of Idaho. All US military who give up now can leave alive. All civilians who want to leave better get out now. Any property they leave behind will be taken by the Republic of Idaho. Rex Faber here called us

terrorists, but we ain't gonna hurt you. We're here to free you. Keep watching this channel for more information. Long live the Republic of Idaho. Long live the Brotherhood! •⌇

⌇• We will defend our liberty . . . •⌇

⌇• Can anyone hear me on this channel? Our comms are still shut off up here. Um . . . Breaker one nine. This is Troy Nolan, two miles up Burke Road in Wallace, Idaho. Look, we ain't Fed. We ain't rebels, but we got a plane crashed up here. Big passenger jet. I think a couple fighters was too close to it, shooting each other up. Listen, we can't call nobody with our comms out. A coupla guys rode down from the fire department on horseback, but they only got enough gas for one fire engine, and that's south of town putting out the fire from where one of the fighter jets went down. People on that plane are hurt pretty bad. We need doctors, like a surgeon, and the fire's out of control. We fightin' it just with like garden hoses, but we ain't makin' a dent. Couple houses are going up. Please. We ain't part of no war. We're just trying to get along in life. Please. Oh, Jesus, help us. The whole town's gonna burn. Please help. This is Wallace, Idaho. Is anybody listening? Anyone at all? •⌇

⌇• Idaho, our lives for thee. •⌇

CHAPTER

THIRTY

As we rode back through town in the Humvee, a flash of tan and green caught my attention. Three Feds had broken cover near a house and sprinted across a street at the western edge of town. I recognized their leader, a face that would haunt my nightmares for the rest of my life. "Alsovar," I said quietly.

When Cal slowed us down to swerve around a burning Ford, I popped the latch on the door, jumped out, and ran. I raised my gun and took a shot at Alsovar, but at the last second, one of the others shifted position, and I clipped his thigh. The other turned and started to bring his rifle to bear, but I blasted him. Alsovar dodged out of sight around the corner of a house. I shot the other Fed in the face as he rolled to his weapon. Then I dove behind a van parked in the driveway right before the major sent a couple of rounds my way.

If I ran around the other side of the house, I might be able to ambush him. Or a guy like that might be waiting for me to round the corner, and he'd shoot me when I did. A bullet whizzed by under the van. Another crashed through the windows. I ran to the side of the house.

The Humvee's engine roared as Cal had finally turned around and was catching up to me. "Wright, you stupid son of a bitch! Get back here, Private! That's an order!" Sparrow shouted from the gun turret.

Alsovar's shooting had stopped. He'd heard the engine. He wasn't dumb enough to hang around when Sparrow's machine gun turned the corner. I ran to the back of the house. "Damn it!" The bastard was fast! He'd cleared the backyard and was almost to the woods near the Abandoned Highway of Love. I aimed and pulled the trigger, but nothing happened. I slapped the magazine up into the well and tried again. "Shit!" I sprinted after him. A shot rang out from the woods, and I dove to the ground, rolling to my right and scramble-crawling behind a little stone birdbath. Shit for cover. I pressed the button to drop my empty mag and slapped a full one in. I rolled back to the left and ran as I fired off three rounds, sprinting for the tool-shed at the back of the property. My last cover until the woods.

The Humvee had jumped the curb and was making its way in my direction, Sparrow unloading heavy machine gun rounds at the trees. With that kind of cover fire, I took off on my best football run across the empty field toward the woods by the river. I crashed into the low scrub brush at the edge of the trees, hitting the ground on a leftover patch of gray snow. My heart beat so heavy I worried I'd never hear Major Alsovar when he made his move. One thing that asshole had been right about: He had a lot more combat training and experience than I did. I'd only been to basic training, which, when compared to all I'd done so far in this war, now felt like preschool.

Where was he? How could I find him in this scrub? When we were kids, we'd build forts and play hide-and-seek in these trees and bushes. Sweeney'd always find the best hiding places, and he loved making us look for him until long after the fun of the game had passed. Later, we came back here to party, drink, and mess around with our girlfriends on the Abandoned Highway of Love. This wasn't a party or a game, though. It was straight-up life or death.

I was pushing a bad position. I would have to search for him, while all he had to do was hide and wait to shoot me. If he scored a clean shot, I might never figure out who won this thing.

No. I squeezed my pistol grip extra tight. The endless hours without sleep. Hot-as-hell room. The damned waterboarding, with no air, no hope. Whatever he'd done to Sparrow that she wouldn't talk about. There were supposed to be rules, even in war. That bastard had bragged about how he'd ruined my shop, casually murdered Schmidty, about how he'd break me, kill me, and then use what I'd told him to find my friends. Torture them too. Hell no. This son of a bitch had to go. I had about eighteen 5.56 rounds that said I'd pull this off.

I bounded to my feet, twisting, ducking, jumping to avoid shrubs, tree branches, and fallen logs. I swept my eyes left to right and back again, rifle at the ready. If anything moved, I'd shoot it.

Where was he?

I tripped on a rock and went down, but I threw myself into the fall, tucking my shoulder and holding my rifle close so I could roll back up to my feet and move.

Then I saw him. Alsovar was scrambling up the far riverbank, using roots and chunks of the collapsing roadway as hand- and footholds. Near the top he swung his right leg up onto the road surface. Before he could pull himself up, I aimed, breathed in and out. In and out and hold. I fired.

Alsovar screamed and rolled up over the edge into the brush. His rifle skittered down the bank until it splashed in the water. Blood soaked into the dirt, but not enough. If I'd hit his leg center mass with a heavier caliber round, I would have damn near shot it off. But at least he was wounded. And unarmed.

"Alsovar! I'm coming for you! See how tough you are when you don't have me chained to a chair!" I pulled the trigger. One-two-three-four-five-six rounds. Sticks and clumps of pine needles fell to the ground as my gun spat fire.

I ran to my left as fast as I could. Maybe Alsovar was dead. Maybe not. But if I tried to climb up that steep bank after him, he'd have the high ground, and he could take me out with a branch or a rock. I smiled as the sweat rolled down my face, down my back, like in football. The game was on my field, my home advantage. I knew this place and he was the shitbag Fed outsider. I ran around onto Party Bridge, happy that the Brotherhood had cut the old roadblock I-beams away. When I cleared the bridge, I made my way back up through the woods. I could have taken the highway, but what if Alsovar had a sidearm? Sparrow had warned me not to do anything stupid. I'd take no chances.

Back at the spot where I'd shot him, I found a patch of pink-white snow and deep red blood smeared on some pine needles, but he was gone. I took a knee with my back to the river, scanning all around, slowly sweeping my rifle back and forth. He couldn't have gone far with his leg like that. *If there's no blood trail, he has to be —*

A dark shape flew screaming out of the shrubbery, knocking me on my back. Alsovar was in my face, grinding his teeth with his nose wrinkled. Spit dripped from his mouth. "You little shit!"

I maxed out my bench press at two twenty. How much did this asshole weigh? I shoved him hard, but he had hold of my rifle with his forearm pressed to my throat. The most I could do was roll him to the side. My grip slipped on the gun, and he almost took it away. If he grabbed my weapon, this was all over. I tried to pull the rifle down, to get the barrel under him and shoot him.

He pushed the rifle back up so the barrel was clear of both of us. Then his fingers found mine on the trigger and he made me squeeze off shot after shot — deafening with the weapon beside my face — until the mag was dry.

Alsovar threw a hard elbow into my face, dazing me for a second. I kneed him in his bloody leg and he groaned. His grip relaxed enough so that I could connect a hard punch. That bought me enough room to slide away from him so I could get a better position for a hand-to-hand fight.

But just as I cleared him and took a few steps out onto the highway, where one whole lane had long ago collapsed into the river, he came at me again. This time when my back hit the ground, my shoulders and head didn't, and I turned my head, frantic that I was falling over the edge to the rubble below.

The major was on top of me, and his hands clamped down on my throat. He was old but strong. I swung my fists down on top of his arms, but couldn't break free. I tried to nail his face. He turned his body and let his shoulder absorb the blow.

"I told you I'd kill you, Danny. I've fought wars for my country." He gritted his teeth and tightened his grip. "Killed for my country. I've wasted Iraqis, Pakistanis, Syrians, even a few . . . Mexicans when I was on a counternarcotics task force. But you're the real prize. Killing the symbol of this damned rebellion. It's good, Danny. Isn't it good?"

Weird little specks of shadowlight danced in my vision. Losing air. He had me. Sparrow and the others. Should have waited for 'em. For Cal. Becca and JoBell'd be so sad . . .

JoBell.

I bent my legs to drag my feet up by my ass. Then I pushed the hardest squat of my life, shoving my body up, arching my butt and lower back off the ground, and dumping us both over the edge of the crumbling road.

Rocks, dirt, sticks, grass. Alsovar lost hold. Air. Some larger stones jabbed my head, back, and legs as I rolled end over end until I skidded to a stop with my legs in the icy water of Freedom River.

I looked up. Alsovar was crouched with his back against a pile of rocks, concrete chunks, and asphalt pavement only a couple feet away. He glared murder at me, but while I stood up and cocked back my right fist, he didn't make a move.

Then I saw the little stream of blood running down from right under his right pec. A red-black, blood-soaked piece of steel rebar stuck four inches out from his chest.

I smiled. "You got a little . . ." I pointed at the rod that had impaled him. "Right there. Might want to get a Band-Aid."

I had to admit, the guy was tough. He tried pushing himself off the bar, and even slid up on it a couple inches before his eyes rolled and he fell back to where he was.

"Oh, did that hurt?" I stepped up and leaned down over him. "Good."

His arm swung at me so fast, I only saw the flash of the blade a second before I felt the burn rip across my chest. I dropped to my knees on the slope right by him, but before he could bring his knife back at me, I grabbed a chunk of concrete twice the size of my fist and blocked his hand so that his weapon flew off into the river.

We looked at each other. I stood and lifted the concrete high above his head, ready to spike it down through his skull like smashing a pumpkin on Halloween.

"Do it, then." Major Alsovar coughed. "Do it, if you got any balls, boy."

I looked down at the man who had tortured me. "I win," I said. "Danny!"

I almost dropped the concrete chunk, but then I realized the voice had been JoBell's. The whole group came to the edge of the collapsed road.

"Wright, you idiot," Sparrow said. "I told you not to do anything like this."

"Yes!" Cal slid down the slope to us, somehow managing to stay on his feet even while carrying the M240. Sweeney, Becca, and JoBell followed. "You got him!"

"Sparrow, you and me will form a security perimeter. Cover them from up here," Kemp said. He yelled down to me, "Wright, what do we do with him?"

Cal kicked the major in the ribs. "Not so tough now, are you? Payback's a bitch!" He elbowed me. "Do it, Wright. It will only take a few hits."

Sweeney touched my arm. "Shouldn't we, I don't know, arrest him or something? Isn't he a POW?"

"Forget that!" Cal put his machine gun down. "Remember how he treats his prisoners? Come on, Wright! Kill the bastard!"

Alsovar winced as his boots slipped in some loose gravel and more of his weight fell on the rebar. I heard his flesh tear like the sound a knife makes when cutting through steak.

"I don't know, Danny," said Becca. "We don't have any doctors, and he's in bad shape. Maybe he's like a horse. When it's hurt, and there's nothing we can do, sometimes it's best to just put it out of its misery."

She said it so matter-of-fact, like an ethics debate at veterinarian school. Alsovar wasn't an "it." He was a person. When had the sweet Becca I'd grown up with gone so cold?

And why was I going soft on Alsovar?

I looked at JoBell, who watched me and said nothing. She didn't offer advice or cry or even look at the major. She just stared at me as the wind whipped her blond hair. My arms shook from holding up the heavy concrete.

"You want to shoot him instead?" Cal asked. "I'll get you a gun. No problem. You've killed tons of Feds before, and he's not just a Fed, he's their damned *leader*. Waste him."

That crazed animal look had returned to Cal's eyes, that violent eagerness that we used to get out on the football field. I'm not gonna lie. I hated Alsovar. I understood Cal's rage.

I met the major's eyes. "You gonna kill me, huh? *I'm* the dead man, you son of a bitch!?" With all my strength, I slammed that concrete down.

It hit the ground right next to Alsovar's head.

"How could you miss?" Cal asked.

Yeah, I understood Cal's rage. It was part of me too. And I worried about what it was doing to Cal and to all of us.

"Let's get out of here," I said. "He's finished anyway."

I took JoBell's hand. "I told you I was getting out of the war, and I meant it," I said. "We finish this battle, and then I'm out. He's no longer a combatant. Killing him would be murder. And I'm not . . ." My throat tightened on the words. "Not a murderer. At least, I don't want to be. We gotta save something of ourselves, of our humanity, if we're ever going to leave the war behind. If we're ever going to get back to real life."

JoBell kissed my cheek, and then we all started climbing back up to the Abandoned Highway of Love. It was a tricky climb, and we slipped a few times when rocks would give way under our feet.

"Cal, you coming?" Becca asked when we had all reached the top.

From behind me I heard a slide-rattle sound and turned to see Cal next to Alsovar with his saber high over his head. "No," he said quietly.

"Cal, don't!" JoBell yelled.

He shook his head. "He doesn't get a free pass." He kicked Alsovar in his bloody leg. The major grunted. "You killed Schmidty! Herbokowitz! Bagley! You try to kill my best friend!?" He stabbed the sword through Alsovar's thigh. It went all the way through his right leg and into his left. The major bit his lip, but kept quiet. Cal twisted the blade. "Huh, tough guy!? You torture him!?" He pulled the sword out and then slashed, opening the major's stomach as blood splattered everywhere. "You mess with my friends! I'll kill you all!" Cal slashed again and again. He left deep cuts crisscrossed all over Alsovar's body. The tough old bastard didn't yell once.

I slid down the slope and grabbed Cal's arm, using all my strength just to slow him down. "Cal. Cal! Enough! He's dead!" Blood was in Cal's hair, running down his cheek, dripping from his nose and lips. His sword and the arm I had hold of were drenched in it.

He swung around to look at me. And just as with the redheaded girl on that horrible night in Boise or the screaming, burning bodies in the tunnel on Silver Mountain, I knew right then that the image before me would be burned into my mind forever. I'd grown up with Calvin Riccon, but when he finally looked at me, covered in sticky, warm blood, I didn't know the person behind those eyes.

I worried for a moment that he'd cut me down, but then something in him seemed to click, like he had just recognized me. He flashed his old goofy smile and patted me on the shoulder. "Don't worry, buddy. I took care of him for you."

✓—• Please note that the list below contains soldiers and combatants only. Civilian deaths are not included, so the total number of dead is much higher. Also, since casualty lists are not being publicly released, please send me a private message to report a confirmed death as a direct result of this war. However, IN ORDER TO REDUCE DUPLICATION, PLEASE READ THE CASUALTY LIST BEFORE SUBMITTING THE NAME OF A CASUALTY!

FEDERAL: TOTAL: 3,615	REBEL COMBATANTS: TOTAL: 7,321
CPT Flora Dixon	CPL Angel Love
PVT Vicki Mood	PVT Cedric Mathis
PFC Nelson Montgomery	PV2 Gary Barnett
PV2 Ricky Giordano	SGT Leo Richardson
CPL Trevor Green	PV2 Tyler Owen
PV2 Kent French	SPC Shen Ho Cheng
SPC Mohammad Samatar	CPL Joseph Lynch
PFC Tomas Austin	SPC Frankie Patrick
PVT Lloyd Mason	PVT Jamal Khoury
PV2 Ralph Simpson	PVT Dustin Rodger
SPC Ian Diaz	SPC Casey Rios
PVT Derek Cho	PVT Martin Sutton
PVT Edmund Valdez	PV2 Erick Greene
PFC Ismail Ahmad	PVT Oscar Freeman
PV2 Shannon Russell	SPC Mark DeAndrea
PVT Aubrey Carson	PVT Roy Gordon
SGT Glen Bowers	PVT Robert Myers
SPC Carl Maldonado	SPC Kim Patterson
PVT Saul Medina	SGT Kenny Hart
PVT Freddie Reese	PV2 Ramiro Simmons
CPL Frank Ponza	PVT Adrian Turner
PVT Ruben Vasquez	SPC Samuel Holland
PFC Matthew Cortes	PVT Marlon Gonzales

PV2 Joey Warren	CPL Guy Blake
SPC Earnest Stephens	SGT Ken Tseng
PV2 Hubert Fleming	SPC Dwayne Jefferson
PVT Dwight Nichols	PV2 Kirk Guerrero
SPC Taher Farsoun	SGT Vernon Allen
PFC Javier Greer	PVT Kenny Kennedy
PVT Jordan Reyes	SPC Erick Lamb
SGT Emmett Cole	PVT Luther Aguilar
PV2 Andy Moon	PV2 Irving Franklin
SFC George Bass	SGT Mike Matthews
PV2 Toby Garner	SPC Earnest Delgado
PFC Isamu Okamura	PVT Bradford King
PVT Antonio Oliver	CPL Joseph Hansen
PV2 Marion Berry	PVT Byron Rowe
SPC Najeeb Kassar	PV2 Joey Webb
CPL Felix Wilkerson	SPC James McLaughlin
PV2 Bryan Peterson	PVT Erick Jenkins
PVT Roland Rizzo	SPC Brandon Walker
SPC Tyrone Guzman	PVT Jerry Willis
PFC Van Moore	SPC Shannon Schultz
PVT Do Won Kim	PFC Tom Pope
SPC Salvatore Chandler	PVT Casey Harrison
SPC Lance Sharp	PV2 Juan Jordan
PV2 Everett Mack	PVT Raul Garner
SPC Wade Barker	PFC Josh Salazar
PFC Rogelio Rose	SGT Ignacio McDaniel
PVT Ron Tran	PVT Everett Hill
PV2 Alfonso Kim	SPC Dave Harrington
PVT Gerard Farmer	PV2 Barry Dawson
SPC Shizuko Hayakawa	PVT Jessie Day
PFC William Brock	SPC Frankie Banks
PVT Jeremiah Moss	PV2 Jane Grady
PV2 Ignacio Sullivan	PVT Lynn Cuzzle

SPC Moses Page	PFC Edwin Jones
PVT Ricardo Salvadori	SPC Morris Harper
SPC Nicholas Kennedy	PFC Brent Parson
PFC Fernando Shelton	PVT Mark Wong
PVT William Hale	SPC Warren Allison
PV2 Don Cain	CPL Noel Gutierrez
SGT Malek Shami	PVT Neal Thomas
PV2 Byron Massey	SGT Jacob Sullivan
SPC Andrew Lowe	SPC Salvador Norris
PFC Cory Sanchez	PVT Orville Turner
PV2 Julian Waters	SPC Roderick Perkins
PVT Doyle Hoshi	PVT Leon Lloyd
SPC Ernesto Douglas	SPC Peter Inaba
PFC Sergio McCormick	SGT Matthew Newman
PV2 Bryant Zembola	PFC Gary Mullins
PFC Donald Hubbard	PVT Bernard Garrett
SPC Elmer Luna	SSG Sydney Lorfel
Scroll down for more . . .	*Scroll down for more . . .*

‒ᴧ‒• *All units, all units. This is talon actual. That noise you're hearing in the background is the sound of heavy artillery rounds leveling the Fed base at Silver Sunset Resort. There were no Fed survivors. We will remain on high alert, but according to our network, we've secured Freedom Lake and surrounding areas from Fed control. Long live the Brotherhood!* •‒ᴧ‒

‒ᴧ‒• *Resistance has taken FIRA headquarters in Coeur d'Alene! The Fed are pulling out. General Thane announced he had orders to redeploy. He left by helicopter. The rest are rolling out by convoy, heading west on I-90. We're letting them go. Long live Idaho!* •‒ᴧ‒

◠—• We're joined now in the CNN Idaho Crisis Situation Room by former secretary of defense David Shima. Mr. Shima, I know we have very limited information from the combat zone in Idaho, but as you can see, we're getting more and more footage of federal military forces leaving the state. Can we draw any conclusions or at least speculate about what might be happening and why?"

"Al, it's simple. I've been on every network that will have me, trying to warn anyone who will listen that President Griffith was making an enormous tactical mistake. One thing I strongly believe we should have learned from the Iraq war is to never send an insufficient number of troops for an occupation and reconstruction mission. The United States military was already stretched too thin from troop cutbacks and overseas deployments. Then they faced a well-armed and determined insurgent force in Idaho, and President Griffith was simply not counting on all these other states declaring independence.

"Bottom line, Al, the US military has suffered significant losses as a result of dozens of well-coordinated surprise attacks. It's time to withdraw, regroup, and reevaluate our important domestic defense priorities. I think the president is making a smart play here by redeploying forces, hopefully to Texas, where we need to protect military bases and oil and gas resources a lot more than we need anything in Idaho. Once critical areas are stabilized, we can return to stop the Idaho insurgency."

"Thank you. That's former secretary of defense David Shima. We're going now to live footage of a number of explosions in residential areas in •—◠

THIRTY-ONE

Back in the Humvee, Sergeant Kemp pressed the radio handset to his ear. "Last calling station, last calling station. This is flashpoint. Say again, over."

JoBell squeezed my hand as we rode in the backseat. "You did the right thing back there."

I looked at Cal in the driver's seat, with his hair matted and shirt stained with blood. "I just want this all to be over."

"It's not over yet," Kemp said. "That was Crocker relaying a message from some Brotherhood guys just north of town. A Fed convoy is heading south on Highway 41. They'll be in Freedom Lake in minutes."

I sighed and exchanged a look with JoBell.

Cal had already turned the Humvee north. "Let's go get 'em!"

"We're going to need some help with a whole convoy," Sweeney said.

"Brotherhood guys and whoever else are on the way," said Kemp.

About a mile out of town, the highway and the land on either side of it was blocked by a mix of old trucks and junked cars. A tow truck had hauled some of the wrecks into place. A few dozen armed men and women were gathered around the barricade. Some of them aimed their weapons when they saw us approaching, but Sparrow was in the turret and held up her fist to show them we weren't Fed.

Cal parked the Humvee on the road, and everybody but Sparrow got out.

A bearded man greeted us. "I hope some more people show up. It's going to be hard to hold the line."

Cal set his 240 on the hood of an old Buick. "This is my last belt of ammo."

"Control your shots," Kemp said. "Go for the gunners. Make it count."

The bearded man pointed to the trees ten yards back from either side of the road. "We have more guys using the woods for cover, but not all of them are well armed. A few only have shotguns."

About two hundred yards in the distance, the Feds rounded the curve.

"Oh shit," Sparrow said.

The Fed convoy consisted of a Stryker armored fighting vehicle leading three armored gun Hummers. Sweeney and Becca crouched in the ditch, taking aim. JoBell and her .50-cal rifle stayed behind a Ford Focus with me. Two of the Fed Humvees moved out to the left and right of the Stryker's rear. That meant three .50-cal machine guns and probably an M240 were coming right at us. I could hear their engines rev up as they prepared to blast through our blockade. I caught a look from Kemp that told me he was thinking what I was thinking.

"This isn't going to work. We're totally outgunned," I said quietly to JoBell. "Hey, we gotta get out of here!" I yelled to the others. "We don't have enough firepower to —"

Our blockade line lit up as the Stryker and Humvees opened fire. Glass shattered. Bullets cut through vehicles. A man right next to me was hit, coughed blood, and dropped. Other bodies fell. Our guys shot back. Cal screamed and sprayed the Fed with 7.62. Sparrow didn't let off her trigger either. But our rounds just bounced off the Stryker, which only sped up.

"They're gonna ram us!" Sweeney yelled. "Get out of the way!"

JoBell was still shooting. "Jo, just drop it! Come on!" I grabbed her by the arm, she dropped her impossibly heavy rifle, and the two of us ran as fast as we could. Our only hope was to reach the trees before a Fed machine gun wasted us.

We reached the woods with seconds to spare. The Feds kept firing as the Stryker slammed into the pickup and cars on the highway, knocking them aside. One Fed tracer round hit a gas can mounted on the rack of an old Ford pickup and burst into flames. I heard screams from the pickup as the convoy rolled past us.

Then suddenly, two major explosions rocked the Fed Stryker, and it rolled off the road. Seconds later, the three Fed Humvees went up in flames as well. JoBell pulled me to the ground. "What the hell?" I said.

"Look!" JoBell pointed back toward Freedom Lake. Four gun Hummers were riding side by side across the road and on the shoulder. Two of their gunners had AT4s cocked and ready on the turrets. That's what must have taken out the Stryker.

"Help!" A scream burst out of the tree line.

JoBell looked at me in horror. "Becca!" we both said together.

We were up in seconds and running back toward the debris of our barricade. "Becca!" JoBell shouted. "Becca, where are you?"

"Help!" Becca said. "I need a medic over here!"

The voice was coming from the other side of a junked Toyota right behind the Ford truck gas fire. As we ran closer, Sparrow, Cal, and Kemp caught up with us.

When we cleared the Toyota, I stopped. "Sweeney. Oh God."

The right side of his face and neck had burned bright red, his hair melted into dark clumps. He must have tried beating out the fire, because the skin of his right shoulder and upper arm had blistered and shrunk back from his pink seared flesh in a mangled purple-black clump. His hips and thighs had burned the same way, only his jeans had sort of melted into his skin.

Becca was kneeling beside him, her coat smoldering at her side. Tears streamed down her face. "I got the fire out but . . . Eric. Oh no. Eric."

I ran and dropped to my knees next to Sweeney, leaning over him to listen for breathing. He was alive. For now. "Sweeney. Hey! Buddy, can you hear me!?" At least the flames hadn't burned him as high as his ear.

"Sweeney!" Cal ran for him, that crazed look on his face. "I got ya, buddy!"

"No!" JoBell screamed. She threw her whole body weight into the big guy, and Sparrow joined her, pulling Cal back. "Cal, no! You can't just rough-handle him. He's been burned and needs careful help!" She slapped his face, and I swear I'd seen punches that were less hard. "You listen to me, damn it!" Awareness came back behind Cal's eyes. He focused on JoBell. "We're going to help him. We will. I promise."

Tears welled up in his eyes. "Eric's all . . ."

JoBell put her hand to his cheek. "I know. I know."

I stepped up to Cal. "We gotta get him to a hospital. Go see if our Humvee's okay. That's the best thing you can do for him right now."

He nodded and ran off with his machine gun.

A captain got out of one of the gun Hummers from Freedom Lake. He saw Sweeney and keyed the mike on a small radio clipped to his chest. "Send Specialist Terry to the front right away. I don't care what he's doing." He nodded at us. "Reinforcements are here, though I'm sorry we weren't sooner. It was a long drive in from Montana. Our mission was to assault US forces here in the north and to secure and open the border with Canada. We also have a truck back closer to town with food and medical supplies for you. Where should they go?"

Cal pulled up in our Humvee. Its hood was mangled and it had plenty of bullet holes, but at least it was running.

"Have them follow us," said Sergeant Kemp. "We'll lead them to the high school. That's where we have our field hospital."

"Roger that," the captain said.

His medic joined me at Sweeney's side. He gloved up, injected Sweeney with morphine, and then ran an IV. "This is about all I can do for him," the medic said to us. "You have to get him to a medical facility soon. These are serious burns. I'm sorry. I have other casualties to get to." He sprinted off down the road.

The captain said, "I'll radio to let my guys in the truck know you're coming and that they should follow you." He remounted his vehicle, and his four Humvees headed north.

I was left there, holding up Sweeney's IV bag. JoBell was crying, her arms around Becca. Kemp looked down at Sweeney. "We're going to have to lift him."

"I got a pickup," the bearded man said. "We can haul the wounded in the back."

I felt completely useless with that stupid IV bag while Kemp and Cal carefully lifted Sweeney into the back of the man's truck. I climbed in with Sweeney and three others who had been shot but were still alive. As we rode back into town with Cal and the others following in the Humvee, I couldn't hold back my tears. "Sweeney. Hold on. We need you, buddy," I whispered.

At the school, an unarmed sergeant in MCUs met us outside the double doors to the gym. Her name tape said MCDONALD. "What do you got?"

"We got wounded!" I shouted. "You gotta help!"

Sergeant McDonald rolled her eyes. "Place is overflowing with wounded. We have almost nothing to treat them with."

"Food and medical stuff is right behind us on a truck from Montana," said Sergeant Kemp.

McDonald let out a little sigh. "Thank God. Dr. Strauss will be glad to hear that. Let's get these people in there."

TJ spotted me as he came out of the gym. "Danny, is everyone —"

"Sweeney," I said.

TJ's tired eyes widened in horror as he saw the burns. "Oh no. Oh shit." Then he snapped to action and ran inside. "I'll get a stretcher!"

He brought out an Army litter, and me and Cal lifted Sweeney onto it. Becca sobbed as she carried the IV bag. The Montana truck pulled up right as we went inside.

When I stepped through the doors to the gym, the smell hit me first — that disgusting, sour-sweet stench of blood that I'd come to know from the dungeon and everywhere else. People crowded almost every square foot of the floor, some of them covered in sheets or coats, dead. Others were bandaged or had open wounds, some moaning or calling out for help. An older major I assumed was Dr. Strauss worked on a patient on a science lab table in the middle of the basketball court, over the Minutemen logo. A spotlight I thought I recognized from the school stage shined light down on the table. We carried Sweeney over to him.

"Sir," said McDonald to the doctor. "Montana Guard has sent food and medical supplies —"

"Did they send a surgeon?" The doctor bit his lip while he worked on the bloody hole in the patient's stomach.

"No, sir, but —"

"You tell them to get me a field surgeon, or we're going to start losing a lot more people!"

McDonald found us a space on the floor to put Sweeney's litter. "How soon until the doctor can get to him?" I asked.

McDonald sighed and swept her hand around the gym.

I crouched down next to Sweeney. He was doped up and had some hydration going. This was probably the best we could do for him until the doctor came around. I looked up at my crew. "Things are bad here. We should help unload the truck, do as much as we can." Everyone nodded except Becca, who sat down next to Sweeney and took his good hand in hers.

"He shouldn't be alone," she cried. She wiped her eyes. "And maybe with my lifeguard and CNA training, I can help here."

The rest of us went to the truck. Gunfire from who knew where continued as we carried boxes into the gym. Cal came up beside me as I pushed out the doors. "Listen to that, man. We gotta get back to the fight. The Fed are still here. We have to kick them out. That's the only way you and me are gonna be able to help Sweeney. We gotta protect him."

A couple of pickups and a wagon drawn by two horses pulled up outside the school. If they were carrying more patients, soon there would be no more room on the gym floor.

"Cal, I know," I said. "But they got one doctor and a couple combat field medics for all these wounded people. Those three can't take a time-out to move this stuff."

"Hey, guys." Dr. Randall opened a door and climbed down out of the pickup, wearing a white lab coat over jeans and a sweatshirt. A handgun was holstered on her belt. "I came to see what I could do."

I closed my eyes and offered a quick prayer of thanks. "Dr. Randall, our best friend Eric Sweeney has been burned real bad.

Becca's in there with him. The doctor is busy with gunshot wounds or something. Can you see if you can help him?"

"I'll do my best," she said, before hurrying inside. I left Cal standing there and went back out to the truck.

Mr. Morgan hobbled up to me as I was bringing in my last box. "Daniel."

"Mr. Morgan, you should really at least get a crutch or something," I said.

Morgan nodded. "An Idaho Guard medic has a wound worse than mine. He's using the one set of crutches we could find to get around while he treats people."

I smiled at the man. "Still, you've been at it all day. Try to get some rest."

The principal nodded. "I might say the same about you, but the fight goes on."

"Hopefully even any Fed holdouts would leave a hospital alone," I said.

"The US Army set up machine gun nests on the roof," said Mr. Morgan. "I've been wanting to bring them down, but we haven't had time."

"We can take care of that," said Sergeant Kemp.

"They get up there using the roof hatch at the back of the stage?" JoBell asked. He nodded. "Follow me," she said to Kemp.

I started after my group, but Mr. Morgan grabbed my arm. "Danny, you have to see if you can use your influence with the governor, er, the president to help us again. I worry about disease. Cholera or fever. Plus the smell . . . It's already nearly unbearable."

"Mr. Morgan, I'm sure people are swamped everywhere," I said.

A loud explosion went off somewhere in the distance, but close enough that we could still feel the shock wave. Morgan led me away from everyone. "We're putting the dead on the floor of the English and math rooms, but those classrooms are almost full. We need at least a truck, a flatbed trailer or something, to move the bodies to a different location."

I swallowed. "Lot of people. And you still have the Fed prisoners in the locker rooms."

"Um, no, actually, we don't," he said. "Some men from the Brotherhood came and took them away. They didn't say where they were taking them. I worry that . . . Well, anyway, they're gone, which at least let us have better access to clean water. Until the water supply ran out. We've switched to bottled drinking water for now."

"The water tower," I said. The Feds had put holes in the tank when they'd been shooting at us. "Yeah, we need to get that fixed. We'll take care of the guns on the roof, and then if you'll let us borrow the welding gear from the shop, we'll get the holes on the water tower patched."

He agreed, and I went to work. I had hoped that staying busy would help keep my mind off Sweeney. It didn't. My group brought two .50-cals, one M240 machine gun, and plenty of ammo for them both down from the roof. We left the M240 to protect the makeshift hospital and packed up everything for the other two guns.

We got a crew together with Skylar Grenke's dad and some men who worked for Freedom Lake. They got the water tower patched and the city's pumps working overtime to get the supply back up. When the power went out, we made sure the town generators were fueled up, and then we transported some generators and fuel to the school hospital.

Sweeney had been treated with some kind of gel, and he'd been bandaged and doped up. I was glad he was still unconscious. His burns would hurt so bad. For the hundredth time, I ran through in my mind all the things I should have done differently to keep this from happening. Becca and TJ were hard at work helping

Dr. Strauss and Dr. Randall, but they never strayed too far from Sweeney's side.

"Becca, TJ," I said when we were finished setting up the generators. "Hey, maybe you two should get some rest."

JoBell put her hand on Becca's arm. "Yeah, come on. He's okay for now. You need to look after yourself too."

Becca shook her off. "I'm staying."

"Me too," said TJ. We knew better than to argue, and we headed back to the Brotherhood base.

Crocker kept relaying messages and news. Where the US military wasn't fighting Guard, Brotherhood, or armed civilians, people were fighting each other. He said there were riots going on in so many cities that the Battle of Boise looked like a spring picnic. A few Texas oil wells were burning like giant blowtorches through the night.

Near dawn, Kemp and Sparrow racked out in the pole barn. Becca finally showed up, having caught a ride with a Brotherhood supply truck passing through. When she joined us in the house kitchen, she looked as fried as I felt. Her sweatshirt and jeans were stained red-brown with blood. Her feet dragged as she walked. Her eyes were red from tears.

"Sweeney?" I asked as she approached us.

She didn't say anything but wrapped her arms around JoBell, buried her face in JoBell's shoulder, and cried.

"Is Eric . . . ?" JoBell asked.

Becca flopped down in a chair near the table. She didn't even look at us. "Eric's alive. Mary Beth Reese and her mom are dead. Randy Huff and his whole family." She sobbed. "Bomb hit his house. Nobody knows why. Lots of people are dead. Someone had enough gas for a pickup and towed down a flatbed trailer. They tried to stop me, but I demanded to help. I wanted to be useful. We moved so many bodies. It took four trips. For now, they're out on the football field under tarps."

"TJ?" I asked.

Becca didn't even look at me. "Went home to check on his family."

JoBell put her arm around Becca and helped her up, guiding her to the living room couch, where the girls plopped down. I took a spot on the other side of Becca. Cal took to the floor, leaned on JoBell's legs, and rested his head on her knee. We sat there together, watching the sky begin to lighten up in the east, all of us but Sweeney, and him being gone put a shadow on the whole new day. We listened without really listening to news on the radio.

"Hey. Hey!" Cal said a while later. "Listen."

I reached for my rifle before I realized we'd been asleep and it was just Cal.

The Idaho national anthem was playing. *"Broadcasting with five hundred thousand watts, AM 1040, the superstation of the triumphant Republic of Idaho. Please stand by for a message from President James Montaine."*

"My fellow citizens of Idaho. I bring you greetings this morning, after our longest and most difficult day and night. We have suffered terrible losses. Our cities and towns have been bombed. Indeed, it is my sad duty to report that the city of Lewiston has been totally destroyed. Thousands of our countrymen and women, civilian and soldier alike, have been killed.

"But I tell you this still with great pride and a renewed hope and profound sense of patriotism for our beloved Idaho. The sacrifice of our honored dead has not been in vain. Idaho lives on. Our enemy, overwhelmed by the new fronts in Texas, Oklahoma, Montana, and

Wyoming, and unprepared for our decisive, determined, and precisely timed strike, has withdrawn most of its forces from Idaho. The United States blockade line, a blight across the northern part of our country, has been obliterated. The ring of US forces around Lewiston has been broken. Four US Navy warships are now trapped on the Snake River after the locks they used to travel were destroyed behind them. They will surrender or be sunk by land-based artillery fire or Idaho air assets. Citizens of Idaho who have endured long months of harsh United States occupation are now free.

"What's more, we have also liberated over half of the territory that used to belong to the state of Washington. The Republic of Idaho has greatly expanded, granting our long-suffering citizens access to new supplies, a greater abundance of food, and the valuable resources of Fairchild Air Force Base and Yakima Training Center.

"Unfortunately, our war is not over. The United States does and will continue to attack our borders and our allies, and so we must remain vigilant in our continuing struggle. But I have been preparing for this day, and even as I deliver this speech to you now, trucks of shelf-stable and fresh food, medical supplies, and other goods are rolling into cities and towns all across the Republic of Idaho from our friends in Montana and Wyoming. After the conclusion of these remarks, please stand by on this frequency for official information about the distribution of these goods.

"My friends, because of your sacrifice and determination, this day will be long remembered in the Republic of Idaho as the day we finally forced the United States from our lands. From this day onward, March twenty-second shall be known as Victory Day, a holiday when we celebrate our great accomplishment — a giant leap toward our shared goal of a peaceful and free republic.

"Today, we celebrate our triumph and look forward to our final and complete victory. Thank you for what you have done for your country. *God bless you all. And may God continue to bless the Republic of Idaho.*"

Cal swung his cavalry saber high over his head and screamed, "Yeah! Idaho! Long live the Brotherhood!" Similar shouts and whoops came from outside as the news spread through the camp. Sergeant Kemp ran in with Sparrow rubbing her tired eyes, looking dazed but almost smiling behind him.

"Did you hear the news?" Kemp asked.

JoBell pointed at the radio. "Yeah, we heard Montaine's whole speech."

"I can't believe it. We actually did it," Becca said quietly, staring out the window from where she sat on the couch. "Idaho is free."

JoBell squeezed her shoulders. "We're safe."

Sparrow leaned against the wall. "For now."

I'd dreamed about this day for months, imagined it a hundred different ways. There would be fireworks and the biggest party I'd ever seen. I would pick JoBell up and swing her around. We'd kiss. Sweeney would maybe shake up a bottle of champagne and spray it all over like in the movies.

I pressed the heels of my hands to my eyes. Sweeney wasn't here for this. Did he even know we'd won?

I had no party left in me. So many people had died. We'd lost so much. And the war wasn't even really over. JoBell sat down beside me, put her arm around me, and laid her head on my shoulder. All of my team listened to the growing celebration outside in exhausted silence — everyone except Cal, who paced around in excitement.

Crocker came into the house. He looked worn out. "Been on for like . . . seventy-two hours or something. Someone finally relieved me." He leaned against the wall and slid down to the floor. "The reports I was getting were all a jumble. Some were wrong. Many were duplicates. We have a marker board and a bunch of maps up in the TOC where we're trying to sort out what's going on. But for now the fighting is far away. I think the Fed is regrouping and making a new plan. They've taken a lot of losses in Idaho, so they're pulling back to just a few areas or they're just keeping some recon units here. A lot of the US military seems to be moving toward Colorado."

"Makes sense," Kemp said. "It's sort of halfway between the two big rebel areas. There are major military bases there. NORAD's there. They can reestablish control and consolidate their assets without worrying about attacks."

"Yes!" Cal shook his sword around in the air. "They're on the run!"

"Cal, can you not?" JoBell had her hands up in front of her. "You're going to hurt someone."

"Oh, right. Sorry." Cal sheathed the saber. "But guys, aren't you pumped for this? We won!"

Finally. As I sat there at alpha base, I could almost feel the relief pass over me like a wave, the way I might feel a warm blanket being pulled up over my body. Suddenly my gun felt heavy on my lap and the new fight was in keeping my eyes open. My part was done. Others could deal with the war now.

╲╱─• *This is a continuing NBC News Special Report. Civil War II. Here's Byron Westbrook."*

"Good evening. It's now been thirty-six hours since the so-called Idaho Crisis spilled over into other parts of the country. We have been wall-to-wall with our coverage, bringing you the information as we have it, and exploring the terrible implications of what some of these happenings mean. At this hour, this is where the country stands. As you can see when we zoom in on this map, the self-proclaimed Republic of Idaho has sent rebel forces into eastern Washington State, and although there is still fierce fighting in the western mountains there, everything east of that range appears to be under rebel control.

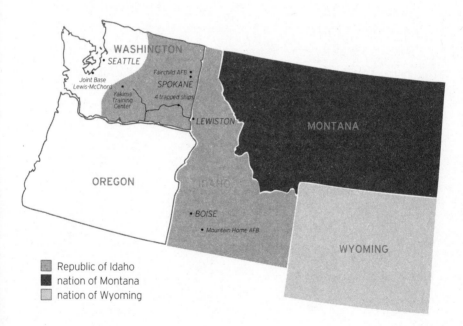

"This advance has created a panic in western Washington cities like Seattle, Tacoma, and Olympia, although with a massive Army and Air Force facility at Joint Base Lewis-McChord and the United States Navy at the sea ports, the likelihood of rebel forces taking the rest of Washington is extremely low.

"The situation in Texas and Oklahoma is much less certain. If we zoom in on the map, we can see the United States has maintained a strong presence around its military bases, but that's not necessarily a help in certain cities. In Texas, the United States has firm control of most of the center of the state from Waco down to San Antonio, including the state capitol in Austin, with primary support from Fort Hood in the middle of that zone and US military resources at a number of bases in San Antonio. As a result, the self-proclaimed president of Texas, Rodney Percy, has moved his government to Houston, and rebel forces have a firm grip on that city and Dallas. Fighting is intense across the state, with casualty reports in the thousands and rising. Even the Alamo was mostly destroyed when a Predator drone accidentally bombed that landmark while targeting rebels.

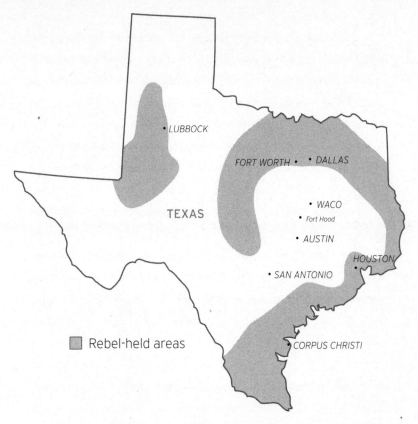

"A look at Oklahoma shows a different, but still disturbing, story. Oklahoma's most significant military base, Fort Sill, has fallen to the rebels, as have the Air Force and Coast Guard facilities around Oklahoma City.

"All of this is troubling enough, but adding to our concerns is the report that two nuclear warheads are somehow missing from the United States' arsenal. A spokesperson for the Northwest Coalition of Idaho, Montana, and Wyoming insists that the leadership of those rebel states are cooperating with federal investigators to try to track down the two missing weapons, probably the most significant cooperation the two sides have seen for months.

"White House spokesperson Kelsey Santos says that President Griffith, now back at the White House, wants to avoid nuclear conflict at all costs, but takes the issue of these missing weapons very seriously. Of course, the rest of the world takes a destabilized US nuclear arsenal very seriously as well, and Russia, North Korea, China, India, Pakistan, and the other nuclear powers of the world remain on high alert. •⌒

⌒• We're going to break away from that story to bring you an exclusive WGN report on several dangerous situations developing very quickly. As in dozens of cities across the country tonight, reports are flooding in of looting and violence at various locations all over Chicago. Several structures are burning near South Ashland Avenue between Fifty-Eighth and Seventy-Sixth. The North Lawndale neighborhood around South Homan and West Roosevelt Road is engulfed in violence. Gunshots have been reported at numerous other locations. Police are attempting to combat looting on a scale never before seen. Stolen items include what one might expect — electronics, jewelry, and liquor — but a greater emphasis has been placed on food. Grocery stores, which were already under pressure from trying to enforce government-mandated rationing, are now being overrun all around the city. Hundreds have *been injured, dozens have been killed, fighting over milk and bread. WGN is begging all viewers to please stay indoors. Mayor Emmons has been in contact with Governor Qualls, requesting reinforcements from the Illinois National Guard, but most Guard forces have been federalized in support of Operation Unity.* •—⌇

CHAPTER
THIRTY-TWO

About ten days later, I used an impact wrench in my old shop to bolt a .50-cal mount to the turret I'd installed in my new tan armored Humvee ambulance. Everything salvaged from the Fed had to go to the war effort, but I'd convinced Crow that the Beast had been a military vehicle sacrificed for the war, and the Idaho Army owed me something. This ambulance wasn't high on their list of priorities, and it wasn't running when I first got it, but I'd fixed the engine, and now it was perfect for what I had in mind.

The thing was like any other Humvee, except it had a huge metal box behind and over the cab. As a noncombat vehicle it had no gun turret, but the Brotherhood lent me tools, and I changed that. I also installed gun ports on both sides and the rear. After an upgrade to the suspension and fuel tanks, I would have a well-armed vehicle that could comfortably, or mostly comfortably, sleep up to five people in back.

It was a lot of work, but I had to have something to do. I visited Sweeney every day. He had regained consciousness and was stable, but he was still in a lot of pain. Dr. Strauss said he'd eventually need surgery, but he would need to be moved to a real hospital for that. I'd tried to contact President Montaine dozens of times to get Sweeney a flight to Boise, but suddenly everybody was so busy that a helicopter couldn't be spared. The situation made me want to punch something, but since the fighting was mostly over, at least around Freedom Lake, working in the shop was the next best thing. I couldn't be like Becca, who stayed by Sweeney's side at the school all the time, helping the doctors and medics when it was time for him to rest.

I put the impact wrench down and enjoyed the quiet for a moment.

"You're crazy, you know that?"

I yanked my nine mil out of its holster and spun around. It was Sparrow. "Ever hear of challenge and password? I about shot you." I put my gun away. "Anyway, why do you say I'm crazy?"

"Are you kidding me?" She pointed at the ambulance. "Rebuilding that thing? And acting like this war's all over?"

"I know the war ain't over," I said. "Why do you think I'm fixing this up?"

"You should be looking for a new place to hide. A better dungeon."

"That's what this truck is all about." I patted the top of the ambulance module. "If shit goes bad again, I'm getting me and whoever wants to come with me to safety in this bad boy. One lesson Schmidty taught me, something I wish I'd paid more attention to before the occupation, is that I gotta be prepared for the worst. And I think the worst may still be coming."

"That why you've got three .50-cal machine guns, an M240, and ammo hidden away somewhere?"

"I don't know what you're talking about."

She rolled her eyes. "You're so full of shit sometimes, Wright. You better not be hiding that stuff down in the dungeon. Crow's going to hear about that place, and he just might want to see it himself. If he finds out you're hoarding captured Fed weapons and ammo, he'll be pissed." My cheeks flared hot. I *was* hiding the weapons down under the shop. Sparrow went on, "You know Montaine will want to use you for publicity now. You're a living symbol. A propaganda piece to get people riled up like you did the morning of the big fight. You might find it hard to ride off into the sunset on that pale horse. And you'll be a target. You need to watch out for yourself."

"I never wanted to be a symbol."

She shrugged and let the silence fall between us for a while. "I came to say goodbye."

"What are you talking about?"

"I got a sister up in Sandpoint. Haven't talked to her in years, but . . . Well, she's got an old sofa bed in her basement. I'm done with the guns and with" — she waved her hand around — "all this shit."

I dropped down into the ambulance and went out the open back hatch. "You're going AWOL?"

She laughed a little. "I'm sure you can smooth that over with the president. We got the Fed to leave us alone for now. We made sure Alsovar . . . But I wanted to say goodbye. And . . . thank you, I guess."

She held out her hand. I shook it, but somehow we soon hugged each other close. "Take care of yourself, okay?" She held me back at arm's length. "Don't be stupid. I hope this big battle wagon helps you stay out of the fight." I didn't say anything. What could I say? She picked up her M4 and a stuffed duffel bag from the ground and slapped me on the shoulder. "Goodbye, Danny."

"Bye, Shawna."

She wasn't kidding. Specialist Shawna Sparrow, one of the toughest soldiers I ever served with, walked off and was gone.

I worked until suppertime, then I drove Pale Horse to the school to visit Sweeney. Becca met me there. "Sweeney was hurting so bad, I finally convinced Dr. Strauss to spare him a little morphine," she said. "So he's out."

"I'm about to head out to his place," I said. "You want a ride? Maybe get cleaned up? Have a rest?" When he'd been awake a few days before, Sweeney asked us to stay at his house. Me, Cal, Becca, and Kemp took him up on his offer. TJ and JoBell went back to live with their parents, even though they spent most of their time with us.

Becca yawned and shot a look back at Sweeney. "I should stay here, but I know you guys could use help with dinner."

When me and Becca got to Sweeney's house, we both took showers. Then, even though everybody tried to get her to relax, Becca insisted on making us a decent meal. It was another one of her creations made from a mix of MRE components and some canned vegetables, but that was pretty good eating for us these days. We bowed our heads and thanked God for the food and for our lives. We asked Him to help Sweeney and everyone else. Then we dug in.

"We thought you'd be in the shop right through dinner again," Cal said. "I don't know why you work so hard on that Humvee anyway. Gas is hard to come by. You should be looking for one of those solar-assist hybrid cars with the super gas mileage."

"Thanks for the tip," I said.

I told the group about Sparrow. Nobody seemed surprised, but Kemp was a little down. "I wish she would have told me," he said. "I would have liked the chance to say goodbye." We raised our glasses of water as a tribute to her.

"So she's going to live with her sister and . . . what? Look for a job? There are no jobs," JoBell said. "Are we just supposed to go back to our normal lives now? After everything that's happened to us, everything we've had to do?"

"All the systems we've always lived by are basically gone," Sergeant Kemp agreed. "I had an apartment before I went to border duty. I had my car in storage. But since the United States invaded, I haven't been able to pay rent. The landlord probably dumped all my stuff out on the curb, if she stayed in Idaho. If she's still alive. My car's probably been repossessed. But then, who was allowed to drive a tow truck during the occupation? Who had the gas? If my bank account still exists, who in the Republic of Idaho is taking United States dollars?"

"It's going to take a long time to rebuild," I said.

"And life will probably never be like before," said JoBell.

I nodded. "Meantime, we'll have to rely on ourselves."

"Ain't nothing new." Cal smiled.

We went on talking like that, daring to think about the future for the first time in a long time. But as I looked around the table at our group, it killed me that Sweeney was not with us.

"Giddyup, partner! You've got a vid call from Nathan Crow."

I really needed a new digi-assistant. Waking up to Hank McGrew was the worst.

"You awake, buddy? I know your alarm hasn't gone off yet."

I raised my head off the pillow and blinked in the light. "Hank, if you don't shut up, I swear I will shoot you."

"Ouch! I hope you don't, but I sure support your Second Amendment rights! Would you like to see a video of a concert I did for a National Rifle Association fund-raiser?"

I reached for my nine mil, but then stopped. "Just put the call on, Hank."

"Private Wright? You there? My screen is all white."

"Yes. Yes, sir. I'm here. Hang on." I sat up and grabbed my comm so Crow would have a view of something besides the ceiling.

"Ah, there you are! Sorry, did I wake you up? I didn't realize you'd be sleeping so late."

I looked at the time. It was zero eight hundred. "I guess a war and torture in a Fed camp wear a guy out. But I'm good now. Do you need us? Something going on?"

Crow held up a hand. "*Relax. Everything's okay. The fighting is clear out by the borders. I have good news! I want you and your squad at Main Street outside my old sheriff station by two p.m. I know Victory Day was a while back, but we were too busy to celebrate then, and we had nothing to celebrate with. Now the Montana and Wyoming cattle associations have sent in some serious steaks, and we commandeered some food from Washington supermarkets.*" Crow laughed. "*We've blocked off Main Street and we're going to grill up a great lunch. We have a lot of hungry people to feed.*"

"So a community picnic?" I asked.

"*A huge community picnic. It's a bit chilly, but my boys have fires going. Everybody's welcome. I don't want to have to order you to come.*" He said it jokingly, but I could tell he was kind of serious.

"It's not that," I said. "Only I wonder . . . The war's not really over."

"*It'll be safe, Private. Two p.m. today. Get your weapons and your team and get on down here.*"

Later that morning, we drove into town in Pale Horse. I'd been reluctant to use more gas, but it was a long walk from Sweeney's to the school, and we didn't feel safe enough yet going in anything but an armored vehicle. We spent a couple hours visiting Sweeney. When it was time for us to go to Crow's picnic, Becca was going to stay with him in the gym, but Sweeney made her leave.

On Main Street, two men wearing black Brotherhood armbands stood in front of a barricade made of scrap lumber and fifty-gallon barrels. SAWs were slung over their shoulders. Looking up and down Main Street, I could see every cross street was blocked off and guarded, and men in civilian clothes manned machine gun nests on the rooftops of nearly all the buildings. Picnic tables had been set up on the sidewalks, and people were already sitting down, talking and laughing, enjoying the sun even if it wasn't super warm yet. Little kids chased each other around the tables.

In Pale Horse, I leaned back against the turret hatch lid and sighed, closing my eyes and letting the sun warm my face, listening to the sounds of almost normal life. Some kid screamed, not from terror for once, but with laughter. With my eyes closed, I could almost believe the war had never happened, that we were about to enjoy a simple town picnic, like a much cooler Fourth of July.

The Brotherhood guys must have recognized me, because they asked us to park by a barricade, where they could watch over our vehicle. We all dismounted and went to join the party, just a bunch of high school kids and a couple of their friends with semiautomatic assault weapons.

My mouth watered at the smell of all kinds of different meats and vegetables roasting on huge grills. Armed Brotherhood guards stood by each of the six cooking stations.

"Sure are a lot of troops around," JoBell said.

Kemp nodded. "These are hungry people. It's important to avoid a stampede."

A stage had been set up in some space cleared by the ruins of Alsovar's HQ. A giant black flag with the white eagle emblem was draped over the back wall behind the stage.

"Private Wright! Sergeant Kemp!" Crow left his conversation with a few Brotherhood guys, and he and Jake Rickingson hurried toward us. Both of them also wore neat black armbands. "I'm so glad you could make it. How y'all doing with fuel? We have to ration what little we have left. We don't have enough to get everybody back on the road, but we have a tanker truck coming up to supply military and Brotherhood vehicles. It's free for the war effort, so just let me know what you need."

"What's with the —" Kemp patted his own right arm where the band would go.

"Just a matter of pride and practicality. The Brotherhood of the White Eagle helped end the United States occupation. We're feeding the people now. We want to let folks know we're proud of who we are and what we've accomplished. But since we don't have uniforms yet, and since we have to be able to recognize other members, the armbands have to do for now."

"Cool," said Cal. "Can I get one?"

"You're not a member of the Brotherhood," Jake said.

Crow smiled. "Not yet, anyway. You have to understand that the Brotherhood takes membership very seriously. We literally have to be able to trust one another like family. Like brothers. You know, the way you all are with each other. There's this whole induction process and ceremony. Anyway, Jake, can you take this squad over to the front of the line to get some good eats? It's time to celebrate." He slapped Cal on the back. "I know this big guy could use a big old steak! He deserves one too. His old man has been running truck for us, bringing back food to feed the people. You talk to him?"

Cal's smile was almost as big as his muscles. "Yeah, talked to him yesterday. He's glad to be back on the road."

Crow laughed again. "Mr. Riccon led a whole convoy right through some serious hot zones. I tried to tell him to wait until we'd cleared the Fed from that area, but he said to me, 'Mr. Crow, we got hungry kids that ain't had a decent meal in months. You keep the Fed busy, and I'll bring in the food.' You ask him! Go take a look at his rig — Fed bullet holes in his passenger side door." Crow shook Cal's hand. "He's a real hero, just like you. But what are you standing around listening to me for? Jake, I told you to get this squad fed!"

Both men laughed, and Jake led us to the head of the line to get our food. We all looked around for a place to sit. A man at a picnic table nearby looked up from his potatoes. His eyes went wide when he saw us, and he hurried to his feet, grabbing one of his sons by the arms. "Boys, get up. Make room. That's Danny Wright."

"Stop!" I blurted out. "No, no, no. Sit down."

"You've been fighting for us and deserve a —"

"We're all in this together," Cal said. "Really. Please sit down."

"It's no trouble," said the man's wife. She looked half-starved and exhausted. Whatever food she'd had must have gone to her sons.

"Stay there. That's an order," I said. I felt bad for acting like a jackwad, but I had to do something. "Sit down. Feed your kids. That's what we fought for." I looked around and noticed people from other tables staring at us. Mr. Hornschlager and his family. Mr. Shiratori and his wife and daughter. There were the Monohans enjoying a meal with Crystal Bean and her dad. Timmy and Cassie Macer and their parents sat on fold-out lawn chairs with plates of food in their laps. Everybody had heard me order these people around. My face flared crimson hot.

"Please," I said to the first family. "Sit down and enjoy this meal. It's what we fought for." I swept my arm at the crowd all around me. "It's what we've *all* been fighting for!"

Kemp leaned closer to me and whispered, "Long live Idaho."

"Long live Idaho!" I shouted.

A cheer erupted from the whole group. People stood up and clapped. Others hugged each other. One Brotherhood trooper was about to shoot into the air, holding up his rifle and pulling the charging handle. Thankfully, one of his buddies stopped him before he pulled the trigger. We'd had more than enough gunfire lately.

We all squeezed in next to the first family, and JoBell's dad joined us. He was slowly getting used to the idea of his daughter being engaged, so he wasn't too warm to me, but it was still the best meal we'd had in months. Cal gave up on his plastic knife and fork and just picked up his steak with his hands. He bit into it like a beast, shaking his head back and forth as he ripped off a giant chunk of rare beef, juices running down his chin.

Becca handed him a napkin. "Cal, there are little kids around. Try to set a good example."

"Care if I join you?" TJ approached with a steaming plate.

"Go ahead," I said. "Where have you been?"

TJ ran his fingers back through his shaggy brown hair. "Talking to my parents. Turns out they're thinking of leaving, going to stay with my mom's cousin or something on a farm in upstate New York."

"You're moving away?" JoBell asked.

I hoped he wasn't. TJ had been a pretty solid guy through this whole war so far.

"That's what we talked about," TJ said. "They told me I had to go with them."

"Well, thanks for all your help," Cal said. "You'll be missed, man."

"Actually, I told them I was staying." TJ stared at his food. "I've been on my own for a while now. I guess I'll make it a permanent arrangement. At least until the war is really finally over. My parents have a cabin. They couldn't sell it now if they tried. They'll never be able to sell the house in town. When the war is over, maybe I'll sort of, I don't know . . ." He looked around like he didn't want anyone to hear him. "Now that we can move around freely, I've been gathering supplies, food, ammo, and all that, hiding the stuff in different secure locations in case we need it in a hurry."

"Don't you think you're paranoiding the situation a little?" Cal asked. JoBell laughed. Cal frowned. "We got the Fed . . . I mean, the United States, on the run now. We're done with that hiding in basements shit."

I hated agreeing with TJ instead of my buddy Cal, but I worried

Cal and maybe others had called victory a little early. "There's still a war going on. The US hasn't given up yet," I said.

TJ nodded. "There's more fighting, so —"

"That's the way to be!" Cal high-fived him. "Stay in the fight until we kill 'em all."

"Cal," JoBell warned.

TJ shrugged. "So I guess you're stuck with me, Danny."

I smiled. "If I've survived the war so far, I guess I can put up with you."

Becca looked like she was about to say something, but then she frowned and looked across the crowd.

"What's wrong?" I asked her.

"Mom?" she asked. We all followed her gaze. The people standing at the edge looked like Tom and Kate Wells, but they were far away. "Daddy?"

The woman elbowed the man and pointed. The two of them had huge smiles on their faces.

"Oh my gosh," Becca cried. "Mom! Dad!" She stood up from the table and ran to them. They rushed to her, and in seconds the three of them were locked in a tight embrace. People all around them clapped. JoBell, her dad, and I stood up, and JoBell led us to the family reunion.

When the Wells finally broke free from their hug, I nodded to Becca's parents. "It's good to see you again, Mr. Wells, Mrs. Wells."

Mrs. Wells's smile vanished. She stepped up in front of me, and I reached my arms out for a hug.

She slapped me hard across the cheek.

"Mom! What are you doing!?" Becca shouted.

I'd seen a lot of hatred lately, but I'd never seen so much anger and rage as was twisted into Becca's mom's face right then, all directed at me. "You stay the hell away from my daughter! Don't talk to her. Don't . . . How could . . . You were like a son to us. We *trusted* you, and you turned her into some rebel, got her wrapped up in the middle of a war." Then she cut me with the most painful words she could have chosen. "Your mother would be so ashamed."

"Come on, Becca," said Mr. Wells. "We're going home."

"Tom, Kate," said Mr. Linder. "I don't think it's as simple as you think. They didn't mean —"

Mrs. Wells pointed a shaking finger at me. "He knew better. He knew what would happen in a war. He should have left my baby girl alone."

I wanted to throw up. How could they say such things, think such things? Worse, were they right?

"I'm *not* a baby," said Becca. "I made my own choices. I took care of the farm for *months*. While you were away on vacation!"

Mrs. Wells put her hand on Becca's arm. "I know you're upset, Becca. Confused. These have been tough times. But that's over now. Everything is going to be okay."

"Nothing is okay!" Becca yanked her arm away from her mother. "The war isn't over, and I've sworn in as a soldier in the Idaho Army."

"Come on, Becca. Let's go," said her father.

"You go." Becca had her tears under control now. "I'm staying with my friends. They kept me alive through all this. You weren't even in the *state*!"

Now Becca's mom started to cry. "Baby, we tried. We came as soon as we could. We were almost shot trying to sneak in this time."

"I've been dreaming of the day when you would come home since all this started, and now you come and ruin it!" Becca shouted. "I'm a soldier, and this is my squad. My team. My family. You don't like them?" She shrugged. "I've been getting along without you for a long time now." She stormed off, heading back toward our table.

"Becca, wait!" her mother called. Then she turned her glare on me.

"I'll talk to her," I said. "I'll get her to calm down and talk to you."

"You guys go ahead and eat," said Mr. Linder. "I'll handle them."

I nodded my thanks to JoBell's dad, who nodded back.

JoBell kissed her father's cheek. "I'll see you tomorrow, Daddy. I have to go help Becca."

He hugged her and kissed the top of her head. We returned to our meal.

Becca did not want to talk, so we mostly ate in silence for a while until I felt a hand on my shoulder. It was Jake Rickingson behind me. "Nathan wants you and Riccon up on the stage." He jerked his head back in that direction. "Come on, we have to hurry."

"What's this all about?" JoBell said.

Jake smiled. "You'll see. This is going to be great."

I shrugged at my team, and me and Cal followed Jake to the stage. When I climbed the steps to the platform, I was surprised to see Mr. Morgan. His suit hung loose on his thin body, and his upper right thigh was still obviously bandaged under his pants. He hobbled over on crutches and held out his hand. "It's good to see you again, Daniel, Calvin. I wanted to take a moment to thank you again for all you've done for us at the school."

I shook the man's hand firmly. "I never did too good in school, but I loved football, and the cool people I got to hang out with. It really sucked to see the Fed turn the place into their base."

Morgan pressed his lips together. "Yes. It certainly did . . . suck."

Nathan Crow smiled and grabbed my arm. His grip was surprisingly tight. "You're a good, loyal soldier, Danny. A great patriot of Idaho. I haven't seen many people who can motivate troops like you can. Your father would be proud."

"Thank you," I said.

"Well," Crow said, "if you could take your seats, we'll get started." He motioned to a row of folding chairs at the back of the stage in front of the giant Brotherhood flag. I took a seat between Cal and Mr. Morgan.

Cal leaned over to whisper, "I'll never get used to you talking to Morgan when you're not in trouble."

"Well," I whispered back, "it is a messed-up world."

Crow stepped up to a podium and spoke into a microphone. "Ladies and gentlemen, people of Freedom Lake, of the Republic of Idaho, welcome to this belated first Victory Day celebration. I hope you are enjoying the food. Please eat all you can. We have plenty, thanks to the father of one young man, a brave soldier I have up here named Calvin Riccon. Cal, can you stand up and be recognized?" Cal stood with his big chest puffed up while the whole crowd clapped. Crow continued, "Matthew Riccon is leading supply convoy runs all over Montana, Wyoming, and the Republic of Idaho, trying to make sure that food gets to the people who need it. Let's let Matt's son know how much we appreciate his father's hard work." The crowd clapped more, but I noticed that the Brotherhood guards at the cross street checkpoints and the rooftop nests were disciplined and kept watch.

Cal sat back down, and Crow spoke again. "It has been a diffi-cult time for all of us through the United States blockade and occupation, and I want you to welcome a man who has been strong and held it together to help our children. Freedom Lake High School principal, Mr. Garrett Morgan."

There was applause again as Mr. Morgan made his slow, injured way up to the podium. "Thank you for that introduction, Mr. Crow, and thanks to all of you for working together to get us through the past challenging months. One thing we've always believed in at

Freedom Lake High School is the power and importance of the arts. That's why, when our band teacher fled the state — um, well, when she fled the Republic of Idaho — I took it upon myself to keep the music playing. Ladies and gentlemen, the marching band of your Freedom Lake High School, augmented by dedicated musicians from the junior high and upper elementary."

Down the street, horns and clarinets took up the new Idaho national anthem. Everyone lining Main Street stood and removed their hats. The band led the parade, but behind them marched a formation of armed Brotherhood of the White Eagle soldiers, nine across shoulder to shoulder and maybe twenty-five ranks deep. They wore civilian clothes and carried mismatched weapons diagonally across their chests, but their identical armbands showed they were all one. They even marched mostly in step.

Our band played okay, but looked strange without the American and Idaho flags flying before it. The Brotherhood soldier marching front and center carried a big black flag with a white eagle, though.

"Shouldn't the Idaho flag be out there too?" I asked Cal.

Crow must have had the sharpest ears in town, because he turned to me and said quietly, "We haven't received the new Republic of Idaho flags yet. When we do, you can bet we'll be flying them. For now, this is the best we can do."

When the band finished with the anthem, the drum section tapped out a simple march. Caitlyn Ericson led the band in front of the stage. When everyone was assembled, she called out, "Mark time, *march.*" The giant procession marched in place. "Group, *halt.*" With a final two steps, they all stopped, the band at once, the Brotherhood a little rougher.

Nathan Crow took the podium again, looking out from the stage over his men and the silent assembly. He read from a piece of paper. "Brave soldiers of the Brotherhood of the White Eagle! You are honored today as our liberators, and history will forever remember and honor your sacrifice and your struggle. You are unique among men, in that it has fallen on you to take charge of your destiny, to fight to secure freedom for your children and for their children. On your shoulders rests the awesome responsibility of the protection of a new and great nation, and never, not even for one tiny moment, have any of you shirked that responsibility.

"On this day, we celebrate a great victory, hard fought and painfully won, but our celebration is tempered with the knowledge that our struggle is not yet over. Our fight goes on! We will continue the battle until every last vestige of the United States military is driven from our land, until every traitor and Fed sympathizer in our midst is brought to justice. My brothers, I salute you!" Crow held his left fist up at an angle over his head. The Brotherhood soldiers in formation immediately brought their rifles straight up and down in front of their bodies as a salute. My own left hand ached. They'd turned part of the memory of my worst, most painful day into a salute? "My brothers," Crow said.

Crow ordered them through military movements until the huge column of soldiers stood with their feet shoulder width apart and their rifles leaning forward, with their right hands near the top of the barrels and the buttstocks on the ground. Crow smiled and motioned me to the podium. He put his arm around me when I joined him. "I believe no introduction is necessary for Idaho Army Private Daniel Wright!"

I'd had a crowd cheer for me before at football games or rodeos. I'm not gonna lie. Back then, I liked the attention. Now, I wished Cal and me could have been back with our friends having a steak.

"And when I said we would bring the traitors to justice, I said so on my honor as a Brother." Crow motioned to someone off to the side, and six Brotherhood soldiers dragged three people up the steps onto the stage. Their hands were zip-tied behind their backs and heavy cloth bags pushed down over their heads. Then four other Brothers carefully pulled down the enormous black-and-white flag behind the stage, revealing a thick wooden beam with three nooses dangling from it.

After a nod from Crow, the hoods were yanked off the three prisoners. One of them was a terrified Fed specialist who I didn't know. The second was Sally, the owner of the Bucking Bronc, who sold me out to Alsovar. The third was Captain Peterson, who had been with me in Alsovar's torture chamber. What I couldn't figure out was, whose side was Peterson on? I had this vague idea that he'd said something nice to me. Or had he only helped Alsovar make the torture worse?

"These two United States soldiers were found hiding in a basement in a farmhouse outside of Freedom Lake," Crow said. "The woman accepted United States ransom money to betray Private Daniel Wright. All three have been convicted of high crimes against the Republic of Idaho and will be hanged immediately."

Hanged? A lot of the people in the crowd clapped and cheered, but it was clear that not everybody was happy about this. JoBell was out of her seat and rushing for the stage. Two Brotherhood guards stepped in front of her. I looked to Cal to see if he was as shocked as I was, but he only smiled and nodded.

"Come on, I'm just a grunt," the specialist called out. "I'm on a six-year contract." Tears started to roll down his cheeks. "I was supposed to be out already, but I got involuntarily extended. What was I s'posed to do? They'd put me in jail if I didn't follow orders."

I stepped up to Sally and Captain Peterson, my heart beating so heavy it throbbed in my ears. The sounds of the crowd died away a little. "Please, Danny," Sally said, sobbing like the specialist. "I'm sorry. I was broke, okay? My bar was shut down. I got a kid at home to feed."

"She says she has a hungry child at home!" Crow shouted. "How many of you were hungry? How many of you watched your children go hungry!? And yet you didn't betray us."

"I'm sorry!" Sally shrieked.

The captain didn't beg. He didn't cry. He just looked at me. "I'm sorry for what happened to you, Danny. I told you that, remember?"

I remembered the heat. I remembered almost drowning. "You were there the whole time."

"This man helped torture Private Wright, in violation of every treaty on the treatment of prisoners of war!" Crow called out to the crowd. More of them cheered now. A bunch of them held their fists up at an angle over their heads.

"How did you get out?" the captain asked me calmly, even as Brotherhood soldiers slipped a rope around his neck. "Do you remember, when you escaped, how your restraints were unlocked? How the door was unlocked?"

I couldn't remember. TJ had shot the door open? He'd fired a round, I think. Stolen a key? From where? None of this made sense.

Now a rope went around Sally's neck. "Please," she cried. "I'll do anything. I'm so sorry!"

"A public execution is not going to help!" JoBell's dad pushed his way through the crowd. "These people haven't even had a trial."

Mr. Shiratori stepped up by Mr. Linder's side. "This is blatantly unconstitutional! And if we don't have an official Republic of Idaho Constitution yet, it is at least contrary to the very spirit of freedom and democracy!"

Two Brotherhood soldiers rushed at the two men with rifles, but

Crow stopped them. "The teacher I recognize, but who might you be, sir?"

JoBell's dad took a deep breath. "Brandon Linder. I'm an attorney."

Crow smiled. "I appreciate your concern, gentlemen. I truly do. We can't be lawless like the United States." He looked up and called out to the crowd. "But the fact is that this is a whole new country in an emergency situation where Fed traitors could cost us all our lives, and we have no legal system in place. Now I promise you that we *know* without a doubt that these three are Feds or traitors."

"I was Spartacus!" Captain Peterson yelled.

"What did you say?" JoBell shouted back. Even Crow turned to him, looking shocked.

"The guy on the inside who told you that Wright and Sparrow were still alive," Peterson shouted. "The guy who told you where to find them. Your source on the inside identified himself as Spartacus. That was me. I'm a traitor, all right. I turned on the Army to save two of your soldiers."

"The source did call himself Spartacus!" JoBell said.

"Yeah, but that doesn't mean this guy is innocent," said Jake Rickingson.

"But you have a reasonable doubt now, don't you?" said Mr. Linder.

"Private Wright, listen to me," said Captain Peterson. "The attack on the mountain base had just begun. Major Alsovar rushed out of your cell. Before I left, I released your restraints and left the door unlocked. I told you to wait until the time was right. Do you remember?"

I did sort of remember, but it was like trying to remember the details of a fading nightmare. I didn't know what to do. The last of the three ropes went over the neck of the specialist. A huge wet spot formed in the crotch of his uniform.

"We can't just let them go," said Jake Rickingson. "And it ain't like we can give them a full trial. We don't have enough people to man the jails. We don't even have courts. They are the enemy."

"That doesn't mean you have to kill them," JoBell said.

"The soldiers tortured Daniel Wright." Crow pointed at Sally. "She sold him out."

"Do it!" Cal yelled. "They deserve it."

That look was back in Cal's eyes. The one he'd had when he cut up those soldiers with his sword. The one he'd had when he killed Major Alsovar. Cal was losing everything that had made him good. He'd managed to dodge the bullets so far, but the war was killing him inside.

We couldn't allow ourselves to go down this road. These people with ropes around their necks weren't combatants anymore. We had to disengage. They at least deserved a trial. "Mr. Crow," I said. "Maybe we should put this off until —"

"Now!" Crow yelled.

The floor under the three prisoners dropped away, and they dangled on their taut ropes like fish gasping on the line. Their faces went red and veins bulged in their foreheads.

"Mr. Crow, please." I ran a couple steps toward the gallows, but Jake Rickingson and a couple of his guys blocked my path.

"Let justice be done!" Crow offered the bleeding fist salute to his men. "Long live the Brotherhood!"

I watched helplessly as the life passed out of the three prisoners. We'd fought hard, risked everything, to win our freedom and start a new country. What kind of society was this?

Hundreds of Crow's men held their left fists at an angle above their heads. "Long live the Brotherhood!"

ABOUT THE AUTHOR

TRENT REEDY served as a combat engineer in the Iowa Army National Guard from 1999 to 2005, where he often thought about the possible conflicts embedded in the Guard's oath, which swears loyalty to both the U.S. president and a state's governor. Those reflections led directly to the *Divided We Fall* trilogy. His other novels include *If You're Reading This* and *Stealing Air*, both Junior Library Guild selections, and *Words in the Dust*, which won the Christopher Medal and was featured on the *Today Show*.

Trent lives in Spokane, Washington, with his family. Please visit his website at www.trentreedy.com and follow him on Tumblr at trentreedy.tumblr.com.

This book was edited by Cheryl
Klein and designed by Christopher
Stengel. The text was set in Sabon,
with display type set in Conduit and
Grotesque. This book was printed
and bound by R. R. Donnelley
in Crawfordsville, Indiana. The
production was supervised by
Starr Baer. The manufacturing was
supervised by Shannon Rice.